Don Henry

The Enchanted Island

THE ENCHANTED ISLAND

NANCY ROSS

POOLBEG

This novel is entirely a work of fiction. The names, characters and incidents portrayed in it are the work of the author's imagination. Any resemblance to actual persons, living or dead, events or localities is entirely coincidental.

Published 2004
by Poolbeg Press Ltd
123 Grange Hill, Baldoyle
Dublin 13, Ireland
E-mail: poolbeg@poolbeg.com

1 3 5 7 9 10 8 6 4 2

A catalogue record for this book is available from the British Library.

ISBN 1-84223-132-4

Typeset by Magpie Designs in Palatino 10/14
Printed by Litografia Rosés SA, Barcelona, Spain

www.poolbeg.com

About the Author

Nancy Ross is the only child of the well-known musician and songwriter, BC Hilliam. After a career in the WRNS, followed by several high-powered secretarial jobs, two marriages and three children, she started out on yet another career – writing.

Her first novel, *Still Waters Run Deep,* was published in 2003.

To my elder son, Edward Paterson Ross

Away with Systems! Away with a corrupt world! Let us breathe the air of the Enchanted Island.

George Meredith
1828 - 1909

PART ONE

Chapter One

Christabel's father, who was a man of the church and supposedly qualified to give advice and sympathy, said rather testily, "I never expected to be faced with such a situation in our family. It is something about which I do not care to give an opinion."

"That's a great help!" said his wife.

"It just seems silly to me." This was from Andrew, Christabel's fifteen-year-old brother.

His sister agreed with him. "It seems silly to me as well." Silly, but nevertheless occupying all her thoughts, so that her concerned mother commented that she did not look well. Her appearance was a complete contrast to her radiance of the last few weeks.

She looked back on the happiness of that time and it seemed to her that this short episode in her life had the substance of a dream, a dream from which she feared she must now awaken. It did not help knowing that she, in a moment she now regretted bitterly, was solely responsible for the destruction of her aspirations for the future. All those hopes now lay in ashes and she did not know how to retrieve them.

* * *

It started when she was invited to a dinner party given by one of Myra's clients. Myra was the owner of an art gallery in Church Street, and Christabel had worked for her for six years. She enjoyed the work; it entailed meeting people and was never dull. Myra always maintained that she could not afford to pay her a high salary, which was probably true, but it was enough for Christabel to pay the rent of a flat on the ground floor of a block of flats in the South Kensington area, and when she made a sale she was given a small percentage. She managed very well, always looked elegant because she had a flair for picking the right clothes. It was an important element of the job.

The invitation from the client was in gratitude for an introduction to a young abstract painter whose paintings had been recently acquired by the gallery. Myra was away when Christabel suddenly had the inspiration to arrange the meeting. Hugh Bramley (she suspected it was not his original name) had acquired several paintings from the gallery, and he had always dealt through Christabel. He hardly knew of Myra's existence.

He arrived at the showroom at half past six, dark, short and immaculately dressed and, there, nervously awaiting his arrival, was a young god. Christabel was never sure whether it was the artist's work or the artist himself that appealed to him most. He seemed enchanted by both. A great deal of money passed hands that evening, and Christabel opened a bottle of champagne in celebration, knowing that Myra would be pleased. A bottle was always kept in the miniscule refrigerator in the office in case such an occasion should arise. She returned home to her flat elated about the success of the evening. Everything had gone just as she had hoped it would. She felt justifiably proud of herself.

She had gleaned information about Hugh from a mutual friend. No one was quite sure how he had made his money, but the general belief was that he had taken advantage of the calamitous slump in property prices in the early part of the twenty-first century, a few years before Christabel met him. He had prospered from other people's misfortunes. He had always been rich, and he became even richer. Now, past middle age, he remained unmarried, and consequently was suspected of being gay. Christabel's confidante thought not. "Nothing," was his assessment. "Everyone has to be put in one category or another, but that is wrong. There are many people to whom sex is unimportant. They fall into no category but bumble along quite happily with no commitments. In my opinion Hugh is one of those people."

Christabel told him of Hugh's obvious fascination with the young Adonis. "Oh, that means nothing," was the airy response. "If you had introduced him to a beautiful woman his reaction would have been the same."

Sex may not have been important to Hugh, but people certainly were. He collected them like he collected other items of value – porcelain, paintings and sculptures – and he enjoyed getting them all together, the names he revered, under the palatial roof of his vast house in Cadogan Square.

Christabel was there for decoration only. She was aware of that. She had swum into his orbit because she had introduced him to a handsome unknown painter whose talent, in Hugh's view, had potential. She had done him a favour and, therefore, warranted an invitation to one of his parties.

"You look wonderful," he said.

He would never guess, of course, that the dress she was wearing was purchased from a shop in Beauchamp Place that sold second-hand clothes. Very special second-hand clothes, and Christabel chose wisely when she shopped there. Her mother, a vicar's wife, wore lumpy tweed skirts and shapeless jumpers, and often wondered why her daughter possessed this talent of looking stunning at all times. She did not look towards her husband for its origins, striding through the village, his black cassock flapping around his ankles, looking every inch the part he wished to portray.

Christabel thought that Hugh would leave her at once to attend to his other, more important guests, abandon her to fend for herself in alien surroundings. To her surprise, he hovered, asking solicitously, "Is there anyone here who interests you particularly?"

"As I know no one here, I must go on appearances alone," she said, her eyes darting from one face to another. The guests, all talking in the rather desperate way people adopt at parties, were thronged in a room furnished in impeccable taste, too perfect to be the genuine article. The faces in the portraits adorning the walls were not Hugh's ancestors, but acquired, no doubt from famous auction houses, for his purpose.

"Take your pick," he said.

She found his attitude rather irritating and faintly insulting. "I feel like a farmer picking out the best pig at the market," she said.

Her eyes fell on a man on the other side of the room. He was bending down from a great height listening to an animated woman who was gesticulating with her hands. Christabel noticed him because of his hair, sleek and almost white in its blondness. She thought that if he did not take so much trouble to make it flat it would spring up like a boy's hair, soft and unruly. His face was half-turned away from her view, but she could just see a straight nose.

"The hair caught my eye," she said. "Unusual."

"Oh, darling," said Hugh, "forbidden territory, I fear. He must have a nice Jewish girl. When I tell you his name you will understand. Ambrose Silveridge."

"I see," said Christabel. The name meant so many

things: immense wealth, philanthropy, university colleges and hospitals with the same name. "Very impressive," she said, "but I was not intending to marry him. Exchange a few words, perhaps?"

"Dangerous," said Hugh, and he linked her arm and steered her in the direction of a group of people standing near them. He introduced them in turn, and she tried to remember their names. A woman amongst them plunged straight into an account of a burglary recently experienced.

"Oh, don't start on that again," pleaded a man who could only be her husband.

"I want to hear," said Christabel quickly.

The story progressed to crime in general and the observation that London was no longer a safe place in which to live, and that led to politics and the inadequacy of the Home Secretary. The conversation was punctuated by the topping up of glasses, and Christabel wondered if she should move on, always a difficulty when you do not know anyone to move on to. Her dilemma was resolved when it became time to eat and everyone started to glide slowly into the dining-room. There was a seating plan perched on an easel, and one of the husbands (she decided they were all married to each other although she could not work out the pairs) found her name on the list.

"Oh," he said, "that is bad luck. I'm afraid we are a few places away from you."

"It is bad luck," she agreed, "as I know no one else

here. But thank you, all the same, for rescuing me. It is daunting walking into a room full of strangers."

They smiled at her benevolently and she made her way to her seat. Her neighbours to the left and right were already seated, and half rose when she appeared.

"Please don't move," she said. "I am Christabel Tooley."

They introduced themselves. The man on her left was called Harry Gaunt (instantly she forgot his name) and on the right of her sat Ambrose Silveridge (a name not to be forgotten).

She caught the eye of Hugh sitting at the top of the table. He gave her a cheery wave and shouted: "I like a challenge."

"What does he mean?" asked a woman sitting opposite Christabel.

"He was telling me earlier," said Christabel coolly, "that he intends to enter his horse in the Grand National. Did you know he owns racehorses, as well as everything else?"

"What a remarkable man he is," said the woman. "So many interests."

Christabel was aware of Ambrose's fingers on her right crumbling bread on a plate; he seemed to overshadow everyone else at the table. Not fat, but large and powerful, taking up a lot of room. He was bending his blond head in the direction of the woman sitting on his other side, and Christabel was interested to see it was the same woman he had been talking to in the other room.

She left them to it and turned to the man on her left. He hastened to explain that he was alone that evening because his wife had recently given birth to their third child.

"How absolutely lovely for you," she said with real feeling because she could not imagine a more complete joy. The situation in which she found herself, all the trappings of wealth, were nothing compared to this miracle and, as always, she was filled with wonder at the thought of such an achievement.

"I must say I am a very happy man," he said. "I was not coming this evening, but my wife insisted. At home we have a rather formidable lady looking after the other two children, and it was quite a relief to get away from her. I seem to have been landed with her every evening since the birth."

Christabel laughed. "Have you boys or girls or a mixed bunch?" she asked. She became aware that other people were listening to their conversation.

"All boys," he told her. "We sort of hoped for a girl, but we are not disappointed."

"Three boys sounds good to me," she said.

"Are you married?" he asked.

"No."

"You must marry and have children," he said. "I heartily recommend it." His own contentment made it easy for him to speak freely with her.

"I'd like it very much," she admitted. "It would be a

great sadness for me not to have children, but it hasn't worked out so far."

"You are very young," he said, giving her a sideways glance.

"Not as young as all that," she replied.

She was conscious that Ambrose Silveridge was hanging on every word. The woman sitting beside him had turned her attention elsewhere, and he was silent, staring straight ahead of him, but listening, as Christabel knew.

She spoke in his direction. "We are getting down to the heart of the matter here," she said.

"Yes, so I hear."

He was rather solemn, she decided, but she did not hold it against him. There were so many flippant people around it was refreshing to come across a serious person. He leant across her and addressed Harry. Harry Gaunt (she had peeked at the name on the card in front of him to remind herself of his name). "Congratulations, Harry. Wonderful news. Is Anne well?"

"Very well, thank you, Brose."

Harry was anxious that Christabel should not feel left out. "Brose and I have been friends for years," he explained.

The woman beside Ambrose suddenly chipped into the conversation. "I could not help hearing," she said. "How absolutely wonderful!" She leaned right over Ambrose, almost in front of Christabel who caught a glimpse of a scarlet mouth and breathed a waft of perfume. She felt more than heard the imperceptible sigh from Ambrose Silveridge. He was bored with her then? For some reason it gave her pleasure.

He was studying the card in front of her. "Christabel," he said. "I don't think I have come across that name before."

"It goes back several generations in my mother's family. Now there is just me and an aunt who lives on a Spanish island and calls herself Bell. I prefer the works." She thought, I'm babbling. She felt unaccountably nervous sitting beside this man. His bulk seemed to take up her whole vision, as if there was no one else in the room. She had always mocked theories about chemistry between the sexes; words from trashy novels she maintained and not like real life at all. In her past love affairs she had never lost her sense of personal power, she had never been taken over completely by another person. She had remained herself. Now, she was beginning to wonder if something strange, never encountered before, was happening to her. The realisation gave her a sense of unreality, as if the room and every person chattering in it were like a dream, and she was not part of it. She felt hot and almost faint. She heard a quick intake of the breath of the person sitting next to her and she thought, with a feeling of relief and joy, he feels the same. She looked straight into his face, studying the features that had suddenly become so important to her.

Then he laughed, and his face was transformed. "Well, what do you think?" he asked.

She felt herself blushing, and that in itself was a new experience for her. "I'm sorry to stare," she said. "It is very rude of me. I suppose I am just interested in people."

Harry came to her rescue with a story about one of his children. "Brose is his godfather," he said.

"Heathen godfather," said Ambrose.

"Well, he calls himself that because he is of a different religion."

"Does it matter?" asked Christabel curiously. The Jewishness of the person sitting next to her interested her, particularly in view of Hugh's comments earlier that evening.

For the first time a cloud passed over his face. He said, "Let's talk of anything but religion. Politics, world affairs, but spare me religion."

Christabel laughed to cover up the slight feeling of tension. "I know how you feel. My father is a vicar, and my brother and I get a surfeit of religion at home."

After dinner, and when people were starting to leave, she went upstairs to fetch her coat. She pulled it out from under a mound of expensive coats, a lot of furs among them despite public opinion, lying on a double bed in what she supposed was Hugh's bedroom. It was a fairly sombre room with heavy draped curtains and ponderous furniture. There was one photograph in a silver frame on the dressing-table. It was of an elderly woman and Christabel guessed it was his mother.

As she came down the wide staircase she saw that Brose (as she had been instructed to call him) was standing at the foot, waiting for her. He stood with his flaxen head bent, as if it was the most natural thing in the world for him to be there, waiting for her. She thought how elegant he looked in the dinner jacket as worn by all the men at the dinner party. Tall, heavily built men looked so much better in this attire than the small insignificant ones who tended to look like waiters. No one would mistake Brose for a waiter.

"May I give you a lift?" he asked.

"Thank you."

Together they went in search of Hugh to thank him for the evening. She tried to avoid his eye as she shook hands with him. "It's been lovely."

She was surprised to see the woman who had sat next to Ambrose Silveridge, standing beside Hugh, chatting with everyone as they stood in line to say good-bye. "Who is she?" she asked, as they walked away together.

"She is Hugh's PA. She organises everything for him, including this party. It is because of her I am here. I know Hugh slightly." Christabel was amused, having got the impression from Hugh that he knew Ambrose Silveridge very well.

"She is very beautiful," she said, giving him a sideways glance.

"Yes," he said.

His car was just as she might have expected. "Nice" she murmured as she sank into soft leather.

"It's over twenty years old years old. The last present my father gave me, and I see no reason to replace it."

She longed to ask questions, but she felt she did not know him well enough.

She was completely relaxed and happy sitting beside him while he drove surely and calmly through the traffic. She had already given him the address of the block of flats where she lived, and he did not ask for instructions. He made his way there without difficulty. He must know London very well, she thought.

They did not speak during the journey. She was tired and there was a stillness about him as if there was no need for light conversation. He parked the car and walked with her to the main door. She put the key in the lock. She toyed with the idea of asking him in for a drink, but then decided against it.

He took her hand in his. She hoped her hand did not tremble. She felt extraordinarily vulnerable and a diminutive figure beside his towering frame.

"Thank you for driving me home," she said.

"It was a pleasure," he replied. "I enjoyed meeting you." He was so polite, so correct, she wondered if she had imagined the magnetism between them.

She opened the door and he turned to go back to his car.

There was a walk across the vast hall to the door of

her flat that was on the ground floor of the building. Once inside, she leant against the door and closed her eyes. He had not mentioned another meeting, and she wondered if she would see him again.

The following evening she telephoned Hugh. She had thought of writing a letter but changed her mind and decided she would speak to him instead.

"Thank you again for such a lovely evening."

She had hoped he might mention Ambrose Silveridge, that was her reason for telephoning instead of writing, and her wish was gratified at once.

"He took you home?" He was longing for a chat.

She thought, he is like a woman in his thirst for gossip.

"Yes." She paused. "Don't read anything into it, Hugh. It was all very circumspect. We parted at the front door, and we did not make any plans to meet in the future."

"I must say I'm relieved to hear it," he said without conviction. "I would feel very guilty if I was the cause of all sorts of ghastly complications."

"Surely, it would not be as bad as that?"

"I assure you it would. You don't know the stubbornness of these Jewish mommas; their religion is second only to their love of their children. It would be a nightmare."

"Well, I'm glad I'm spared then," she said lightly, "although, if what you say is true, your mischievousness is more dangerous than I thought. You are a very naughty fellow."

She heard his cackle of laughter as he put down the receiver.

Although as a child she had been taught to pray, and it was hard to break old habits, she did not pray for Brose to get in touch with her. She was too grown up, too experienced to sink to such depths, but she thought of him a great deal during the next few days, and when the days turned into weeks she did not stop thinking about him. Before she fell asleep at night she summoned up a picture in her mind of his sensitive rather angular face, the blue eyes and the amazing shaft of light that was his hair.

Because he was so much in her thoughts she was convinced he was thinking about her in the same way. It seemed inevitable that they would see each other again. She waited for the call she knew would come. He would have doubts, but eventually he would look for her name in the telephone directory, and he would dial the number.

She waited patiently, so certain of the outcome, and then one evening she lifted the receiver of her telephone and she heard his voice at the other end, asking her if she would have dinner with him.

Chapter Two

Christabel had never known such happiness in her life. She felt that every part of her body was working at double time, her heart, her pulse and the blood racing through her veins. Even her skin seemed to have acquired a new radiance, her hair shone with life and vitality and she could not restrain a smile of satisfaction when she thought no one was looking. She wished she had the power to stop time so that she could sit back and survey what had happened to her from the moment Brose stepped foot in her flat.

They had dined together, at his telephone request, and afterwards she had suggested they have a drink together in her flat. He could not know how hard she had worked the previous evening, polishing the furniture, even washing down the paintwork. Arranging flowers in a vase her brother had given her for Christmas. On the following morning she had risen half an hour earlier than usual so that she could put clean sheets on her bed before she went to work. Why had she done that? A part of her was annoyed with herself.

And she felt even more annoyed when she filled her lunch hour by rushing to the shops and purchasing a new dress and a pair of shoes, both more expensive than she could afford. She did not go to the second-hand shop because she wanted everything to be new and special for him, even her clothes. If there had been time she would have had her hair done, something she never did, being content with a cut every six weeks and washing it herself under the shower. This she did after returning from the gallery, and she was pleased with the result. She had easy hair; it curled naturally, soft and fine, framing a rather small pointed face.

It had been a wicked extravagance buying a new dress and shoes, but it added a frisson of excitement to the evening ahead of her. She peered at the finished article in the long mirror and decided she looked good. When the doorbell pealed through the flat she went to open the door feeling confident. And she could tell at once that he thought she looked good as well. She had forgotten how big he was – he seemed to fill the doorway – and she had almost forgotten about his dramatic hair. It did not look quite as sleek as the last time she saw him; there was a substance to the tow-coloured mop, almost falling on to his forehead. He looked younger, less intimidating, expectant. His wide smile told her he was glad to see her again. He was the man she had been thinking about for the past few weeks and his presence made her feel weak. Supposing he had never telephoned her? It was unthinkable.

Of course they dined expensively. She had expected that. She wondered if at an earlier age he had ever eaten at one of the cheap bistros in the side streets. Perhaps he had never experienced the satisfaction of a giant plate of pasta washed down with rough red wine. It was a deprivation suffered by the very rich, that and the loss of their privacy, but the Silveridges were not film stars, they were treated with respect by everyone in the media. Doing good in the world only merited a small mention.

The waiters knew who he was and they hovered like anxious mother hens. Had he everything he wanted? Was the wine satisfactory? He brushed aside their administrations and ploughed stolidly through his food. She was glad to see that he plainly enjoyed eating. Would he, she wondered, in time become fat? At present his largeness was all muscle and sinew, but might this, with age, turn into flab? So concerned was she that she asked him if he took exercise.

"Squash three times a week," he told her, "and the occasional cricket match when I'm asked."

That's all right then. By comparison she led a sedentary life.

He wanted to know about it, her life, and she told him about Myra and the gallery. It was an interesting job and she liked it, but Myra was a hard taskmaster, expecting her to work long hours and never allowing her to have a proper holiday. She did not mention the low salary, as she thought he might find that hard to believe. "I have not had a holiday for three years," she said. Only visits to her parents, living from hand to mouth in the draughty cold vicarage, just managing to scrape up the money to see her through university, and now wondering whether they could do the same for their son. She was about to explain these problems to Brose, but stopped herself. She sensed that rich people must regard such disclosures with suspicion. Instead she tried to describe the beautiful countryside surrounding the village where her parents lived. The strange lives they led, completely bound up with the parish and the irritating bureaucracy of the church. Her father read books, composed sermons, skimmed through the newspaper and never went to a theatre. His wife interested herself in child welfare, the local cottage hospital and its survival, and followed the soaps on television.

"I'd like to meet them," said Brose.

It was easy to chatter about her family, harder to talk about his. Everything that could be said had been said about his father; his obituary had occupied a full page in all the newspapers. He had left his mark in so many different ways. Because of him exciting new buildings, designed by young architects, had sprung up in London. Because of him a modern college had come into being in Oxford, specially catering for gifted schoolchildren from comprehensive schools, giving them a chance to do well in the world. In a London teaching hospital a ward had been named in his honour, in a country hospital a scanner had been installed to detect breast cancer. His munificence knew no bounds. What could Christabel find to say about such a man? What could his son say about such a father?

"Nothing, really, except that I miss him more than I can say. He was as kind at home as he was in the world. When he died I felt as if nothing could ever be the same again. I know my mother and sister felt the same."

He paused and looked steadily at her. "I'm only sorry he missed seeing you," he said.

The significance of the statement made her feel as if all the strength had left her body. She stared at him across the table, clutching the stem of her wineglass. She knew in that moment that everything she had ever wanted was there for the taking; it was laid in front of her ready for her to accept and glory in it. There was no impediment to her extraordinary prospect of happiness.

She heard her voice, as if coming from the end of a long tunnel, disembodied, "And your mother? You love her in the same way?"

"Yes, of course," he said calmly. "I have had to take on where my father left off. He was devoted to her. She is a very vulnerable, rather pathetic old lady, without him. My sister and I share the responsibility of looking after her."

There was a small area of dance-floor in the restaurant, and they danced. At last she was where she had longed to be, in his arms. They both knew it was the preliminary to something much greater.

"Let's go," he said impatiently. He paid the bill, and the headwaiter accompanied them to the door.

Afterwards they were able to laugh about their hasty exit.

"You were just about to tell me about your mother," she said.

"Well, you'll meet her soon enough."

Of course he stayed the night. The crisp white sheets, so carefully ironed and folded, were not wasted. They did not talk until the early hours of the morning when the sunlight was edging the curtains, and it was nearly time for Christabel to go to work.

"Ask the lady who owns the gallery to give you two weeks' holiday," he said. It was more like a command than a request.

"I don't think she will like that very much," she said, her mouth against his ear.

"Remind her you have not had a holiday for three years. I want to take you away with me, to France, Italy – we can take the car and drive wherever it pleases us."

It was an intoxicating idea. "What about you? Can you be spared from your work?" What was his work?

Committees, decisions, all things that could be put on hold if the master dictated.

She lay very close to him and drifted off to sleep. When the alarm shrilled she was instantly awake and she put out her hand to find an empty space in the bed where, shortly before, there had been a substantial form. She must have been very soundly asleep because he had managed to get up and dress without disturbing her. And he had left a note propped up against the mirror on the dressing-table.

The writing was unfamiliar to her and because every small detail about him was important to her she studied it closely. Legible, neat, she could imagine him sitting on the stool in front of the dressing-table, head bent, writing on the back of an envelope he had retrieved from his pocket. Probably using a gold pen, which had been given to him by his father.

'Please tell you boss your holiday starts on Monday. We will go from Dover on the ferry. If you want to see what my mother looks like go to the Summer Exhibition at the Royal Academy. There is a portrait of her there by Penfold. Very good.'

* * *

Myra noticed a change in her at once. "What is wrong?"

"Wrong? Nothing is wrong. Why do you ask?"

"You look different somehow."

Christabel plunged into an explanation that she knew Myra would understand. "Well . . . I have something going. Something important. At least, for me it is important, and I want to go away with him for two weeks. Starting on Monday, if you agree."

There was a silence. Myra was beset with problems concerning the gallery.

Christabel felt it was a case of leaving a sinking ship.

"Do you have to go away at such a time?"

"Yes, I think I do." Christabel tried to sound firm. "I haven't had a proper holiday for years."

"I know that, darling." She looked searchingly into Christabel's face. "Who is this man?"

Christabel knew that the name Silveridge would be recognised immediately; there would be instant interest, endless questioning.

"Just a man I met a few weeks ago, at a party given by Hugh Bramley."

"Hugh Bramley?" Myra was suspicious. "Why wasn't I asked?"

"It was nothing special. I introduced Hugh to Lyonel Jones and he bought a couple of his pictures. He was grateful, perhaps in more ways than one, so he asked me to dinner."

"Oh, that sort of dinner," said Myra, satisfied, "and I suppose you have fallen for some poverty-stricken painter who wants you to tour Italy with him, at your expense."

"Italy is right," said Christabel.

"Well, go with my blessing," said Myra, "although how I shall manage without you remains to be seen.

There was a time when I would have loved such a holiday. No longer, I fear. I must be getting old." The prospect made her look disconsolate for a moment.

To bring her back to reality, and also to satisfy a whim, Christabel said, "What about the Summer Exhibition? We have not been this year. Shall we go in the lunch hour?"

"I suppose we ought to see if there is any new talent," said Myra, falling comfortably into the trap laid for her. "It is such a bore. The same old names, year after year. It gets a bit much."

"We might spot something . . ."

"Of course we might, and afterwards we can treat ourselves to smoked salmon and scrambled eggs at Fortnums to celebrate your new young man and your new radiance."

Christabel thought, she has noticed then, the radiance. It was hard to hide, even if she had wanted to.

They wandered around the rooms of the Royal Academy, bathed in light, embellished with gold leaf. Myra was anxious to hurry through the landscapes and portraits; the modern art interested her most. The portrait of Lady Silveridge took up the middle section of one wall and could not be ignored.

"What do you think?" asked Christabel tentatively.

Myra was plainly impressed. "The folds in the material of her dress, the texture of the velvet. He paints like an old master."

"What about the subject?" Christabel persisted.

"He hits the nail on the head every time. I have never met Lady Silveridge but I am sure she looks exactly like that."

"A sweet old lady?"

"Sweet old lady, my foot. Have a good look at that face. He has managed to convey in that gentle expression the sheer determination of the sitter. Her husband was a philanthropist, she is not. She would not give away a farthing if it would do her no good. I would not like to cross that lady. I think I might be the loser."

Christabel studied the face closely. Despite the elaborate clothes, the erectness of the figure, almost as if she was a queen sitting on a throne, the sparkle of the diamonds at her throat, in her ears and on her misshapen fingers, the face was simple, reposed. It was startling in its pallor; every line was visible as if she had asked the painter not to disguise her age in any way. There she was, an old woman for all the world to see, an old woman who had once been the wife of a great man, and now was left to face life without him.

"I think it's an amazing picture," said Christabel. "I'm so glad I've seen it."

"I agree," replied Myra, "but we have these portraits by Penfold year after year. They are always good, always like the subject. It is very tedious."

"But surely we should appreciate real talent . . ." Christabel followed Myra into the room containing the abstract paintings.

"Just look at that," said Myra, pivoting on her high heels. "The size of it! How does he expect anyone to buy that? You would need a castle or an outsize barn for this one painting."

"I suppose he wanted it that way."

"Maybe, but it is not good economics. Imagine the amount of paint he has used, layer upon layer. Very expensive, and his wife must have despaired. I feel sorry for the women who share their lives with these mad men. Let it be a lesson for you."

Afterwards when they were eating lunch at Fortnums, Myra said, "He is not an impoverished painter, is he?"

"No."

"I guessed as much. You are not the type to get involved with anyone who has not got both feet firmly on the ground. I put it down to your parochial background."

"I'd like to tell you, but . . . " Christabel began.

"Don't worry, darling. You can tell me when the moment is right. Be happy, that is all I ask. Happiness is such an elusive ingredient. We must grab it when we can. Too often it has disappeared before we have time to grasp it."

Christabel stared at Myra, the red slash of lipstick, the lines at the corner of the mouth. They clashed glasses, both of them slightly tipsy.

"To us," said Myra, encompassing, as Christabel

thought, all the lonely ageing people whose past was all they had left to console them.

* * *

"She agreed to the holiday," Christabel told Ambrose triumphantly when they met that evening. "She did not ask any questions, she just hoped that I would have a wonderful time. I can hardly believe it."

He was not as impressed as she was by the victory. He had never envisaged there would be a difficulty. She formed the impression that he usually got his own way when it was something he desired very much. And the fact that he desired to be with her for two whole weeks was almost too wonderful to be true.

Chapter Three

Ambrose did all the driving, through France and into Italy. Christabel offered to take over, but she sensed he did not want her to. He liked to be in control of the situation and he would not have been happy sitting beside her while she was at the wheel of his precious car. She did not mind. She loved sitting beside him, sometimes with her hand on his knee, watching the amazing countryside flash by. She was relieved not to have to drive in Italy where everyone drove at such high speed. The fact that she was not in control did not concern her in the least; she was perfectly content to allow him to do all the driving, make all the decisions where they should go and where they should stay. She made an attempt at being the navigator, spreading the map on her knee and trying to make sense of it. Eventually, with a wry smile, he took the map away from her and she never touched it again.

They visited places Christabel had never seen before – Florence, Venice, Naples; they were not new to him, but he delighted in observing her enjoyment. She only had to express a desire to visit a gallery or look around an old church and he fell in with her wishes at once. She marvelled at his even temper and thoughtfulness. When they were in Florence she said she wanted to visit the Casa Guidi, the home of Robert Browning and Elizabeth Barrett Browning, and he went to a great deal of trouble to find out how to get there. Her interest in the two poets fired him with enthusiasm as well, and she had managed to find a place he had not been to before. In fact, his knowledge of the Brownings was sketchy and lying on their big bed in the hotel bedroom, before they went down to dinner, she told him the story of that wonderful love affair between people of like minds, as much in love all those years ago as they were themselves, now, in the present.

During the long car journeys they talked and talked, but sometimes they were content to sit in companionable silence. There was never any constraint between them. They constantly assured each other of their love. It was a miracle they never tired of discussing. The meeting at Hugh's house, the days before he finally decided he must telephone her, their first night together; it was a story told over and over again, and it never ceased to delight and amaze them.

One day he explained why he had allowed several weeks to elapse before he telephoned her. She thought it was caution, but she was wrong. He felt it was necessary for him to break off the long-standing relationship he had with the woman he was with at Hugh Bramley's party, before arranging to meet her. This he had done in the kindest way he knew how. It was so like him, and it made Christabel realise that he had known at once, when he first met her that evening, that she was the person he wanted to be with; he made that his objective, and he did not let anything dishonourable stand in the way.

Because of the intense heat they decided to abandon the car in Naples and take a train to Rome. They hoped it would be a cooler form of transport, but it stopped in the depths of the countryside and did not move for three hours. The Italians on board got very excited, leaning out of the windows, shouting and demanding to know what had gone wrong. Brose and Christabel sat patiently, from time to time giving each other a wry smile. The compartment was like an oven and it appeared that the air conditioning had broken down as well. A small amount of warm air came through the tiny open window. Brose made his way down the corridor to see if he could get some water, but he was unsuccessful. The buffet car was firmly closed.

Christabel reflected, with her damp back stuck to the seat, that it was the only time during the holiday they had suffered real discomfort. They never had any difficulty in finding accommodation; the best hotels were always able to find a room for them. She thought her father would not approve of such luxury; he was fond of saying that the rich enjoyed themselves at the expense of the poor. When she told Brose this, his reply was, "Rich people can't help being rich. It is a fact of life for them. All Jewish people give one tenth of their income to charitable causes; that is the rule of the Torah. I don't know what proportion my father gave to establishing places of learning and building new hospitals, but I do know he tried to spend his money wisely and for the good of humanity. Your father would accept that, I'm sure, and forgive him for being rich."

Eventually they reached Rome. By the time the train arrived apologetically at the station it was dark, and they went straight to the best hotel where they managed, of course, to procure a room. They dined outside at a table with a pink tablecloth in a garden festooned with lights. In this beautiful setting he asked her to marry him.

For the first time since she met him she detected he was nervous, and she was glad to see it because it showed her how much her answer meant to him. She accepted his proposal without hesitation. She loved him with every fibre of her being, and she told him so.

"I'm frightened," she said. "Such happiness can't last."

All his usual self-assurance had returned. "It can and it will," he told her firmly.

He insisted on taking her shopping in Rome and buying her a ring. The idea of buying an engagement ring in such a city was unbelievable, and she felt she must be dreaming. The practical side of her nature could not be lost in this world of make-believe. "Nothing elaborate," she said nervously.

He was perplexed, and she realised that the spending of money meant nothing to him. It was immaterial whether a great deal of money or a small amount was spent so long as the item acquired was appropriate. Christabel had been brought up to believe economy was essential, that extravagances were for Christmas and special occasions. She did not think she would readily lose the habit of studying the right hand of the menu before reading what food was on offer, but already she was becoming accustomed to a new set of rules.

She chose the ring she liked best. It was exquisite and very expensive. It was so valuable she was afraid to take it off her finger. She gloried in it, studying it in every light; her hand took on a new importance with the addition of the ring.

The journey back to Naples was uneventful and they were glad to pick up the car again. Their holiday was drawing to a close now, and before embarking on the long journey home they spent a few days at Sestre Levante. This was a small seaside resort with narrow streets and crumbling walls overhung with mimosa. Their hotel, which must have been at one time the home of an Italian aristocrat, stood on the top of the hill overlooking the sea. It had a private beach. They lay side by side on the sand, like effigies of a man and wife in an old church. Christabel was deeply tanned, but he had fair skin and had to be careful. He did not mention it, but lying in the sun did not appeal to him. When she slept, like a cat in the sun was how he described her, he sat in a deckchair and read a book. When she awoke she liked to look at him when he was unaware of her gaze, sitting in the shade of a big umbrella, his hair almost bleached white. The hard work in the gallery seemed very far away.

On their last night in the hotel they discussed their future. They had eaten and drunk wine and gone to bed and made love, and now they were lying, side by side, hands clasped.

Christabel told Brose what Hugh had said to her when she first saw him, standing talking to the animated woman who she now knew was in love with him.

"He is such an old woman," was his comment.

They lay naked on top of the duvet; the windows wide open because of the heat. A little breeze stirred the curtains. There was a moon and the room was not completely dark; they could see each other in the half-light.

She persisted, "But is there any truth in what he said?"

"Well, I suppose my mother would prefer me to marry a Jewish girl, there is no way of avoiding that fact. But it is too bad, isn't it? I'm marrying you, and that's all there is to it."

Christabel gave a soft laugh. "She will not have bargained for the daughter of a minister of the Church of England."

"No, that would not have been one of her aspirations for me. My grandparents on either side were Orthodox Jews, my parents more on the Reform side. My sister did the right thing, marrying a Jew." He paused. "I remember going to the seaside when I was about eleven years old. We made friends with the family who had the beach hut next to ours. The grown-ups sat in deckchairs, four in a line, chatting and watching their children. There were four of us boys, and my sister was the only girl. She was then about thirteen years old. She particularly liked the eldest boy who was her own age. Although only eleven I remember finding it interesting to watch the innocent feelings they had for each other. They were too young to recognise the implications, but they were aware of something between them. It manifested itself in a form of horseplay, racing each other on the beach, colliding, touching and a great deal of laughter. They were completely happy in each other's company. Like we are, but they were children. It did not worry them that the boy was a Gentile and she was Jewish. My parents, sitting stolidly side by side, took in what was happening. Our holiday was cut short and we went home."

"But, as you say, they were children. What harm could there be?"

"Evidently they thought there was a danger, and as

Ingrid became older they became more vigilant. She never met any people other than Jews, young eligible Jewish men were put in her way and, sure enough, she fell in love with one of them, and married him. Very happily, I may say."

Christabel said, "And they hoped for the same with you, but it didn't happen. Now you have reached the age of forty-two and you are still unmarried."

"But not for long." He turned to her.

But she wanted to know more. "How important is the Jewish religion to you?"

He replied, "It has no importance whatsoever. At the age of thirteen I had my barmitzvah, and it was during that ceremony, with all it's traditions and mumbo-jumbo, that I realised I was incapable of affiliating myself with any religion. Strangely enough, I think I do believe in God, but he seems to have become lost in a mass of conflicting principles. I longed to be out of it, and I expressed my feelings to my father. He may not have understood, but at least he was sympathetic and not judgemental. My mother did not take it so well. For her sake I have continued going to the synagogue on special occasions, but it means nothing to me, nothing at all."

"It is the same with me," she said. "My brother, Andrew, and I are a disappointment to my father because we refuse to take an interest in the church. I was the first to make the decision, I think at about the same age as you, thirteen years. Andrew followed suit."

"Well," he said, "it all points to our getting married in a registry office, my darling, and the sooner the better."

"Of course," she said, "and do not suppose I shall miss the white wedding with all its frills and speeches, because I shall not, and yet . . . " she spoke a little wistfully, "there are words in the Church of England marriage service that go straight to my heart. They express how I feel for you – so apt, so wonderful for the occasion."

"It is the same with me. There are aspects of the Jewish ceremonies that I find intensely moving."

"It is a little saddening," she said, "that neither of us can enter into it with the wholehearted enthusiasm our parents would like."

He laughed quietly. "Perhaps it is just as well, considering our circumstances. As it is, we can stand aside and go our own way and, hopefully, not tread on anyone's toes."

Her fingers caressed the fair hair, now tousled and untidy. "You don't look like a Jew," she murmured.

Suddenly she was aware he was very alert. Instinctively, she knew that it was an observation he had been waiting for her to make. She waited, very quietly lying beside him, waiting to hear what it was he had to tell her.

"There is a reason for that," he said, "and I should have told you before this. That evening in Rome, I knew I should have told you the truth before I asked you to marry me." He sounded distressed.

"Nothing you can tell me will make any difference," she said.

"It's nothing bad, I'm sorry if I gave you that impression. It is just that it is important that we know everything about each other, and for some reason I find hard to explain I have kept this from you. Force of habit, I suppose. I am so used to keeping it to myself I have just got used to not talking about it. There seems no reason why anyone should know, but that does not include you of course. My parents were unable to have children. In those days they were not as clever about infertility as they are now, there was no solution to their problem except adoption. My sister, Ingrid, and I are both adopted."

Chapter Four

Lying in the semi-darkness, her body tucked against his long frame, she held her breath, waiting to hear something which, she was convinced, he had never discussed with anyone, apart from his sister. She was right, for he said, "I never tell anyone that I am adopted, and neither does Ingrid. Of course there are members of the family who know the facts, but we have never felt the need to talk about them to anyone else. We feel wholeheartedly that we are the children of our parents, and it hard for us to feel otherwise. It has always been that way and I can say, with all honesty, I do not think either my father or my mother gave it a moment's thought. We belonged to them, and that was enough. Because of their attitude it was not something that concerned us greatly, although my sister became curious at one stage.

"I'm sure you are aware, Christabel, that my father was a Life Peer. When I was a small boy he was offered an Hereditary Peerage. It was felt that he was deserving of this honour because of all he had done for his country. He was a proud man and I think he would have accepted it – but there was one obstacle in the way: I could not inherit his title and this was an admission, in his view, that I was not his son in every sense of the word. He declined the honour, and took a Life Peerage instead. When, in later years, I questioned him about it, he made light of his decision, saying he did not approve of hereditary titles, and anyway they would count for nothing in the future. How right he was.

"Ingrid, who is two years older than I, was the first baby to be handed over to them. My mother has described many times the momentous day when they received this little creature into their family. They were enchanted with her, particularly, I think, my father. Nothing pleased him more than when an unsuspecting person commented on how like the child was to him or to his wife. It was true; Ingrid did look like them, and still does. I'm sure when you meet her (and I'm longing for you to meet her because I know you will love her as much as I do), you will see at once that she is a typical Jewish girl. The Adoption Society did well when they chose her for my parents.

"I think my father and mother decided to adopt a girl because the idea of a strange boy becoming a member of the dynasty and inheriting all that it entailed was a bit daunting. The success of Ingrid made them brave, and it was only a year later that they approached the Adoption Society and said they wanted a son. My father, in his eternal gratitude, had given the society large sums of money. Because of his generosity they were able to buy a house where the expectant mothers could stay during their pregnancy. Before then they had been billeted on families, which proved to be an unsatisfactory arrangement; now they could afford to have the house and a housemother to supervise the girls and attend to their needs.

"Like many powerful men my father was impatient. Once he had decided to take the giant step of procuring for himself a son and heir he wanted it to happen quickly. I have no doubt he pestered them with telephone calls. How they must have longed for a dark-haired Jewish child, or anything resembling one, but the weeks went by and turned into months and no infant of that description became available. They settled on me, and assured my parents of a good background and intelligent parents. Even at the age of three weeks I must have looked undeniably fair, and my blue eyes did not change colour.

"I was accepted with love and pride. Both my father and my mother were delighted with their blond boy. I am quite sure they did not have a moment's regret. Once in the family I do not think they ever considered I was anyone's child but theirs. Ingrid and I had an idyllic childhood, indulged and adored beyond the adoration received by our peers. We heard mothers declare, 'Thank goodness the holidays are over!' Our parents said, 'Oh dear, the end of the holidays!' Neither of them could have borne to send us to boarding-school, so we remained at home and attended a local school. When we were naughty we were humbled, not chastised. A nanny was employed to look after us, but only because our mother was a busy woman with many charitable interests. She and my father spent every possible moment with us, and the nanny was told that making herself scarce was part of the job.

"From an early age, as soon as we were old enough to understand, we were told that we were adopted. We would say, 'Tell the story . . . ' and my father or my mother, depending on which one of them happened to be there when one of us asked the question, would immediately embark on telling us about the day we were collected from the society. The story never varied, every detail we knew by heart: the signing of the forms, the moment my mother took each of us in her arms, the journey back in the car to our new home.

"We were chosen and, therefore, we were special. When we went to school, for some reason, we never told the story to anyone, even our best friends were not let into the secret. We liked it that way. I suppose it is every child's dread to be different. Not even the headmistress of our school knew that we were both adopted.

"Ingrid was seventeen when she decided she would like to find out about her background. I don't know what prompted her. She was an imaginative girl, and perhaps she thought it would be exciting. I am quite sure that she had no wish to upset our parents by her enquiries and her curiosity was not spurred on by any dissatisfaction with her life. She was always a very contented girl and she loved my father and mother. She just wanted to know more about her beginnings, it was as simple as that. I had no interest whatsoever, and it irritated me when she always wanted to talk to me about it, drawing me to one side, cornering me in an empty room so that we would not be heard. I thought that my parents, my father in particular, would be hurt if they knew what we were discussing so furtively. Eventually my complete lack of enthusiasm made her give up the quest and the whole thing was forgotten for several years.

"It must have been lurking somewhere at the back of her mind though, because after the death of my father, when we were both in our twenties, she brought up the subject again. I told her to go ahead and find out what she could about herself, but to leave me out of it.

"Surprisingly, she had no success. There are no religious orders in Judaism, no Jewish monks or nuns, but there are countless movements where Jewish people follow their own line of spirituality. One of these sects, consisting of men and women, aimed to attend the three daily services, *Sacharit* in the morning, *Mincha* in the afternoon and *Aravit* in the evening. The Adoption Society confirmed that Ingrid's biological mother was a member of this sect. The movement was still in existence when Ingrid made her enquiries, but she came up against a blank refusal to help her in any way. It was felt that by revealing information they would be betraying a sister. When she asked to look at records she was refused permission. It was disappointing for her, but she accepted the failure with resigned cheerfulness. After all, she was completely happy, had the fierce and protective love of our mother and tender memories of our father.

"Then, to my dismay, she decided to find out about my background. It was to be her next project, and she was determined. She had just finished a rather unfortunate love affair, and it was shortly before she met Ramon. I suppose she felt her life was meaningless at that point, and she needed something to occupy her. Perhaps I felt sorry for her and that was why I did not make it clear to her at once, as I had done years before, that I did not want to know – the present was quite enough for me. I think I had the idea that as she had failed to trace her own biological mother, she would fail to find out anything about mine.

"It was not the case. Triumphantly, she told me that she had discovered that my mother was Swedish, that she lived in Malmo. Her name was Kirsten Erikkson and she had come to England as a young girl to be an au pair in a family, and to learn English. The English family she lived with consisted of a doctor and his wife and two children. The doctor was my biological father.

When her pregnancy could no longer be hidden she went to live with several girls in a similar position in a house which had been bought with my father's money. In that house I was born, and then handed over for adoption.

"Erikkson was her married name. She had two children, one at university and one still at school. Her husband was a successful businessman in Malmo.

" 'Let it be,' I begged.

"But my sister refused to be deterred. She is stubborn and likes to get her own way, but I must confess, by this time, I was beginning to be interested. Ingrid and I flew to Copenhagen and then got the hovercraft to Malmo. We stayed in a very nice small hotel, and I was unpacking my bag in my room when there was a sharp rap on the door. It was Ingrid who told me that she had already telephoned Kirsten and the lady had changed her mind. She no longer wished to see me. However, she did want to see Ingrid the following day, and she asked if she would bring with her a photograph of me.

"Well, that's impossible," I said shortly.

" 'No, it isn't,' she said, and she produced a photograph. 'I thought she might want it,' was her explanation.

"I could understand so well the feelings of the poor woman who had given birth to me so many years before. It was in all probability an episode in her life she had never divulged to anyone, perhaps not even her husband, certainly not her children. Now there was a danger of exposure, and I did not blame her for losing her nerve at the last minute. However, curiosity is a human trait, and I could not help being a little disappointed.

"Ingrid set off the next day, and I was left alone to wander around a strange city. It was the middle of December and bitterly cold. The temperature was displayed on one of the buildings, and I saw it was ten degrees below freezing point. My sister and I had anticipated this and had bought suitable clothes with us. I was wearing a long thick coat and a fur hat. I was reluctant to bring the fur hat, but Ingrid had persuaded me. Now, looking around me, I noticed that most of the men were wearing fur hats so I did not feel ridiculous. The cold was penetrating but peculiarly invigorating. The air smacking into my exposed face was fresh and pure. I strode along taking healthy gulps of it. The streets of Malmo were wide and free of traffic congestion. There were cars, but they were not head to tail as in other cities. Perhaps it was the lack of petrol fumes that was so refreshing. The place was ablaze with Christmas decorations. Trees covered in sparkling lights and every house had a triangle of lights in the window. In one square I found an ice statue and in another there were braziers, cheerful fires, and stalls alongside where one could purchase a warm alcoholic drink.

"The people walking along the streets were mostly good-looking and smartly dressed in furs and boots.

There was an air of prosperity about them. All of them looked unquestionably Scandinavian. It intrigued me to see so many men like myself, tall and fair. I, who had always felt different from everyone else, felt completely at home in this place. I had found my roots.

"When I returned to the hotel I found that Ingrid was already there. Her meeting with Kirsten had been brief. As I had expected she confided to my sister that she did not want to disrupt her happy life. She looked at my photograph, studying it carefully for a few moments, and then she handed it back to Ingrid.

" 'What was she like?' I could not help asking.

" 'Tall and big-boned.' Well, I was not surprised to learn that. 'She has the faded hair that has once been blonde. The house is situated in a good area. It is a substantial house with many rooms. The room we were in had a big fireplace containing a wood-burning stove, the doors of which had been flung wide open, showing the flames. The floor was wooden and there were a few scattered rugs. On the white walls were some abstract paintings, and the room contained comfortable sofas and chairs, and not much else. Minimalism in the Swedish tradition, and in very good taste.'

"Ingrid continued, 'I told her that you have had a very happy life so far, and that neither of us ever worried about being adopted, although I became curious to no avail. She was sympathetic about that, and said she was glad I had got in touch with her. It had given her peace of mind. She wished you all the luck in the world, and said she would always think of you.'

"I asked, 'What did you think of her, as a person?'

"Ingrid replied, 'Nice. Charming, in fact, but rather dour.'

" 'Dour? Do you mean humourless?'

" 'Well . . . perhaps a little."

* * *

Brose, lying on top of the bed in an hotel in Sestri Levante, said, "That figures, doesn't it? I am like my real mother."

Christabel snuggled up close to him. "No, it does not," she said defiantly. "Sensitive and serious perhaps, but not dour. And certainly not humourless."

"We returned to England," he continued, "thoroughly sobered by the whole experience. We hardly mentioned it on the journey back, and we have never discussed it since. I was possessed by a terrible fear that my mother would find out where we had been, perhaps someone we knew had spotted us on the aeroplane, or something of the sort. I imagined her asking questions that would be hard to answer, but it did not happen, I'm glad to say."

Christabel turned and put her arms around him. "Thank you for telling me," she said. "I like to think of you being born in the house which your father donated to the Adoption Society. He deserved to get a son like you." She paused. "You would like to have children?"

Instead of answering her question, he countered with another in the same vein. "You want children?"

"Two," she answered happily. "A boy and a girl would be ideal, but I'd settle for any combination of the two."

"I don't want two children," he said decidedly. She felt her body stiffen. Everything had been so perfect up to that moment. She had always felt there must be a flaw somewhere. She distrusted absolute happiness and had been waiting for something to break the spell. Now here it was, the fact that he did not want children. She envisaged that it would cause a great rift in their relationship.

At once he was sensitive to her change of mood, and took her face between his large hands. "Of course I'd love to have two children," he said, "but why can't we have more than two? I'd like a big family."

It was such a relief. "Oh, my darling," she said, "of course we can have a big family." She added inconsequently, "As many as you want!"

She thought, that is what rich people should do, have lots of children. No worries about educating them, people there to help when you wanted them to help. She thought of her poor mother, harassed because she did not know how to clothe and feed her children. Those anxieties would not exist for her and Brose.

"Lots of children," he said burying his face into her soft neck. "That's the Jewish tradition."

Chapter Five

The return to England after such a sun-drenched passionate holiday could not help being anticlimactic. Sitting opposite each other on the ferry, watching the rain splashing on the thick windows, they hardly spoke. Both were occupied with their own thoughts. Christabel was wondering, not for the first time, what Lady Silveridge's reaction would be to the news of their engagement. Although that lady featured foremost in her thoughts, she thought of her father's response as well. Would he be able to wish his daughter, unreservedly, every happiness in marriage? The idyllic fortnight was over, and reality had to be faced. She told herself that the opinions of other people did not matter, but although she was sure she could deal with any objections her father might raise, she knew that Brose would be upset if his mother did not give her blessing to the marriage.

The journey from Dover to London seemed long, and the windscreen wipers worked overtime all the way.

Brose, straining his eyes to see ahead on the flooded road, looked tired.

"Shall we stop for a while, so that you can have a rest?" suggested Christabel.

"No, darling, I think I'd rather get there."

It was a typical man's reply, but not one he would have made in Italy where everything was relaxed and unhurried.

Before he dropped her off at the block of flats where she lived he suggested that she remove her engagement ring until he had spoken to his mother. He spoke casually, but she knew that it was hard for him to make this request. Suddenly she felt sorry for him, thrust into what might turn out to be an awkward position between two women. She fingered the ring lovingly, and said, "Of course, darling. I understand."

He got out of the car to take her to the door. "I won't come in."

"No, my sweetheart, you go home and get some sleep." She watched him through the glass doors, head down against the rain, returning to his car parked on a double yellow line.

It occurred to her that she had said nothing about their time together, never even thanked him for the most wonderful holiday in her life. But he was the man she was going to marry, he would understand. When she was in her flat, which looked small and unlived-in after her absence, she went into the bedroom and sadly dropped her ring into a soft pile of underclothes in the top drawer of her dressing-table.

Its rejection obviated endless questions from Myra, who, as it was, spied the band of white on the finger of her deeply tanned left hand, but this was a source of amusement, not speculation. Christabel knew that Myra had much on her mind. The gallery was running at a loss, and she did not know what to do about it. She must be more concerned about paying Christabel's salary than she was about her romantic life.

It was arranged that Brose should take Christabel to meet his family on Friday, Friday being the evening Jewish families choose to get together. He had already told his mother that they were engaged, but he did not say how she had taken the news. Christabel longed to ask him, but she was too frightened to hear his answer. She did not want Friday evening to start with her feeling at a disadvantage. Perhaps it was better not to know. His silence made her fear the worst; surely if she had been pleased he would have mentioned it?

He drove through the drizzly London streets to the magnificent house in Halkin Street where his mother lived. Christabel had dressed carefully and she felt confident about her appearance. Simple elegance was what she had aimed to achieve, and she felt she had been successful. She had debated whether to put the ring back on her finger now that the news had been broken, but at the last minute decided against it. Now, sitting beside him in the car, her ringless hands folded on her lap, she knew that she had made an error of judgement. She missed the ring so terribly, and it would have given her a sense of power that, at the moment, she did not possess.

An elderly manservant, who looked at her with obvious interest, took her coat. She noticed in the hall there were a number of abstract paintings hanging on the walls; so Lord Silveridge had been interested in modern art then? She did not have the time to study them closely, but she knew Myra would have been excited.

She was surprised to see so many people congregated in a vast drawing-room and she was aware that all eyes were turned on her. Brose escorted her to an upright chair in which his mother was seated, and Christabel observed the familiar features of the portrait; small black eyes regarded her closely.

"Mother, this is Christabel."

"How do you do?" The fingers barely touched hers. Lady Silveridge turned to a figure by her side. "This is my daughter, Ingrid."

Ingrid bestowed on her a wide friendly smile, and Christabel took an instant liking to her. Brose had said she would love his sister, and at that first meeting she felt it would be true. Ingrid was very beautiful, olive-skinned with high cheekbones. Her eyes were brown like her mother's, but Ingrid's eyes had a deep velvety softness with long lashes. There was a voluptuousness about her that was very attractive and she had a slightly husky voice and a deep laugh. Her husband was just behind her and Christabel was introduced to him as well. Like his wife, he gave her an encouraging smile. Hovering in the background, somewhere, were their three children, as interested as their parents, and Christabel was aware of three pairs of brown eyes regarding her with curiosity. Of course they were intrigued; they, Ingrid especially, had waited a long time for Brose to choose a future wife.

Evidently children were part of the Friday night festivity because there were many children in the room, mostly being restrained by anxious parents.

The old lady said, "How young you are, and so pretty!" Her voice was so low it was difficult to hear her. Christabel noticed that people leant forward in order to try and catch what she was saying. Somehow the small weak voice made her more intimidating.

She realised she was being congratulated on her engagement.

"Thank you very much," she said and, when there was a little awkward silence, she filled it with the words, "I'm very happy."

"It cannot be," said Lady Silveridge. The three words, spoken in an undertone, but nevertheless with great firmness, made Christabel's heart turn to ice. She felt the colour rise in her face, and sensed the embarrassment of Ingrid and her husband. Brose seemed either to have not heard or to have not noticed their significance.

He took her elbow and steered her through the

people, introducing her with pride in his voice to everyone they met.

What had she expected of such a gathering? Old men with long beards and young boys dressed in black with pallid faces and skullcaps? There was no one of that description to be seen. They were a happy lot and, when not too near the old lady, laughed and chatted at the top of their voices. Brose introduced her to a rabbi, but she was a middle-aged woman wearing a turquoise silk trouser suit, not at all as Christabel had imagined a rabbi to be. The men wore dinner jackets and the women were expensively dressed and bejewelled. The diamonds sparkled in the ornate room, with its dark panelling and high ceilings.

Lady Silveridge made a sign to her son, and he took her arm and they led the way into the dining-room.

There were name cards so Christabel had no difficulty in finding where she was seated. She hoped she would be beside Brose, but she was not. He was a little further down the table, on the opposite side, and she was conscious of him watching her closely. Was he worried that she felt awkward in such company or that she was not enjoying herself? Her neighbour was Ingrid's husband whose name was Ramon and he was an agreeable person to have sitting next to her.

Ingrid was on the other side of the table, opposite her. She leaned over and said, "It is wonderful to see my brother so relaxed and happy. You have done that to him."

It was a very nice thing for her to say, and Christabel warmed to her. She thought about the brother and sister brought up in this atmosphere of opulence and restraint. Surely, if there was dourness in Brose's character it was due to this upbringing, and not to the inherited genes of his serious-minded Swedish mother. Ingrid, on the other hand, seemed very much at ease, sitting at the long table aglitter with crystal and silver and flickering candles. Her loud uninhibited laugh rang out from time to time. Except for a momentary lapse of curiosity about her forebears she had accepted this specialised society with good humour and understanding. Christabel thought she, unlike her brother, would cause no disturbance in the status quo.

During a gap in the conversation she was able to study the large portrait of Marcus Silveridge that dominated the room. He was standing with his hand on a table, obviously not a tall man, but with great presence. His eyes were very penetrating as if he would not suffer fools gladly. It was a kind face, but forbidding as well. Christabel wondered if the oil paint had darkened with the years. Only two points of colour, the yellow of the gold wedding ring on his finger and a splash of bright red that was his bow tie, relieved the sombreness of the painting.

She could not get over how friendly everyone was towards her, anxious to meet her and to hear what she had to say. When Brose joined her again after dinner (she was relieved to have him by her side once more) there was a great deal of companionable talk and plans made for future meetings. Some of the older members of the family approached them and she found them charming and sincere in their wishes for their happiness. The clasp of hands and benevolent looks conveyed only approval and good intentions. She became conscious that their hostess, sitting in her high-backed chair, was bidding the early leavers goodnight.

"I think I should have spent more time with your mother," she whispered to Brose.

"We'll go and talk to her now," he said.

They had to wait to speak to her. At last they were in front of her, bending over to hear what she said. "We're leaving soon, Mother," said Brose. "It has been a good evening."

The old lady turned her attention to Christabel. "I hope you have enjoyed meeting the family."

"I have indeed," said Christabel. "Thank you very much for inviting me this evening."

She wondered how to make her retreat. It was an uneasy moment. Eventually she decided on the kiss, and she leant forward, her mouth meeting a powdery furrowed cheek. To her surprise her hand was grasped and given an affectionate squeeze. "It has been a joy meeting you, my dear," said the old lady.

On the way home, sitting beside Brose in the car, Christabel thought of that farewell. There was warmth and love in the pressure of the old fingers on her hand. There had been no need to display such emotion with someone so recently encountered. Perhaps she had overreacted to the three words, "It cannot be." They could be taken in a different connotation, such as, how amazing that my son, at the age of forty-two, is at last to be married. It cannot be! And yet, her mind reasoned, Ingrid and her husband had been clearly discomforted by the words.

In the darkness, Brose said, "You are very quiet. Is something worrying you, darling?"

"No, I don't think so. I find your mother a bit of a sphinx. It is hard to know what she is thinking."

"Don't worry about her. She is not nearly as complicated as she would like you to believe. I'm sure my happiness is important to her."

"More important than the big religious gulf between us?"

"I can't believe that will affect her deeply. She must know by now that I am an outsider. It can be no surprise to her that I am marrying someone who is not of the faith."

He did not come in. They were both tired and, although neither would admit it, a little strained. They kissed at the doorway of her flat. A desperate kiss, both conscious of something they had lost since returning to England.

"I love you so much," he said. "You were a great success this evening. Everyone adored you."

She wished she could be back on holiday with him, where people's reactions did not matter, where only their feelings towards each other were of consequence.

"I liked them very much," she said, "especially your sister. She is everything you said she would be."

After she shut the door of her flat, she thought of the strange evening. She had enjoyed seeing so many well-meaning faces, but they had not been able to override an underlying feeling of tension. The words of the old lady came back to perplex and disturb her: "It cannot be."

Slipping between the cool sheets of her solitary bed she thought of Brose's departure that evening; his expressions of love before he left her gave her a feeling of security. But he had not stayed, and that was because his mother had effectively stepped in between them. He was not aware of this fact, but Christabel knew it to be true. It was an insidious intrusion, but it was real, and lying alone in her bed she vowed that she would not allow this to happen. Her hand lay in the empty space where he should have been and, fully awake, she conjured up the happy times they had spent together and envisaged they were only the beginning of years of contentment in each other's company. No one could come between them. The words 'It cannot be' had no meaning; they were the empty words of a pathetic old woman and could not influence the future of two people so bound together in love and compatibility. This was the comforting thought she had before she finally fell asleep, and it was with her when she awoke in the morning. The sun was shining and she and Brose were spending the day together.

Chapter Six

The following day was Saturday, and the day they had chosen to drive to the country so that Brose could meet Christabel's parents and her brother. Brose had to work that morning and he asked Christabel to meet him at his office. It was the first time she had been there because although she was familiar with the place where he lived, an unpretentious very masculine little flat in a block of flats like her own, she had not yet seen the place where he worked. As she climbed the steps to the heavy glass door she felt slightly nervous. It was very impressive, the spacious entrance hall with soft leather sofas and armchairs, and Brose's secretary, who greeted her with spurious warmth, was undeniably attractive. Long-legged and impeccably dressed, she exuded efficiency as she led the way to his office. Christabel was glad of the ring on her finger, the confidence it gave her, so solid and personal, hers alone, a symbol of love. She thought that, in her usual way, she had exaggerated the events of the previous evening, invested them with an importance they did not possess. It was so like her to get worked up over three innocent little words that could mean anything. She had been overtired, that was probably the problem. Today she felt rested and more certain about the future.

She was alone with him in the room that must have at one time belonged to his father. The secretary left, closing the door quietly behind her, and before Christabel had time to take in the big desk and the heavy curtains, she was enveloped in his arms. He pressed her against the wall, kissing her with great enthusiasm.

"I missed you," he said, "last night, I missed you so much."

"Stop!" she cried. "That girl . . . she may come in again."

"She won't." he said, and went on kissing her, pinning her arms to her sides.

She managed to say, "I missed you too."

Over his broad shoulder she could see a strange face leering at her, a face full of colour and distortion. "We're being watched," she said.

He turned and looked at the face in the picture. "Picasso," he said briefly. "He, of all people, would understand."

Later, when she was sitting beside him in the car (it was so good to be back in that comfortable seat with all the happy memories of the miles they had travelled together), she thought about the fact that he had a genuine Picasso in his office. Somehow, since accepting that invitation from Hugh Bramley, she had been catapulted into a completely different world, a world of immense wealth, intense religion and a Picasso on the wall.

"Sometimes I find it a bit bewildering," she said, speaking her thoughts aloud.

He looked sideways at her. "What puzzles you, darling?"

"Power and money," she said, "they puzzle me, and I hope you will like my parents. They are a very simple pair, and power and money do not enter their lives at all."

He took his hand off the wheel, and pressed one of her hands folded in her lap. "Don't let it worry you," he said. "We are all the same underneath. I know I will like your family and I only hope they will like me. I would not like to think that power and money would get in the way of that."

"That is the only thing I'm sure about," she said. "It means very little to my mother and nothing at all to my father. They will know about your father, of course, but they will be more interested in the good he did than the money he made."

"Then everything will be fine," he said.

He was right. They hit it off from the start. Christabel was startled to see how clean the house looked; a real effort had been made. The vicar shambled off to the kitchen to fetch a bottle of wine to drink to their health and happiness. Andrew quickly found out that Brose enjoyed a game of cricket, and immediately embarked on a long saga about a recent village cricket match. Brose listened intently. Then they went into the dining-room, cold, draughty and damp, like the rest of the Georgian vicarage. Christabel's father carved a brace of pheasants (a present from a parishioner) and Christabel's mother, comfortable in a worn tweed skirt and a sloppy cardigan, scooped the vegetables on to their plates. The conversation was as warming as the wine. There were no awkward moments.

Afterwards in the vicar's study, encased by shelf upon shelf of books, they got on to more serious topics. The ring was examined and exclaimed upon. "What a rock!" said young Andrew, and, "It is so beautiful," from his mother.

Brose explained that they would marry in a registry office because of the differences in their religion. "I hope you will not mind that too much," he said.

Christabel's father said, "I do not mind where the ceremony takes place as long as you love each other and aim to stay together. It concerns me that differences of religion should make it necessary to marry in a registry office, but I am well aware of those differences. We have put up with them for many hundreds of years. We should all be able to live in harmony together. I do not think God intends his children to bicker over small discrepancies."

"I agree with what you say," said Brose, "and I think

that is partly the reason your daughter and I have broken away from the beliefs we were brought up to respect. The fact that these beliefs are poles apart means that we must abandon them altogether, but we had almost done that before we met."

"I am the same," chipped in Andrew, not wishing to be left out of the discussion. "I have no beliefs."

"Then I am sorry for you," said his father, "for if you do not believe in anything it is difficult to understand the reason for your existence."

"The old ways of one's childhood are never forgotten," said Brose. "When I said we almost abandoned them, that's what I meant. Almost."

"And any children you may have?" asked Christabel's mother. "How will this attitude affect them?"

Christabel answered this time. "I think we should leave it to them to decide, when they are old enough to do so."

Her mother sighed. "A great pity, if I may say so. I suppose you will not teach them to say their prayers before they go to sleep. A very good idea to bless all their relations, brings it home to them the importance of the family."

"It did not do me any good," said Andrew.

"You have not had your children yet," replied his mother with spirit. "When you do, you may change your mind about saying prayers. Thank goodness I was brought up in a Christian family where doubt was never an issue. It was much happier that way."

Her husband said impatiently, "But these two cannot do that, Jessie dear, you must see there is no solution for them but to distance themselves from the ideologies of their families." He went on, "I think we should draw this argument, or rather I should say discussion, to a close, and just concentrate on the happy aspect of your engagement. I understand, Ambrose, your close family consists of your mother and sister?"

"That's right. My father died over twenty years ago. I think of him a great deal, and wish he could have lived to meet Christabel."

"Oh, I know about your father," said the vicar, "although, of course, I never had the privilege of meeting him. He left his mark on the world, that's for sure – medicine, education, social reforms, they all benefited from his generosity."

"He could afford to be generous," said Brose.

"Many people can afford it, but they never achieve what he achieved during his life. He was a force for good, and this country was a better place because of him."

"Thank you," said Brose. He looked humbled. He felt it was right that his future father in-law should know everything about him because he was aware that, if the circumstances had been different, he would have asked Brose for details of his income and whether he was able to keep his daughter in the style she deserved. Obviously in this case it would be nonsensical, and it was a foregone conclusion between them they would ignore the financial aspect. To Christabel's surprise, Brose told him that he and his sister were both adopted. He even described their trip to Malmo. The vicar, his wife and their young son listened to the story with rapt attention.

"How very interesting," said Christabel's father when Brose had finished.

His wife could not help exclaiming, "You could have gone anywhere, but you were adopted by the Silveridges! That was very fortunate for you."

"Yes, to be part of such a loving family was, as you say, Jessie dear, fortunate," said her husband hastily, anxious that his wife's comment would not be misconstrued.

"My mother does not know of my visit to Sweden," said Brose.

"Of course." With these two words his future father-in-law pledged that not one word of what he had just been told would ever pass his lips. A confidence entrusted to him was sacrosanct.

"The other thing that may concern you," said Brose, "is the difference in our ages. I am much older than your daughter, as you can see."

"Well, that does not concern us at all," said Mrs Tooley. "David is ten years older than me, and it has not worried us."

"As usual," said the vicar, exasperated, "my wife speaks without any thought."

"What do you mean?" she demanded.

"Well, it may not have worried you, but the difference in our ages has created difficulties in my opinion."

"Difficulties?" Her voice rose. "What difficulties?"

"Yes," said Andrew, interested. "What difficulties?"

"You, my boy, for one. It cannot be easy for you to have such an elderly father. I am completely out of touch with you over so many things. If I were younger I would have more understanding."

"What rubbish you do talk," said his wife. "If we had had both our children during the first years of our marriage you would not be able to make such an outlandish statement. It is not my fault," she finished determinedly, "that I gave birth to Andrew at the age of forty-five."

* * *

"They are delightful," said Brose on the way back to London. "I could not like them better and I felt completely at ease with them. I like the way they bring all their arguments and little points of dissension out in the open. I'm not used to that, it never happened in my family. We kept out opinions to ourselves."

"You have not heard them in full flow yet," she said. "The Resurrection and the Virgin Birth are favourite topics of discussion."

"And your father believes utterly in these events?"

"Not at all. He is full of doubts, as are most of the clergy, but he believes in the principle, and I think that is important. The church is not financially rewarding, but it has its advantages. My parents enjoy village life, and being a vicar of a country parish holds no terrors. He will not be made redundant unless he does something really dreadful, and that must give a sense of security."

"He must have had a calling or he would not have taken on the job," said Brose.

Christabel replied, "Andrew and I think he would have liked to have been an actor. But that would not have suited him because, as I said, security is important to him. The way he floats around in that black cassock every day is very theatrical. He is a direct contrast to our mother who doesn't give a damn what she looks like."

"I thought it important to tell him about my background," said Brose.

"You were certainly very honest with each other," said Christabel.

"The fact that I was adopted might just have made a difference, but it was obvious that it did not. Your father, though intolerant in many ways, is amazingly understanding about things that matter."

"I expect he was relieved that he did not have to ask you about your financial position. He really hates talking about money. It drives my poor mother mad. She has to do the worrying for both of them. Now she is concerned about Andrew going to university. Neither of them wants him to start a career with an enormous debt."

"When I know them better, perhaps they will let me help," he said.

When they got to Christabel's flat they found there was a message on the answerphone. It was from Ingrid. *'Mother wonders whether Christabel can come and have supper with her this evening, seven o'clock.'*

It was then six o'clock, which meant there was only an hour to change and get there. She felt she needed more time to think about the request and the significance behind it.

Brose telephoned his sister, "What is this about?"

Christabel leaned against him so that her ear was near the telephone receiver and she could hear Ingrid's reply.

"She said she did not have a chance to talk to her the other evening. She wants her to come alone so that they can get to know each other."

There was a silence while Brose stood, telephone in hand, frowning slightly.

Ingrid persisted. "I don't think you should read anything into this. She means what she says."

"All right, I'll take your word for it. Does she want Christabel to telephone her?"

"No, neither of you have to do a thing. I'll let her know I have talked to you. Just ask Christabel to be at Halkin Street as near to seven o'clock as she can manage."

"In which case, my darling," said Christabel, "you

must make yourself scarce for I want to have a shower and change, and if you are here I'll never be ready on time."

They kissed at the door.

"I'm sorry," he said.

"What a day!" she said. "Perhaps after this confrontation with two sets of parents we can relax and be together."

When she was ready and the taxi was waiting at the front door, the telephone rang. It was Brose.

"I'm just leaving," she told him.

"I hope everything goes well."

She sensed anxiety in his voice. "Of course it will. I don't want you to worry."

"Then I won't. I'll telephone you later tonight. I love you."

"I love you too," she said.

Chapter Seven

She asked the taxi driver to take her to the address in Halkin Street. He was talkative. "Nice part of London, that. Rich people live there."

"I know."

"The house I'm taking you to used to belong to Lord Silveridge. He often took my taxi. He was a fine gentleman and always had a few words to say to me."

"His widow still lives there."

"Is that right? Well, I was really bowled over when I heard that he had died. It must be some time ago now."

"Nearly twenty years."

"All that time? I can hardly believe it. Just shows how long I've been trundling this cab around. I've never forgotten him. He cared for people and did a lot of good. There's not enough of his sort around today. I hope you have a good evening, miss."

She thanked him for his good wishes when she paid the fare. She felt he was a kindred spirit, and she thought the same of the butler who took her coat.

"I hope I'm not late."

"Right on time, Miss Tooley."

She followed him to a part of the house she had not been to before; she was expecting to be ushered into the large gloomy drawing-room. Instead it was a small room, almost cosy in fact, with comfortable armchairs and sofas and numerous family photographs in evidence on every available space. There were a couple of lamps, but no other illumination, so there were pools of darkness in the room.

Lady Silveridge took her hand, "My dear, how good of you to come, and at such short notice. This is my private sitting-room. Marcus and I spent so much time here. Sometimes we had our suppers on trays, watching the television." It sounded reassuringly normal.

Christabel became aware of someone else in the room; a man in a lounge suit, who rose from one of the sofas and extended a hand. She was surprised because she had understood this was to be a meeting with Brose's mother on her own: to get to know each other better had been the reason for the invitation. Now it seemed there was a third party. She wondered, had he arrived unexpectedly? Such things do happen, and she wanted to give her hostess the benefit of the doubt.

"This is Rabbi Daniel Wiseman," said Lady Silveridge.

He did not look like a rabbi, more like a successful

businessman; dapper, rather fat, with a shock of white hair.

Her head spun. How should she address him? "I'm so pleased to meet you, Rabbi," she said hopefully.

"And I to meet you," he replied with excessive politeness, "and I must congratulate you on your engagement to a most excellent young man whom I have known for years."

They all sat down. There was a little awkward pause. "And what have you two being doing today?" asked Lady Silveridge.

"We have been to the country to visit my parents."

"Did that go well?"

"Very well, thank you."

The butler appeared with three glasses of sherry on a tray.

"You will have a sherry before supper?"

"Yes, please."

The tray was put on a coffee table, and as well as the three glasses there was a plate of cheese straws and a bowl of olives. Christabel took one of the olives. "I got addicted to these when we were in Italy," she said. "We ate them like sweets."

"You were in Italy with my son?"

Christabel thought, surely she is not going to preach morality to me? One word in that direction and I will have no hesitation in reminding her that Ambrose is forty-two years of age.

Afterwards, when she thought about the evening,

she realised that she had been on the defensive from the beginning. She had entered the room expecting to feel at a disadvantage, and the presence of Rabbi Daniel Wiseman did not improve the situation.

Lady Silveridge went on to recall happy holidays she and her husband had spent in Italy. Sadly, in her quiet voice, she said, "We both loved it. The climate, the countryside, the food, everything was perfection."

"I agree with you," said Christabel, and she thought, perfection, and a long way away from this room and its occupants.

"Your father and mother? Do they enjoy travelling?"

"Not at all," Christabel replied. "He is a country parson, and not well off. They have a young son, my brother, aged fifteen, and until he is settled in a career I'm sure they will not think of going abroad. Maybe when my father is retired, but I doubt it. They are set in their ways."

"Such a pity," sighed Lady Silveridge. "It is so rewarding to travel. Marcus and I had some wonderful trips. Now he has gone I have lost my enthusiasm."

Rabbi Daniel Wiseman was silent, and Christabel did not know what to say to him. She did not like to ask him if he had a family in case rabbis were celibate. She wished she was not so ignorant about Judaism; if she had known beforehand of his presence that evening she could have asked Brose to put her in the picture about Jewish laws and customs.

Her doubts were resolved when Lady Silveridge

said, "Tragically, Daniel lost his wife last year."

Rabbis led normal lives then. Bully for them. "I'm so sorry," she murmured.

"He has grown-up children to comfort him," went on her future mother-in-law, "as I have. I would not be able to survive without Ambrose and Ingrid."

They moved in to the dining-room and sat at one end of the long table. As well as gloomy the room now seemed rather chilly. Marcus Silveridge with his dark suit and flamboyant bow tie looked down at them with fierce appraisal.

The butler who had taken Christabel's coat waited on them. Fish-pie was served and it was delicious. The white wine had been chilled and the glasses were replenished at intervals. Christabel noticed that the rabbi enjoyed the wine and, after his second glass, he relaxed and lost some of his pomposity. She ventured to ask about his family, and he told her he had a son and a married daughter.

"She has just had her first child," he said proudly. "A son. I am looking forward to the Redemption ceremony which takes place next week."

Christabel said, "I'm sorry, you will have to explain that to me."

"It is a service for the first-born male child, and symbolises that the suffering of the Jewish people leads to salvation."

"I see.

Lady Silveridge took tiny bites of her fish; consequently she was still pecking at it when Christabel and the rabbi had finished. Conversation lapsed. Christabel could think of no words to fill the gap. The rabbi stared into the middle distance and sipped his wine. Fruit salad was eaten in silence, and the coffee was served in delicate coffee cups.

At the end of the meal no one stirred. Christabel decided that the procedure must be that they remain at the table until it was time to leave. She hoped some indication would be made when that time came.

Lady Silveridge wiped her mouth with her napkin and they waited for her to speak. "I imagine," she said, "that before your marriage to my son you will wish to embrace our faith, and I have asked my dear friend Daniel here this evening as he will be happy to instruct you."

Somehow she had known all along that this moment would come. She was conscious of two pairs of eyes studying her closely.

She took a deep breath. "I'm afraid not," she said as calmly as she could. "You see, as I have explained, my father is an Anglican minister. My brother and I have made a conscious decision that we not longer wish to attend church. Of course, this is a sadness to my father, and I certainly do not want to add to that sadness by taking on another religion. Apart from the fact," she added hastily, "I do not wish it myself."

"Have you explained this to my son?" The voice was so small and low that Christabel and the rabbi had to lean forward to hear her.

"Of course we have discussed it, and we are in complete agreement."

"And what about your children? I'm sure Ambrose will want to have children – are they to be left in this wilderness?"

"They can decide when they are old enough to make that sort of decision," said Christabel.

There was a great sigh, a sigh that seemed to fill the small frame and was almost like a groan of pain. Daniel looked concerned.

"Your father may be saddened," said the old lady, "but it is nothing to the despair I feel. Presumably he will stay in touch with you, still regard you as his daughter?"

"Yes," replied Christabel wondering where this conversation was heading.

"Which is not possible in my case. If you marry my son, in your present state of mind, I shall have to distance myself from him entirely."

Christabel felt anger welling up inside of her. She clasped her hands in her lap to stop them trembling. She tried to speak without a tremor in her voice. "Do you mean that you will cut him off financially? That is the usual procedure, isn't it, in all the old-fashioned books?"

The old woman made a little tut of irritation. "You are so dramatic," she said. "I'm sure you are aware that Marcus left his two children well provided for, whereas I live on the proceeds of a trust fund which will pass to them when I die."

She turned to the man sitting on her right. "I'm afraid this is very distressing for you, my dear old friend. If I had known about the stubbornness of this girl, I would have spared you."

Christabel said, "I would be obliged, Lady Silveridge, if you would tell me what it is that you object to about me. Is it solely that I am not Jewish, or is there some other reason?"

For the first time the old woman's voice rose a little. "The fact that you are not Jewish is a very valid reason for my objection to the marriage, not because I dislike you. If you really love my son you will wish to become part of our faith. It is not a terrible thing I ask of you. Of course I do not dislike you, that is a figment of your overworked imagination. It is just that you do not begin to understand the importance of the teaching I have been brought up to love and respect. By marrying him, you will be taking away the birthright of my only son."

"That is not true," replied Christabel hotly. "It is not his birthright, as you well know. His birthright lies in Sweden with his biological mother. Nothing you can say can take that away from him."

The shaft had gone home, the already pale face was now drained of all colour. A thin, almost transparent, hand fluttered in distress and settled on her breast. At last she said in a whisper, "I am surprised he told you.

It is something we do not find necessary to talk about."

"I am to be his wife," said Christabel. "Of course he told me."

"There is no 'of course' about it," said Lady Silveridge, stronger now. "Ambrose and I have not discussed it because we both felt it was of no importance. It made no difference."

"It was important enough for him to make a trip to Malmo twenty years ago in the hope of meeting his mother."

As the words came out of her mouth, she regretted them. Fervently, she wished she could retract them, that they had never been said. She had betrayed a trust, and the realisation was sobering. Her anger against the pathetic old woman dissipated in the face of her own shame and humiliation.

She carefully placed her napkin on the table, and rose to her feet. She was aware that the man sitting opposite her had risen also. She wondered if her legs would carry her to the door. Outside in the hall she leaned against a table, feeling faint. As the feeling receded she saw that Rabbi Daniel Wiseman was standing in front of her. She had to admit he had a kind face. The butler hovered, and he too looked concerned.

"Please may I have my coat," she said.

He fetched it and held it out for her and she put her arms in the sleeves. She looked up at him and thanked him.

"Come," said the rabbi. "We will go outside where there is fresh air, and I'm sure you will feel better."

It was true that the cold air on her hot face was refreshing. She began to breathe normally again.

The rabbi regarded her sadly. "It has been an ordeal for you," he said quietly.

"Yes."

He took her arm. "Let us walk for a few minutes." They set off slowly in the direction of Belgrave Square.

"Before you came," he said, "Lady Silveridge informed me that she has cancer. She is about to embark on a long treatment."

"Do her children know about this?"

"No, she has not told them yet. It is her intention to tell them, of course. I was wondering whether you would consider delaying the marriage until she is better?"

"Now you are employing blackmail tactics," she said bitterly. "What other tricks and devices have you two got up your sleeves?"

His arm tightened on hers. "It is not blackmail," he said. "More like a gesture of conciliation. She is a very unhappy obstinate old lady. You must feel sympathy towards her."

She withdrew her arm from his. "I have to think," she said fretfully. "Please leave me now. Go back to her. She needs you at a time like this."

"I'll stay and get you a taxi."

"No, please. I want to walk for a while."

"Are you sure?" he asked. "I could walk with you."

"No . . . please."

He looked earnestly into her face, and then seemed to make up his mind.

"As you wish," he said. He turned and started to walk back to the house.

She walked for an hour, trying to concentrate her mind on the events of the evening.

Eventually, she saw the lights of a taxi and she hailed it. As she stepped out opposite her block of flats she saw a familiar car parked outside. Brose and Ingrid got out of the front seats.

"Thank God, you've come," said Ingrid.

No explanations were necessary. They followed her in to her flat, and she removed her coat and threw it on a chair. Then she kicked off her shoes. She felt utterly weary. "Sit down," she said, sitting down herself. "I think we need a drink. I have a bottle of whisky somewhere. Brose will deal with it."

She heard his heavy footsteps in the kitchen that was familiar to him, pouring the whisky into three glasses and topping up with water from the tap. He came in carrying the glasses on a tray that he knew Christabel kept in a space near the sink.

They all sat down, glasses in hand. Christabel glanced at Brose's face. It was expressionless, and it was impossible to know what he was thinking.

"Daniel telephoned us," said Ingrid. "He was worried about you."

"And he told you everything?"

"Absolutely everything, even about Mummy's illness which was a bit of a shock."

Christabel shivered. How anyone could call that woman 'Mummy' was beyond her comprehension.

"We thought she had become very frail, but we never guessed."

Christabel looked at Brose. "Breaking off our engagement would make her feel better," she said.

He did not reply, just stared, head down, at a patch of carpet between his feet. She felt, with a terrible dread that she had lost him.

"I suppose he told you that I mentioned the trip to Malmo?"

Again he was silent, and his sister replied for him. "Yes, he did tell us that," she said.

"I was provoked," said Christabel. "I had to lash out at her in some way. That was the first thing that came to my head. I knew it would hurt her. It was unforgivable, and I am truly sorry." She searched their faces for some response from either of them, but there was none. "I did not know then that she was ill," she said lamely.

Ingrid spoke at last. "I'm afraid you have had a perfectly horrid evening. I know how intractable my mother can be about the Jewish question. I have often wondered what would have happened if I had married someone not of the faith. I hoped, or rather we hoped," she looked at her brother, "that because old Brose here had been an outsider for so long, it would not worry her. We were both completely wrong."

"It is so late," said Christabel. "Do you mind if I go to bed?"

"There is no point in staying up to argue about what has happened," agreed Ingrid. "Nothing will change Mummy's attitude, that's for sure." She got to her feet, and Brose did the same. Christabel thought, for the first time, he looked quite old, as if all the cares of the world were on his broad shoulders. What a burden to him she had turned out to be!

She accompanied them to the door of the flat.

"We can let ourselves out of the main entrance," said Brose. It was the first time he had spoken.

Ingrid took Christabel's face between her hands. "Sleep well," she said, "and don't worry too much. We are on your side, remember that."

Brose bent down from his great height and kissed her on the lips. She felt his lips were cold against hers. She watched them walk across the hall; then she closed the door. There was nothing she could do except go wearily to bed.

Chapter Eight

Before she opened her eyes on the following morning she knew that something had changed in her life. Behind her closed lids dawned the memory, menacing in its clarity, of the events of the night before. When her eyes were wide open and she could make out the familiar contours and contents of her bedroom, the terrible realisation came to her that the happiness she had experienced during the last weeks had disappeared. Before she had become accustomed to the daily feeling of well-being, like a twitch on a thread it had been snatched away from her.

She examined her face in the bathroom mirror. She saw a woman who looked as if she had not slept the night before, but it was not true: she had slept uneasily not waking once. Last night she had felt so tired that all she wanted was sleep. This morning she still felt tired, her bones ached with despondency and exhaustion.

While she ate a piece of toast and drank a cup of

coffee she willed the telephone to ring. But it remained silent. Brose was angry with her, and he had every reason to feel that way. Perhaps at this very moment he was reviewing the situation and their relationship and wondering if he had done the wrong thing. It had been a very hurried courtship; momentous decisions had been made in romantic settings when passions ran high. It would be understandable if he were having second thoughts in the darkening light of a wet Sunday morning in London.

She did not leave her flat for the whole of that day. She stared at the telephone willing it to ring, hating the inanimate object for its silent immutability. The rain beat on the windowpanes so there was no incentive to go out. Loneliness and self-pity engulfed her. She sprawled on the sofa, the Sunday papers scattered all over the floor around her. She had read all the sections, even the sports one which normally she never glanced at, and there was nothing left for her to do except contemplate the misery of her situation. At midnight she realised that Brose was not going to telephone her that day and she went to bed, knowing that she would get very little sleep that night.

Christabel had intended wearing her ring when she went to work at the gallery on Monday morning. She had anticipated showing it to Myra, and enjoying her amazement when she told her who had given it to her. Now, it did not seem an appropriate moment, and she removed it from her finger and put it back in its old hiding-place among her underclothes in the top drawer of her dressing-table. It was a sad little gesture that exemplified her thoughts at that moment.

The underground was a seething mass of humanity, and in the train she was crammed between strap-hangers who, like herself, were on their way to work. When, at last, she pushed herself forward on to the platform she was buffeted by hordes of struggling people all determined to escape this hell under the ground. Eventually, when she emerged into the street, it was raining, and she quickened her steps, holding an umbrella over her head.

When she reached the glass door, to her surprise, she could see the figure of Myra, standing on the other side of the wet glass, waiting for her.

Myra opened the door and said, "Come quickly. I must talk to you." She almost pushed Christabel towards her tiny office. A small corner of the gallery had been partitioned off so as to hold two small desks (one for her and one for Christabel), two chairs each and a filing cabinet. There was a little refrigerator and also a built-in cupboard where the women put their coats. Myra called it her cubby-hole. Here she studied the catalogues, did the accounts and wrote out the receipts for people buying pictures. She motioned Christabel to sit down, and she took the seat behind her table.

Without preamble she announced, "I have sold the gallery."

Christabel was astonished. "When did this happen?"

"While you were abroad with your young man."

"And you did not think of telling me that this was your intention?" There was no partnership involved, but Christabel had been working for Myra for six years and the two women had become close. Christabel knew every detail of the running of the gallery, and Myra was well aware how much she depended on her.

"It all happened so quickly," was the excuse offered, "and you were away. I was not sure it would go through until the end of last week. We signed the contract on Friday evening." She paused, looking, for her, almost shamefaced. "I could not do anything else, darling. This place was running at a loss, as you know, and it is a relief to be shot of it."

"So, I haven't got a job?"

"I'm afraid that's so."

"Shouldn't I get a month's notice, or something of the sort?" There was an edge to her voice when Christabel asked the question. Under normal circumstances she would have tried to be understanding, but this was no ordinary day.

"He wants to move in right away," said Myra bleakly. "We have to clear the place today so that he can take over. All our hard work over the years has gone down the pan. I feel as bad about it as you do. Worse, because it's my baby."

But you have the compensation of a big cheque, thought Christabel.

As if reading her thoughts Myra took her cheque book from the top drawer of her desk. She wrote out a cheque and handed it to Christabel. It was for one thousand pounds. "Take this, darling, with my love – it will tide you over until you get another job."

"Thank you." In the harsh light of the cubby-hole Myra's face, with its pancake make-up and scarlet slash of lipstick, looked old and vulnerable. What would she do now, an ageing woman with no children who had now lost her 'baby' as she called it?

"Have you any plans?" Christabel asked.

"I'm going to work for Sam Hirsch." Sam Hirsch owned a gallery in the next street.

They had been rivals and Myra always maintained she hated him. "It won't be too bad," she said, on the defensive. "The money I made from the sale of this place won't keep me in my old age. I have to do something."

Christabel collected the few items in the cubby-hole that belonged to her: a notebook, pens and pencils, a calendar and her coat in the cupboard. There seemed no point in staying any longer. Myra accompanied her to the door. "Don't let's lose touch, please," she said. There was a pleading note in her voice as if she was conscious of the poignancy of the situation.

"Of course not." They embraced and wished each other good luck in the future.

And so six years of working together had come to an end. It seemed a fitting beginning to such a day. The underground train was almost deserted. Christabel sat with empty seats on either side of her and studied her indistinct reflection in the window opposite.

Her feet echoed as she hurried towards the escalator. It was eerily quiet after the hustle and bustle of the early morning. They echoed again on the tiled floor as she walked across the hall to the front door of her flat. When she entered, it felt cold and unwelcoming. It was not the right time to return; missing was the sense of relief at getting home after a hard day. In the kitchen was a mug half full of cold coffee and a plate with the remains of a piece of toast she had eaten only two hours before. There were no messages on the answer-phone, but that was to be expected, Brose would think she was at work.

Christabel sat on the edge of her bed and allowed herself the luxury of tears. She howled with misery, disappointment and anger at the way things had changed for her. Copious tears are only beneficial if there is someone with the person doing the weeping. Sobbing alone leads to nowhere very quickly, and it has to stop. When she had recovered sufficiently she wondered whether she should telephone Brose. It seemed the obvious thing to do. But the practical side of her character reasoned that if he had wanted to speak to her he would have called her. She had apologised, that was all she could do. Now it was up to him.

Christabel telephoned her mother. "I'm coming home. I'll be with you this afternoon. Don't worry to meet me, I'll walk from the station."

"Are you all right?" The voice at the other end was anxious.

"Not really, but I'll explain when I see you."

Then she sat down and began to write.

My darling Brose,

The fact that you have not telephoned me or left a message makes me certain you are still angry with me, and you have every reason to be. I know only too well that I betrayed a precious confidence when I told your mother that you have visited Malmo. I wish I could undo the moment when I uttered those words, but I know I can't.

This morning I find I no longer have a job at the gallery, so this afternoon I am going to hop on a train and go home. I feel I need time to think about what your mother said to me, about her illness and its implications, and also about us. I'm sure you feel the same. You know where I am if you want to talk to me.

I love you very much. That is the one thing I am sure of at this moment.

Christabel.

With hardly a pause, she started on a second letter.

Dear Lady Silveridge,

Thank you for inviting me to supper last night. I enjoyed meeting Rabbi Daniel Wiseman.

I am sorry we cannot agree on so many important

things. Because they are so important I am going away for a while to try and work out how they will affect Ambrose's and my future. I am able to do this because the art gallery where I worked for six years has been sold, and I no longer have a job. In a way it is a blessing as it means I have time to myself, which is something I need at present.

Also, of course, I am very sorry to hear about your illness. I do hope the treatment will…

She crossed this out and began the letter again.

I wish you a full recovery.

Trite, but it remained.

Yours sincerely,

Christabel Tooley.

* * *

Her mother had tidied the vicarage for Brose's visit. Dusted and polished the furniture and vacuumed the carpet. Now it was returning rapidly to its former state of chaos. Andrew's cricket clothes, bat and school-books were scattered around his father's study. The hairy dog had resumed its usual place on the sofa. It was good, after the walk from the station, to sink into one of the unbelievably comfortable chairs, shabby and soft to the touch. A mug of tea and a slab of fruitcake were put by Christabel's side.

Her parents were good listeners and they did not interrupt her story. Andrew listened as well.

When she had finished the vicar made the remark, "I never expected to be faced with such a situation in our family. It is something about which I would not care to voice an opinion."

His wife said, "That's a great help!"

"It just seems silly to me," said Andrew, and he sidled out of the room, intending to go and practice in the nets before supper.

Walking to the village cricket ground he decided the world would be a better place without religion. He hoped his sister would refuse to be upset by such nonsense. He did not know much about Jewish people except that they had been persecuted for hundreds of years. Perhaps that made them supersensitive about everything outside the boundaries they had made for themselves.

They had been reading about the Holocaust at school, and it was pretty horrific; enough to make a person distrust the human race. He wondered if any member of Brose's family had been affected by it. He thought not. He had shown no signs of oppression, just the natural confidence of the very rich. The Rolex watch on his wrist had not escaped Andrew's notice. He thought his sister would be mad to let such a man slip through her fingers. Why take notice of a spiteful old woman, anyway?

* * *

After Christabel had said, "It seems silly to me as well," and Andrew had left the room, there was a long silence while the three adults contemplated the position.

At last the vicar's wife ventured an opinion. "I can understand him being annoyed by what you said. It was a very silly thing to do, if you don't mind my saying. I know you were provoked, but that is no excuse. I am often provoked and I have learnt to hold my tongue. It is the only way."

"You have to remember the poor woman is ill," said her husband, "perhaps dying. She ought not to be bothered by you and your problems at such a time. Leave her in peace."

"That is what I am doing," replied his daughter. She began to wish she had stayed in London.

The vicar gave a great sigh as if all the religious disputes throughout the world were taking place in his study. "It cannot be," he said.

They were the exact words Lady Silveridge had used. "You mean you think that Brose and I should not be married because he is a Jew and I am a Gentile?"

"No, I don't mean that. I have said over and over again that God did not intend it to be that way. I am just saying that it raises enormous difficulties. You would not be here now if that was not the case."

"I can't believe what I'm hearing!" She almost shouted the words. "You profess to be a man of God, and yet you believe that differences between people of separate cultures and religions must come between them, in spite of their feelings for each other?"

"I'm afraid I do believe that," he admitted. "It is a sad fact, but a true one."

"Then you are a bigger coward than I thought you were."

Her mother took on the role of peacemaker. She came up with a suggestion. "Give it time," she said. "Your father is right when he points out the poor lady is very ill. Let her children help her through this ordeal. In the meantime, you have the money Myra gave you – why don't you use some of it to visit Aunt Bell?"

Her mother was referring to her elder sister who lived on an island south of Mallorca. The island was called *La Isla de la Fuga.* She lived in a house she had inherited years ago. The lady who left her the house was her employer, and Bell had cared for her before she died. At one time the impoverished Christabel (Bell as she liked to be called) had eked out a living by looking after decrepit and sad old ladies (and sometimes old gentlemen) and she was in her fifties when to her delighted surprise she discovered she had been left a little house on a Spanish island. She had never married, and she left England without a backward glance. There were a few happy memories of childhood, and in her adult years when she and her father had shared a home, but after his death there had been nothing but despair and humiliation. She remembered her family, her sister and brother-in-law and their two children every year at Christmas when she sent them a card usually emblazoned with the words *'Feliz Navidad!'* They inferred she was so happy she did not want to travel to see them, or maybe it was that she could not afford it. Certainly, in their case, they maintained a lack of funds was their reason for not visiting her. The Christmas cards they received from her over the years always contained the same message: *'Come and visit me. I have the room.'*

"She would love to have you," said Christabel's mother encouragingly.

"Yes," said Christabel thoughtfully, "that's a good idea. I'll go and see Aunt Bell."

There was no doubt her father was visibly relieved. He disliked family traumas interrupting the even tenor of his life, and he considered this a good solution.

"I'll telephone her," he said, "and let her known you are coming."

"How can you do that?" asked his daughter.

"I'll get the number from Directory Enquiries," he said quite cheerfully. He closeted himself in his study where the telephone was situated, and it seemed to Christabel that he was gone for hours.

"Leave him be," said her mother placidly. "He likes to have a project."

That's all very well, thought Christabel, but supposing Brose is trying to telephone me and the number is engaged all the time?

Her father returned at last and announced that he had failed to get through to Bell.

"When she first lived in that house she had no telephone," said his wife.

Her husband ignored her.

"It may be the explanation," ventured Christabel.

"No, no." He could not believe Bell was not on the telephone by now. "Don't change your plans though," he said hastily. "I'll try again tomorrow and I'm sure I will be successful."

Christabel did not have the heart to argue with him.

As soon as Andrew appeared they all went to bed. She lay between the sheets in the bed where she had slept as a child, and she tried to convince herself that Brose had telephoned her while her father had been trying to get through to Spain. But in her heart she knew the truth: if he had wanted to speak to her he would have managed it somehow. There had been many times during the day and the day before when he could have rung her, but he had not done so, and his silence filled her with fear, fear of an uncertain future without him. They had been so confident of their prospect of happiness, their rightness for each other. Now all those hopes had been destroyed because of one foolish unguarded moment on her part. She stared into the blackness of her old room and asked herself: *What have I done?*

Chapter Nine

Christabel sat in the aeroplane waiting for it to taxi along the runway. A long time seemed to have elapsed before reaching this point. During the previous evening her parents had impressed upon her, over and over again, the importance of leaving Ambrose's mother to deal with her illness, with the help of her children and no interference from her. For once, they appeared to share the same opinion, and perhaps this unusual concord made them anxious to emphasise the point, and their daughter longed for them to stop. Andrew was able make his escape, but his sister could not.

She had to remain where she was in case the telephone rang. It did, once, but it was a parishioner wishing to speak to the vicar. She became even more irritated when her father left them for a long time while he was attempting unsuccessfully to get through to Bell.

After a restless night she left early to return to London. She sensed that her mother was worried about her and she felt guilty that she had been so critical of both her parents. They had wanted to help her with good advice and she had just felt exasperated with them. Even Andrew was beginning to get on her nerves; he did not say much, but she could tell that he thought she had blown it this time.

She hugged her mother before she left to go to the station.

"I'm sorry I have been such a wet blanket."

"Oh, my darling child," replied her mother, "of course I understand. Please give my love to Bell when you see her."

Christabel went to her flat, and the first thing she did was to telephone and book a ticket to Palma, Mallorca. She paid for it on her credit card, and she decided that she would collect the euros for her trip at the airport. Then she put Myra's cheque into an envelope and addressed it to her bank. There was nothing else for her to do except pack her suitcase and put her passport into her handbag. She tried not to remember how recently she had done all these things. As she gathered up the light summery clothes she had taken to Italy, so redolent of happier times, she began to wonder if she was making a mistake, but the memory of the previous Sunday strengthened her resolve. She could not face another day like that one, and until she got another job every day would be like a Sunday.

The telephone standing on a little table in her flat was silent, and she thought of picking it up and dialling Brose's number. What was he doing now? Probably he was with his sister and they were deciding how best to tackle the big problem in their lives, the illness of their mother. She could not help with that, and it was best to leave them to it. By now he would have received her letter. Would he respond to it? Resolutely she closed the front door and double-locked it. The wheels of her suitcase squeaked on the tiled floor of the lobby. Outside the doors of the building she hailed a taxi and asked to be taken to the airport. The die was cast. There was no turning back now.

* * *

They were airborne and soon the girls appeared with the drinks trolley. Christabel asked for a brandy and ginger ale, something she would not have dreamed of ordering in normal circumstances. She tried not to think about the reason for this journey; she only had to remember Brose's cold kiss on her lips to feel the tears spring to her eyes. She stared fixedly out of the window at the mountains of cotton-wool clouds in an effort to prevent the tears from bursting their banks and sliding down her cheeks. She remembered her outburst on the day before when she had sobbed alone, and she did not want to repeat the episode in public. She clutched at the glass of brandy and ginger ale, warm and faintly comforting.

Stepping out of the aeroplane at Palma was like stepping into a warm oven. The heat came to meet her like an embrace. The airport was iridescent with shiny steel and acres of glass windows. She had been allowed to take on board her small suitcase on wheels so there was no waiting at a carousel. With a feeling almost like hope she trundled it along the seemingly endless moving gangways, following the signs marked 'Taxi', for taxi is the same in any language.

She had to stand in a queue for the taxi and when it was her turn she had her speech prepared. *"Plaza España, estacion ferrocarril, por favor,"* she said, having studied a map obtained from the Information Office at the airport.

"You want the station?" said the driver airily as she stepped into his cab.

"Si, gracias," she replied, determined not to be outdone.

During the drive to the station the beauty of Palma amazed her. She had imagined it to be a brazen uncultured city, and no doubt there were areas that fitted that description, but the route to the station passed tall elegant buildings made of a pinkish stone and green parks full of flowers. All the streets were lined with trees. Majestically, rose the cathedral, fronted by a giant fountain. It was a city bathed in sunshine beneath a cloudless blue sky.

The station itself was a curiously humble affair and she approached a man who was collecting tickets at the entrance to one of the platforms. "Colonia de Sant Jordi?" she asked hopefully, but he shrugged his shoulders and pointed her in the direction of a timetable on the wall of the ticket office. She craned her neck to look at it and, with a sinking heart, realised that the name Colonia de Sant Jordi, the port where the boats left for the Isla de la Fuga, was not mentioned. In her agitation she abandoned her attempts at speaking Spanish and said in English to the girl behind the ticket office, "I wish to get a train to Colonia de Sant Jordi."

"No, no is possible," replied the girl. "There is no train to that place. You must get a bus. The bus station is near, a very short walk." She gave her a timetable, marking the bus she required with a pencilled circle. "The journey takes one hour and twenty minutes and will cost three euros."

Well, that sounded reasonable enough, and it was true, the bus station was no distance. Christabel dragged her suitcase across the baking tarmac until she found herself surrounded by bright orange buses. "Colonia de Sant Jordi?" she asked, and was immediately directed to a bus marked IB33, standing empty and unmanned. A quick glance at the note the girl had given her informed her that it would not leave for another twenty minutes. She wondered whether she would fill in the time by going for a stroll, perhaps seeing a bit more of this fascinating city, but a gathering queue made her decide to stay.

The sun shone relentlessly on to the top of her head, and she wished she had the hat stowed away at the bottom of her suitcase. She was uncomfortably aware of the sweat running down her back. There was no shade anywhere, and other coaches moved away or drove into the area causing exhaust fumes and a film of dust. She thought of her recent holiday in Italy where, except for a slight hiccup on the way to Rome, everything had been so luxuriously simple. Now, she realised for the first time that she was not alone on this journey. Brose had been with her every inch of the way. During the taxi drive to the station she had said to him, 'How beautiful it is,' and now, when she felt hot and impatient, 'What a bummer!'

At last she was settled in a window seat in the coach. In no time at all they had left the city and the harbour behind, and the land stretched for miles on either side of them. Christabel was reminded of a painting by Paul Klee she had seen in a gallery on one of her trips abroad – slabs of colour, terracotta, yellow and drab green – very like the hot barren countryside she viewed from the window of the coach. The earth on Mallorca was like the earth in Devon, red, but the dark green of the olive trees was so different from the vibrant green of English foliage. The brilliant blue of the sky relieved the slightly sombre Spanish landscape.

The coach turned off the main road to drop off passengers at little towns on the way, quiet places with sleepy churches and few inhabitants. The frenetic nature of the tourist industry had not yet affected these places because they were inland and not on a railway line.

They arrived at Colonia de Sant Jordi and the coach

parked outside an hotel. Christabel retrieved her case from the locker above her head. She stepped off the bus and surveyed the scene. Ahead of her was a road flanked by giant palm trees and, beyond, a stretch of beach and the sea. In the distance she could see the indistinct grey shape of an island. She walked towards the beach, dragging her suitcase behind her, and saw, as she had hoped, a small kiosk with the large initial 'I' on its side. To her relief it was open, and behind the small window sat a middle-aged man with a big aquiline nose, shaped like an eagle's beak, and a melancholy expression.

"Is there a boat going to the Isla de la Fuga?" she asked tentatively.

"You have missed it," he said laconically.

That was a blow. She pointed to the grey mass of land just visible on the horizon.

"Is that it?"

"No, no," he sounded impatient. "That is Cabrera."

"I see," she said. "When is the next boat to the Isla de la Fuga, please?"

"Not tomorrow, but the next day. In the morning."

That meant she would have to stay two nights in this place. It was disappointing, but there was nothing she could do except to thank him politely and retrace her steps to the hotel. She saw the other occupants of the bus were collecting their luggage from the hold, and they were all waving their arms and shouting at the tops of their voices. She deduced they were mainly

Spanish holidaymakers; perhaps Colonia de Sant Jordi was too inaccessible for European tourists. The hotel was white with green shutters and the positioning of the windows and the balconies gave it an art deco appearance. The entrance hall was cool and spacious. Christabel decided it would meet her needs very well during her enforced stay.

The girl behind the desk, smart, efficient and fluent in English, told her that there were no rooms to be had. It was the peak of the season and she doubted whether she would get accommodation in any of the big hotels. Seeing Christabel's stricken face she said kindly, "Why don't you try the information kiosk on the beach? He may be able to help you."

So back went Christabel to the man with the big nose. By this time she had given him a name (shared of course with Brose): Mr Punch. It suited him very well, particularly as his place of work was a box situated on the beach. She told him of her quandary, and she tried to sound as pathetic and defenceless as she could. It was not hard, as she was beginning to think nothing would ever go right for her again.

He stared at her for a second, then slammed shut the partition across the window. At first she thought he was being unbelievably rude, but he emerged from a door at the side and, with quick robotic movements, removed a key from his waistcoat pocket, locked the door and with great precision returned the key to his pocket. Then he grabbed the handle of her suitcase, saying, "Follow me, if you please."

He sped across the sand and on to the road, the case bobbing up and down behind him. He quickened his pace, down one street, up another, then turning left and left again. Christabel found it hard to keep up with him. She wondered if she had fallen into the hands of a madman. At last, when they were both out of breath, he stopped in front of a terrace of narrow white houses. He rang the bell of one of them, waiting impatiently, stamping his feet and whistling through his teeth until the door was opened and a hand appeared and parted the beaded curtain inside. The hand belonged to a stout elderly lady, white-haired and dressed from head to foot in black.

"Mi madre," said Mr Punch proudly. "Here you have a nice room. Clean. Not expensive."

He exchanged rapid words with his mother and, although Christabel listened attentively, she could not understand what they were saying. Then she realised they were speaking mallorquin. She hardly had time to thank him before he was striding away down the road.

Christabel followed the woman up a narrow staircase. She was shown into a room that was darkened by a slatted blind across the window. As Mr Punch had said it was spotlessly clean. There was a white crocheted runner on the dressing-table and the bed was made up in the old-fashioned way, with sheets and one blanket. The door of a free-standing cupboard was opened for her to see inside. The hangers clattered on the bar, and the woman said, "Much room." In a little room adjoining the bedroom was a shower, surely an unexpected bonus in a house like this? The white walls were bare except for a religious print over the bed, the Madonna and Child.

"It is so nice," breathed Christabel, immeasurably relieved and grateful. *"Me gusta mucho, Senora. Muchas gracias."*

Then she remembered Aunt Bell, and as she said, "Have you a telephone? *Tiene usted un telefono?"*

"Si, en la planta baja."

"Downstairs. I understand. Have you a telephone directory? *Directorio?"*

The woman did not seem to comprehend, and left the room, closing the door quietly behind her. Christabel raised the blind and the sunshine streamed into the room. She partially unpacked her case, laying her nightdress on the bed. There was a discreet knock on the door and her hostess reappeared with the telephone directory in her hand.

"Give me later," she said.

The book was divided into three sections, one for Colonia de Sant Jordi, one for the island of Cabrera and the third for the Isla de la Fuga. The name Graham was nowhere to be seen. No wonder her father had not been able to get through to his sister-in-law on the previous evening: it appeared that Aunt Bell was not on the telephone. No doubt he would have discovered that fact by now. Knowing him as she did, Christabel was sure he would not be duly worried. He would write a letter instead, a form of communication he much preferred. But it was a further minor irritation to add to Christabel's anxieties; her aunt would not be expecting her.

When she went downstairs she found Mr Punch's mother sitting behind a desk in the hall. Christabel returned the telephone directory to her, and was handed instead a menu. "For you, here? This evening?"

"Yes, please." She could not be bothered to go out and find somewhere to eat. The woman wrote a large nine on a piece of paper. Dinner was served at nine o'clock. She realised then how hungry she was. Her last meal had been Serrano ham and salad on the plane, the accompaniment to the brandy and ginger ale. It seemed a long time ago.

She decided to go in search of a shop, and she found a small supermarket a couple of streets away. There she purchased a bag of potato crisps and a bottle of still water. Back in the bedroom she stretched herself on the bed, reading her book, sipping the water and nibbling at the crisps. She heard several clocks in the neighbourhood striking the hours and the quarters in unison; seven o'clock passed, then eight and at last nine.

The dining-room was surprisingly large, the narrow house went back a long way. All the people seated at the tables were Spanish, mostly families with well-behaved children. The adults were not in holiday attire; the men wore ties and the children were impeccably dressed. Seated alone at one of the smaller tables was Mr Punch. When he saw Christabel he rose to his feet, napkin in hand. He gave a slight bow in her direction and said, "I hope you are happy in my mother's house?"

She smiled at him. "I am," she said. "Very happy, thank you."

The first course was soup, and was a substantial meal in itself. It had a thick consistency with a great many beans in it. It was quite delicious. Next came a large portion of lamb, slightly greasy and with no vegetables to accompany it. There was a carafe of red wine on Christabel's table and she replenished her glass at frequent intervals. Brose was with her all the time, and she was beginning to feel better about him. After several glasses of wine she was sure he would forgive her. The last course was a sponge trifle with a dollop of cream on the top. With her coffee she was given a glass of brandy.

She wondered how the children managed to keep awake so late in the evening. She decided they must have had a *siesta* during the day. She had not had a *siesta* and it had been quite a day. The bed was unbelievably soft and comfortable; she sank into its warm depths with a tired sigh. She did not wake until the sunshine filtered through the slats of the blind and fell upon her sleeping face.

Chapter Ten

When Christabel came downstairs for breakfast she found a long table in the dining-room, covered with a pristine white cloth. She walked the length of it surveying an amazing array of dishes containing scrambled egg, fried tomatoes, bacon, mushrooms, several kinds of cereals and big jugs of milk and juice. At one end of the table there was a coffee machine. Christabel helped herself to a bit of everything; one of the joys of being on holiday is having a big breakfast.

The same people were in the dining-room as had been there the night before, and now they were all dressed casually as if prepared for a day at the beach. Christabel felt quite expectant as she hoped she had devised a plan that would occupy her for most of the day. As she passed through the hall on the way out she stopped in front of her landlady, sitting in her usual position behind the desk, and she conveyed to her that she would be dining elsewhere that evening. She decided that she would eat at one of the restaurants on the seafront.

She made her way to the beach and to Mr Punch's box. "I'd like to go to Cabrera," she told him. There was a sign on the front of the kiosk advertising boat trips to the island and mentioning *una memoria meurta y un museo*. This interested Christabel who could not understand why there should be a memorial to the dead and a museum on an uninhabited island that had been turned into a national park.

To her surprise her request was turned down. Vehemently, he almost shouted at her, "*No es posible!* Impossible! You must have a permit to visit Cabrera and you have not the time to get one. Only those people interested in bird life and the rare plants are allowed to go."

She felt disappointed and rather annoyed. "That does not seem very fair," she said.

He explained, "They want to keep the island free from tourists – too many people would spoil it."

Christabel had to admit there was logic in that. So much of the beauty of Mallorca had been destroyed by the tourist business, perhaps, at last, the government was beginning to acknowledge that certain parts of their lovely land should remain intact.

"Very well," she said grudgingly, "I understand. But what about my trip to Fuga tomorrow? Has that been arranged?"

Immediately, the window was slammed shut just in front of her nose, but she was ready for it this time. Mr

Punch emerged and went through the usual procedure, standing as if to attention, locking the door with a precise movement and replacing the key in his waistcoat pocket. Then he set off across the sand with Christabel closely behind him. When they reached the little harbour he stopped in front of a boat. It was white and very smart, and had the words *L'Imperial Jet* written on its side. It looked as if it might have come from the South of France. It was conspicuous among the other boats bobbing on the water.

"That is the boat that goes to Cabrera," he said. A handful of people were climbing aboard her, and Christabel, listening to their voices, realised they were all, without exception, Germans. Presumably they had permits. They were talking earnestly amongst themselves, burdened with cumbersome cameras and binoculars. Twitchers, she thought.

They continued around the rim of the harbour and came to a halt beside a more humble vessel. It was a very big boat made of wood and painted a terracotta colour. There was a vast amount of room on the deck. A middle-aged man was working on it and when he saw Christabel's companion he jumped very nimbly on to the jetty. He was slim and quite handsome with a weatherbeaten face. The two men exchanged words, speaking at a rapid rate.

"This is Francisco," said Mr Punch. "He will take you to Fuga tomorrow."

"Thank you," she said.

"I am delighted," said Francisco. "The charge will be twelve euros." She started to delve into her handbag and he said, "No, no. I prefer you pay me tomorrow. Please to be here at half past ten."

* * *

She had the rest of the day to fill, so she decided to explore the town, and that did not take long. She found that nearly all the houses were square white buildings with cascades of bougainvillea and oleander falling over their walls. The streets were wide, and the aspect of the place made her think of Miami. She had been there once when on a trip for Myra. She decided that Colonia de Sant Jordi was more like America than Spain. There was a New World feel to it that she had not encountered before in her travels in Europe. Even the churches were architecturally modern. Then, turning a corner, she saw, ahead of her, an old one. She pushed open the heavy door and stepped inside. She blinked in the dim light, her eyes becoming adjusted after the glare of the sun outside. The cool silence was very restful. Like all Spanish churches the altarpiece was a blaze of gold leaf. Above were brightly coloured paintings of the saints. On impulse, she put money in a wooden box for a candle, and she lit this for Brose. Her thoughts reaching out to him were very akin to prayers. In her heart she recognised that this action was against all her principles. She had always decried a person who turned to God when the going was hard; now she had become that sort of person. As she stared at the bright little flame she wondered if she and Andrew would have felt closer to God if their father had been more convincing.

Outside in the sunshine again she decided it was time for something to eat and drink. After such a big breakfast she was not at all hungry, but she was very thirsty. She went back to the seafront and sat at a small table on the pavement. She had a plate of *tapas* washed down with a glass of white wine and a bottle of still water. It was quite pleasant sitting and watching the people go by, and she spun it out for nearly an hour. She wondered why eating on one's own in a foreign place was such a lonely business.

In the afternoon she purchased a strip of matting from one of the garish shops on the front, and she contemplated spending the rest of the day on the beach. The sight of hundreds of brown glistening bodies with the same idea deterred her. She made her way to the rocky shore on the other side of the harbour. It was volcanic stone and she spread her piece of matting on it, and wriggled herself into a fairly comfortable position, her back against a boulder. There she sat, reading her book or just looking out to sea and thinking. Her thoughts did not make her feel happy, and the bright sea under a fiercely hot sun gave her a headache. When she got up stiffly, to return to *la pension,* the guesthouse, she noticed three small stone cottages on the foreshore. They looked like fishermen's dwellings; two of them were derelict, but one was obviously still inhabited, as there were lace curtains at the windows. Christabel thought they and the church she had visited in the morning must be all that remained of the old fishing port, and it seemed sad to her that at some time in their history the people of Colonia de Sant Jordi had lost their heritage and sense of tradition.

Later, she discovered that going out that evening was a mistake. The restaurant was packed with people, noisily enjoying themselves and, once again, she was conscious of being very much on her own. She did not hear an English voice, and she thought the sound of an English accent would have been welcome to her ears. All around her were the Spanish talking, as usual, at the tops of their voices, interposed with a few, very few, German voices. The children were not as well behaved as they had been the evening before, and they ran between the tables, sometimes pursued by their distraught parents. Christabel thought dolefully, I am in a bad way if I am irritated by the behaviour of children. From her table she could see couples passing by on the street, under the palm-trees and the lights, their arms around each other. The food was good, but it did nothing to assuage her feeling of hopelessness; this time the wine did not raise her spirits, it only increased her headache. Further down the street there was a giant trampoline for the children, and this remained open far into the night, with the music and shrieks of delight filling the air. After a time she admitted to herself that it was the happiness of the people around her that was making her feel depressed. She decided to give up the struggle, and she paid the bill and left.

Christabel could not get to sleep that night. The bed that had seemed blissful the night before was now too soft for comfort. She heard the clocks strike the hours and the quarters and she lay awake, wondering why she had come to this place and how, in one foolish unguarded moment, she had forfeited her one chance of happiness. Towards the dawn she must have fallen asleep from sheer exhaustion.

The bill for her stay of two nights and one dinner came to forty-five euros and she could not complain about that. She held the hand of the *madre* and thanked her for everything. The son was present, and his sad clown's face cracked into a smile of pleasure. There was much smiling and handshaking. Christabel thought them delightful. She had heard it said that Mallorcans are inclined to be unfriendly and offhand, but she had certainly not found this the case. Mr Punch insisted on taking her suitcase and escorting her to the harbour.

A tall good-looking boy, tanned like his father, accompanied Francisco this time and he was introduced to Christabel as Fernando. She handed over twelve euros that were acknowledged with a little bow of thanks. The deck was covered with boxes, one on top of the other, and she could see that some of them contained fruit and vegetables. A mailbag was leaning against the side of the small cabin. She had expected there would be other passengers, but she soon realised she was the only one.

She turned to say good-bye to Mr Punch.

"You have been so kind," she said. "What would I have done without you?" It was a sentiment straight from the heart; he had been her saviour.

She could tell from the expression on his lugubrious face that he was sorry to see her go. He gave his customary little bow, and she watched his black-suited elongated figure lope off down the beach, like a marionette on a string.

Fernando fetched a cushion to place at her back, and she sat in a small space on a wooden seat hemmed in by boxes. The last of the cargo was heaved on to the deck, and the boat, low in the water because of the weight, chugged slowly out of the harbour.

When they were further out to sea the movement became more pronounced. She was glad that she was not prone to seasickness, but the smell of the engine fumes made her feel slightly queasy.

She wondered how long the journey would take, and was embarking on the sentence, "*A que hora . . . ?*" when Francisco interrupted her by saying, "The trip takes one hour and a half."

She laughed. "How can I ever learn your language when you will not even let me try?"

He laughed too, showing even white teeth. "I am so sorry."

As they passed Cabrera he said, "It is called the

Wilderness Island. All the islands have special names. Mallorca is *La Isla de Calma*, the island of tranquillity, although I think it is no longer a good name for it. *La Isla de la Fuga* is the island of escape and the port is called *Esperanza* which means hope."

"I tried to get to Cabrera," she told him, "but I was not allowed."

"It is difficult," he said. "You must have a permit. My ancestor came from there. I am half Mallorcan and half French." There was a note of pride in his voice.

After a while he said, "I hope you will not mind my asking, is it with Mr Patterson you are staying?"

"No, with Miss Graham who is my aunt."

"Ah! She is a very nice lady, *muy simpatica*. You will enjoy your stay with her very much. She has a beautiful garden."

They were now in the open sea. Christabel closed her eyes. She was so tired she felt like sleeping. Time passed quickly. Sitting on her hard seat with her eyes shut against the glare of the sea, she did not sleep but was on the edge of it, or so she thought. Perhaps exhaustion made her lose consciousness for a while, for suddenly she was aware of a change. She remembered the stories of old mariners who saw a cloud on the horizon and knew they were approaching land. Eyes wide open now, she observed a small cloud hovering over the island, that was gradually drawing nearer and nearer.

"We arrive very soon," Francisco told her.

Soon she could see the jetty and a group of people standing there. One of them was a stout lady who resembled her mother. Instinctively, she started to wave, and the lady cheerfully waved back.

"Your aunt is glad to see you," said Francisco.

"Yes."

When she stepped on shore, rather shakily because of the movement of the boat, she was greeted with the words, "You are Christabel?"

"Yes. Were you expecting me? Somehow you heard from my father?"

"No, no letter. Perhaps it is in the mailbag."

Christabel was amazed. "How did you know it was me?"

"You haven't changed much since you were a little girl, my dear. I am so pleased to see you. I can't believe my luck."

"Why are you here?" It was very difficult to understand.

"I came to see if Francisco has any mail for me." The straggly grey hair and the ample form were so like Christabel's mother, but Bell was dressed in a cotton skirt and a T-shirt that her sister would never have worn.

It was like coming home, and Christabel felt close to tears. She was enveloped in a warm embrace.

"You are here, and I am so happy," Bell told her. "Your bed is made up for you, and I hope you will stay with a lonely old woman for a long time."

Chapter Eleven

Bell's chalet (in England it would be called a bungalow) was only a short walk from the tiny harbour. To Christabel's surprise Francisco insisted on walking with them so that he could carry her suitcase. He and her aunt kept up a lively conversation in Spanish all the way. Christabel listened hard to what they were saying, but could only pick up a word or two. She could make out, however, from Bell's excited tones, that her aunt was very pleased to see her.

The three of them walked up an English-type garden path to a front door that was open. "We don't lock our houses when we go out," explained Bell. "In fact when I first came here we used to leave the key in the lock to show visitors we were not at home. For some reason that is not done any more. I suppose you could call it progress of a kind."

Over the front door there was a sign that read '*Sunnybanks*'. "It was the name of the cottage my father rented in Dorset," Bell explained. "I wanted to have a little piece of England on my island."

"It's appropriate," said Christabel, "in view of all the sunshine you get in this place."

The interior of the house looked as if it had not been altered since its owner took it over. Christabel thought that was probably the case as Bell had inherited it when she was in her early fifties and now she was in her seventies. It was simple and comfortable but furnished in no particular taste, as if the person living there did not worry too much about colour schemes and the choice of curtains. That is like my mother, thought Christabel.

Francisco followed the two women into the house, as if he knew it well, and walked straight into a bedroom where he deposited the suitcase on the floor. As Bell had said, the bed was made up as if in readiness for her arrival.

"I am always hoping that someone will come and stay with me, so I am prepared." Bell explained. "Now it has happened, and I am very happy."

There was a clothes cupboard and a chest of drawers, both in white painted wood. On top of the chest of drawers was a photograph in a silver frame which Christabel recognised: it was of a small girl holding the hand of her much older sister. Bell and Christabel's mother, standing close to each other, staring into the camera over all the years. There was a bookcase too, crammed with orange and green Penguin books dating back to a time when they cost half a crown.

"This is so nice," she murmured. A very faint breeze stirred the chintz curtains. The shutters outside were wide open.

Francisco shook her hand and looked keenly into her face. "You have a happy time here," he said, as if stating a fact rather than wishing for her enjoyment.

Then he turned to her aunt. "You have company at last," he said. He kissed her twice, a kiss for each cheek. "*Hasta pronto.*"

"Thank you for bringing her here to me."

After he had gone Bell said, "He is a dear man, but I'm so glad we are alone. Now I can have a real good look at you. I never thought when I awoke this morning what joy lay ahead of me. I am so glad to see you, my dear!"

It was so obviously a heartfelt admission that Christabel felt warmed by it and, for the first time, was glad that she had made the journey. Suddenly, it seemed all worthwhile.

The sitting-room had comfortable chairs and one long sofa. Because there was no dining-room a table and chairs occupied one side of the room. There was a wood-burning stove, unlit now of course, but Christabel had noticed a pile of logs stacked up against the side of the house. The walls were unadorned except for one watercolour that was obviously a local view; it was plainly the work of an amateur. The room felt pleasantly cool. The tiled floor made it look Spanish, but there was also an English feel to the house.

Her aunt showed her the kitchen, again the sixties image reflected in old-fashioned glass-fronted cabinets and an antiquated electric stove. She was relieved to see the stove because the lack of a telephone made her wonder if the house also lacked electricity.

"From a generator," said Bell, opening the back door and pointing to a shed near the house. "My dear neighbour, Rex Patterson, keeps an eye on it for me. As you know, dear, there is no telephone. I hope that will not worry you too much. It does not bother me at all."

She set about preparing lunch.

"Can I help?"

"No, not this time. I just want to spoil you. Later you can do lots of things for me. Anyway, there is nothing to do. We will have salad and *sombrasada* – that is a locally made sausage, very good. I have tomatoes and a cucumber and there is lots of fruit. We won't starve." She opened a cupboard and took out a bottle of red wine. "And of course we can have this."

"Oh, please, don't open it for me . . . "

"I have a glass of red wine with my lunch every day," said her aunt firmly, "and with my supper. In fact, in the evening I have several glasses."

While she was tearing the lettuce and slicing the sausage, she asked Christabel about the family.

"Mother is very well," said her niece, "and sends her love, of course. It was her idea I should come and see you. They lead busy lives, but they are content."

"I wish they would come and see me," said Bell, "but

they never do. However, I can't talk – I have not been to England for nearly thirty years."

"You are completely happy living here?"

"Completely. I love the beauty and the peace of the place. We have everything we need on the island. One shop, supplied by Francisco, a church, a small restaurant that provides delicious fresh fish, priced according to the size of the catch that day, and a *farmacia*, which is a chemist's shop, in case we need medicines. You can buy a lipstick there if you want one."

She carried the plates and the salad bowl out on to the terrace at the back of the house. Christabel followed with a tray laden with the bottle of wine, glasses, knives and forks and a little jug of oil and lemon dressing. They sat at a wooden table that Christabel's mother would have described as having 'seen better days'.

For the first time, Christabel had a chance to see the garden. It was a dream. An enormous olive tree dominated the scene and other trees and shrubs surrounded it. A very tall strawberry tree sheltered one half of the bottom of the garden and a eucalyptus was on the other side. In between the trees and shrubs (Christabel did not know the names of most of them), there were beds of roses and clematis winding everywhere, everything looking perfectly healthy in the environment in which they found themselves. Even the grass looked a robust green, like an English garden, and Christabel thought this must be unusual.

"Do you have to keep watering because it is so dry?"

"I have a complicated sprinkler system. It has been my one big expenditure since I came here. It will come on at five o'clock and you will see for yourself how magical it is. It has already watered once today, at six o'clock in the morning. I wake up when I hear it starting to work. I'm afraid you may grow to hate it, disturbing your sleep. It groans and splutters before it gets going."

Christabel laughed at this.

"I hope you will not be bored, dear," continued Bell. "It is a very tranquil life here, not what you have been used to at all. About two hundred people live on the island, and there are very few young people. There are children, of course, enough to make the school worth maintaining. When they grow up they tend to move to the mainland.

"About twenty years ago a couple, both in their twenties, decided to settle here. They made a living, she by cleaning and he by doing odd jobs. He installed my sprinkler for me. There was great rejoicing when they had a baby. When the baby became a child it attended the school with about ten other pupils, but when the child grew up it left the island. The parents left as well. It is a common story and fills me with foreboding. People are no longer content to earn their living by fishing and cultivating the land – they think that is thankless work. Perhaps, in time, the island will be left on its own. Not in my lifetime though, I'm glad to say."

Christabel began to relax. Sitting in the sun, that was not overpoweringly hot and tempered by a warm breeze, she could smell the *arizonica* that formed a hedge around the garden. That and the red wine made her sleepy.

Presently her aunt told her that every afternoon she had a siesta. "You can do the same, if you wish."

"I may stay out here for a while. It is so lovely."

"Well, that chair you are sitting in can be made into a lounger. Just press the handles. That's right. You can have a nap out here if you feel inclined."

She stumped into the house, and Christabel stacked the tray with the dirty plates and the empty salad bowl and carried the whole lot into the kitchen. She was glad her aunt had left her this job to do because it made her feel useful. She filled a plastic bowl with hot water and did the washing-up, finding, after a while, that the dishes could be left to drain in a rack above the sink. She would have liked a drink of water, but she did not know if the water in the cold tap was fit for consumption.

When she returned to her chair she found she could not keep awake. Her eyes closed in spite of herself, and she slept sweetly and deeply, breathing in the scents of the garden.

Bell arose from her siesta at half past four to see the sprinkler work its magic. It was a daily ritual she would not wish to miss. Christabel had to admit it was quite spectacular, fountains of water spurting in all directions, and anyone standing in the line of fire would have got very wet indeed. When the show was over the garden looked grateful and refreshed.

"It lasts fifteen minutes," said Bell proudly. "We are not short of water on the island. It comes from springs and a river flowing from the hill. It is the purest water in Spain. You need have no concern about drinking it straight from the cold tap." She was such a considerate hostess, and anticipated her guest's needs before she had time to express them.

That evening Bell made a delicious stew, *guisada* she called it, and it contained many delicious ingredients: a basis of lamb with tiny carrots, small onions and white beans. Christabel marvelled again how she had managed to produce such a magnificent meal when she had not known she was going to have a visitor in her house.

She was amused that Bell changed into a silk navy blue and white dress for dinner, which was served on the table in the main room. It was exactly the sort of dress her mother wore for special occasions. It was reminiscent of the Raj: the English person changing for dinner long after the custom had been abandoned in England. Christabel put on a white blouse and a black skirt in deference to the tradition. She wondered if this was Bell's only posh frock, or whether she rang the changes; later she was to discover there was one other that she wore when invited out for the evening.

Promptly at six o'clock Bell poured two schooners of

sherry for them. Also, she produced a terracotta dish containing olives. They sat on the terrace overlooking the garden.

"Are there many Brits living on the island?" Christabel asked.

"Not permanent residents. There are a few who come here for, say, six months of the year, but I know only one couple that live here all the year round. They are my greatest friends, the Pattersons. A very interesting pair, and I shall enjoy introducing them to you. He is a talented man and painted my picture over the fireplace."

"But a lot of Spanish people live here permanently?"

"Oh, yes. They are mostly families that have lived here for centuries; you will see their homes when I take you round the island tomorrow. Picturesque white-washed cottages. Not like this, of course; my house was built in the sixties. The locals still call it *la casa moderna*."

"And the lady who left you the house in her will? Tell me about her."

"Well, her name was Mrs Baldwin, and she was a saviour as far as I was concerned, but at the expense of her own happiness, which has always played on my conscience although it was no fault of mine. She and her husband visited *La Isla de la Fuga* on one of many trips they made before his retirement. They loved it and vowed to come and live here one day. When he died she revisited the place and purchased a piece of land. A local builder constructed the chalet to her specifications. Unfortunately the poor woman got ill and could not make the journey. Sometimes she managed to let it, but only for short periods. The island is not a tourist attraction and there are not many visitors. Mostly the house was unoccupied."

"How long did you look after her?"

"Ten years, but I was thankful to have a steady job. I had been living from pillar to post all my adult life. Neither your mother nor I had any qualifications – it did not seem important for girls in those days. Our mother died, Jess got married and I cared for our father. He had been in the Merchant Navy and one of his fellow officers allowed us to live in a rented property for a peppercorn rent: it was a thatched cottage near Dorchester called Sunnybanks. We only had Father's pension, but we managed and, oh, we were so happy. It was a double blow when he died because I was left with nothing. His pension died with him, and I was not allowed to live in the house any more."

"How awful for you," said Christabel. It was a situation hard for a woman living in the twenty-first century to visualise.

"It was devastating, and that is when I started my wanderings, as I now call them. I worked in boys' prep schools as an assistant matron. I liked the children, but sometimes the matron was hard to get on with and, when I found life impossible, I moved on to another school."

"I suppose that must be about the time when I remember you, when you used to come and stay with us. I was a little girl, and Andrew was not born."

"No, I have never seen Andrew. I was very fond of you though, although, I hope you will not be offended, dear, if I say the visits do not stand out in my mind as being particularly happy. You see, there is nothing so awkward as a poor relation. It is hard for everyone concerned. Your parents were not well off themselves, and my arrival added to the household expenses. I felt it keenly. Also, they were secure, married to each other, whereas I was completely alone. An old maid was the derogatory way people described someone like me. I know your father wondered what they would do with me when I became too old to earn a living."

Yes, Christabel could imagine him becoming agitated at the thought of such a burden. Bell was his wife's only relative, and it would fall on him to look after her in her old age. She conjured up a picture, maybe an indistinct memory, of her mother being faintly patronising with her elder unmarried sister.

"When I was in my late thirties," went on Bell, "I found that by looking after frail old people I could make more money. On the whole, it was more comfortable too, a soft bed in a nice bedroom instead of a hard cot in a draughty back bedroom in a school miles away from anywhere. I looked after a succession of old people until I was sent to Mrs Baldwin. We often talked of her house on the island and, to my surprise, she left it to me in her will together with a tidy sum of money, enough to live fairly comfortably for the rest of my life. She was a lonely lady whose whole life had been wrapped up in her husband. They had no children. She left the house in England to a niece who never bothered to come and see her when she was ill."

And my father's worries were over, thought Christabel. The spinster sister was catered for and he could turn his attention to other anxieties. His nature was such that he must always have something to worry about.

When the sherries were drunk, Bell fetched two bigger glasses, and they started on the red wine. Several glasses had been downed before they went into dinner at half past eight.

It was quite early when Aunt Bell staggered off to bed. Christabel did the washing-up and put away the remains of the food. The red wine had stimulated her rather than made her sleepy as sometimes happens, depending on the mood of the person drinking it. It made Christabel think more clearly, had sharpened her brain so that she was arguing with herself, justifying her actions before she left England.

She had a bath, hoping that would have a soporific effect. Brose was so much on her mind she knew that if there had been a telephone in the house she would have rung him. What was the time difference? Only one hour. What was he doing while she was thinking of him?

When she climbed into bed she hoped for sleep, but it was impossible. The only difference between the night before and this one was that she could not hear the clocks of the town striking the hours. Here, there was silence, oppressive silence. Then she realised the silence was not as complete as she had supposed. From Bell's room came the rise and fall of robust snoring. She got up and shut her door, hoping that would block it out. It did, but sleep was still elusive.

She lay in bed and reviewed the situation. Her immediate reaction was to return home as quickly as possible. She had been too hasty in her retreat from an uncomfortable situation. But she had just arrived, and her aunt was clearly delighted to have her company. It would be discourteous to talk about leaving after just one day. Of course she must stay longer. The very little problem of how long she should stay became a very big problem and occupied a great deal of the night. It was early morning before, exhausted, she fell asleep.

Kind Bell, peeping into her room at nine o'clock found her sleeping soundly, and decided to leave her.

Chapter Twelve

She got up at eleven o'clock, full of apologies. She could not understand how she had slept so long. It was so unlike her.

Bell gave her a steaming cup of coffee and that revived her. "We have a busy day ahead of us," she was told. "I am going to show you my island."

She was preparing a picnic, putting a piece of lettuce, a slice of tomato and a hard-boiled egg between pieces of crusty bread and filling a thermos. "I thought we could have our lunch on the beach," she said. She put the food into a basket, and went off to fetch a straw hat. "The sun is very hot today. You ought to wear a hat too, dear."

Obediently her niece went to her bedroom to fetch it. She insisted on carrying the basket. Together they set off, leaving the door of the chalet unlocked, but not open. It was slow progress because Bell was no longer able to walk quickly.

"There was a time," she said, "when I could have

walked all round it with you, but now I am getting old and cannot manage that distance. However, I can show you the best bits."

Their first stop was at the shop that stood in the little square. Bell wanted to purchase chocolate there for them to eat after their *bocadillo*. The shop reminded Christabel of the village shop of her childhood, since replaced by a small supermarket, which sold everything anyone could want under one roof. The Spanish shop was crammed with goods, and all the shelves were full of tins, packets of tea, sugar, raisins, and cereals and, hanging from the ceiling, *jamons* and *chorizos*. As well as the comestibles there were items an ironmonger might carry, pots of paint, packets of nails, hammers and screwdrivers. In another corner Christabel spied garden tools and packets of seed. Francisco must have made many trips to supply all this merchandise, and a little area of the counter was sectioned off with a grille, denoting it to be the post office where he collected his bag of mail.

Bell was greeted by the man and wife, the owners of the shop, with much gesticulating and raised voices. Other people joined in, and Christabel could not understand a word they were saying. They all spoke very fast, but she could tell by their wide smiles they were talking about her.

"They are interested," said Bell. "It is not often a stranger comes here. They are very welcoming. When I first arrived at my cottage a neighbour had left a plate of figs on my doorstep, a token gift to greet me at my new house. They don't do that any more, but some of the old customs remain. No bills are sent out, for instance – someone comes round to your house to collect the money. Everyone is kind and happy, there is very little dissension on the island, and people live too close to each other to quarrel."

At last they were able to make an exit from the busy shop and step out into the sunshine of the *plaza* once again. People were sitting outside the one restaurant, leisurely watching their children play in the square. They too knew Bell, and called out to her and rose to their feet when they saw her approaching.

She introduced Christabel to a man who was sitting alone drinking a glass of beer. "This is our *panadero,*" she explained, "the baker. He is a very important person on the island. We would not get far without our daily bread, and absolutely delicious it is. *El pan Moreno* and he makes it in the *panaderia* that is next to the chemist over there, on the other side of the square. Senor Garcia can speak English very well."

He was a small pale floury man who indeed looked as if he made bread for a living. He rose to his feet and bent over Christabel's hand. "I am happy to see you," he said.

"Encantada," she murmured, feeling rather foolish as most English people do when they attempt to speak another language, particularly when the other person is so proficient at doing the same thing.

"I am taking my niece to see the tower," said Bell.

"That you will like very much."

As they walked away Bell told her, "We buy our fruit and vegetables at the market which is held here every Sunday. Francisco brings the fresh produce with him on his Saturday trip."

"Apart from the shopkeepers, what do people do here?" asked Christabel. "How do they make a living?"

"It is hard," said her aunt, "but they are mostly *campesinos* and *pescaderos*, that is farmers and fishermen. Then there is a teacher who runs the small school for a handful of pupils. She is a good friend of mine, the wife of one of Francisco's uncles."

They made their way slowly down to the sea. "Behind us," Bell said, "you can see the hills where the farmers graze their goats and sheep, and also one mountain. We call it a mountain, but it is really only a very high hill, and can be climbed by steep steps. I'm afraid I'm too old to attempt that now, it is quite a climb, but you can do it on your own one day when you feel inclined."

"It is so beautiful," said Christabel and, as before on this trip, she wished Brose was there to see it with her. Although everything was so hot and dry, the landscape was luxuriantly green, and the grass was lush beneath their feet.

"That's because we have had a lot of rain this year, much more than usual," explained her aunt when

Christabel commented on the greenness. "Almond trees thrive here, and in February they are a sight to behold. Everything flourishes on this island and, as you can see the bougainvilleas and oleanders are wonderful at this time of the year, but in the autumn pampas grass and flowering vines make it just as beautiful. Every season has its special charm." She spoke proudly. It was her place and she enjoyed showing it off.

Christabel noticed that Bell was out of breath by the time they reached the tower. However, she insisted on climbing to the top. The stone steps were very high and narrow and the inside of the tower smelled damp and musty. Christabel was glad when they stepped out of the claustrophobic atmosphere into the clean fresh air at the top. There they faced an indescribably magnificent view of the clear blue sea, the horizon only broken by the island of Cabrera in the distance. Looking to the west and east they could see rocks and inlets and small areas of stony beaches. There seemed to be hundreds of birds, perched on rocky ledges or swooping over their heads.

"Local people used to keep watch here for pirates," Bell told her. "They used to land here to plan their pillages of Mallorca. In the early days Barbary corsairs raided this island relentlessly. The peace we enjoy now is a direct contrast to those days."

"I can see a house," said Christabel suddenly, "on the promontory over there. What a magical place for a house!"

"And it's a magical house," said her aunt. It is called *La Casa de las Hermanas* and it is the only big house on the island. It is very old and in the eighteenth century it was a convent. After the sisters moved out during the Franco regime it was bought by a rich businessman from Madrid, and he and his family used to come and stay here for months at a time. He sold it to my friend, Rex Patterson. He and Faith have lived here for nearly as long as I have. You will meet them, not tomorrow evening but the evening after that, when we have been invited to dine with them."

"When was this planned?" asked Christabel, mystified. How could her aunt accept an invitation without a telephone?

"While you were sleeping I went to the shop and met Faith there. She was so interested to hear of your arrival, and she and Rex can't wait to meet you."

So much for Christabel's vague plan that she would leave the following day; it was obvious that the old lady expected her to stay longer. There was no way she could disappoint her, and she had a sneaking curiosity to see the inside of the house and meet its occupants.

"I think we should descend and go and find a place for our picnic," said Bell.

* * *

They sat with their backs against two flat rocks, with the waves lapping on the beach a few feet away from them. The food was delicious, and Christabel wondered if a bottle of wine was hidden in the basket, but the thermos was produced and it contained ice-cold homemade lemonade that was very refreshing.

Bell had told her that she reckoned that on Francisco's next trip he would bring with him the letter from her father warning of her niece's arrival. Christabel wondered if he would mention the underlying reason for her visit. She thought not. He would think confiding in a sister-in-law he had not seen for years would serve no purpose at all (she was right and his letter, when it arrived, contained no reference to recent events). Now, sitting on the beach with Bell, whom she felt she had known for ever, Christabel came to a sudden decision to tell her all about Brose.

"I noticed that beautiful ring on your finger," said Bell, "and I wondered about it, but did not like to ask. I felt you might be in some sort of trouble."

Christabel laughed. "That is the phrase my father would use. It implies so many things, but I assure you the trouble is my own making. I have been very foolish."

It was a relief to tell the whole sad episode to a good listener. Bell did not utter a word until the narrative was completed. Then she sat quietly for a few moments, in deep thought.

At last she said, "I think you were impulsive, and I am sure you are right in thinking he was annoyed. Put yourself in his place: he told you something in confidence and you went and blabbed it to the one person he did not want to know. It must have enraged him, but if you love someone, and I'm sure he loves you, that sort of anger does not last forever. My guess is that he has recovered from it already."

Christabel said nothing. She was sceptical about what her aunt had just said. By now she had convinced herself that Brose would never forgive her.

"You think because I am not married I do not understand such matters," said Bell, "but I loved a man for ten years and I know about quarrels between people who love each other."

Christabel was astounded. "When did you meet this man?"

"Here, on the island. He was a *pescadero,* a fisherman. In fact, he was the father of Francisco."

"I'm amazed," said her niece. "Why have I never heard about this before? Did my parents know about it?"

"No," replied her aunt calmly. "I did not tell them. I do not think your father would have approved of an alliance with a Spanish fisherman. And as your mother follows him in everything she does, she would have been of the same opinion. I did not think there was any need to tell them. He was married when he was very young to a Mallorcan girl. They had one child, Francisco. His wife could not stand the solitude and boredom here and went home to her family. Jose, that is Francisco's father, saw his son infrequently, but when the boy became an adult he decided for himself that he wanted to get to know his father better.

"Jose's brother had the boat in those days and made the trip here once a week. Now Francisco and his son, Fernando, have a bigger boat and make the journey there and back from Mallorca every two days. As you know it is always laden with provisions for the shop, the mail and orders from people living here. In bad weather, of course, they cannot make the trip, and we have to manage without them. Most of us grow vegetables in our gardens, so we are fairly self-sufficient."

Christabel was curious to know more about Jose.

"We were happy together," said Bell simply. "We just got on well, that is all. It was an uncomplicated relationship, and he was an uncomplicated man. Neither of us were young and he loved me and, as I had never been loved by a man before, I counted myself lucky."

"Did he live with you, in your house?"

"No," Bell sounded quite shocked. "We both valued our independence. I think that was what made the relationship so special. He had his house at Colonia de Sant Jordi on Mallorca, but he visited here on business quite frequently. Sometimes he stayed overnight before returning to the mainland."

"What happened to him?"

"There is a terrible wind that blows up around the Archipelago. It is called *la gota fria* and the locals are terrified of it. It blew Jose's boat on to the rocks and he was drowned."

"How terrible!"

"I was devastated. I did not think life was worth living without him, but here I am, twenty years later, still going strong. I think the arrival of Rex and Faith helped me. They are unusual in that although they are English they live here all the year round. Rather, I should say she goes to England twice a year to visit her sons, but Rex refuses to stir. He it was who pulled strings and got the telephone brought to the island. They both maintained they could not exist without it. It was useful for the shop too. Everybody had to contribute towards it, and it was quite a lot of money. I felt I could not afford it and, anyway, what was the point? There is no one I want to keep in touch with by telephone, so I decided to do without it. Sometimes I get anxious about living alone in my old age. There are no facilities here for caring for old people and nursing them. I would be shipped off to Valencia or Barcelona, and I would not like that. I hope to die in my little house."

"Perhaps you should think again about the telephone," suggested Christabel gently.

"You may be right," said Bell. "It was awkward for you and your father not being able to get hold of me. And there are other reasons why it would be better for me to be on the telephone; especially now I am getting old. I can see that."

They were quiet for few moments. It was very still and Christabel said, "It is so peaceful."

"Yes, it is, and sometimes, I must confess, a little too

peaceful. That is why it is so nice for me to have you here, my dear, although I am sorry it is your unhappiness that had brought you here to me."

"What can I do about my situation, Bell?" asked Christabel. "I can't force a wedge between a mother and son, especially when I know she is ill and needs him. Are all Jewish people so taken up with their religion that they cannot see anyone else's point of view?"

"Of course not," said her aunt. "It is nothing to do with the Jewish religion. It is entirely to do with the lady, and if she belonged to the Roman Catholic faith she would be just as dogmatic. It is a great pity that people of different faiths cannot be more tolerant of each other."

"It certainly is," said Christabel bitterly. "Even my father seems to understand how she feels."

"Your father has followed a certain path all his life, and any diversions from that path are hard for him to accept."

"I know what you mean," said Christabel. "The ordination of women, for example – he cannot accept that change. My brother and I argue with him about it, but he remains obdurate. Women should not be ordained, and that's the end of it. Of course, he has had to bow down to the inevitable, and that has made him bad-tempered."

"Oh, dear!" Bell laughed. "You are surrounded by a lot of narrow-minded old hypocrites, and you must not let them get the better of you. What a pity Marcus

Silveridge is not still alive. I'm sure that wonderful man would have shown more sense."

She tipped the straw hat over her face, and said, "I'm going to have a little nap, dear. You could do the same – and try not to worry. I'm quite sure if your Brose is the man I think he is, he will not let a bit of religious humbug stand in his way."

Presently the rhythmic snoring competed with the sound of the waves breaking on the shore. Christabel did not feel inclined to sleep. She sat quietly with a sort of resigned tranquillity, thinking of Brose and London and the gallery, and they all seemed a long way away.

Chapter Thirteen

Christabel detected in her aunt a suppressed excitement about their invitation to dine at *La Casa de las Hermanas*. No excursions were planned for the day before or for the day of the event. The two days were spent very happily in the garden, but Christabel had many idle hours to think about her situation, and she became more determined than ever to return to England.

"Do they dress for dinner?" she asked as the time approached for them to leave.

"No, no, it is quite informal," was the reply, "only it is polite to dress up a little bit."

Christabel had little choice about what to wear: she had brought with her a silk trouser suit that Brose admired when she wore it on their holiday in Italy, and she wore that. Bell appeared in a burgundy-coloured dress, except for the colour an exact replica of the one she changed into every evening.

"I think we'll have a glass of sherry before we set off," she said.

"Won't we get one when we get there?"

"Sure to, dear, but that doesn't mean we can't have one now."

* * *

Christabel realised that to get to the house overlooking the sea they would have to walk the same distance they had two days before. The walk there and the walk back, at her aunt's pace, was a daunting prospect. However, it was not be: Bell informed her proudly that the Pattersons owned a pony and trap and employed a man to drive it. It arrived at eight o'clock to pick them up.

"Hola, Miguel," Bell said cheerfully, as she put her foot on the little step and heaved her heavy body on board. *"Te presento a mi sobrina de Inglaterra."*

"Inglaterra! Increible!"

I'm enjoying this, thought Christabel, sitting bolt upright on the wooden seat, moving up and down to the rhythm of the pony trotting in front of her. They were following a narrow track, a different route from the one over the fields she and her aunt had taken.

Bell's cheeks were quite pink with the excitement of it all. "Of course, you know about Rex Patterson, our host for this evening?"

The name was familiar. "Should I?" asked Christabel doubtfully.

"I am surprised you do not recognise the name," said

Bell a shade reproachfully, "but perhaps he is too much before your time."

"You don't mean the playwright?" Christabel could hardly believe it when her aunt nodded her head. "Of course I have heard of him. Who has not? One of his plays is on at the Olivier now – Brose and I were planning to go and see it."

Uttering Brose's name made her feel almost unbearably sad.

"You will be able to see it together when you get back," said her aunt briskly.

"I can't believe I am about to meet Rex Patterson," said Christabel. "They say that his plays never date. They are as fresh now as they were when they first appeared on the London stage. Felicity Kendall is in the one at the Olivier."

"Well, when you see it you must write and tell me all about it."

"I will," she promised. "He must be quite an old man now."

"He is eighty-four. We live to a great age on this island, and he has his lovely Faith to look after him, and she does it so beautifully."

"Faith is the name of his wife?"

"No," said Bell, "she is not his wife. She has a different name from his, and is always known as Mrs Agnew. I have never known why they did not marry, and I have never wanted to know. It is a mystery, but no one here is the slightest bit curious: to their neighbours they are Senor Patterson and Senora Agnew. It is good enough for them and good enough for me."

Christabel who, during the short time she had known her aunt, had begun to understand her character very well, decided that *'the lady protests too much'* and that, in reality, Bell was intensely interested in everything to do with Rex and Faith.

"All I know," went on the old lady, "is that they are utterly devoted to each other and for some reason they are not man and wife. This island is not called the Island of Escape for nothing."

The house, when the pony and trap stopped outside it, was an enchantment. Pink, mellowed with age, with wide steps leading to an imposing front door. The garden was wildly luxuriant with olive-trees, orange-trees and masses of colourful shrubs leading down to the sea, which could be seen, through the foliage, as a bright blue streak. Christabel could imagine an artist like Matisse living in such a place, transferring the vivid colours to his canvases. Instead it was owned by an English playwright who no doubt gloried in the beauty of the place every day of his life. Christabel had always admired Rex Patterson who had brought a mixture of passion and dignity to the English theatre. She thought he deserved to end his life in the mature tranquillity of this strange island.

Miguel had leapt from his seat and now pulled the doorbell, producing a sonorous peal which echoed through the house. A young girl opened the door and greeted Bell by name. A granddaughter? No, a sort of secretary-cum-housekeeper, Bell whispered to Christabel. They found themselves in a large hall with a stone floor, uneven and with the sheen of hundreds of years of wear. Ahead of them was a wide staircase with a wrought-iron banister.

"You know the way," said the girl to Bell.

It was like being in church. The house had a peculiar feel to it, as if the prayers of the sisters still pervaded and had never been banished. They walked slowly up the stairs, and Christabel felt as if she was taking part in a film or in one of Rex Patterson's plays. She was acutely aware of the momentousness of the occasion, and an adequate reason for a sudden attack of nerves.

Her apprehension was instantly assuaged by the appearance of the two people greeting them in the salon, or drawing-room as it would be called in England. They stood, side by side, in front of an empty stone fireplace. Hands were clasped and kisses exchanged. It became obvious to Christabel that her aunt was much loved by these people.

She noticed that the room was furnished with antique furniture from England. The pieces were not as heavy as the usual Spanish furniture, and the effect was to make the room look lighter than most salons. A desk, a corner cupboard and a number of small tables fitted happily into the charming room and the very English feel to it was surprising and delightful. No doubt the floor was tiled, but a fitted carpet and oriental rugs concealed it.

Christabel became conscious of the very old man; his hand in hers was as light as thistledown, the bones like the bones of a bird, the veins erupting from thin parchment skin. Faded blue eyes surveyed her speculatively and with appreciation.

"The niece," he said. His hair was sparse, like a thin covering of snow on a skeletal head.

The girl who had opened the door to them appeared now with drinks on a tray, the inevitable glasses of dry sherry that precedes the wine at every Spanish dinner party. Alongside were olives and cheese straws.

"This is Angela Maitland," said Faith. "She is an actress who, fortunately for us, needs a break from the stage. She has been so helpful, sorting out all Rex's stuff, and next week when I go to England to see my sons she is going to be here."

"To keep an eye on me," said Rex whimsically. "I am not allowed to be on my own."

Faith seated herself in one of the many comfortable armchairs scattered around the room. "Sit down, all of you. Rex finds standing a strain." She smiled a sweet intimate smile in his direction. She was much younger than him, and Christabel reckoned she was probably in her sixties. There were strands of grey in her hair, but they were only strands, and her face was browned by the Spanish sun and remarkably free of wrinkles, except for fine lines around her eyes, eyes the same colour blue as his.

Christabel's chair was next to hers.

"We have been so looking forward to meeting you," said Faith. "Bell was so excited by your arrival. I go to the shop every morning, Rex always has letters to leave for Francisco, and the last two days she has been there and we have had a little chat, mostly telling me how happy she is to have you with her."

"Did she tell you all about me?" asked Christabel, wondering how much her aunt had divulged.

"Well, we only had a few minutes, but she did manage to cram quite a lot of information into that short time. Do you mind?" She glanced anxiously at Bell, as if to reassure herself that she had not made a blunder, and Christabel understood that Bell had indeed told Faith about Ambrose.

"I did not know it was a secret," said Bell, on the defensive.

"And it is not," said Christabel. "In fact, it is something about which I would welcome an opinion from an outsider."

"Here you have a couple of outsiders, Rex and myself, who have braved all odds to be together," said Faith, "so we feel qualified to help in any way we can." She quickly touched Christabel's left hand. "It is the most beautiful ring. I don't think I have ever seen anything so exquisite before."

"I'm not even sure whether I am entitled to wear it," said Christabel.

"I'm sure you are. I met Lord Silveridge, years ago

when I was on the stage. He had put up the money for a play I was in. I only had a minor part. On the first night he and his wife came backstage to meet the cast. He was the most charming man, I'm sure a son of his must be delightful also. His wife, I remember, was very shy."

"Shy?"

"Yes, she seemed overawed by him. A little mouse-like lady who spoke in a whisper." Faith laughed. "Sometimes, I think they are the worst kind."

Christabel felt curiously close to this woman, although she had only just met her. She liked the direct way she had plunged straight into the problem Christabel was facing. Faith was aware there was a problem and she had not skirted around it.

They moved into the dining-room, which was adjacent to the drawing-room, Angela going ahead of them and opening the heavy door that separated the two rooms. Faith clutched Rex's hand and steered him to his chair at the head of the table. Bell sat on his right and Christabel on his left. Angela's seat was next to Bell and Faith was in the chair at the other end of the table.

"How long are you staying on the island?" Rex asked Christabel.

"I don't really know . . . it depends . . ."

"She has only just arrived," said Bell with determination. "I'm not allowing her to return for some time yet."

Angela brought in the dishes and placed them on mats in the centre of the long table. The meal was delicious. The main course was fish. "We eat very little meat, for obvious reasons, " Rex told Christabel. "Our fishermen bring us their catch and we eat it on the same day." Christabel was sure that the person who had cooked the meal was hovering in the kitchen. Angela was not responsible for that.

"This is the room where the nuns used to eat," said Faith. "They had a vow of silence, and sometimes we feel their quiet contemplation is still with us. It is quite unsettling. That is why Rex and I usually have our supper on trays in another room, which is free of saintly spirits. However, you need not worry. If there are more than two people in the room the ghosts disappear. They do not like company."

"You feel the place is haunted?" asked Christabel.

"We know it is, especially in the garden. There is a very spiritual feeling there, but it is tranquil and does not worry us. In here, on the other hand, there is a definite aura of discontent. It is not remarkable when you think about it; it is not in the nature of women to remain silent for hours at a stretch. When they sit down to a meal they love to talk."

"My dear, " said Rex, "are you determined to frighten poor Christabel out of her wits?"

"Not at all," said Christabel. "I am not easily frightened by unexplained sensations. My father is a vicar, and I know all about the spookiness of old churches when they are empty of people. I am certain neither of you have ever seen an apparition in this house, but the conviction there are spirits around is still very strong. I don't believe people when they say they have seen a ghost, but I believe them when they say they have been aware of one."

"Yes," said Faith, "we are aware, but they are so friendly and benign it does not concern us at all. Just a group of unrequited ladies."

"And the strangest thing of all," said Rex, "is their reaction to children. When Faith's boys come with their children, the nuns settle back into a state of complete contentment."

Christabel mentioned the play at the National Theatre on the South Bank.

"Oh, yes," said Rex, "I gather it is doing well. It is out of copyright, which is why they can bring it back after so many years. I had a nice letter from Felicity – she is a very sweet person."

"And you do not feel an urge to go to London and see it?"

"Not at all. Faith can go and see it if she cares to, when she visits England to see her sons and grandchildren. She will represent me."

Bell decided it was time she was included in the conversation. She volunteered, "The day before yesterday I took Christabel to the tower."

"It is impressive, isn't it?" said Rex. "And you saw the Wilderness Island in the distance?"

"Yes, and we passed it on the way here, in Francisco's boat."

"Not a wilderness any more, a National Park no less. Do you know the history of Cabrera? Has Bell already told you?"

"If she has not," said Faith dryly, "you are about to hear it."

"No," said Bell, "I could not remember the details."

"Please tell me," said Christabel.

"When Napoleon marched into Spain the last thing his army expected was an humiliating defeat at the Battle of Bailen. It was their first failure and a bitter blow to their pride. The prisoners taken were confined to eight prison ships anchored in the Bay of Cadiz. The local population resented their presence, and plans were made to move them. The original idea was to keep them on Mallorca, but they were not welcome there either, and the island had no facilities for a large contingent of officers and men. Eventually, after a year of indecision, they were taken to the deserted island of Cabrera. It had not been named the Wilderness Island without reason. Nine thousand men were abandoned in that God-forsaken place. Sparse rations were delivered by boat from Mallorca every four days. Ten of them planned to escape. They built a makeshift craft, and one day set sail for the small piece of land they could see on the horizon. It was their only hope. The weather was in their favour and they landed safely on these shores. It was inhabited by a scattering of farmers and fishermen eking out an existence in this solitary place. The island must have had a name, but when the strangers arrived it was renamed 'the island of escape', *La Isla de la Fuga*, and it has been called that ever since. The escaped prisoners merged into the scanty population, married and produced children."

"My Jose was a direct descendent," said Bell proudly.

"Of course!" said Christabel, "That is why Francisco told me he is half Mallorcan and half French. I wondered where the French came in. What happened to the ones that were left behind?"

Rex said, "After five years, of the nine thousand only three thousand and six hundred remained, and they were in bad shape. They were shipped back to France, but the French government took no interest in them. Defeat was no reason for compassion; the ten who escaped to *La Isla de la Fuga* fared much better."

"Oh, darling," said Faith, "it is such a romantic story, and I never tire of hearing it."

"And I never tire of telling it," he said.

"I know," she said fondly.

Although he was so frail his voice was strong. He held his audience; no one interrupted him while he was talking. "There is a monument on the island," he continued, "to the memory of the soldiers who perished there. I hope it still stands now that it is a National Park."

"They would not destroy it, darling," said Faith.

"You can never tell with bureaucrats – it is the same

all over the world. What does it say, Faith?" He explained, "Her French is better than mine."

"It says '*A la memoire des Français morts a la Cabrera.* Something like that."

"It is still there, said Christabel. "I saw a notice about it on the information kiosk at Colonia de Sant Jordi."

"I am so glad to hear that."

"It is a very sad story," continued Christabel. "Those poor fellows, so many miles from home, how desperate they must have felt. To have been in Napoleon's army must have been a tremendous honour, and then it all went wrong. It is the same through the ages; soldiers always got a raw deal. I would like to see the memorial stone. How does one get to the island?"

"With difficulty from here," said Faith. "Francisco may agree to drop you off for an hour or two, but he is not keen. He, like many people here, thinks it is haunted."

"On second thoughts, I don't think I fancy it," said Christabel. "I might disappear, like Mary Rose."

Rex laughed at that. "I did not think anyone of your generation knew about poor Mary Rose!"

Slowly, in procession, they made their way back to the drawing-room. Angela brought in a jug of coffee, which she poured into very English cups.

"Would anyone like Pacharan?" asked Rex. "It is a Spanish liqueur, very good."

"I would," said Bell promptly.

When it was time for them to leave the pony and trap and the driver were there waiting for them.

"What a wonderful way to travel," said Christabel.

"It is the only way, other than walking," said Faith. "So far we have managed to avoid cars on the island." She took Christabel's hand. "Come and see me! Perhaps you could walk over here tomorrow afternoon when Bell is having her *siesta.*"

"It is very kind of you," said Christabel. "I wonder if I might use your telephone? I would very much like to telephone England. Of course I will pay for the call."

"We'd be delighted if you would call from here. Rex has a swim in the morning –"

"Goodness!"

"I always go with him, although I don't swim. I sit on the beach. We have the only tiny strip of sand on the island and we guard it like a jewel. I'll show it to you tomorrow afternoon when he is having his rest."

"Thank you very much, for everything."

"Dear Bell," said Faith, kissing her, "It is so lovely seeing you look so well and happy. And we have enjoyed meeting your niece so much."

"I am enjoying having her with me," said Bell.

"What wonderful people," said Christabel on the way back. "I'm so glad to have met them."

"Yes, they are very special, but I thought Rex had aged since I last saw him. He looks so frail. What a bore getting old is, it creeps up on us, relentlessly, and there is nothing we can do about it." She sighed. "He will be all right with Faith to look after him. She will never agree to him going to a home for old people. However, I am not so fortunate and I can see myself ending up somewhere in a *residencia de ancianos*." She sounded as if it would be the worst fate possible, and the prospect of it, possibly exaggerated in her mind by fatigue, silenced her for the rest of the journey back to her home.

CHAPTER FOURTEEN

Christabel had got used to rising late in the morning. Her aunt was always up at an incredibly early hour, admiring the sprinkler at work from the kitchen window, making herself a cup of tea.

At about eleven o'clock it was their custom to sit on the terrace in the morning sun, enjoying cups of coffee and toast with English marmalade. They did not have lunch until three o'clock. It was a routine that suited Christabel very well. Sometimes her aunt pottered in the garden when the air was cooler in the late evening. Then she came in and prepared the evening meal. She refused to allow her niece to help her with the cooking. Christabel had the feeling that she enjoyed cooking for someone after spending so many years on her own. Christabel helped in numerous other ways, with the washing up and sweeping and dusting Sunnybanks, and she insisted on doing the shopping and paying for the goods she bought. Bell did not protest and they evolved a very happy arrangement that suited them both.

The morning after the dinner at *La Casa de las Hermanas* they were even later than usual. It was nearly noon before they carried their cups of coffee outside. They sat in a companionable silence, which was suddenly interrupted by the noise of a helicopter overhead. Christabel found nothing unusual in this, but her aunt jumped to her feet, shading her eyes to stare into the cloudless blue sky.

"Oh, dear, what can it mean?"

The significance did not dawn on Christabel until Bell explained, "It has come to take someone to the hospital on the mainland."

They watched the helicopter, circling now, as if the pilot was looking for a good place to land.

Bell said, "I'll go to the shop, dear, to see if I can find out who it is."

"Do you want me to come with you?"

"No, you wait here." She was gone in a moment, as fast as her stout legs would carry her.

Christabel carried the cups into the kitchen and washed them up. She thought of the importance of the helicopter arriving on the island, a link with the outside world, when reality took over from an idyllic existence. Soberly, she wondered if this would happen to her aunt; the helicopter would whisk her away from her little home, the beautiful garden and the sprinkler, all the things that mattered so much to her. Perhaps her gloomy prediction of the previous night would come true, and she would find herself in the harsh real world from which there was no escape.

Bell was gone a long time, and the helicopter passed over the house once more and chugged away into the distance. No doubt there was someone on board who was in need of help. Christabel looked at her watch, and wondered anxiously about her assignment to see Faith that afternoon. She was just deciding to leave a note for her aunt, when the old lady reappeared. She looked old, distraught, and flopped into a chair, covering her face with her hands.

"What is it?" cried Christabel, alarmed.

"It's Rex," she said, raising her head. "He went for his swim, as usual – only about ten minutes in the water every day, and Faith waits for him on the beach. This morning, when he came out, he sat down beside her, and said, 'I'm exhausted!'" She helped him back to the house, and there he collapsed. She managed to get him into bed while Angela telephoned the hospital. But, oh, this is what is so sad, Christabel dear: the helicopter arrived too late. He was dead when they got to him." She broke down and sobbed.

"How did they know all this at the shop?" asked Christabel wonderingly.

"Angela told one of the women who work in the big house, and she told them. News travels fast on this island."

Bell continued to sob noisily. "That wonderful man!" she said brokenly.

Yes, that wonderful man, thought Christabel, and she felt privileged to have met him the night before. It was tragic, but a part of her acknowledged that he was an old man who must have enjoyed much good fortune during his life. His career in the theatre had been hugely successful, and his declining years on the island had been blessed by having a woman at his side who clearly adored him. The young Napoleonic soldiers on Cabrera, of whom he had spoken so eloquently, were more to be pitied.

Of course there was no question of her going to the house now; the telephone call to England would have to be put on hold for the time being. She resigned herself to comforting Bell as best she could. Old people find it hard to face the death of someone close in age to themselves; it is a preview of what must inevitably happen to them, and it is very disturbing. Eventually, Christabel persuaded her aunt to go and have her rest as usual, and the old lady tottered off to her room. It had hit her badly, and her niece faced the fact that she would have to stay with her a while longer at any rate.

The next day Bell made several sorties to the shop to find out what was happening at *La Casa de las Hermanas*. Eventually, she returned with the news. "Faith's two sons arrive tomorrow, and the funeral is two days after that."

"If you don't mind," said Christabel, "I thought I'd go to the shop myself and telephone from there. I'd like to ring home."

"You'll need an awful lot of change for that," said Bell doubtfully.

"I think I have enough to cover it."

"You won't go dashing off before the funeral, will you? I could not face it without you."

"Of course not," said Christabel patiently. She could not help thinking that less than a week ago her aunt had hardly known of her existence, but now she seemed unable to manage without her.

The telephone call to England was remarkably quick and easy, and only the noise in the shop made it difficult to hear. Two women chatting together sounded as if they were having a violent quarrel. She heard the word Patterson mentioned, and guessed that they were discussing in excited high-pitched voices the sudden death of someone in their midst. Through the noise of their shouting, Christabel heard the familiar tones of her father.

"Is Mother there?"

"No."

"Andrew?"

"No."

"I just wondered if there had been any messages for me?"

"None that I know of, but your mother may have taken one."

She took a deep breath and plunged in with the question most important to her. "Has Brose telephoned to ask where I am?"

There was a silence at the other end, and then her father said ponderously, "I thought we'd been through all this before."

"Father!" She found herself shouting at him, in competition with the women in the shop. "I just want to know! Has he telephoned?"

"No, he has not. More importantly, did your aunt receive my letter?"

"Yes, she did, but it arrived after I did."

"Oh, I hope that did not inconvenience her too much."

"I don't think so. Is everyone well?"

"I think so."

"Give my love to Mother and Andrew. Tell them I rang."

And that was that. No one cared how longed she stayed on the Isla de la Fuga. That selfish old Lady Silveridge had won. Defiantly, she put in a call to Brose's office.

His secretary answered, "I'm so sorry, he is not here at present. Can I give him a message?"

"No message, thank you."

Bell noticed something was wrong as soon as she saw her. "An unsatisfactory telephone call?" she hazarded.

"Let's say an unsatisfactory parent," Christabel replied. "My father shows no understanding whatsoever."

"I never cared for Jess's choice," said Bell shortly. "A

man of the cloth he may be, but a man of substance he is not."

Christabel did not know how to answer that and, seeing her face, Bell said at once, "I'm sorry, my dear. I should not criticise your father. I'm sure he has many good points."

"He has. He's just a bit weak, that's all."

"And you won't be running off and leaving me just yet?" said her aunt anxiously, wishing for more reassurance.

"No, if you can put up with me a bit longer, I'd like to stay."

* * *

The funeral was quiet, dignified. A Catholic funeral, and Christobel wondered if Rex had been Catholic, or indeed any religion at all. It was the only church on the island, so there was no choice. Angela telephoned and asked if Christabel would mind walking, it was not far, and Bell could share the pony and trap with someone else who found walking difficult. Miguel was going to make several trips.

The melodious words flowed gently from the mouth of the grey-haired priest, demonstrating the beauty of the language when spoken in a modulated tone. Christabel enjoyed listening to the words rolling off his tongue although she could not understand most of them. There was a dramatic quality about the service, the coffin standing in front of the altar, covered in deference to the English tradition. The flowers laid on the top were from his garden. The church was packed with people who had grown to love the man. Christabel studied them, a mixture of old, middle-aged and very young. There was a whole swathe of twenty and thirty-year-olds missing from the congregation, and she remembered her aunt telling her about the people in that age group who had made their escape from the island.

She glanced in the direction of Faith, sitting between her two tall sons. She looked elegant, dressed in black, grave but not prostrate. What must it be like to lose a companion so much older than herself? It was something Christabel was beginning to feel she would never now experience. She thought that Faith must have envisaged this day many times. It was the inevitable conclusion to a relationship with a man many years her senior.

Ben, Faith's elder son came to the front of the church and read a poem. The fact that it was a poem and not a verse from the bible convinced Christabel that Rex had not been a religious man.

'Life! I know not what thou art
But I know that thou and I must part;
And when, or how, or where we met
I own to me's a secret yet.
Life! We've been long together
Through pleasant and through cloudy weather;
'Tis hard to part when friends are dear -
Perhaps 'twill cost a sigh, a tear;

Then steal away, give little warning,
Choose thine own time;
Say not Goodnight;
But in some brighter clime
Bid me Good Morning.

Later in the service the younger son, Giles, left his mother's side to deliver his contribution. Unlike his brother he was visibly nervous and he faltered when, surprisingly, he read an extract from Rex Patterson's most famous play, *Summer Storm:*

'Please do not leave me.'

'I have to go, it cannot be avoided, but in time you will become accustomed to being without me. We are blessed in this existence with the capacity to remember, but with the passage of time our memories become less of an anguish to us, until at last they become like old friends to whom we can always turn when we need them.'

Christabel thought it very poignant, especially as both the readings were directed solely at a very small proportion of the congregation. The Spanish sat in respectful ignorance about what was being said. She wondered about the relationship between Rex Patterson and these two men, both obviously very moved by the occasion, and she remembered they were not related to him in any way and were not even his stepsons.

Afterwards, they went to *La Casa de las Hermanas.* Angela escorted them into the garden. Under a giant tree a long table was covered with plates of *tapas* and bottles of red and white wine. Angela was much in evidence, bustling around attending to everybody's needs. Christabel felt awkward; she was, after all, a comparative stranger in this house of grief. This feeling was dispelled when Faith came over to her and Bell and embraced them both.

"I want you to meet my sons."

They were both married, and had three children apiece. They looked alike, and Christabel wondered if they were twins, but she was told there was a gap of eighteen months between them.

"It was like having twins when they were babies," Faith said lightly. "An absolute nightmare!"

Ben, the elder of the brothers, and a doctor, seemed to be in control of the situation. Christabel got the impression that he was quietly steering his mother through a difficult time.

"You must be a comfort to her," said Bell. "Did you have an awful journey getting here?"

"We are used to it," said Ben. "We have been here many times before."

"Nevertheless it was good of you to come so quickly," said Faith.

"Rex has been wonderful to us since we were children," was his reply, "and we wanted to be with you, Mother." He stood beside Faith, his arm linked in hers.

"How do you like our island?" he asked Christabel, as if anxious to move away from more personal subjects.

"I like it very much," she replied, "and I think this old house is perfection. A dream place with a fascinating history."

"Yes, it was a good find," he smiled at his mother, "and we have Faith to thank for that. It was all her doing."

"I am completely fascinated by the tree we are standing under," went on Christabel. It had large bright green leaves, and was like a roof over their heads, a roof with slivers of blue sky shining through. Its gnarled roots had broken through the grass beneath their feet.

"It is a Catalpa tree," Faith told her, "and it's size and age make it unusual. I think it may have been a sapling when the sisters were here, perhaps not big enough for them to enjoy its shade. Rex loved to sit under it." She mentioned his name casually without a tremor of emotion in her voice. "In the winter when it loses its leaves it is a bit stark, but at this time of the year it is magical. I shall miss it terribly when I leave this place."

"Leave?" cried Bell sharply. "You are not thinking of leaving?"

Faith replied calmly, "I'm sorry to upset you, Bell, dear. Perhaps it was wrong of me to mention it so soon. Of course I shall miss my friends on the island, particularly you, but Rex and I planned it this way. I shall return to England and buy a house not too far away from my children and grandchildren. I could not bear to live in this beautiful place without him. We always knew that."

Bell's disapproval hung like a cloud over the conversation.

Pretending to be unaware of it, Faith want on, "Unfortunately, Ben and Giles have to return to England straight away, but they are returning to help me with the sale of the house and the move to England." She turned to Christabel. "I shall feel very flat after the boys have left. Francisco is coming to collect them in the morning. Could you manage to come and see me sometime during the afternoon, if Bell can spare you?"

Christabel was astonished by the suggestion. She had imagined Faith would want to be alone at such a time.

"You can telephone England from the house. I believe you said you wanted to do that."

Christabel explained, "I telephoned from the shop. I did not want to bother you."

"Oh, well, come anyway. I shall be badly in need of company."

Bell was vehement in expressing her feelings when they got back to her cottage. "How could she decide so soon to leave this place? And to tell us like that when poor Rex is hardly cold in his grave!" To announce such a proposal so soon after the funeral seemed almost obscene to Bell, as if, now that Rex was out of the way, Faith was ready move on. "I hope she realises she will not be able to sell the house until probate is granted. And that takes a very long time."

Christabel got the impression that her aunt was very disappointed in Faith, someone who, up to that moment, she had loved and admired.

"Have you thought that the house may belong to her?" she said gently, remembering that the son had said his mother was responsible for its purchase.

Christabel thought she understood how Faith felt. The island was for two people, bound up with each other, not for a solitary soul dependent on memories. People on their own must live in the real world. Beautiful surroundings are wasted if they are not shared. She did not express these feelings to Bell, for she, except for the ten years when she had enjoyed a comfortable relationship with a man, was a being on her own, and likely to remain so. The loss of Rex, and then Faith would be very hard on her.

* * *

She did not leave the house the next day until she heard the comfortable sound of snoring coming from Bell's bedroom. The old lady was sleeping peacefully then, and she was free to leave. She walked quickly along the little path, through the glade of olive-trees and down the hill towards the sea, She met no one and the only sound she heard was her own soft footfall and the slight movement of the leaves in the trees overhead. The sun was so hot that day she wore a hat to shade her face. Suddenly, she felt indescribably lonely.

She could not stay much longer in this place. Whatever decision Brose had come to about her future, she must go home and face it. His ring was still on her finger; she felt it was her only link with him, but she was beginning to recognise the fact that probably she had no right to keep it there.

Faith came to the door to greet her. Gone were the funereal clothes and instead she was wearing a cotton skirt and a white shirt, and on her head a wide straw hat.

"I'm glad to see you have a hat," she said. "You need it on a day like this. I thought you might like to go to our beach. You haven't seen it before."

They descended narrow wooden steps, and there, as she described it, was a strip of silver sand. It was flanked on both sides by rocks, and the sea lapped benignly on the shore. Apart from the little line of white foam at the edge it was a deep blue stretching to the horizon and the sky beyond.

"As I told you before, this is the only sandy cove on the island and Rex and I guarded it like a precious jewel," said Faith. "You know, we have been saved from a tourist invasion by two things: the size of the place, not big enough to make a resort, and the fact that there are no sandy beaches. Sometimes I had nightmares of this little strip being packed with bodies, like sardines in a tin of oil, but, thank God, it never happened. I can't tell you how many hours Rex and I have spent here, looking at the sea." For the first time

Christabel detected a break in her voice.

"I'm so sorry," she said.

Faith tilted her hat over her nose, and Christabel recognised it as a sad little gesture to hide her tears.

Christabel felt no words were appropriate, and she remained silent.

At last Faith spoke in an almost normal voice. "Let's go back to the garden."

They retraced their steps and Faith removed two wicker chairs from a garden shed and she placed them beneath the Catalpa tree. "It is better here," she said. "The beach has too recent memories."

They settled themselves in the comfortable chairs, the leaves of the old tree sheltering them from the intense heat of the sun.

They sat in silence for a while until Faith said, "I wanted to talk to you when dear old Bell told me about your problems with Lady Silveridge. I'm afraid she was not very discreet. You, I am sure, would have preferred to keep it to yourself. I think I was remiss in not stopping her, but I was interested, and it occurred to me since then that my own story might be helpful to you. Now, I want to tell it to you for another reason, to help *me*. Can you bear to listen?"

"Of course I can," said Christabel.

"It's rather long, I'm afraid."

"I have all the time in the world," Christabel told her.

"It all started," said Faith, "during the blitz in London. It was 1941, the year that I was born. My father, George Foster, was a managing clerk in a firm of solicitors called Gowers in Arundel Street, just off the Strand."

PART TWO

Chapter Fifteen

George was the youngest member of staff at Gowers, a fact that set him apart from everyone else, giving him that sense of being 'different' which he had experienced most of his life. Here at Gowers he was different because he scurried from room to room whereas his colleagues walked slowly and sedately, as befitted their age. He was different from them in another respect: he was profoundly deaf, and most of them had partial hearing at least. His deafness had prevented him from going into the armed forces, which was the reason he was still working at Gowers when his peers were serving their country. He was like the schoolboy who cannot play games because he has a weak heart: he would have given anything to be there in the centre of the scrum. He tried to do his bit for the war effort by doing ARP work and refusing to leave London now that the bombing had begun.

He was not all that young; he was in his late thirties, and he had been married for ten years. He and his wife, Daisy, lived in a neat suburban house in Notting Hill. Daisy was house-proud and the house smelled of polish. He looked after their small patch of garden, and it always had a manicured appearance, the edges cut and the path swept. Everything about the house and the garden pointed to one fact of life – there were no children in that orderly establishment.

George knew, although he would never utter the thought to his wife, that this orderliness could disappear in a flash if their little house got a direct hit one night. George thought that Daisy should go to the country, but she steadfastly refused. Nothing would induce her to leave him, and they both knew that he felt committed to stay at Gowers during a difficult time. 'After the war…' was a phrase people used many times, and George was no exception, "After the war," he told Daisy, "we'll buy a little shop in a country village somewhere." It was a dream, and he saved up for it.

He travelled to work every day on the Circle Line, eight stops before alighting at Temple Station. He could have done the journey in his sleep, it was so familiar. He had taken that route for nearly a decade. He had gone to Gowers as a tea-boy and risen, by stint of hard work and ambition, to the status of managing clerk. It was a routine: kissing Daisy goodbye at the front door, then putting on his bowler as he walked down the garden path; closing the gate carefully behind him, and then a brisk walk to the underground station; looking to the left and right before crossing the busy street, for deaf people must take extra care in traffic.

When he went through the swing doors of Gowers he acknowledged the greeting of the old chap sitting inside, and put his head around the door of accounts and said, "Good morning, ladies!" to the women sitting at their desks. They raised their grey heads when they saw him, and gave him a smile. George was popular with everyone in the office.

When he described his work to anyone interested he said he did all the dirty work for the partners. That was the way all managing clerks thought of themselves, and there was some truth in the assertion. They oiled the wheels that kept the old place running smoothly. With the exception of George, all of them were elderly, like the partners, as all the younger members of staff had joined the forces. They longed for the end of the war when they could retire. In the meantime, they 'kept the ship afloat' as they said, and, at the weekends, joined their wives in the country.

George had met Daisy in the Temple gardens, at a time when there was no thought of war. There was a sandwich shop by the station that did a nice line in salt-beef sandwiches. Every lunch hour he joined the queue, purchased his sandwich and then took it to his special bench by the statue of a pretty little girl holding a bowl in her hand. It was a fountain and sometimes it was working, sometimes not. When it was operating on a summer's day the sunshine glinted on the water and it made a sweet tinkling sound. Underneath were written the words *Lady Henry Somerset* and, at first, George thought the little girl must have this high-sounding name, but then he realised the fountain was dedicated to this lady because of the work she had done for the Temperance League cause.

He ate his sandwich, but did not bother with a drink; there was an endless supply of cups of tea in the office all day long. The pigeons gathered around his feet in expectation, and he always threw them the last bit of crust.

One day as he was sitting in the sun, his bowler hat by his side on the bench, he saw a young woman wheeling a big pram along the path, a small boy walking by her side holding on to the pram handle. She was dressed in the austere grey of a nanny: flannel overcoat and felt hat. The child by her side was in the attire chosen by most rich parents for their children, a Harris tweed coat with a velvet collar. But George was not interested in the appearance of the little boy; he was struck by the clean rosy face of the girl who looked as if she came from the country, and did not belong to a smoky city.

The next day he was in the same place, and he looked out for her. His heart lifted when he saw her. This time the boy was playing with a ball, running in front of her, bouncing it up and down on the path. It came flying through the air in George's direction and, by a fluke of fate, for he was not usually very coordinated, he managed to catch it. The child stood in front of him, and George returned his property.

The nanny stopped. "Say thank you, George," she said.

He did as he was told, and George said, "That's my name too. I'm George."

"Well, fancy that!" she said, and smiled. The next minute she was gone, walking briskly with the pram, little George running in front of her.

He did not see her the following day, or the one after that. Then it was the weekend, and he had time to think about her and wonder if he would ever see her again. Then on Monday there she was, and she recognised him at once and rewarded him with her bright smile. The little boy was back at her side, one hand holding the handle of the pram.

"Where is the ball?" asked George boldly.

"We lost it," she explained, stopping in front of him, "on the Round Pond in Kensington Gardens. George threw it in by mistake, an old gentleman tried to reach it with his stick, but it sailed out into the middle of the pond." Then as if embarrassed at having said so much to a complete stranger, she was on her way with her charges.

Next time he saw her George was prepared. "Here, young George," he called, and he threw a new ball in the child's direction.

"Oh! You shouldn't have . . ." she protested, and to

the little boy, "Say thank –" But George was already shouting out his thanks and running around with his new ball.

George Foster watched her hesitate and then, to his delight, she steered the pram towards the bench where he was sitting. He got to his feet while she parked the pram, putting on the brake with a neatly shod foot.

"Perhaps I'll wait here for a while," she said, "and we can watch him play."

George could hardly believe his luck. Hastily, he removed his bowler hat so that she could sit in the bench beside him. The trouble was that, although he had become adept at reading the lips of people in front of him, he knew that in order to understand what she was saying to him he would have to turn and look hard at her. He was afraid she might find that disconcerting. There was nothing for it but to make the usual confession.

"I'm sorry," he said. "You will have to speak at me, as I'm deaf."

"Oh!" She turned her face towards him and he saw the colour come to her cheeks. "You don't talk like a deaf person." Now that she knew, she thought she noticed a slight slurring in his speech, but nothing more.

"That's because I did not become deaf until I was seventeen years old. I had a motorbike accident and landed on my head. I was unconscious for days, and when I came to I was deaf. I can hear very faintly in one ear, but mostly I have to lip-read." He had saved up for the motorbike from his first earnings at Gowers. He had been so proud of it, but a patch of black ice on the road had put an end to all his dreams.

"Am I sitting on the side of the good ear?" she asked.

"Yes, you are."

"My name is Daisy," she told him. "Daisy Flower."

That was a bit of a shock. "I know," she said. "I have to live with it. My dad has a warped sense of humour. My sister is called Rose."

He told her his name, and they shook hands formally, laughing nervously at the same time, both aware of the unusual circumstances of their meeting. He told her he was a managing clerk with a firm of solicitors in Arundel Street, not far from where they were sitting. He hoped this information would give him an air of respectability. To cover up their confusion they got to their feet and played with little George, throwing the ball backwards and forwards between the three of them. The child invariably missed the catch and had to run after the ball, leaving the grown-ups standing awkwardly, not knowing what to say to each other.

Finally, she said, "We must be off."

"Me too. Back to work."

She rocked the pram, gazing into it. "This is Amy," she said. "Isn't she lovely?"

He did not know much about babies, but this one looked all right, and when he gave her chest a little prod she smiled at him. "She's a wonder, no mistake," he said, and knew at once that he had said the right thing. Encouraged, he said, "Shall I see you tomorrow?"

She nodded. "We'll be here." She remembered to look at him when she spoke, and from that day onwards she never forgot. He watched the little group until they were out of sight, around the corner of the path. He admired her back view, the little knot of hair under the plain hat, the slim legs and ankles.

He felt exhilarated. He walked back to the office with a light step. All the rest of the day he felt his mouth twitching at the corners in a secret smile. He felt he was master of the universe, and it showed.

"I think our Mr Foster is in love," said the senior partner's secretary. "Am I right, George?"

It was the usual office banter, and he fielded it by saying, "You may be right or you may be wrong."

The women surrounded him, asking questions and demanding answers. "What is her name?" they wanted to know.

"Daisy Flower." Of course they laughed, and one of them said, "The sooner you change that the better."

Daisy worked for Mr and Mrs Anderson. Mr Anderson was a backbencher at the House of Commons. "They say he has a great political future," she told George. "We are never in the same place for long. Either at their flat in Westminster or at his mother's house in the Cromwell Road, and then during the weekends we go to the country to their house in Sussex. It must be upsetting for George, all the moving around, but he does not seem to mind."

She was full of praise for her employers. Surprisingly, she had been with them for four years, in fact since the birth of George. "They are wonderful people," she said, and George, always loyal, said, "They must think the world of you." It was true, because when she told them she was leaving to get married they gave her a cheque for one hundred pounds as a wedding present, a great deal of money in those days.

George had been right when he guessed she was a country girl. They were married in Devon, and both sets of parents hit it off from the beginning. Everyone was delighted when they heard a baby was due, exactly nine months after the honeymoon.

Daisy loved being pregnant; she was over the moon at the idea of being a mother, for she adored babies. That was the reason she decided to train as a nanny. When she left work she missed little George and Amy, and often went to visit them.

"George can't understand what has happened to Nanny," she said, patting her swollen stomach. "He was quite concerned about me, bless him."

They moved into a little house in Notting Hill. A good solid house, but in the words of the estate agent's blurb 'in need of refurbishment'. Those four words made it possible for George to purchase the house, and immediately he set to work on it. He started ripping out the old kitchen cabinets and building new ones, but then he had to leave the kitchen and concentrate on the nursery. He painted the second bedroom pale yellow, suitable for either sex, and he built an elaborate piece of nursery furniture to his own design, a flat surface for changing the baby, with shelves below for piles of fleecy napkins, Harrington squares and little garments. The whole thing folded up so that it could be stored when it was no longer needed.

George Foster wanted to take part in the miracle that was about to happen to his wife. It was his dearest wish to be present at the birth.

"You'll never be allowed," said his wife.

She was right. Like all expectant fathers he was left to pace up and down the waiting-room. Then a doctor appeared and told him that there were complications. Suddenly, it was borne upon him that Daisy, his Daisy, was fighting for her life. He was taken to see his daughter, lying spread-eagled in an incubator. She looked unbelievably frail, and he felt a wave of resentment towards her for endangering the most precious thing in his life. In his distress he felt no bond with the little creature, no awareness that this was what he and Daisy had waited so eagerly for, their own flesh and blood. At last, he was persuaded to go home for the night and, when he returned the next day the news was no better. Daisy was still very ill, and a nurse took him into a ward, and handed the baby to him. "Hold her, Mr Foster, for I'm afraid she has not long to live." He held the weightless bundle, and saw two pale blue eyes looking at him. He handed her back to the nurse, tears streaming down his face. They had planned to call her Mary, which was Daisy's second name. When she died, George could hardly take in the fact of her death so relieved was he to learn that his wife would recover. "She cannot have another child," the doctor told him.

What followed had to be endured somehow. The funeral, the small coffin lined with satin, closing the door of the yellow bedroom, and carrying the contents up into the loft. Daisy, always a cheerful person, became depressed. So depressed that her husband did not know how to deal with it. Eventually, he hit upon the idea of her becoming a nursery teacher at the local kindergarten. She got the job, and with it came the satisfaction of working with small children. But it was a baby she yearned for, not a child, and she could not explain that to George. He was just glad to see her smile again. She did not believe the doctor who had told them she would never conceive again. She believed that God would bless them with a child, but George privately had more faith in the doctor's verdict that in the munificence of the Almighty.

The years passed, happy years except that each month Daisy hoped, and each month she was disappointed. George suggested they should adopt, and Daisy visited an Adoption Society. She came home and said, "They told me we are not suitable."

"Not suitable, why?"

"I don't know, dear," she lied. Daisy, who never told a lie, lied for his sake.

But he knew; it was his deafness that made the powers that be decide he was not a suitable father. The unfairness of it made him bitter, but he kept his thoughts to himself, and a time came when they did not talk any more about babies, missed periods, hopes and disappointments.

When the war came the kindergarten closed down. George suggested that Daisy should leave London, go to Devon where her family lived, although the distance had prevented them from seeing any of them since the wedding.

She said, "You daft ha'p'orth, I'm staying here with you. It's not as if we have a child to think of."

When he saw the children leaving London with their gas-mask boxes and labels on their coats, he was almost glad he was not a parent. This is no world for a child to grow up in, he told himself.

It was Daisy's birthday, and during the lunch hour on that day in February 1941 he went to the Civil Service Stores to buy her an umbrella. She had left hers on a bus. Carrying it back, unwrapped to save paper, he noticed that everyone in the Strand had started to hurry; the pavement was jammed with people on the move. Nobody ran, but they quickened their pace and, from time to time, looked anxiously at the sky. George himself walked quickly to Arundel Street, and when, at last, he reached the office he found that it was deserted. Chairs had been pushed back, and typewriters left without their thick covers. Desks were piled with unfinished work, ledgers left open. George knew that the entire staff of Gowers had gone to the basement, and there he found them all, partners included, huddled together, surrounded by shelves of yellowing dusty files.

One of the ladies gave him a cup of tea, and said, "We were worried about you, George."

"I just nipped out to the Civil Service Stores to buy the missus a brolly. It's her birthday today."

"Oh, wish her many happy returns of the day."

Walking home from the underground, clutching the new umbrella, he felt a familiar twinge of fear. Turning the corner, he saw that his house was still standing, as were all the others in the street. There was Daisy to greet him with his evening kiss, and the house smelled reassuringly of cooking.

He sat down in his special chair, and they had a drink together in celebration of her birthday. A whisky for him and a medium sherry for her. She told him she was delighted with the present, it was 'just what she wanted'. That night they made love, even though it was not a Friday, which was their night, but a Tuesday and a birthday.

Afterwards George turned to kiss her, and felt her cheeks were wet.

"What is it?" he asked. He turned on the bedside lamp so that he could see her lips.

"What's the matter, love?"

"Nothing."

"The same old thing?"

"Don't worry about me," she said, "I'm just silly." She leaned over him and turned off the light. After she had gone to sleep, he lay awake staring into the darkness. He knew what was wrong. She felt time was running out for her. Birthdays were milestones leading the way to a childless old age. No amount of kissing and comforting from him could do any good, he was powerless to help. He would have made any sacrifice to give her what she wanted.

Chapter Sixteen

The following night he was on ARP duty, and neither of them wanted to leave the other. George reminded himself that there were men serving many miles away from their wives and families, and he had no right to complain about his lot. Daisy was particularly afraid that night because there was an air raid in progress. She could hear the sound of gunfire and the unmistakable throb of German bombers overhead. She felt fear for them both, but mostly for George having to step out into the thick of it.

She helped him on with his heavy greatcoat, and he put on the tin hat which made a red mark on his forehead. Daisy handed him the little flask containing brandy and he put it in his pocket. He always took it with him just in case, but so far it had not been touched. The last thing he did before he left the house was to see that she was sitting in the cupboard under the stairs. A wooden chair just fitted into the cupboard, and there was a bare bulb overhead. He left her there with an eiderdown over her legs and her knitting in her hands.

Outside it was bitterly cold, and he clapped his hands together as he marched down the street. Despite being worried about Daisy left alone in the house, he felt exhilarated, a sense of doing something worthwhile. This was the next best thing to being in some army camp on the other side of the world or shivering on a minesweeper in the North Sea.

At the corner of Addison Road, which was two streets away from where he lived, he met his friend, Alec, a colleague in the ARP. The two men did not speak because Alec knew that he would not be understood in the darkness, but they spoke to each other in their minds, and Alec said, the buggers are busy tonight, and George said he could hear the faint sound of gunfire in his good ear so it must be pretty loud.

They stood together watching the searchlights arching over the black sky. Alec heard the scream of the bomb, and both men rocked on their feet with the force of the explosion. Then there was another bomb screeching down to earth, and another. They ran to the tall Victorian house on the corner, which was soon engulfed in flames. Down the street another house had been hit, and another; it was as if a light had been turned on in Addison Road. Alec was able to turn to George and mouth the words, "The big house is empty, leave it to the fire service boys."

He made off down the street, and George was left

surveying the destruction of what had once been someone's home. Alec had said it was empty, but how could he be sure? Homeless people often found shelter in abandoned houses. He decided to stay there until the firemen had extinguished the flames. Obviously they had been informed there was no one living there because they moved on quickly; their assistance was needed in so many places they could not afford to waste time searching an empty house.

George went into the smouldering skeleton of the house. Only one half had been badly affected, the other half was almost intact. His torch, an inadequate beam in accordance with the regulations, swept across the charred remains of what must have once been the drawing-room. A family portrait had been wiped out, but the gilt frame remained, hanging grotesquely on a section of wall still standing. Two armchairs and a sofa stood stolidly in their places. A door hung precariously over the entrance, banging in the wind. George moved it carefully to one side and stepped into the room. The smell of ashes assailed his nostrils. It was hard to see in the semi-darkness which was overhung with a pall of smoke and dust. His Wellington boots sploshed in the water left by the hoses, and he stepped gingerly over the broken glass which scrunched beneath his feet.

He passed from that room into what must have once been the hall. It was completely gutted due to the fact that the staircase had collapsed and part of the roof above it. George could see the black sky through a gaping hole. He guessed there would be a cupboard under the stairs; he could just make it out and he forced himself to peer into it. He knew it was the place where people were advised to go during an air raid. It gave them a small hope of survival. The advice had not worked on this occasion though.

He turned his face away from what was inside. He had seen many terrible sights during the Blitz but he could never become hardened to such tragedies.

There were two bodies and he felt instinctively they were both dead, but he had to be sure. He put his hand inside – they were entwined, clinging to each other during their last moments, a young couple by the looks of them. His hand felt a movement, something stirred beneath his touch. He had to put his torch on the ground while he fumbled in the dark and removed a sodden bundle.

He carried it into the other room and laid it on one of the dusty armchairs while he went back to retrieve the torch. When he returned the object was still moving. If he had been able to hear he would have known it was making noises as well.

He took off his greatcoat and removed the thick pullover underneath, a pullover that Daisy had knitted for him for his last birthday. Tenderly, he wrapped the little thing in it and laid it on the armchair again while he put on his heavy coat again.

"No need for us both to perish in the cold," he said aloud.

The atmosphere in the room was not conducive to easy breathing so he made haste to negotiate the hanging door, carrying the bundle in his arms. He stepped outside into the pure cold air of the garden and laid his little burden under a bush.

"I'll be back in a minute, love," he said.

He knew he had to return, to take another look at the young couple and also to make sure there were no other occupants in that house.

He examined the bodies, in each case feeling for a pulse, as he had been taught to do, making certain there were no signs of life. Then he walked around the ground floor of the house where it had received a direct hit; the hand holding the torch was shaking as he shone it into the corners. He thought of the cupboard under the stairs in his own house, two streets away, and he was terribly afraid.

He left the derelict house, picked up the bundle from under the bush and made for home. He noticed people emerging from the shelters so he knew the All Clear must have sounded. They were all anxiously hurrying to get back to their homes, and they did not notice a man walking quickly, carrying what looked like a bundle of rags.

* * *

He was not surprised to find that Daisy was no longer under the stairs. She was often disobedient about staying in the cupboard, which she thought was claustrophobic. He hoped that she had stayed there until it was safe to come out. He put his jersey and its precious contents on the sofa in the sitting-room, and then he ran up the stairs, two at a time. As he had expected, Daisy was sitting up in bed, waiting for him.

"Quick," he cried urgently. "I have something downstairs for you."

She got up at once and put on her dressing-gown. Then she followed his lumbering form down the stairs, and with a shaking hand he pointed at the sofa, "There."

She knelt, parted the jersey and then undid the soaking wrapping. The baby did not move.

"Is it dead?" she whispered, pressing her ear to its small frame.

"It wasn't dead when I found it," he said. "Perhaps it's in shock, that's all."

He felt there was a note of reproof in her voice, as if he had neglected to do something important.

She leapt to her feet. "We must warm it. Light the fire."

He knelt to ignite the gas fire with a match, his hands trembling so much he could hardly perform this simple task. Daisy gathered the baby to her, pressing it against her breast, trying to instil some life into it.

"It can't be dead!" she cried. She started rocking it, backwards and forwards, holding it against her body.

It let out a cry. It was like the first cry of a newborn baby after emerging from its mother's womb. George did not hear it, but he saw Daisy's face.

"Thank God," she said.

The baby started to cry in earnest then, filling the room with its thin wails. George stared fascinated at the open mouth and the little face gradually changing colour.

"It's hungry," said Daisy desperately. "Go and warm up some milk."

He did as he was told, and she tried to spoon the liquid into the tiny mouth with a teaspoon. It sucked ineffectually and, watching its efforts, George found his own mouth working in a desire to see it take nourishment. The pursed-up little mouth rejected the teaspoon, and George thought sadly of the girl in the cupboard, her breasts no doubt engorged with milk ready to satisfy her baby.

Then Daisy handed the baby to him while she went into the kitchen to wash her hands. When she returned she dipped her finger in the warm milk and put it in the baby's mouth. "This'll work," she said. She was right for it started to suck eagerly. When it was used to the finger she reverted to the teaspoon. At some time the baby fell asleep in her arms.

They both stared at it, hardly daring to breathe. Thick lashes fanned a grubby cheek. The tiny nose was smeared with ash, and the hands were small black stars. The clothes that had once been white were blackened by smoke. The baby smelled of smoke and something else which George could not identify.

"We must clean it and change it," said Daisy. She

looked at her husband and he understood at once. He did not need to be told what to do. He went upstairs and removed the steps that were hanging on the wall next to the loft. He propped them up and climbed up through the sliding hatch above. There was no electric light but he had his torch, and he found the bassinet and the changing contraption he had invented, neatly folded, and the nappies put away in an old pillowcase. In another pillowcase were the matinee jackets and the baby clothes lovingly made for Mary. With care he lowered all these things to the floor below.

They filled the bathroom basin with warm water. Gently Daisy peeled off the damp dirty clothes. "It's a little girl," she said.

Of course George had known from the first it would be a girl. She did not cry now, but just stared at them with blue unfocussed eyes.

There was a pad over the belly-button. "She can be only a few days old," said Daisy wonderingly. George watched, fascinated, as she sponged the little body and wiped the face with cotton wool. Then she wrapped the baby in a towel.

"Those clothes may be damp, up in the loft all that time," said Daisy, "put them around the fire for a while." She was in charge, giving the orders, and he was only too happy to obey. He fetched the clotheshorse and put it in front of the gas fire, then hung on it a nappy, a Harrington square and a change of clothes.

Then they sat together on the sofa and looked at the baby. George could not believe how wonderful she was, and he had found her. When the clothes were warmed through, Daisy put on the nappy (George had to rush around the house in search of a safety pin) and then the clothes. She objected to being thrust into the clothes; she had been happier wrapped in the towel. Soon, safe and warm, she drifted off to sleep again. George fetched the bassinet, and they decided she should sleep in the room with the fire.

"That room hasn't been slept in," said Daisy decidedly. "She would be cold in there."

George nodded agreement.

"Where did you find her?" Daisy asked, and George told her about the bombed house, and when she heard about the dead parents in the cupboard under the stairs she hid her face in her hands for a moment.

They both gazed at the sleeping baby. "The poor little scrap," whispered Daisy, "left alone in the world." She looked at her husband. "You saved her life," she said, her face full of pride and adoration. "You should get a medal for this."

Daisy took George's hand. "Let's go to bed, love. She is warm and cosy now, happen she will sleep until the morning."

She did not. They had just settled themselves down under the covers when Daisy heard the cries from downstairs. They both padded down, and George lifted the baby from the bassinet and held her against his shoulder. "There, there," he murmured in an ineffectual way.

They had no more sleep that night. The baby was feeling hungry, and the milk on the finger was not what she wanted. "We must buy her a bottle in the morning," said Daisy with a note of desperation in her voice.

The next morning, tired and anxious, George instructed his wife to telephone Gowers to say he was sick and could not go to work that morning. In all the years he had worked there this was the first time he had feigned illness in order to have a day off.

Daisy wrote out a list for him. "You can get everything from Colin's down the road."

Colin, the local chemist, was a friend. "I know he stocks everything we need."

George nodded, but when he was outside in the road the thought struck him that Colin, being a mate, would want to know why he wanted a baby's bottle and suchlike. He'd likely make saucy remarks and ask questions. After consideration, George decided to walk to the nearest bus stop, and he took a threepenny ride to another street and another chemist.

There were so many items on Daisy's list he was glad she had given him a shopping bag. Then he had to wait a long time for a bus to take him home. Hurrying along the road to his house he met a neighbour, a large comfortable lady who was eager for a chat.

"Not at work today, Mr Foster?" she said.

"No," said George, "I'm not well. I've only come out to fetch some medicine." He felt the woman's eyes on him, he imagined with suspicion.

"You look tired," she said.

"Well, I am. I came over all queer in the night, didn't have a wink of sleep." Like all unpractised liars he did not know when to stop. At last he managed to escape from her. The little episode filled him with guilt, but only for a short while. He made up his mind to forget it as quickly as possible. Clasping the shopping bag, he hastened up the path to his front door. He was already taking the first steps to a great deception.

Chapter Seventeen

As he walked up the garden path he saw Daisy's anxious face peering through the window, waiting for him. She was holding the baby to her shoulder, trying to pacify her, and George could see from the colour of the baby's face that she was not having much success.

"Where have you been?" she demanded.

He started to explain about going to another chemist, but she cut him short and handed the child over to him. "Here, you have her," she said, and she snatched the bag and hurried into the kitchen with it.

George walked up and down, while his wife sterilised the bottle and the teat by boiling them for two minutes, then making up the feed with Carnation milk, a teaspoon of sugar and cool boiled water. The whole process seemed to take an age, and George did not know what to do. He realised that Daisy must have had an awful morning, waiting for him to return with the things she needed. The evident distress of the baby made him feel agitated, and he felt utterly useless because he had no comfort to offer. He continued walking up and down, turning her this way and that way, his clumsy hands sensing the desperation of the small squirming frame. Her head shot back and she stared at him with what he felt was angry hostility.

At last, Daisy appeared with the bottle in a jug of cold water. She settled herself into the old sofa, a cushion at her back, and George thankfully handed the infant over to her. She thrust the nipple into the open mouth, and George felt the relief himself as he watched, fascinated, as the little creature fastened on to the rubber teat like a limpet to a rock.

"Ah!" he said.

"Ah!" repeated his wife. "That makes her feel better." She assumed the contented dreamy look of a woman feeding her child. The baby held tightly on to one of her fingers. "Such a little mite it is," she said.

When the baby had drunk half the milk in the bottle Daisy expertly put her against one shoulder, covered with a Harrington square, and firmly patted her back. Then she gently laid her in the bassinet and moved it slowly backwards and forwards. It was lined with pale yellow muslin, and George remembered her buying the material and painstakingly sewing it during the evenings of her pregnancy.

The baby slept, and Daisy said calmly, "You'd best be off again, dear, to report this at the police station."

George took a deep breath. "The parents are dead," he said, "both of them. I know that for a fact. What will become of her? She'll be put in some home, most likely. Why can't she stay here? We'll look after her. There's no one better with babies than you are."

She looked at him directly, and he could see that she was almost cross with him. He knew he would have to tread carefully with her as she was scrupulously honest at all times, insisting that the bills be paid on the day they arrived and never trying to cheat the system of a penny. When the bus conductor forgot to ask for a fare she called out to him.

She spoke patiently to him, as she might have spoken, years before, to one of her charges. "Of course we would care for her, and love her in time, but that's not the point. This little girl has probably got grandparents who will want to have her with them. If not, perhaps we could get permission to foster her."

"You know what the answer will be to that," said George, remembering their experience with the Adoption Society.

"Well, we can't keep her, that's for sure," said Daisy decidedly, taking a sideways glance at the occupant of the bassinet.

"But we could keep her for a while," pleaded George. "There is no hurry, surely?"

"If she stays with us too long we will get fond of her," reasoned his wife, "and that won't do anyone any good."

"We'll wait and see if there is anything in the local paper about her family," said George. "There is bound to be something about the bombing of a big house like that, it's the biggest in Addison Road. You agree to that?"

Daisy agreed, but she did not let the matter rest there. "You can't steal a baby, just like that. She has to be registered and have a birth certificate. I remember when Amy was born Mr Anderson went to the register office to register her birth and brought home her birth certificate signed by the registrar of births and deaths."

"I saved her life, you said so yourself," George pointed out. "If I had not rescued her from that house she would be dead by now. That's not stealing, that's giving."

"Yes, love," said Daisy, putting her arms around him, "and I understand why you want to keep her. To make me happy. I am always such an old misery, and I'm sorry."

"It would make me happy to," her husband told her.

The next day he returned to work and everyone was very sympathetic. "It's not often you're away sick," someone said, "and you look as if you've come back too soon." George realised that lack of sleep and anxiety had made him look ill.

He worried all day in case Daisy took matter into her own hands and telephoned the police. On the way home he picked up a local paper from the newsagent's shop. As he expected, there was a column devoted to the bomb on the house in Addison Road.

'No 1 Addison Road suffered a direct hit on Wednesday

night. It is the home of Group Captain and Mrs John Patterson who live in Harrogate, Yorkshire. The house had been shut up since the beginning of the war, and the fire brigade, thinking it was empty, left the scene after extinguishing the fire. Later, after a busy night during which there were three direct hits in the same street, the police inspected No 1 Addison Road and found the bodies of a young man and a young woman. They were sheltering in a cupboard under the stairs. A police doctor was called and he surmised the force of the explosion had killed them both instantly. They have since been identified as Miss Mary Patterson, aged sixteen, and Mr Donald Beeching, aged seventeen. Miss Patterson was the only daughter of Group Captain and Mrs John Patterson and Mr Beeching the younger son of Mr and Mrs Brian Beeching who are neighbours of the Pattersons in Harrogate. The two families have been friends for years, and yesterday Mr Beeching said, "We are completely devastated by the news, and have no idea why the young people were at the house in London. My son was due to be called up next month, and we can only suppose he had gone to London to report for duty. My wife and I have not seen him for a year as he was working in Kew Gardens gaining experience in horticulture which he hoped to take up as a career after the war."

Group Captain Patterson, who is stationed at an airfield somewhere in the north of England, came home to be with his wife when the news was broken. Both were too grief-stricken to make a statement.'

"It is strange that the baby is not mentioned," said Daisy after she had read the news item. "And the mother was only sixteen years old!"

"I know why the baby is not mentioned," said George triumphantly. "It is because they did not know about her. The only place those two children could go with their baby was that empty house. And what was a sixteen-year-old girl doing in London during the blitz I'd like to know? Were her parents worried about her being away from home?"

"They loved her," said Daisy slowly. "It says here they were too grief-stricken to talk to the press."

George thought long and carefully. Daisy had said the baby was only a few days old.

Where was she born? He guessed at the local hospital because her mother and father would have moved into the house in Addison Road to await the birth.

The next day he left Gowers early in the afternoon saying he was 'not feeling too good'. No one was surprised. They all agreed he had returned to work too soon. "Give yourself time to get better' was the general advice. They were genuinely concerned about him, and their sympathy would have made him feel ashamed were it not for the fact he had so many other things to think about. "Don't come back until you are really well, George," said one of the elderly secretaries.

He took a bus to the hospital and boldly walked up to the reception desk. "I'm deaf," he said to the woman behind the desk, "so please will you speak at me so that I can read your lips. I want details of a baby girl, born here at the beginning of the week."

"The name please?" she mouthed the words, no doubt shouting at the same time.

He took a deep breath. "Beeching, that's my name, Donald Beeching." He spelt the name. He felt his heart thudding in his chest as he watched the woman stand up and reach for a big red book on a shelf behind her. He had taken his first big risk. The girl might have given her own name, Patterson.

"Here we are," said the woman. "Baby Beeching born on the 7th February, 1941. Is that correct?"

He nodded. He felt he was drowning.

"Mother – Mary Beeching?"

"Yes, that's right."

The woman rummaged around in a drawer until she found a form. Then she started writing on it, copying from the book. When she had finished she handed the sheet of paper to him, and he began to read it slowly. He thought it best that he should not appear agitated or in a hurry.

The words swam in front of his eyes, only gradually making some sort of sense. The paper was headed with the name of the hospital.

'Baby Beeching. Normal delivery. Date 7.2.41. Girl. Weight 6lbs 7 ozs. Period of gestation 38 weeks. Healthy. No physical abnormality noted. Breastfed four hourly.'

The woman slid the heavy read book over to George.

He watched her lips. "Please sign here," she said. She indicated the place with her finger and handed him a pen. He wrote Donald Beeching and, as instructed, repeated the name in capital letters below the signature.

The woman's lips formed a smile. "Thank you, Mr Beeching, and congratulations on the birth of your daughter."

"Thank you," he said.

He made straight for the register office where there was a queue. He stood waiting, knees knocking, feeling sick. The thought came to him that he felt so rough he was justified in taking the afternoon off. At last his name was called and he went to the desk allotted to him. He wondered if he would be able to speak. He stared into the face of a young woman whose skin was caked with make-up; her mouth was a purple slit, and she had an expression of bored disinterest. She did not look friendly like the woman at the hospital.

He felt his courage ebbing away but he managed to give the explanation that had worked for him before. "I'm deaf. I have to lip-read and sometimes I do not understand what is said to me." He slurred the words and the girl looked disconcerted. He handed the paper to her.

She glanced at it, then looked up and spoke distinctly, "You are the father?"

"Yes."

"Mr Beeching?"

"No, that was my wife's name. The mother of the child. Since the birth we have married. I want to register the child in my name, Foster."

She had already pulled the familiar red and white form towards her. "I have to have the Marriage Certificate."

"What did you say?" The sweat came out on his forehead.

"The Marriage Certificate, Mr Foster. Have you brought it with you?"

He knew she was shouting because the person sitting at the next desk looked in his direction.

"No, I didn't know I had to . . . "

She was pushing the form away from her. She mouthed the words, "I can't fill this in without it."

He looked straight into her face, noting the plucked eyebrows and the eruptions beneath the pancake make-up, and then he saw her expression change. Her eyes glazed and she acquired a listening look. He knew the reason, and already he was aware of movements behind him. The queue was breaking up and people were leaving. The girl behind the desk had moved her chair back. She wanted to leave as well, and no doubt she would soon make for the cellars of the building.

"Look here," he said, the slurring of his words more pronounced than ever, "my wife's dead scared. I can't leave her alone after the baby. The air raids and al . . ."

There was a new expression on her face. Pity. It

transformed her, and he exulted in it. She drew the form back towards her.

She copied the date of birth from the paper he had given her. "Name?" she asked.

"What?"

"The child's name?"

"Faith Mary." It came to him in a flash of inspiration: that was the name of their child.

"Your full name?"

"George Henry Foster." He felt in his pocket and pulled out his Identity Card. She glanced at it quickly.

"Your wife's maiden name?"

"Daisy Mary Beeching."

"Now Daisy Mary Foster?"

"Yes," he said, glad to be able to answer truthfully.

"Your occupation?" The pen was poised as if she was anxious to get the matter over as soon as possible.

"Solicitor's managing clerk."

She got to her feet. "Wait," she said.

He saw her teetering across the linoleum floor on her absurd high heels. She stopped at the desk of another girl and said something to her; he guessed she was asking her to wait for her. The room was emptying rapidly. She disappeared into another office, closing the door behind her. After a few minutes she reappeared, this time accompanied by a middle-aged man; he had a harassed expression and he was hurrying, with an armful of ledgers and papers. She did not bother to return to her desk, but just handed the birth certificate to George.

He ran out of the building and into the deserted street. He leant against a wall, hardly able to breathe. The sounds around him must have been very loud because he could hear them, very faintly. He realised he was in danger, and he thought, perhaps I am going to die listening to the sounds of war. He huddled against the wall, and when there was a gap in the bombardment he ran to the air-raid shelter on the other side of the street.

It was dank in there, and smelled of bodies and fear. He sat on a plank beside a woman and child. Both were terrified out of their wits. The child, a boy, clung to his mother, the tears coursing down his cheeks. Why are they here? thought George. Perhaps the woman had not had the courage to send her son away when the other children were being evacuated. Perhaps she had been lulled into thinking there was no necessity. Now she could not afford to escape to the country. Those who did not take advantage of the evacuation scheme were given no second chances. They were left to sink or swim, and no help was offered to them.

George searched around in his pocket and found a toffee in a screw of paper. He offered it to the boy and the mother looked grateful. He was too drained by his recent experiences to embark on the rigmarole of explaining his deafness. Anyway the light was too dim for him to lip-read. He sat with his bottom on the hard plank, head bent in hands, the precious document hidden in the breast pocket of his jacket. He thought of Daisy, the softness and tenderness of her. He thought of Faith.

It was a good name, and he was proud of it.

CHAPTER EIGHTEEN

At last George emerged into the street again and joined a line of weary-looking people waiting for a bus. When he entered his house he found his wife and the child in the cupboard under the stairs. Daisy came out, holding the sleeping baby in her arms. She put her head on his chest, and he put his arms around the two of them.

"It's been such a terrible day," she said. "I thought it would never stop. I was really frightened. The All Clear only went as you came in."

"Never mind," he said, "they won't be back for a while now."

She looked up. "Why are you home so early?"

He did not answer her, but waited until they were both sitting down in the front room before he removed the document from his inside pocket and handed it to his wife. Then he took the baby from her while she looked at it. "Read what it says about our daughter," he said nervously.

"What is this?" she cried at once. "Daisy Mary

Beeching, whose name is that?"

He might have known she would spot that right away. "Don't worry about it," he told her, "it is only a slight discrepancy, no one is going to notice it. Everything else in there is just the ticket, and the main thing is that she has a birth certificate. As you said, everyone needs one of those, and she will always be able to produce hers if necessary."

Daisy read aloud the words in the left-hand corner of the document. *"Any person who (1) falsifies any of the particulars of this Certificate, or (2) uses it as true, knowing it to be false is liable to prosecution under the Forgery Act, 1913 or the Perjury Act 1911."*

"I've read that," said George shortly.

"You are a criminal! You could go to prison for this."

But he was not worried. He knew that many people managed to escape punishment for crimes in wartime. "I haven't done a bad thing," he reasoned. "What I've done is beneficial to everyone."

"How did you manage it?" She wanted to know, but he could not begin to explain all the complications to her. It's done, he thought, let it be. He felt physically and emotionally exhausted.

Daisy knew that she was in a very awkward position. If she went to the police now, as her conscience dictated, enquiries would be made and certainly George would come under suspicion. The small print on the birth certificate filled her with terror. She could not risk him being arrested and put into prison, for something he had done for her sake. Of course her heart swelled with the realisation of what had been achieved. The baby lying so peacefully in her husband's arms belonged to her, to them. She felt it was the truth, but her instincts and upbringing told her it was far from it. In Yorkshire there were people who had a rightful claim with regard to Faith. Faith, she savoured the name and, as George had done, recognised from the beginning that it was perfect. Daisy did not know how to reconcile her feelings of joy with her feelings of fear. She knew that although George would soon accept the situation and rejoice in it, she never would, and the shame of it would hover in the background of her life, like a menacing shadow.

"We must leave here," George told her decidedly. "It is not safe, for more reasons than one. No one must know we have Faith, no neighbours, no family, no one."

"My sister, Rose . . . "

"We'll write to her in Devon later on, and tell her you've had a baby. But not now. We're out of touch anyway because of the war, so it won't look strange."

George telephoned the office. "I'm sorry, I'm still not feeling up to scratch." It was amazing how adept he was becoming at telling lies. They rolled off his tongue without him even thinking about them. He knew he had one clear day before he would be expected to produce a medical certificate.

He, Daisy and Faith left early in the morning so that

the people living next door would not see them. They took the underground to Waterloo station, and then travelled to Southampton. The port had been badly bombed, and everywhere they looked there was evidence of destruction. They had to step over the hoses in the road, and try and avoid the puddles of water. The Pirelli rubber factory near the station had received a direct hit, and the acrid smell of burning rubber still pervaded the atmosphere. Daisy put her handkerchief lightly over the baby's face, so that she would not breathe in the fumes.

They made their way to the Green Line bus station and, on impulse, took a bus which was going to the New Forest. It was wonderful to get away from the smouldering city and into the fresh pure air of the countryside. Neither of them had seen the New Forest before, and they thought it was beautiful. The bus stopped at the village of Lyndhurst, by a pub called The Fox and Hounds, but they decided to stay on for one more stop, and alighted in the village of Annesley.

The place where the bus stopped was outside another pub, this one was called The Royal Oak. They walked straight into the forest, and sat down under a gigantic oak. The sun was shining and they felt happy and confident. Daisy carried a bag containing all the baby equipment – bottles, nappies, gripe water – as well as a thermos of tea and packets of sandwiches for themselves. They were a little family, and Daisy rejoiced in that concept. How she had longed for it over the years! On that magical day in February, when the sun appeared for the first time since a cold unforgiving winter, her former doubts disappeared. It gave her intense pleasure to see her beloved George carrying Faith in the woven basket that had been brought ten years previously for the anticipated transport of Mary. They sat under the old tree and fed the baby, and when she was dealt with and comfortable and full, they ate the sandwiches and drank their cups of tea.

George went into the pub and spoke to the landlord. He was in the public bar sweeping the floor in preparation for opening time at six o'clock. "Sorry to disturb you," said George, "but we are looking for a place to rent. Have you any ideas?"

The landlord took his time, considering the matter carefully and studying George at the same time. He saw a skinny chap with an honest face. He knew from his way of talking that he was deaf. He decided he looked all right.

"Mrs Wiltshire's father has just died in the cottage next to hers. The Wiltshires own both the cottages, and I have a notion they'll want to rent the empty one."

He accompanied George to the door so he could point out the way to Mrs Wiltshire's cottage. Daisy was standing outside waiting, the baby sleeping on her shoulder. George could not help thinking how right and natural the two of them looked like that, and he said proudly, "This is my wife, Daisy, and our daughter, Faith. My name is George Foster."

"Mine is Albert Thurlow," said the landlord, "and I'm pleased to meet you both, and the little one. Mrs Wiltshire will be pleased to see her, as she dotes on babies."

Mrs Wiltshire was a very fat comfortable lady and, as the landlord of The Royal Oak had predicted, went into ecstasies when she saw Faith. "Oh, the little love!" she exclaimed, peering at the sleeping baby in Daisy's arms.

There were two Victorian terraced cottages looking out on a green sward with a winding lane leading to a canopy of beeches and oaks beyond. Mrs Wiltshire's own house had a neat garden in front of it, still looking very wintry although there were snowdrops to be seen growing in the grass near the wooden fence and gate.

The adjoining cottage did not look so well cared for and, when they entered, the dampness and coldness hit them like a wet rag in their faces. The small windows were so covered in grime it was impossible to see out of them. The owner of the property apologised for its deficiencies. "My dad was very old, and did not look after the place. He was that stubborn he would not let me clean it up for him. My husband was always offering to do the repairs that was needed, but he would have none of it. However, we did get him to agree to get a bathroom put in." This was an extension over the kitchen, very basic with a white bath, basin and lavatory, but compared with the rest of the cottage it was luxury. Thinking of their orderly house in Notting Hill, George and Daisy tried to imagine what magical changes could be made with a bucket of soapy water and a paintbrush.

As if reading their thoughts Mrs Wiltshire said, "We was going to get it decorated throughout before we let it. When would you want it by?"

"Right away," said George, looking at Daisy.

She walked to one of the front windows and wiped away the dirt with her finger. A shaft of sunlight penetrated the gloom of the room, and through the gap she had made she could see the trees. "Let's take it," she said.

"We want to get away from the London, bombs and all that," George explained to the woman. "It's no place for a baby. I shall have to stay because of my job, but I'll come weekends."

"Well, you'll not escape bombs living here," she replied, as if indignant that he should imagine such a thing. She went on to tell him proudly, "There have been bombs galore over Southampton, nine miles distant, and an incendiary dropped here only last week, not a mile away. If it's peace you're after, you won't find it here."

"We'll risk it," said George. Walking with her to the broken-down gate, Daisy and Faith following behind, it was hard to believe the war had ever touched that place.

"It's so quiet," said Daisy wonderingly.

"We watched the Battle of Britain from here," said Mrs Wiltshire determined to get the last word.

"What about the rent?" asked George, looking straight at her so as to be certain of her reply.

She hesitated. "Would thirty shillings a week suit, considering the bathroom and all?"

Daisy repeated the amount for her husband's benefit. "Thirty shillings. Is that all right, dear?"

He thought it a bit steep. He supposed country people thought folks from London were made of money. "I would take it for twenty-five shillings a week," he said. Even that was more than this tumble-down cottage was worth.

Mrs Wiltshire agreed at once, and seemed perfectly satisfied with the arrangement. George thought, probably she did not expect to get more than a pound a week.

They were tired by the time they got back to their London house, and Faith was fractious.

I hope we've done the right thing, thought Daisy, who did not share her husband's unfailing optimism. When she heard the German planes droning overhead in the night she was convinced they had. She nudged the sleeping form of George to find out whether he thought they should get up, but he was so tired he did not waken, and she lay and listened until there was silence again, and then she too fell asleep.

The move to the country required a great deal of

planning and a certain amount of deviousness. There was a bad moment when their neighbour came to the door to borrow some tea. Daisy peered through the side of the net curtains and saw her standing on the front step. Faith was hastily carried to the bedroom upstairs, and the door shut. Daisy was fearful that she would start crying and be heard, or that there would be some of her garments or part of her paraphernalia left around which would arouse suspicion. When Daisy went into the kitchen to fetch the tea from a cupboard she saw the baby's bottle standing by the sink, and she did not have time to remove it before her friend followed her into the room. She put a teacloth over it, and hoped her gesture had not been noticed. She need not have worried because the woman, who lived in the adjoining house, was not on the lookout for anything unusual in that most usual of households. Daisy would have liked to say good-bye to her, to explain their reason for moving away, but George had impressed upon her the importance of secrecy.

That weekend George borrowed a van from a friend and, in the early hours of Sunday morning, he and Daisy loaded it with the essential furniture, bedding, clothing and bits and pieces they would need at the cottage. What could not be fitted in the van had to be left behind. They also took a bolt of black material to put over the windows of the cottage because they did not want to irritate their new neighbours by breaking the regulations. They knew these to be as stringent in the country as in the towns and cities.

Heaving furniture and heavy suitcases was hard work for the physically unfit George, and when he climbed into the front seat of the van his skinny frame was drenched in sweat and his heart was thumping, partly from exhaustion and partly from nervous anxiety about what lay ahead. A place in the van was found for Faith, lying in the bassinet with furniture stacked on all sides of her. They hardly glanced at their home, so anxious were they to get away before people started stirring and looking out of their windows.

It was easier the other end because Mr Wiltshire helped lift all the stuff out of the van, while his wife happily kept an eye on Faith. Mr Wiltshire told them his name was Len, and he was a cheerful fellow, chubby like his wife. He informed Daisy and George that they had no children, which was a great sadness to them. Daisy was too busy to feel guilty; all she wanted, at that moment, was to get 'straight' as she put it.

They found to their delight that the Wiltshires had worked hard on the previous day, which was Saturday, and everything had been scrubbed and Mrs Wiltshire (she asked them to call her Lily) had lit a fire in the old grate. She told them the chimney had been swept and they owed the sweep three shillings. She had cleaned the little windows with rolled-up newspaper and turpentine, and they were able to see the view of the green in front of the cottages and the trees beyond.

The sad moment came when George had to leave his little family. Daisy stood in the doorway of her new home, Faith in her arms, and watched the van drive away. She was terrified that some evil would befall him. It was part of her upbringing to believe that a sin such as they had committed would have repercussions. She did not say 'look after yourself' or 'take care', for these were phrases that became popular years later when the country was at peace. She and George, like many others, believed that nothing could be done if a bomb 'had your name on it'.

George had to sleep on an old mattress, which he dragged down from the attic. Their tidy house was unrecognisable, bereft of most of their belongings, which they had collected over the years. Alone in the empty house, staring into the blackness, he was conscious of feelings of discomfort and nervousness. So far, everything had gone amazingly right, and he prayed such good fortune would continue. It was hard to believe their lives had changed so much in less than a week.

He told neighbours and friends at work that Daisy had become scared of the bombs, and he had sent her to the country to live. Everyone agreed it was a sensible decision.

The following weekend he went to the New Forest again, by train and bus this time. He found Daisy contented, but missing him. She had purchased some remnants of material from a local jumble sale, and she was busy making them into curtains. At the same sale she had bought an old pram, and now Faith was left under the old apple-tree in the garden, from half past nine in the morning until she was brought in for her midday feed. In the afternoon Daisy could be seen trundling the rickety pram along the lane, the baby's little pink nose appearing over the top of the blankets that covered her. It could never be said that Faith was deprived of fresh air, and George noticed a change in his daughter every time he saw her. He could hardly believe how pretty she was becoming.

On the third weekend he was with them he told Daisy that he had decided to leave Gowers. He missed his family too much to allow the present regime to continue. It was a risk he had to take, the uncertainty of a deaf man being able to obtain a job at once. He felt bad about his decision because the firm had been good to him, and he liked old Mr Gower who had lost his only son in the war, and must have felt many times that he could not go on.

The task of giving notice was made easier for George when he returned home one evening in March 1940. As he walked from the underground in the gathering dusk he suddenly noticed the change in his street. For a moment he stood stock still on the pavement, wondering what had happened to it. Where there had been buildings there was nothing. The sky was open and vulnerable behind the place which had once been his house, and the house on the left and the house on the right. All gone, except for rubble and the remains of people's homes, bedrooms open to the world like those in a doll's house.

Alec found him staring at the wreckage and took him home. He conveyed to him the news that the friends next door had escaped because they went to the shelter in time. The people on the other side had not been so lucky. When George went to view the remains of his house in the daylight he found that the staircase had collapsed into the cupboard beneath, and he felt sick.

He arrived late at the office that day, and he went straight to Mr Gower's room. In his agitation he slurred his words more than usual, but he managed to make the old man understand that he had lost his home and must join his wife in the country. Mr Gower, a true Christian gentleman, was sympathetic, although in his heart he despaired at the thought that the firm was going to consist of elderly men and women; the young secretaries were all working in factories and even the office boy was due for his call-up. He was generous enough to give George a cheque for fifty pounds and, more importantly, a letter to take to his old friend, Archie Cotton, the senior partner of a firm of solicitors in Southampton.

When George was eventually reunited with Daisy and Faith, having worked his month's notice at Gowers (Alec kindly accommodated him during the time) he showed her the envelope Mr Gower had given to him. Then he boiled the kettle on top of the range and proceeded, very carefully, to unstick the envelope with the steam from the kettle. Daisy was shocked. She felt that her man had lost all moral integrity, and she tried to stop him committing this infamous act. But it was too late, and he was already extracting the paper, and reading it aloud under the dim light in their little front room.

Dear Archie,

I hope all is well with you and your family in these troubled times. You will have heard that we lost our son, James. It was a blow from which we thought we would not recover but, sadly, life must go on for the ones left behind, and my wife has been wonderfully brave, and her courage shames me into trying to be the same. He was not so young, in his mid-thirties, and leaves a wife and two children.

But enough of my troubles … this letter is to introduce George Foster. He is leaving here because his house has been bombed and his wife is in the country, settled in a village in the New Forest, nine miles from Southampton. George has been with Gowers for fifteen years, first as an office boy, and then training as a managing clerk. I am sorry to lose him because he has been a reliable and conscientious worker. The poor fellow is deaf, hence his exemption from any of the services, although I understand he is an ARP worker. Sometimes it is a strain talking to him, but he is remarkably adept at lip-reading.

If your firm is, like ours, woefully short of manpower, you may be glad to employ George Foster. One thing I can assure you about him: he is incapable of a dishonest act.

Yours ever,
Henry Gower.

"I hope you feel ashamed of yourself," said Daisy, watching her husband slip the letter back in the envelope, and carefully press down the damp paper so that no one would guess it had been tampered with. It was a small rebuke, made with loving affection and no malice. In the years to come she was to repeat it many times, but with increasing asperity.

CHAPTER NINETEEN

Daisy wanted Faith to attend the village school, which was conveniently situated just down the lane from where they lived, but George was adamant that his daughter should go to a private school, and so when she was six years old she went to Miss Chambers' school in Lyndhurst. Miss Chambers shared the responsibility of teaching ten small pupils, boys and girls mixed, with her friend Miss Pickard. Bizarrely, morning lessons took place in a downstairs room of the big hotel in Lyndhurst, and during the mid-morning break the children played in the grounds of the hotel, and sometimes the more venturesome ones approached the windows and spied on the guests sitting in the lounge.

Faith was not happy on her first day at school and clung, weeping, to her mother's skirt. Daisy was glad that work prevented George from taking her, as she knew he would never have been able to withstand her grief, and he would have brought her home as soon as he saw her tears. Daisy was made of sterner stuff and realised in a short time Faith would settle down. Of course, she was right, and soon Faith loved school and made new friends. Her best friend was called Hermione and her parents actually lived in the hotel, and Faith thought this must be the most wonderful existence imaginable, living in the luxurious splendour of an hotel, and eating hotel meals every day.

George never uttered a cross word to Faith, and she knew he never would. He had wanted a baby for Daisy's sake, but from the moment he extricated the little damp bundle, protected by the bodies of her parents, he knew the meaning of real happiness. After the accident in his adolescence he had become a lonely boy and then a lonely man. The miracle of meeting Daisy and marrying her had changed that for him. Now there were other important milestones in his life, the joy of peering into the old pram and seeing Faith's toothless smile and the pride he felt when she took her first steps. Daisy had witnessed these small miracles before – she had been a nanny, and she took them in her stride. She soon realised that all the discipline must come from her. Even at the age of six Faith appreciated the worth of having one malleable parent, and George was like the Plasticene she played with at school, soft and yielding. When she misbehaved, the threat 'I'll tell your father' held no fears for her.

It was a constant source of wonder to George that Faith was such a beautiful child. Daisy was aware that she had a fineness of features which neither she nor her husband possessed. She had dark hair and blue eyes whereas she and George were both brown-eyed people with the same nondescript-coloured hair. When Faith was small she was always laughing and running, she never seemed to slow down. "Like a blooming clockwork toy, wound up all the time," George said of her. Even when she was holding her father's hand she was bouncing up and down.

It seemed as if after their move from London everything had gone right for them. George had a good job with Cottons. They had made many improvements to their little cottage, most importantly, a telephone had been installed so Daisy could keep in touch with her family in Devon and Faith could ring her friends. They had put up new fencing and there was a shed in the back garden for George's tools and the mower. The garden was now full of flowers in the spring and summer. The Wiltshires were wonderful neighbours, so kind and helpful, and they loved Faith and would do anything for her.

George counted his blessings, but his contentment was marred by one worry. He was aware that Daisy was too weighed down with guilt to enjoy contentment to the full. In the moments when they were alone together she railed at him for what he had done. "No good will come of it," she warned. "You'll see, God will make us suffer." She blamed herself for going along with the deception and she blamed him for orchestrating it. He, for his part, could not see that it was an evil act. His wife's constant recriminations were his only reminder that Faith was not his child.

George was convinced that if he had not rescued Faith that night she would have died of cold before help arrived, and if they had informed the police she would have been taken from them and put into an institution. Daisy did not agree. She insisted the child's grandparents would have brought her up, and she would have had advantages they could not provide.

"I suppose you mean she would have a posh accent," was George's response. "Well, she has picked that up at school, she speaks better than you or me, that's for sure."

"We have given her a very different sort of home," said Daisy. "It is not what she would have known if they had looked after her."

"She's happy enough with it," retorted George. "You could not find a happier girl than our Faith."

But Daisy could not be convinced, and many times she went to the secret drawer where she kept the newspaper clipping about the bombing of the house in Addison Road. Over and over again she read about Group Captain and Mrs Patterson who were too grief-stricken to make a statement to the press.

George was sceptical. "What sort of parents were they when they did not even know their daughter had a child of her own?"

But his wife wondered and wondered. Supposing

they did know? Supposing the loss of a daughter and a granddaughter had altered their lives so much that every chance of happiness was lost to them? Daisy anguished that perhaps these distraught people were always looking for the baby who disappeared one night in 1941. Faith in her little room heard her parents whispering to each other, but the walls of the tiny cottage were thick and she could not hear what they were saying, and if she had been able to make out the words she would not have understood them.

Faith was completely oblivious to any discord in her family. George was correct when he said she was a happy child. For her seventh birthday her parents took her and her friend Hermione to see *Peter Pan* which was at the Empire Theatre in Southampton. The performance made a deep impression of Faith. She was certain she could learn to fly like Wendy and her brothers, and she practised on the wide grassy paths in the forest. Sometimes she fancied she could manage a few steps without her feet touching the ground. When she told her father of this achievement he came to watch her. Daisy could not be doing with such nonsense.

Faith quietened down when she went to her big school in Southampton. "At last she is walking like an ordinary mortal," commented her mother. George was sorry to see the end of the exuberance of childhood, but there were compensations. A new routine was established which pleased him greatly. Each morning

Faith and her father walked to the bus stop together, Faith very neat and tidy in her school uniform, its dark-green blazer with a badge on the breast pocket; George in his suit, his bowler hat fixed firmly on his head, furled umbrella in his hand. At first he always accompanied her to school, leaving her at the gates, returning in the late afternoon to pick her up for the return journey. When she was ten she started going to school on her own, parting from her father at the Hants and Dorset bus station, meeting him at the same place in the evening. He usually left Cottons at about the same time as she finished school. Sometimes he was late and she waited for him, but it was never longer than ten minutes. When she became a prefect she took life very seriously, her brown satchel crammed with homework, always finished by the morning. She was a conscientious student.

They both enjoyed the journeys on the bus together. They always found a lot to talk about. Daisy was aware of their closeness, and she occasionally had pangs of jealousy. When she had been particularly sharp with them both at breakfast, she wondered sometimes if they talked about her, maybe giving a sigh of relief to get away from her nagging tongue and be together. Her fears were groundless; George was fiercely loyal to his wife and no one was allowed to criticise her. Faith understood this. When she argued with her mother, George always put an end to the dispute by saying: "Your mother knows best." On their journeys home to Annesley they talked about the events of the day, his day at work and her day at school. George was completely happy. He had managed to find the baby so wanted by Daisy, but the child was his.

One day George was delayed at Cottons. There was nothing he could do about it. Mr Cotton wanted his opinion about a document, and he could not say, "I have to go because I am meeting my daughter, and she will be worried about me." As the old man took his time, George kept glancing anxiously at the clock in the office. He could picture in his mind the forlorn figure of Faith waiting, looking out for him. Already they had missed their usual bus and would have to catch the next one.

At last he could leave. He hastily put on his coat and crammed his hat on his head. He walked as quickly as he could towards the Civic Centre. It began to rain, but he did not stop to put up his umbrella. Usually he was very careful in traffic, but his lateness had made him flustered. He did not hear the lorry heading towards him, and because he did not hear it, he made a sudden turn and walked straight in front of it. In a flash of understanding he realised what he had done, but it was too late; he felt the impact of the unyielding mass of metal, he had a mental picture of his family and then the darkness settled around him.

The horrified driver saw a figure lying on the road in front of his vehicle. "It wasn't my fault," he said, over and over again. A few people gathered around the motionless body, someone rescued George's bowler hat and his brolly and laid them by his side. An ambulance was called for, and it arrived in ten minutes, exactly as the clock in the Civic Centre was striking six. The distraught driver went on protesting his innocence, first to the ambulance men and then to a policeman who appeared on the scene. "He just walked straight in front of me, there was nothing I could do." Carefully, the ambulance men lifted the body of George and put it on a stretcher. The crowd watched as the stretcher was stowed into the ambulance, and the door shut. Then, as there was nothing more to see, the bystanders moved away.

Poor Faith waited and waited. The next bus came and then the next and the one after that. She decided to walk to Cottons. Unknowingly, she stepped across the place where her father had lain, two hours before. Of course she found the office firmly closed; everyone had gone home long before she got there. She retraced her steps to the bus station, and there she decided there was only one thing to do and that was to go home. Trying to fight back her tears, she sat on the bus, watching the raindrops on the window next to her seat.

At last she was running up the garden path to the front door of the cottage. Daisy was standing in the lighted doorway, waiting for her, waiting for them.

Faith stammered out the explanation for her lateness,

how she had waited at the bus stop, then made her way to Cottons to see if her father was there.

"Why didn't you telephone me?" demanded her mother.

"I didn't think . . . and I haven't got any money for a telephone call."

Had Daisy become intolerant over the years? She blamed her daughter, for what it is difficult to understand. Neglect? Not doing the right thing? Fear made her say things she would afterwards regret, and the girl stood, weeping, not putting up any defence.

When the police arrived, and the terrible truth was revealed, Faith felt what had happened was somehow her fault.

Chapter Twenty

Daisy was sorry she had spoken sharply to Faith at such a terrible point in their lives, particularly as she knew she had been completely unreasonable. She waited until after the funeral before she made a half-hearted apology.

"I did not mean to say those things to you. I know you were not to blame. I was upset and worried, that's all."

"Don't worry, Mum." But words spoken in haste are like feathers in a down pillow; once they are out in the open they cannot be retrieved and stuffed back in the bag. Always, for the rest of her life, Faith had an uneasy feeling that she could have acted differently on that dreadful day.

Life was very different after George's death. Daisy was constantly complaining of their poverty, how they could not manage on his meagre pension. Faith was taken away from her private school, and started at the local school which she did not enjoy. The other children in her class thought she was 'stuck-up' because she talked differently from them, and also they resented her because she was so much ahead of them in almost every subject. She walked to school alone, along the little lane opposite their house, and she walked home slowly with her head bent. The happy carefree child had gone for good, and Daisy was too preoccupied with her own troubles to notice her disappearance.

In time the situation improved, and Faith was accepted. She made a friend and they were always together. Laughter came into her life again, but it was tinged with sadness. She did not tell anyone about the aching void left by the death of her father. At night in her little bed she wept into her pillow and, hearing her one night, Daisy came in and switched on the light. When she saw the tears glistening on Faith's face, instead of gathering the girl into her arms and comforting her, she said abruptly: "We did a very bad thing by you."

"What do you mean?"

"Nothing. Just go back to sleep, there's a good girl." She spoke to her as she would have done to a child, but Faith was no longer a child. She was eleven years old, and growing up. Faith turned her head away, and Daisy closed the door.

To make money Daisy took on cleaning jobs in the village. She worked five days a week while Faith was at school, and three of the days she cleaned the house belonging to rich people who had recently come to Annesley. The villagers did not approve of them because they had made their millions from manufacturing electrical goods, not like the local gentry whose money had been handed down from generation to generation. Daisy was very pleased to have this job, however, as it was well paid. Soon the lady of the house realised that she had found a treasure in Daisy, that she could leave her alone in the house, certain that on her return everything would be spotless. The kitchen floor would be scrubbed and the surfaces washed; nothing escaped Daisy's eye for detail. Pictures were straightened, and old newspapers tidied away.

One day when Daisy was polishing the furniture in the living-room she noticed a magazine lying on the floor by the sofa. She carried it over to the window so that she could have a glance through it. The glossy society magazines always intrigued her, and this one was full of pictures of balls and smart people attending race meetings.

Suddenly her eye was caught by a caption under a photograph: *'Mr Rex Patterson, the well-known playwright, at the first night of his new play,* The Captive Audience. *Mr Patterson is seen with his leading lady, Miss Chloe Adams, and his mother, Mrs Patterson, whose husband, Air Vice-Marshall John Patterson, CBE, died recently.'*

So that it would not be noticed Daisy carefully removed two pages, one of which interested her, and she put the magazine in a canterbury. When she got home she placed the cutting in her secret drawer. Then one afternoon she visited the local library and looked up the name of Patterson in *Who's Who*. She wondered why she had never thought of doing so before.

'PATTERSON John Air Vice-Marshall CBE, DFC. AOC and Commandant Royal Air Force College, Barnwell, Yorks. Born 12 Oct 1896 son of Arthur and Mary Patterson m 1921 Kathleen (nee O'Neill) one s one d (dec).

Then a list of his achievements and finally, most importantly from Daisy's point of view, his address: Coley House, Harrogate, Yorks.

She copied the address on a slip of paper before she looked up Rex Patterson.

PATTERSON Rex DFC born 3 Feb 1923 s of John and Kathleen Patterson. Playwright and Director. Served in RAF 1942-1947. Plays: The Human Conflict *1948 (Stage);* Understanding Nature *1950 (Stage);* The Anniversary *1950 (Radio);* Sea of Discontent *1951 (Stage);* Christopher's Story *1952 (Stage);* Come to the Party *1952 (Television). Screen productions:* Bless this House *1949 and* Unfair Verdict *1951.*

Recreations. Painting, cricket.

Address: 1 Peacock Mews, London, SW7.

And now, thought Daisy, he has written a play called *The Captive Audience*. She looked it up in the newspaper and found that it was at The Strand

Theatre in the Aldwych.

She announced to her daughter, "We're going to London, to go to the theatre."

Faith was astounded. She had only been to the theatre once in her life, and that was to *Peter Pan* in Southampton. She remembered it was at her father's insistence that they went at all. Daisy had not been keen at first, although she had enjoyed herself on the day.

"We've been moping too long," Daisy explained, as if justifying the sudden decision. "We both need a change. I'm writing for tickets."

"What is the name of the play we are going to see?"

"It is called *The Captive Audience* and it is written by someone called Rex Patterson."

"Why have you chosen this play particularly?"

"Because the author is very famous," replied Daisy, "and don't keep asking questions, just be happy we are going."

Faith was more than happy; she was so excited she could hardly wait until the day arrived when she and her mother travelled by train to London. All she knew about that city was that she had been born there.

She was thrilled to be sitting in the theatre, watching the people filing in to take their seats, mostly grey heads because it was a matinee. The murmur of conversation petered away to silence as the heavy curtain rose slowly, revealing the stage set, a room bathed in light. The play was difficult for her to understand; sometimes when there was a gale of laughter she wished she knew why the audience was laughing. Nevertheless, she enjoyed it, and during the interval she and her mother went to the bar and Daisy had a glass of medium sherry and Faith an orange juice. It was all part of the treat, Daisy told her, and you never know, you might see someone interesting.

Travelling home in the train from Waterloo station, crowded with commuters (there were people jammed tight in the corridor as well as in the carriages), Faith sat in the corner next to her mother, and tried to peer through the grimy window at the countryside flashing past. She thought of the last few hours, sitting in the hot darkness of the theatre, watching the exquisite Chloe Adams in the leading role acknowledging the thunderous applause at the end of the play. She was the most beautiful person she had ever seen in her life. Faith came to a decision - when she grew up she would be an actress.

She did not mention this aspiration to her mother because she thought it would be met with disapproval. Daisy did not think much of stage people, vain and slightly disreputable in her view. That is why her daughter had been so surprised when it was suggested they should both go to the theatre. She did not think it would happen again, certainly not within the next six months.

"Rex Patterson has another play in London, this time at His Majesty's in the Haymarket. I thought we'd go to it. I'm writing for tickets."

"Couldn't we go to a play written by someone else this time?" asked Faith.

"Didn't you like *The Captive Audience*? I thought you enjoyed it."

"Oh, I did. I just thought it would be fun to go to something different."

"I'm sure this play is very different from the one we saw. And I've heard it is a beautiful theatre. It is worth going just to see the theatre."

Faith was satisfied. She was too sensible to quibble about a treat so soon after the last one. "Of course, Mum, I'll love it. Perhaps next time we could go and see something written by William Shakespeare?"

"Humph," replied her mother, "perhaps there won't be a next time."

As Daisy had predicted (without being sure of her facts) this play was very different from *The Captive Audience*. It was a serious straight play dealing with real life people in a situation that had actually happened. It was about the painter, Millais, and his love for Effie Gray, the wife of John Ruskin. Faith knew about Millais from History of Art lessons at school. Before the curtain went up a man walked on to the front of the stage and announced that Chloe Adams was indisposed, and her understudy, Rachel Fleet, was taking her part.

"Really!" muttered Daisy, as if she was being short-changed on the price of the tickets. Faith shared her disappointment; she had been looking forward to seeing Chloe Adams again.

Rachel Fleet was excellent in the part of Effie, a bewildered naïve girl who did not understand why her husband was repulsed by her. When at the end of the play Millais rescued her from a life of bewilderment and shame, Faith's heart went out to her. Perhaps she had grown up since seeing *The Captive Audience* but she felt utterly involved in the play. Already she thought she knew the importance of a sexual relationship in marriage. She was not sure what it was all about, as Daisy had not initiated her into the secrets of sex, but she comprehended its significance.

Recently she had taken on a paper round in the village and, for the first time in her life, she had money of her own – not much, but it enabled her to buy a programme. Daisy had thought it an unnecessary luxury, but Faith revelled in the shiny pages and had studied it closely before the curtain went up. On one of the pages was a photograph of the author, Rex Patterson.

"He looks nice," said Faith thoughtfully.

As before they went into the bar during the interval, the matronly Daisy wearing her sensible country clothes and her long-legged awkward daughter, dressed in her school uniform, leather strap shoes and ankle socks on her feet.

Sipping her orange juice, Faith said suddenly, "There he is."

If she had not said those three words to her mother,

'There he is,' everything in their future lives would have been different.

"Who?" demanded Daisy.

"Over there, Rex Patterson." It was the face she had been studying so closely before the beginning of the first act. Looking at it now, she decided her first impression had been right. It was a very nice face.

Daisy looked, and it is impossible to imagine her feelings at that moment. Perhaps she thought atonement was within her grasp. "Come on," she said roughly to her daughter, "we'll go over there."

There was a long seat. Surprisingly it was empty, and Daisy and Faith, clutching their glasses, made for it. Faith was faintly embarrassed. Of course, Rex Patterson had not noticed them, but even so she felt it was an intrusion.

He stood alongside them, nonchalantly elegant, talking to another man.

"Why are you here?" asked the man. "We are greatly honoured."

"I wanted to support Rachel Fleet. She deserves success. I think she is doing brilliantly."

"I agree. It is a splendid breakthrough for her. I'm sure she appreciates your presence."

"Not at all," Rex Patterson sounded impatient, as if flattery irritated him.

"How is your mother?" asked the man politely, perhaps sensing that a change of subject was expedient.

"Thank you for asking. She is well, but lonely since

my father died. She refuses to sell the house and move into something smaller. I have managed to persuade her to advertise for a companion-housekeeper."

"In *The Lady,* I presume?"

"You've got it. In *The Lady*. I don't suppose anything will come of it, but it's a step in the right direction."

"Old people are a worry to their children," said the man. "I am constantly worried about my parents, but I have a sister to share the burden."

"You are lucky," said Rex Patterson. "I am the only one."

The bell sounded, summoning the people to return to their seats.

Faith, like her mother, listened avidly to every word of this conversation, but she did not find it particularly edifying. She liked looking at Rex Patterson, the spare figure, the rather aquiline features and straight smooth hair. She enjoyed listening to the sound of his voice. She thought she would enjoy thinking about him before she went to sleep that night, and already she was planning to remove his picture from the programme and pin it on the wall by her bed.

She might have known that her mother would not approve of such an action.

"What is he doing there?" she demanded when she came in to switch off the light.

"I like him," said Faith lamely.

"Take it down at once," said Daisy. "He is old enough to be your father."

Chapter Twenty-One

Rex looked at the bundle of letters on his mother's desk.

"These are from *The Lady*?" he asked.

Kitty was sitting in an armchair not far from him. "Yes," she replied.

"Have you read them?"

She had the grace to look slightly ashamed. "No," she said.

"Not one?"

"I'm afraid not. I'm so sorry, darling."

He looked indulgently amused. "I suppose you have left them for me to sift through," he said amiably.

"There is no need," said Kitty, a note of triumph in her voice. "I have already engaged someone to come and look after me."

"Oh," he said, "and who is that?"

"Her name is Daisy Foster. She wrote me such a nice letter, I felt she must be the right person. She was sensible enough to put her telephone number by her address, so I rang her up, and she sounded a pleasant homely body. You can read the letter she wrote – I have put it in the little drawer on the left so that it would not get muddled with the others."

He found the letter and read it carefully. The first thing he noticed was the way it began: *'Dear Mrs Patterson...'* He glanced at the other letters on top of the desk, and saw that they were all addressed to a box number.

"This is very odd," he said, "how did this woman know your name and where to address the letter?"

Kitty put her spectacles on the end of her nose, and took the letter from him. "I see what you mean," she said. "She has written to me personally. The other letters came separately, in a big envelope." She handed the letter back to him. "It's a mystery," she said lightly, content to leave it at that.

She was right when she said it was a nice letter. Written in an educated hand it explained that the writer was a widow who had been left with very little money. She and her child would welcome a change of scene, and Daisy wanted the job. She was prepared to do anything that was required of her. She gave as a reference the name of Mrs Anderson at an address in London.

Daisy had given a great deal of thought to the question of a reference. She knew if she asked her present employer she would get a glowing one, but it would be for her virtues as a cleaning lady, and perhaps that would not appeal to someone who was advertising for a companion-housekeeper. Eventually, she decided to name Mrs Anderson as her referee, despite the fact they had been out of touch for so many years. The job of nanny sounded very respectable.

"We should take up the reference," said Rex. "And a child? Do we really want to be burdened with a child?" He found the whole thing deeply suspicious, and envisaged awful problems ahead which he would have to sort out.

"Oh, darling," said his mother, a little impatiently, "we have lots of room for a child. They can have the two bedrooms at the back of the house, and a sitting-room of their own. It is like a small flat with its own bathroom. It will be an ideal place for them to live, and there is a school nearby. The child is no problem." She paused. "It will be good to have a young person around the house." She ended on a defiant note.

"All right," he said, "we'll settle for the child. But I'd like to chase up the reference she gives. We should write to the woman she mentions in her letter."

"I am not a complete fool," said Kitty with dignity. "I don't like the idea of strangers in my house, any more than you do. It's your idea that I should have a carer. I think Annie and Ruby are quite enough, and Harris when I want him. If you look in the same drawer you will find the letter I received when I wrote asking for a reference."

Dear Mrs Patterson,

I have your letter about Daisy Foster. I remember Daisy very well; she was nanny to our two children, George and Amy, and she was with us for nearly five years. But this is over twenty years ago, and I am wondering if anything I say can be of use to you over such a long passage of time.

Daisy was called Daisy Flower in those days, and she left my employment to marry George Foster. We continued to see her from time to time until the beginning of the war when we left London. We returned to this house when the war was over and we have lived here ever since. We must have been out of touch with Daisy for about fourteen years.

Daisy was a good-natured extremely responsible young woman. The children adored her, and I never had any misgivings about leaving them in her sole care. I was confident they would be well looked after, and Daisy was capable of dealing with any emergency that might arise.

My own view is that you would do well to employ her, as I do not think the good qualities of a person alter over the years. If she does come to work for you please give her my warm regards – my husband and our two children, now grown-up, join me in this.

Yours sincerely,

Elizabeth Anderson.

"Sounds good," said Rex, but doubts niggled in his mind. The letter written personally to his mother and, by all appearances, not connected in any way to the advertisement in *The Lady*. The fact that the Andersons still lived in the same house they had occupied over twenty years ago – surely that was unusual? It was certainly very fortuitous for Daisy Foster that her old employers had not moved, and therefore received her letter asking for a reference.

He expressed this thought to Kitty, and she replied, "We have lived here, in the same house, since just before you were born."

"I know that, darling," he said gently, "but there was a reason for that."

The three of them, in a tacit understanding, had resolved to stay in the house that held so many memories for them. The uncarpeted passage from the kitchen to the dining-room echoed with the clatter of her shoes (she was invariably late for school) and the garden was redolent with the sounds of childhood, the two of them playing cricket together (she was always able to keep up with him) and, in earlier years, games of hide-and-seek among the giant rhododendrons. It was unthinkable that they should ever leave that place, although Rex had purchased a small mews cottage when pressure of work made it essential for him to live in London. When his father died, he wondered whether Kitty would consent to leave the family house but, as he expected, she was adamant in her refusal.

"They are coming next Monday," she told him.

"Well, that's that, then," he said.

"For a month's trial," said Kitty, "to see whether we like each other. She rents a cottage in the New Forest, and she is keeping it on until we decide if the arrangement is going to work."

"That seems a good idea," said her son. "You have dealt with all of this very efficiently, darling." He bent down and kissed the top of her head. He loved her very much, and he thought she had changed since the death of his father. Her mind was agile, but her body had slowed down. She was plagued with arthritis, mostly in her knees, and this had aged her prematurely. She had always been a frail woman and he had never imagined she would outlive her robust husband. It was her frailty which had decided him that she must have someone in the house to look after her.

"I'd like to stay and meet them," he said.

"I thought you said you had to go back to London for the new production..."

"It can wait," he said firmly.

* * *

Faith was devastated when she was told of her mother's plans for their future. By this time she had settled down in her new school, and the thought of having to face another change, to a strange place hundreds of miles away, filled her with apprehension.

"But why?" she wanted to know. "Aren't we happy here, in the place where we all lived together, Dad, you and me?"

"It's not practical any more," said Daisy. "Where we

are going we will have a place to live, and all our food paid for; we'll have security, and that's something we haven't got at the moment."

"I thought we were doing all right," said Faith miserably.

"We're going on trial for a month," Daisy told her briskly. "If we don't like it, we can come back here."

"I hope at the end of the month we'll be back," said Faith, showing a stubbornness in her nature which Daisy had not encountered before.

* * *

Harris took the car, an ancient Ford, to meet them at the station. Harris was not a chauffeur – the Pattersons were not the sort of people who would have enjoyed having a chauffeur – but he drove the car for them, kept it sparklingly clean and in good order, worked in the garden, mowed the lawn and generally did any odd jobs that were necessary around the house. He had been the Air Vice-Marshall's servant during the war, and he had wished to stay by his side. Now that he had gone, he wanted to stay and help his widow. He was a bachelor, and lived in very comfortable quarters over the garage.

He was standing on the platform when Daisy and Fa[illegible]rived. He heaved their suitcases into the boot, [illegible]limbed into the back seat of the car. They [illegible]roughout the journey, Harris because he [illegible] non-communicative individual with [illegible] know, and Daisy because she was feeling overwhelmed by the audacity of the step she had taken. Faith was too choked to utter a word. When she thought of the cottage and the village, the kind Wiltshires and all the friends they had made over the years she could not stop the tears welling up in her eyes. She turned her head away and stared out of the window of the car, so that her mother would not see.

The house was impressive, solid Edwardian brick in a fashionable road in Harrogate. There was a drive sweeping to the front door and, although Daisy and Faith could not see it on that first sight, there was a very big garden at the rear of the house. Harris parked the car neatly outside the front door. He rang the door and a maid answered it. This was Ruby, and she said, "They are both waiting in the drawing-room."

The suitcases stood in the spacious panelled hall while Daisy and Faith were ushered into the room to meet Mrs Patterson and her son.

With one quick glance Daisy took in the room, the quiet elegance of it, comfortable sofas and armchairs, well-polished furniture and vases of flowers, many silver frames containing photographs. This was a room that was to become very familiar to her, and in time she would be able to examine the photographs, the large one of the Air Vice-Marshall in his full dress uniform and the one of a young girl standing in the garden, her hair blowing across her laughing face.

Of course Faith recognised Rex at once. Had she not had his picture on the wall of her bedroom before her mother removed it? Daisy had not expected to see the son so soon so she had neglected to tell Faith about the connection. The realisation brought a quick change of colour to the girl's pale face.

Kitty saw a small rather dowdy woman with rosy cheeks and a sweet expression. She took her hand. "I hope you are not too tired after the journey."

"No, we enjoyed it," said Daisy. She introduced her daughter. "This is Faith."

For the first time Rex Patterson looked at the girl. He had expected a child, but he saw a twelve-year-old schoolgirl. She stood in an ungainly way, long legs encased in wrinkled stockings, one leg straight, the other at an angle. Somehow the stance evoked a memory he thought had gone forever. Someone else had stood in that same awkward way until she had learned to be graceful. He looked into the girl's face and he saw the blue eyes, and above them the thin black eyebrows, now creased in a gossamer frown. He thought, she is ill at ease and wishes to be miles away from this place. It was as if she had transferred her grief to him, and he felt inexplicably sorry for her.

Suddenly he felt a deep concern for his mother. Quickly he turned to her, sensing her reaction. The colour had drained from her face; she looked confused and in need of care. He longed to take her in his arms and comfort her, to assuage the confusion she was suffering by trying to convince her that all twelve-year-old girls look the same.

Chapter Twenty-Two

When Rex returned to visit his mother three weeks later he perceived at once that Daisy and her daughter were there to stay. They had become so part of the household it was hard for Kitty to imagine life without them.

Rex was told that Daisy had severed all connections with their life in the New Forest, and the arrangement with Mrs Wiltshire had been terminated. She and Faith had gone down there for one day to say good-bye to their friends and to arrange for a carrier to take the bits and pieces they wanted to keep to Harrogate. There was not much of any value, and Kitty readily agreed to an extra table and what had once been George's special chair being put into the flat. She impressed upon them that they did not have to ask her permission, the flat was theirs now and they could do what they pleased with it. Daisy was asked to choose new curtains for the windows, paid for by Kitty of course, and the flat was given new carpets throughout. Even Faith was impressed by this generosity, and she was beginning to warm towards her new home. Also, she recognised that her new school offered more scope than the country school she had just left. Grudgingly at first, she began to enjoy living in Harrogate.

Rex could not help but be impressed by the way Daisy looked after his mother. She cooked her delicious meals, small portions as she preferred, and she made sure that she took the pills for her arthritis at the right times and generally attended to all her needs. It was all done in a quiet unobtrusive way, and when Rex arrived she made herself scarce.

Over the months that followed he hardly ever saw the daughter, and he suspected that Daisy made her stay in their part of the house, fearing that she might be a nuisance. One day when he was driving towards the house on one of his visits to his mother, he saw Faith furiously peddling her bicycle up the hill – no doubt she was returning from school. He sounded the horn, discreetly so as not to startle her, and she looked round and gave him a cheerful wave. He thought then that his mother had been right when she had said it would be a good thing to have a young person in their lives.

Daisy need not have worried about Faith being an annoyance to the lady of the house; it was quite the reverse. Kitty took a great interest in the girl. "She is doing so well at school," she told Rex, "and I think she is getting very pretty, don't you think so, darling?"

"Well, I see her so seldom, I haven't noticed," he said.

"We have become quite close," continued his mother. "After she has done her prep in the evening she comes and sits with me. We talk about so many things. Daisy did not approve at first, but I managed to persuade her it is beneficial to both of us."

"It strikes me that Daisy is quite hard on her," said Rex. "Would you agree that Daisy, with all her virtues, is a little bit humourless?"

"I think you are right," agreed Kitty, "and I might find that just a little trying if it were not for that wonderful added bonus, Faith. She provides the laughter."

"I'm glad you get such pleasure from her company," he said, "and I can see I must try and get to know her better."

"She wants to be an actress!" Kitty gave him a mischievous look, knowing what his reaction would be when she told him that piece of information. It was true, his heart sank a little, and he felt sure he would be called upon to further her career in some way.

The next morning he came down early and found her sitting at the kitchen table eating cornflakes and milk from a bowl. Daisy at once became flustered and said, "Hurry up, girl, and be off to school."

"No," said Rex firmly, "finish your breakfast in peace. I'll join you, if I may." He fetched another bowl and emptied some cereal into it. A jug of milk stood in the centre of the table.

Then he was stumped. What do you say to schoolgirls? "Do you like school?" he asked, and knew how pompous the words sounded.

She smiled, as if appreciating his difficulty. "It's not bad," she said.

Of course, that had always been the stock reply to the conventional question he had asked. Not bad. He felt he had let her down, she was disappointed in him, and he tried a bolder tack.

"My mother tells me you want to be an actress," he said.

"Yes."

He watched, fascinated, as the colour suffused her face. He was not used to blushing – none of the women associated with the theatre seemed capable of blushing. In fact, now he came to think of it, he had never seen an actress blush on the stage. Crying they seemed to manage quite easily, but blushing was out of their range.

For no particular reason, he remembered an incident, years before, when he had an exeat from school and invited two of his friends over for the day. He had found his sister's bra, a recent acquisition, in the bathroom, and he had raced around the house brandishing it in the air. She had been mortified and angry at the same time, and her face was scarlet. Afterwards, he had felt ashamed for upsetting her just because he wanted to show off to his friends. When they had gone, he tried to make a lame apology, because he loved her very much, but she did not forgive him at once.

He said to Faith, "Would you, and your mother of course, like to come to the first night of my new play? It is in three weeks' time."

She looked pleased. "Thank you very much, Mr Patterson."

"I'd prefer it if you called me Rex," he said.

"Thank you, Rex." She was composed now, very sure of herself. He felt her eyes were on him, studying his features.

"Well?" he said, amused.

"I have a photograph of you which was in the programme for *Effie Gray*. I was wondering if it does you justice."

He laughed. "Those terrible stage photographs! How I hate them! They all look the same, like Ivor Novello on a bad day!"

"That's true," she said. "I hadn't noticed it before." She remembered how she had treasured the photograph, and how her mother had torn it from the wall of her bedroom.

"If you don't hurry, you'll be late for school," interrupted Daisy.

Faith got to her feet and put her arms into the sleeves of the unattractive school blazer. Rex could not help noticing from the contours of the white blouse she was wearing that she had reached an age when she probably thought a bra was necessary.

The three of them sat in the front row of the stalls. His mother looked elegant, as always. Daisy was dressed in a blue and white silk dress, obviously her best, and Faith was wearing a deep blue blouse and a very full multi-coloured ankle-length skirt. Kitty had told him proudly that she had taken her shopping and bought her the clothes. "The child had nothing to wear," she said. She had even bought her flat-heeled shoes, which showed off her pretty ankles. "I thought the blouse was exactly the same colour as her eyes," she said.

Rex watched from the side. He was always nervous on the first night of his plays although, after so many successes, the critics expected to be impressed. He would have been even more apprehensive if he had known that this play was to be his first failure. On the following day every reviewer of every newspaper slated it, and one of the most important critics walked out before the end of the play.

If someone had been able to tell him, on that first night, what he was going to read the next day, he would not have been surprised. He felt his luck had changed. With a heavy heart he watched the exquisite Chloe on the stage. As usual she was putting her heart and soul into the part, a part he had written especially for her. It was over between them. A relationship that had survived many years had, at last, come to an end.

They had never cohabited; she had her flat and he had his little house in a quiet mews off the Cromwell Road. During rehearsals for the play he was watching at present, she had told him she wanted to go away for a few days. She was so accomplished, so quick to learn her lines, such a professional, he knew that time away from the rehearsals would not affect her performance, and he did not hesitate in granting her request. There was a very good understanding between them. She was funny and companionable and, when away from the theatre, amazingly uncomplicated for an actress. She liked to lounge around his house or her flat in old clothes, her face devoid of make-up, and managing to look just as beautiful as she did on the stage. He had loved her for years, and there was no doubt she loved him too. He wanted to marry her, but her career got in the way. Just when she was deciding to settle down another part came her way and she could not resist the challenge. As the part usually came from his pen, he was as much to blame as her when a decision was made between a career in the theatre and domesticity and motherhood.

She told him that she was going to Brighton with her best friend, another actress called Ruby Gates, who was not in any production at the time.

He had not been curious. They respected each other's privacy. But she volunteered the information, "I have not been feeling well lately, and I thought Brighton would do me good. All that lovely ozone, darling – Ruby and I are going to fill our lungs with sea air, walk along the front every day."

When she returned he was struck by her appearance.

It was as if all the blood had been drained from her body. Even her skin looked muddy and unhealthy. "You look awful," he said. "Are you all right?"

She answered peevishly, "No, I'm not all right."

He was terribly concerned. "Can I help?"

"No, you can't." She flopped into a sofa, his sofa as she was in his house, and laid her head against a cushion. If he had not known her so well he would have thought she was suffering from a hangover. Fear clutched his heart that she might be really ill.

She must have guessed what he was thinking because she said, "If you must know, I've had an abortion." She pressed her face into the cushion as if her head was aching.

He was astounded. He stared at her as if he could hardly believe what he was hearing. Never, for one moment, had he imagined such a thing.

"My child?" he managed to ask.

"Of course." She sounded affronted.

"Why didn't you tell me?"

"I didn't tell you because you are such an old softie I thought you would try and persuade me against it."

"And would that have been such a bad thing?"

"Just when I am about to start in a new play? No, Rex, this part is important to me, and I do not want anything to interfere with it. Feeling sick and getting fat is not my scene at the moment."

They had talked about getting married and having children, and she had always said that was what she wanted. Now he knew that she had not meant what she said; children were all right as long as they did not get in the way of her career. She had killed his child without even telling him of its existence. It was a small entity that had half belonged to him, and he had a right to know about it.

"I never meant to tell you . . ." she began. She looked at his face, and understood in his eyes she had done a terrible thing. She began to cry.

Her tears did not move him; he felt that his body was wracked with unshed tears of sadness. He remembered he had once asked her how she managed to cry so easily on the stage. Like all good actresses she could summon grief without difficulty. She had told him, "I had a dog when I was a little girl, and it died. I only have to think of Benjie and I start to cry."

He wondered if she was thinking of the dog. He felt ashamed for having such an uncharitable thought, but it was indicative of the change in his feelings for her.

* * *

Kitty became tired after so much excitement, and she declined to attend Rex's party after the play. When her husband was alive they had gone to the first nights together, and had enjoyed talking to the cast at the dinner after the performance. Now, she no longer felt up to it.

Rex put the three of them into a cab to take them to the hotel where they were staying overnight. He hoped his feeling of despair did not show in his face. Perhaps he had an inkling that this play was going to be a flop, perhaps he had noticed the critic sidling out of the theatre or the slightly unenthusiastic applause at the end. He saw the look on his mother's face. She knew, she understood.

He dreaded the evening ahead of him. Entertaining the cast and trying to behave towards his leading lady as he had always behaved towards her, so that the gossips would not suspect a rift between them. He felt vulnerable, as if his outer skin had been removed and all could see what he was really like. It is hard to be in the public eye, especially for a naturally reserved man like Rex. Writing was something he enjoyed doing, success gave him a feeling of achievement, but all the frills that went with it – the extravagant praise, the false acclamations, part of the theatrical career he had chosen for himself – they meant nothing to him. He recognised it to be a nebulous fame that could disappear as quickly as it had arrived.

He wished he could return to his little mews house and spend the rest of the evening on his own.

Chapter Twenty-Three

Kitty telephoned her son from Harrogate. "It is Faith's last term at school. She is in the school play, two weeks from now, on Saturday. You will come, won't you, darling? She has a big part and I know it would mean a lot to her, and Daisy, if you could be there."

He hesitated, "Mothe . . ."

"I don't want to disappoint her."

He recognised the wheedling tone of her voice, and knew that he would not be able to withstand it. "What is the play?" he asked.

"A Midsummer's Night's Dream." It was his least favourite Shakespearean play. He had seen it many times, and he found the humorous scenes increasingly irritating. And a school production! Could he really subject himself to a whole evening of such torture? He knew that he would agree to be there for his mother's sake; she was so taken up with the girl. Every time he spoke to Kitty on the telephone Faith's name was mentioned several times. She had brought a new

interest into a rather sad lady's life, and Rex was glad of it.

"What part is she playing?"

"The leading role," said Kitty proudly.

"Titania?"

"No, Puck."

"Too tall," he said.

"She's not very tall," replied his mother with spirit, "and she is slight."

As he knew he would, he found himself promising, "I'll be there."

The production took place in the school gymnasium. The seats were hard, it was cold and there was a faint smell of sweaty socks. He was the guest of honour, so they sat in the front row – his mother, Daisy and himself. He noticed Daisy was wearing the same blue and white dress she had worn on that disastrous first night, when he had felt everything was going wrong with his life. Since then he had experienced success with two productions, and he had found himself a new leading lady. It was strictly a business relationship though, and he did not intend to repeat the mistakes he had made with Chloe. He resolved that if he did marry, it would be to someone completely unconnected with the stage.

These haphazard thoughts drifted through his mind as he sat waiting for the play to begin. He could imagine the feelings of panic backstage at that moment. Daisy did not seem to be at all nervous for her daughter, and was more concerned about the draught and how it would affect her charge.

"Oh, do stop fussing," said Kitty impatiently.

The two women had been together now for over four years, and the relationship between them had never wavered. It was a loving companionship, and Rex wondered how he could have had doubts about it.

People are usually genuinely surprised by the excellence of school productions, and this was no exception. The amateurish efforts to create a country scene, the painted background of blue sky and clouds, fragile trees suspended on strings from the ceiling and the unrealistic sound of birds twittering, added a certain realism to the performance, an essence of how it must have looked when the play was first shown at the old Globe Theatre in London. The young actors made a very good showing, a few lines were forgotten, but very few.

There was no doubt that Puck stole the show. Rex noticed that Faith's hair had been cut short for the occasion, and it suited her. She darted hither and thither like a will-o'-the-wisp – he had been wrong when he pronounced her too tall for the part. She appeared like an elfin being, and he thought that showed real talent, the ability to hoodwink the audience into thinking you are something you are not.

The drama teacher had shown insight when she chose Faith to take the part of Puck. She uttered the words *'I'll put a girdle round about the earth in forty minutes'* with the same abandoned arrogance Peter Pan had shown when he said, *'To die would be an awfully big adventure'*. When she came centre stage at the end and stretched her arms wide and said, *'Give me your hands if we be friends, and Robin shall restore amends'*, Rex felt quite moved, and clapped as loudly as anyone in the audience. When the young people gathered on the stage to take their bows he wondered why he had been so affected. He remembered an incident in his childhood, when he was five years old and his sister two years younger. There was a summer storm, and he, Kitty and Mary stood, hand in hand, at the open glass door in the dining-room, watching the sheet lightning darting across the sky. Then there was calm, and an eerie light descended over the garden and it began to rain. Suddenly, the little girl released their hands and ran outside. She danced round and round the lawn, pirouetting and raising her arms like a ballet dancer. Her small bare feet splashed in the water, which was falling on the grass like silver globules. They could hear her laughter, laughter of sheer unadulterated joy at being alive at such a magical moment. Common sense prevailed and Kitty called her in. She came at once, her thin frock clinging damply to her small frame, and her mother gathered her in her arms and took her upstairs to put her into a hot bath.

Rex thought of this event as the cast acknowledged the applause and the makeshift curtain clattered to the floor. It occurred to him how often he thought of Mary these days, and wondered if it was a sign of growing old. Memories which had seemed forgotten came to the surface out of the deep recesses of his mind, and sometimes before he went to sleep or fully awoke in the morning he imagined he could see her face appearing to him behind his closed lids.

Afterwards there were refreshments in a small bare room in the same building. Faith appeared, dressed now in a white blouse and a cotton skirt, and she thanked him for coming. It was apparent that she was still quite shy while in his company, lacking the self-assurance she had shown on the stage. He thought that was because of her youth, and if she did eventually realise her ambition and become an actress, she would soon lose that young lost look and become like all the rest of the breed. Rex did not have much time for actresses; there was a sameness about them, a falseness and conceit, a propensity, like their brother actors, to talk endlessly about themselves. He had thought Chloe was different, and he had been proved wrong. The fact that he had been so mistaken still hurt.

Faith introduced him to the person who had organised the production, Miss Carroll. She was flushed with the success of the evening, and flattered that Rex Patterson had deigned to be there. Later he managed to speak to her on her own.

"Faith has real talent," he said. "What does she intend to do with her life after she leaves school?"

"She has no idea," said the teacher, trying not to

appear overawed in the company of such a famous person. "Of course she should go to a drama school, but that would be expensive, and I do not think her mother would even consider the possibility."

"Surely Faith could get a scholarship?"

"Yes, indeed she might, but that does not include everything, only a proportion of the fees, and then there are the living expenses to consider. At the drama school I have in mind for Faith the course is for three years, and living in London does not come cheap." She looked earnestly, almost pleadingly, at Rex, the successful playwright who had amassed a fortune. Powerful, knowing all the right people, she knew he could help.

He discussed the matter with his mother. "I have decided that Faith should go to a drama school. I talked with Miss Carroll, the teacher at the school who trained all the actors tonight. She is keen that she goes to the Victoria School of Dramatic Art. As a matter of fact I am on the committee, although I did not tell Miss Carroll that. I think that Faith may well get some sort of bursary but, in any case, I am prepared to pay her fees and living expenses."

"Oh, darling Rex, that is so generous of you . . . "

He said awkwardly, "This has nothing to do with your feelings about the girl. I know how fond you are of her. I think she has a gift and it should be recognised. I would do the same for any young person showing talent."

"Of course," she said placidly. "I'm just a little worried about Daisy's reaction. She is such a prickly person, and perhaps in her eyes this will smack of charity."

Daisy was called in the drawing-room. By this time a very weary Faith had gone to bed. Rex explained the position to her and, as Kitty had predicted, she was immediately hostile.

"It's very good of you, Mr Patterson –"

"Rex, please."

"We could not possibly accept."

"Why not?"

"It would not be right."

"If you think it would put you under an obligation to me, you are quite wrong. We are obligated to you, Daisy. Since you have been looking after my mother she is a different person. This is a very small way of saying thank you for all you have done. Also, you must know, Daisy, that your daughter is a very clever girl. It would be a tragedy to see such cleverness go to waste. I hope you will allow me to prevent that from happening."

His charm and tact won the day. Daisy capitulated, and Rex opened a bottle of champagne to celebrate the victory. They stood, the lady of the house, her son and the housekeeper and drank a toast to Puck.

The next day he had to leave, to drive back to London. Daisy waylaid him in the hall.

"Faith wants to thank you," she said.

"Where is she?"

"She's in the garden."

He went into the garden and, at first, he could not find her. He began to feel impatient; he wanted to be on his way, not delayed by grateful schoolgirls. He found her, at last, sitting on the bench beneath his mother's favourite tree, the Catalpa tree. The big leaves of the tree threw shadows over her face. When she saw him she got to her feet with the same effortless grace he had observed in her performance on the previous night. She was dressed in the school uniform, the shapeless skirt, the school blazer, but somehow it seemed wrong on her, as if she had grown out of it, and was now playing the part of a schoolgirl. For the first time he agreed with his mother when she had commented that Faith had become very pretty. He thought she was almost beautiful.

"You are very kind," she said.

"Not at all."

Gently she contradicted him, "No, it means everything to me."

Suddenly, to his surprise, she put her arms around his waist. Her head came to the level of his chest. She lifted her face and kissed him lightly on the lips. "Thank you," she said again.

He did not know what to say, so he left as quickly as he could. Driving back to London he could still feel the cool lips against his, young innocent lips, not moved by passion. As yet, he thought cynically.

But the memory of that moment remained with him, and he could not get it out of his mind. Everything else in his unreal life seemed false and empty compared to that unrestrained expression of gratitude and affection. Fervently, he hoped that was all it was, but a little suspicion nagged in his brain. He was wary of ambitious young women, he had encountered them before. When he went to see his mother he made certain beforehand that Faith would not be there. When she started at the Victoria School of Dramatic Art it was easy – he visited during the term-time when he knew she would not be at home. He wondered if she noticed his absence from the house when she came home for the holidays. For some reason, Faith had ceased to be the youngster with talent he aimed to help. Since his last encounter with her he felt a slight reluctance to let the relationship develop; he thought it wiser to keep everything in a low key.

His misgivings resulted in him not seeing her again for three years.

Chapter Twenty-Four

Although Rex did not see Faith during her three years at the Victoria Academy of Dramatic Art, his mother kept him up to date with her progress.

"She is doing so well. Why don't you go and see her some time? The poor child must be lonely on her own in London."

He suspected that she was not lonely, and he reasoned he was doing a great deal for her, and there was no necessity for him to do anything more.

"I would so like to be a grandmother before I die," said Kitty plaintively, not once but many times. He did not say so, but he understood her feelings.

The talented young man who had taken London by storm was now nearly forty, and although he had met women since Chloe none of them had matched her for beauty, charm and the simple enjoyment of being in her company. He knew that she had married a rich American and, ironically, she had a child and had given up the stage. Rex began to think that he was becoming a confirmed bachelor. He recognised the signs with mixed emotions: the desire to be on his own and his growing reluctance to share. Friends tried to persuade him to move, but he stayed in his tiny house, surrounded by possessions he had grown to love. He was very fastidious. His clothes were valeted by a firm, the suits collected and returned in perfect condition. His shirts were laundered and his hand-made shoes were always highly polished. He could afford such luxuries. He remembered Chloe saying to him with affection, "You are such an old fusspot!" and he had thought it funny at a time when he was in the throes of a torrid sexual relationship. Now he did not find the memory so amusing and when his mother used an old cliché, and described him as 'set in his ways', part of him had to agree there was a vestige of truth in what she said.

However, if he had been honest with her, and with himself, he would have admitted a longing to have children, a family of his own. Each godchild he acquired made him more aware of this void in his life. A great deal is written about a woman's obsession to have children, but very little about a man's, and the longing is as strong. Rex felt that his success meant nothing if he could not achieve this last important objective.

He received a letter from Faith:

Dear Rex,

I am nearing the end of my course here, and there is an

end of term play in which I have a leading role. I would love it if you could come to the performance. The enclosed gives you all the details, date, time etc. I am not asking my mother or your mother and, when you see the play, you will understand why.

I know how busy you are, and if you can't make it I will understand. I have enjoyed being here so much, and am endlessly grateful to you for giving me this wonderful opportunity. I hope I will not let you down.

With love from Faith.

This letter amused him because he knew at once why she was unable to ask Kitty and Daisy. He could never understand why drama schools invariably chose a lewd play to round off the course. He supposed it was because they wanted to show that their students could face up to a challenge.

He wrote a short letter to Faith accepting her invitation, and asking her to have dinner with him after the performance.

As usual, an honoured guest, he sat in the front row. The small theatre was a slight improvement on the school gymnasium, but the lighting was very harsh and Rex felt uncomfortably near the stage. A man sitting on his right made snorting noises throughout the first act, whether from disgust or embarrassment he could not tell. During the interval he turned to Rex and said, "Do you know if the parents of that girl are here to see this?"

"She has a mother," said Rex, "and no, she is not here."

"Just as well," said the man. "I would not care to see a daughter of mine copulating on the stage in that fashion."

"The students cannot choose the play," Rex pointed out. "It is chosen for them, and they have to make the best of it."

This observation was greeted with a grunt.

Rex could not help asking, "Who have you come to see this evening?"

"My son. He has the doubtful pleasure of playing opposite the leading lady." He held out his hand. "My name is Robert Agnew. If I may say so, I have enjoyed your plays for years."

"Thank you very much," said Rex, taking the hand.

"Better than this rubbish, that's for sure. I was against Tony becoming an actor, but he was determined. It's a very dodgy career in my view, no substance to it."

"Someone has to do it," said Rex.

"His mother is not here this evening, I'm glad to say. She wanted to come, but he would not hear of it."

"That shows sensibility," said Rex, "which is a good quality in an actor."

The curtain went up again and they had to sit through the last act, which Rex had to admit to himself was an unique form of punishment. Afterwards they were escorted to a vast room where the cast walked around filling glasses with red wine and offering small eats on plates. Faith appeared, three years older than when he had last seen her. She was thin, her face was finer, the cheekbones very prominent. She had obviously scrubbed the stage make-up off her face, as if getting rid of something distasteful. The lack of it accentuated her pallor, making the weariness in her face more noticeable. "I'm sorry I put you through that," she said.

He could not say he had enjoyed the performance, that would be completely dishonest, but he said, "I'm very glad you asked me to come."

He felt pleased to be there on his own, without his mother and Daisy. It gave him an odd sense of freedom, the prospect of an evening alone with her.

Rex spotted the Agnews, father and son, on the other side of the room and gave them a friendly wave. Robert Agnew raised his glass and beckoned them over. Faith saw the gesture, and said hurriedly, "Do you want to stay particularly? Would you mind if we left now?"

"Of course," said Rex. He took her elbow and steered her towards the door. He passed the Agnews on the way, and called out, "Sorry, we have to leave. Well done, Tony!"

"Do you know those people?" Faith asked.

"No, I have never met them in my life. I sat next to the father this evening and he told me his son was your leading man."

Sitting in the warmth and the dim light of the restaurant she started to relax.

"I'm so glad that's over," she said. "Now I can enjoy myself."

"You were brilliant," he told her. "Not an easy part to play."

She looked at him over the menu she was studying and gave him a wide smile. Her face when lit up with amusement was very beautiful. "Particularly difficult for me," she said, "as I am still a virgin."

"Congratulations."

"Not fashionable though – you must remember we are now living in the sixties. If I allow the situation to carry on much longer I shall be a sort of freak."

"No, you will never be that," he murmured.

She tucked into the food with evident pleasure. He was amazed how much she managed to eat. "Don't they feed you at the place where you live?" he asked.

"Not like this."

"You are thinner since I saw you last."

"I don't know why, the students all eat unhealthy food – we survive on fish and chips and bacon sandwiches." She went on to tell him about the course, the people she had met, "All sorts," she said. "I have made lots of friends. It has opened up a whole new world for me, all due to you of course."

Halfway through the meal he began to realise he had not enjoyed himself so much for years. She was very easy to be with, completely natural and seemingly not at all overawed by his presence. He often found that actresses tried too hard when they with him, so anxious were they to give a good impression. Faith treated him like an old friend, and he appreciated it.

"Your mother is always kind to me," she said, helping herself to another plateful of salad. "I love her. And of course my mother is so happy looking after her."

He asked her about her father, and she was eager to talk about George. "He was a dear man. Nothing special about him, very reserved and hampered by deafness. I learnt to speak at him, looking straight into his face, otherwise he did not understand what I was saying. We got on so well, never a cross word between us. I was devastated by his death. A lorry in Southampton ran him down. It wasn't the poor driver's fault – Dad just didn't hear him coming."

"And your mother?" he asked. "You are close to her?"

"Oh, Mother is wonderful," she said loyally.

The wine brought a faint colour to her cheeks. With her coffee she had a liqueur.

"I should not have this," she said, for the first time betraying her youth. "I don't want to disgrace you."

"You have had a very exciting evening. You deserve to relax at the end of all that activity."

"Don't remind me of it!" She looked at him. "Regarding my lack of experience, except when I'm acting of course, I suppose you would not care to initiate me? I can't go on like this for ever, and I would like it to be you."

He was startled, and then interested to see the colour come to her face. She had not lost her old habit of blushing then. He thought she had two sides to her character, one rather unassuming and shy, the other outspoken and not afraid to say what she thought.

"My dear," he said in an absurdly avuncular manner, "I am very flattered, but I'm afraid the answer is a definite no."

"Why?"

"You are so young," he said, and then realised he could not have said anything more hurtful. The young, with all the advantages and expectations that youth brings, hate to be reminded of the fact. He could see the look of dejection on her face, and shame too, and he knew that with one sentence he had spoilt the evening for her.

"I'm so sorry," he said, making it worse.

"No, don't be sorry," she said briskly. "Please, do me a favour and forget what I said. It was very foolish of me, and no doubt I have had too much to drink."

He drove her home. She sat in the seat beside him and chatted about things they both knew: the house at Harrogate, the two ageing ladies who were both so close to them. When they reached the place where she lived (giving directions had been a welcome diversion) she said, "I can't ask you in. We are not allowed visitors after eleven o'clock."

"That sounds very old-fashioned and sensible," he said. By this time every word he uttered sounded pompous in his ears.

She thanked him again for coming to the play. "And for all you have done for me," she said again. He watched her skip up the steps and open the front door with a key. She did not look back.

A week later he telephoned her. He wanted to speak to her before she returned to Harrogate at the end of the course. He had a good excuse for doing this. He asked her if she would like to have a small part in his forthcoming play.

She was ecstatic. "When do I begin?" she wanted to know.

"Turn up at the Garrick Theatre on the third of next month," he said.

"Do I have an audition?"

"No, just be there at ten o'clock. Don't get too excited, it's a very small part, but it's a beginning."

"Thank you, thank you! I am always thanking you."

He wasn't directing the play, but he turned up for some of the rehearsals. He took care not to speak to her personally. He did not want it to appear as if he was distributing favours. The gossips were on the lookout for a new romance in his life. They would love to link his name with a young girl like Faith. She was good in the small part, and he did not regret his decision. His mother and Daisy came to the first night. As usual

Daisy was more concerned with Kitty's wellbeing than with the success of her daughter.

He did put his head round her dressing-room door to wish her luck. She was shaking with fear. "You'll be fine," he said, taking her trembling hand. He noticed she had lots of flowers; none of them were from him though. Sometimes he regretted being so cautious.

Afterwards he drove his mother and Daisy to the hotel where they were staying, as was their custom after first nights. Faith came with them and she sat in the back with her mother. Kitty sat beside Rex, her stick by her side. She was never without it now. She had difficulty in getting out of the car, and Rex took her arm, and very slowly they mounted the steps to the hotel. Faith and an anxious Daisy followed behind.

He walked with her as far as the lift.

"We'll be all right now," said Daisy.

"Yes, darling," said his mother, "don't worry about us any more. Daisy will look after me." She kissed him, and then she kissed Faith.

"Oh, dear," said Rex, as they walked away. He had got used to his mother hobbling about at home but, somehow, in a public place her deterioration was more apparent. It upset him to see it. "Thank goodness we have your mother," he said to Faith when they were in the car. "What would we do without her?"

They were not seated together at the party; he was at one end of the table, she at the other. He took covert glances at her from time to time and she seemed to be enjoying herself. After dinner he saw her go upstairs in the restaurant to collect her coat. He waited at the foot of the stairs for her to come down. When she appeared he offered her a lift home, and she accepted.

She had moved to a bed-sitter and she told him that this was a great improvement on her old room. "No silly restrictions," she said. "And you'll be glad to hear," she announced cheerfully in the darkness of the car, when he could not see her face, "I have sorted out that problem I told you about, with someone who seems to care about me, Tony Agnew. He has even asked me to marry him, although how he thinks we could afford to do that, I can't imagine."

He felt all his self-assurance and urbanity crumble as if to dust. His voice, when he managed to speak, was a thin croak. "I hope you enjoyed it," he managed to say.

"Not much," she said, "but I don't love him, and that must make a difference."

His hands tightened on the steering wheel, and he did not speak. It was absurd, of course, she was lying. Young impoverished actors, straight out of drama school, did not ask the girl they slept with to marry them. It just did not make sense; but the fact that she had slept with him, that did make sense.

As in a dream, he heard her giving him directions to the house where she lived. Without protest, he followed her into the bed-sitting-room. It was very stark, but she had managed to make it more comfortable by putting posters on the walls and covering the drab armchairs with throws. The bed had been disguised as a sofa, with lots of cushions piled on it. There was no sign of any of her clothes; they must be hidden in a cupboard somewhere. In one corner there was a little cooker. "I never use it," she told him, speaking very fast, "in case it makes the room smell."

He looked around him. He had never had to live in a room like this. Boarding school and the RAF had not provided creature comforts, but after that success had come to him almost immediately. During most of his adult life he had suffered no deprivations. Life had been very easy for him.

"There is a bathroom on the other side of the passage," she said desperately. "It is shared between the tenants."

"I don't need it," he said.

"I'm afraid this is not your sort of place," she said.

"I like it," he said, taking her in his arms, "because you are here."

Chapter Twenty-Five

After that first night in the bed-sitting-room he had no difficulty in convincing her that they should meet in future at his mews house. "The bed is bigger," he said, "and you must remember I'm getting old and I appreciate such niceties."

She got cross with him when he mentioned the age gap. He was apt to mention it quite frequently, as it was something that preyed on his mind. He was by nature a worrier, and he considered it the only flaw in the perfect love and understanding that existed between them. He knew it did not concern her at all.

They had to be careful. He did not accompany her to the theatre because he did not want people to start linking their names. He waited at home until she returned after the evening's performance. Sometimes they went to a little bistro nearby, mostly he had cooked a meal for them both. He was a good cook.

He trod warily. He was afraid of such happiness, that it would be snatched away from him, disappear as quickly as it had arrived.

One morning he awoke and turned to see her face on the pillow beside him. He gazed at her for some time, and then she opened her eyes wide and smiled at him. "I love you," he said simply.

"I have loved you for years," she said.

Like all people who discover each other, they never stopped talking about every aspect of their lives before they met. He heard in detail about Faith's childhood, her schooling and her childish memories, mostly connected with her father. He never tired of listening to her talk about such things; every memory brought him closer to her.

In return he told her about his sister, Mary, her enthusiasm and love of life. "We had these neighbours," he said. "They moved away, years ago, soon after it happened. The son, Donald, was crazy about my sister. He loved her from a very early age. I think both families were at a loss as to how to deal with the situation. Girls are difficult, you know – when we have children I hope they will be sons."

When he made this statement, quite casually, as if it was the most natural thing to say to her, she felt as if all the breath had left her body. She resolved to challenge him later, but for the present she was anxious to hear what he had to say about his sister. She knew about her existence of course, Kitty had mentioned her from time to time, but always with such heartbreaking sadness in her voice that it seemed better to move hastily to another subject. Daisy had said to her, "Don't ask her about her daughter, it upsets her too much," so she had not probed into a tragedy that was of profound interest to her. Now, at last, she was about to hear the full story.

"She was fifteen," said Rex, "and at a boarding-school in Yorkshire. My parents were not in favour of boarding-schools for girls, but the war made them change their minds. My mother was busy with war work and my father was in the RAF – there just wasn't the time to take Mary to her day school and collect her in the late afternoon. This, together with the problem of Donald Beeching, made boarding-school the ideal solution. The school was not far from Harrogate, so they were able to see her from time to time, and she came home for two weekends each term.

"I don't know whether she was unhappy or not. My parents did not notice any discernible difference in her; perhaps the old exuberance was a bit subdued, but they put that down to the fact that she was growing up.

"Then one day the headmistress of the school telephoned to say she was missing.

"Can you imagine the consternation this caused? My mother and I travelled by train to the school, but they had no explanation to give, just that one sunny afternoon she must have walked through the main gate, and was gone from us forever. Neither of us thought for a moment it was forever though; we fancied it must be a childish prank and that she would return to us with some explanation for her outrageous behaviour. Before real anxiety set in my mother gave sighs of exasperation; Mary had always been an unpredictable child. We questioned her friends, but they were remarkably unforthcoming. I remember that one mentioned that she had a photograph of Donald Beeching in the locker by her bed. It was against the school rules to have photographs of members of the opposite sex; even brothers were forbidden. It is hard to imagine the restrictions of those days. Any youngster with spirit rebelled against them.

"As my father was away from home, serving in the RAF, it was left to my mother and me to make the decisions. At the age of eighteen I decided when it was the right moment to seek the help of the police. I was about to telephone them when we heard the thud of letters falling from the letterbox.

" 'Wait!' shouted my mother, and she rushed to the hall, as she did every day, to see what the post had brought.

"On that day there was a postcard from Mary. It was addressed to my mother, and it said: 'I am well and happy. Don't worry. Love to Rex. I love you. Mary.'

"After that Kitty received a postcard once a week. Always the same message, always posted from somewhere in London. My father got compassionate leave, and he came home to deal with the situation in the way he knew best. He was certain that Donald Beeching was behind it all, and he strode over to the

Beeching's house to confront them with his theory. Donald's mother was adamant that Mary's disappearance had nothing to do with her precious son; Donald's father was not so sure. They had not heard from him for months, but they said he was a poor letter writer. He had been working at Kew Gardens, gaining horticultural experience with a view to a future career. Telephone calls were made to Kew and they were told that Donald had left there two months earlier. He left at about the time Mary absconded from school, so it looked as if my father's suspicions were right.

"Dad decided that neither Mary nor Donald had enough money between them to pay for accommodation, and his thoughts turned to the house in Addison Road. Six months before the outbreak of war my mother's maiden aunt died and left her this house in her will. It was my parent's intention to live in it for a few weeks each year so that they could have a taste of London life, the theatres and the shops. The war intervened, and immediately the house became a problem. There was no chance of selling it for anything like a decent sum, and so it was left empty.

"The family car had been put on bricks for the duration, but my father had an RAF vehicle and a driver, Harris. We all piled into the car and went to London. I remember that day so well. The sun was shining, and it was an adventure going out in a car. People imagine the war to be a saga of exciting emotions and they do not realise there were vast tracts of intense boredom.

As a young man yearning to be in the fray I welcomed this diversion. As for my sister, I had no worries about her. I thought she would be all right, especially if she was with Donald Beeching for whom I had the highest regard. She had kept in touch with us, that was the main thing, and I had no doubt she would return to the family circle when she felt like it. I thought my mother and father were making a fuss about nothing. I was so young myself I could not appreciate that in their eyes she was a child. In 1941, a fifteen-year-old was still a child, and Mary possessed an air of innocence in common with her friends of the same age. My mother was mortified that her little girl celebrated her sixteenth birthday away from home.

"We arrived at the redbrick Edwardian house, and my mother put the key in the lock and we all trooped in. Harris was prepared to stay with the car, but my father indicated that he wanted him to accompany us. It smelled dank and musty, unlived-in, and the furniture, which belonged to the aunt, was large, old-fashioned and covered with dust. We tramped from room to room, and then climbed the thinly carpeted stairs to the rooms above. The main bedroom was very spooky as it was exactly as my mother's aunt had left it before she was taken to hospital, where she died. There was a square of faded pink satin material trimmed with rather grubby lace lying on one of the chairs, and I asked Kitty what it was. "Old-fashioned people used to put their underclothing under it," she told me. "It was the Victorian view that those sort of things should be kept out of sight."

"I shuddered; imagining what sort of awful item of clothing belonging to the old lady was hidden beneath it.

"We explored each room, but found nothing. I think we were all anxious to leave, before the darkness descended and it was difficult to see the roads with our dimmed headlights. Now, I wonder so much about that day and whether we missed a vital clue. I can't help thinking they saw us coming and hid from us. Perhaps if we had lifted the lace cover we would have found some of my sister's clothing underneath. There was a shed at the bottom of the garden; they could have been in there, peering through the grimy windows, waiting for us to leave. I remember I looked into the cupboard under the stairs before joining the others leaving the house. The key was turned in the lock, and we started for home. My father was silent throughout the return journey; his theory had been shattered and he did not know what to do next. He had not discovered the whereabouts of his only much-loved daughter, and he had to return to duty with nothing solved. His suffering was acute. It was two weeks before the house in Addison Street was bombed.

"The police came to tell my mother and me what had happened. My father, back at the RAF base where he was stationed, was recalled and made a statement to the press requesting that we be left alone with our grief. They complied; they were more considerate in those days. We had a kindly letter from the fireman who had discovered the bodies of Mary and Donald, and he said they must have died instantly. These were comforting words, said many times over in wartime.

"I cannot express to you, my darling, the grief I felt. I had been taught not to show my feelings, and I endured in silence a permanent lump in my throat and the sensation of being unable to breathe. At night I was convinced I was dying; anxiety made my heart beat faster and I imagined the darkness in the room was closing in on me. My mother stayed in her room and sobbed, and I envied her the luxury.

"Mary was a very special person, and we were close. The gap of two years between our ages was of no consequence; a girl is always two years ahead of a boy and so we were equal. She had a sort of radiance about her, and when that inner light was extinguished forever, we, the ones left behind, were plunged into darkness.

"The call-up rescued me from having a breakdown. Before Mary's death I had longed for it; now it was a necessity for my very existence. It was a relief to get away from the sombre atmosphere at home, the endless questions we asked each other – had it been a mistake sending her away to school, did it cramp her ebullient nature? My parents felt themselves to blame. I did not want to cause them any more heartache, and I determined to survive the war. At the age of nineteen I joined the RAF, as my father had done, and learnt how to fly an aeroplane. My companions had a devil-may-care attitude. I was different. I was cautious."

"You still are," said Faith lovingly, "but being cautious did not prevent you from getting the DFC."

"That was a calculated risk," Rex told her. "I did not go in for heroics. Of course I realised in the hazardous lives we led no one could be sure of anything, but I never allowed myself to think about dying, not for one moment. I concentrated on one thing, staying alive. Perhaps it helped."

"Thank you for telling me about Mary," she said. "It is a very sad story, and one can only hope that she and Donald were happy."

"I think they were," said Rex. "They had loved each other since childhood. My father and mother could not begin to understand such love; they felt it was wrong, different from the norm, and it worried them. You know, a person can spend years and years looking for the perfect soul mate. With Mary and Donald it happened very quickly. If they were destined to die young, I'm glad they were together." He paused. "They were hiding from the bombs in a cupboard under the stairs. They would have thought it the safest place. The staircase and the roof above it caved in on top of them. I hope the fireman was right, and they did not have too many frightened moments."

She put her arms around him; she felt that even after so many years he was still grieving. Skilfully, she returned to his previous remark about them having sons.

"You want children?" she asked.

"Yes, I do," he said, "but what about you? You are very young, and have a career ahead of you. I'm sure you don't want to give it up, so it would be a question of juggling the two things, a career and a family."

"No," she said decidedly, "I would not like to do that. If I had a baby I would give up the stage without a backward glance. I am not particularly ambitious; I expect I take after my father in that respect. I just want to be a wife and mother."

Instantly, she regretted saying these words. They sounded very presumptuous, as if she expected him to ask her to marry him.

"I'm sorry," she said. "I talk too much."

"No," he said. "I like it. Will you marry me?"

"Yes."

"In spite of the fact that I am eighteen years older than you?"

"If you mention that again I will not marry you," she told him.

They decided not to tell anyone straight away. It was their secret, and they wanted to keep it that way, for a short time at least. Rex cursed the play which kept them apart for so many hours during the day, and prevented them going away on a holiday together. He wished he had never written the damned thing. Then an article written by a well-known critic caused him concern. It was headed 'Star in the Ascendancy' and it hailed Faith Foster as a young actress with a great future. "Although only in a minor role, her star quality shines out for anyone to see'.

"There you are," said Rex gloomily, "you can't give it all up."

"I can and I will," she said, "because all I want is to marry you and have your children."

Eventually, he telephoned his mother.

"Darling," she said, "how wonderful to hear from you." Perhaps she had been wondering why he had not been in touch lately.

"We thought we would come and see you next Sunday, if that suits."

"We?"

"I'm giving Faith a lift. We are coming together."

"That's lovely," said Kitty. "Daisy will be pleased."

He thought Faith seemed a little silent on the journey. Driving along the seemingly endless road he put his hand on her knee. "Is something worrying you, darling?"

"I'm just wondering how your mother will take to the idea of your marrying the daughter of the housekeeper."

"I think she will be more worried about the difference in our ages," he said.

"Rex!"

Faith need not have worried.

Kitty looked at them quizzically, standing side by

side in front of her.

"We have news to tell you," said Rex. "We are going to be married."

Her face was transformed with happiness. She embraced them both, and then hobbled to the door, calling, "Daisy, Daisy, come at once!"

Daisy appeared, her expression, as always, enigmatic, slightly disapproving. Nowadays she had only one concern, the wellbeing of her mistress. Now, she saw in front of her the daughter she had always wanted. Yet, she did not greet her with affection, but stood aside waiting for a sign from the woman who meant so much to her.

"Daisy," cried Kitty, "they are to be married!" Her voice was filled with excitement, with joy at the prospect of future happiness.

Faith moved towards her mother as if to embrace her, but the gesture was ignored. Rex felt the ominousness of the moment. He took Faith's hand and held it tightly.

There was a long silence. Daisy's face was expressionless. Then she uttered three words only.

"It cannot be."

CHAPTER TWENTY-SIX

"Why are you against them marrying, Daisy?" asked Kitty gently. "Is it because of the difference in their ages?"

"Yes, that's it," replied Daisy stubbornly. "It's not right."

Faith spoke, immediately on the defensive. "Anything you say, Mother, makes no difference. Rex and I are going to be married, and that's all there is to it."

Rex was still holding Faith's hand, and he pressed it encouragingly. He decided he did not like Daisy's attitude. He was grateful for all she had done for his mother, but there had been kindness on both sides. Daisy had comfortable quarters in the house, she was treated like a member of the family, and security in her old age, should she outlive Kitty, had been promised to her.

"I'm sure Faith wants us to feel comfortable with the arrangement," said Kitty, trying a conciliatory approach. "It will spoil her happiness if she knows you are opposed to it."

Daisy said, "I am completely opposed to it. This marriage must never happen." She glared at Faith. "Your father would agree with me if he could be with us today."

"That's not true," cried her daughter hotly. "Dad would always go along with my judgement and wishes. He would understand how much Rex and I love each other. The age business would not bother him at all. It is your own opinion you are expressing."

"Maybe I am," said Daisy, "but nothing will alter it."

Rex spoke at last. "Faith is over eighteen, and so she can marry whom she chooses. Would it not be best to abide by her choice, whatever you may think privately, rather than cause a rift between you?"

"After all," interrupted his mother, "John was ten years older than me, and we had a very happy marriage."

"That's not relevant, Mother," Rex pointed out rather sharply. "We are talking here of a gap of eighteen years, not ten." He began to feel weary of the whole fruitless discussion. As Faith had said it made no difference to them. They had discussed the difference in their ages at great length, and had decided it could not get in the way of their future life together. He thought, after all, I'm only thirty-nine, not an old man, as this woman seems to imply.

"I'm sorry, Daisy," he said firmly. "Of course it

would have been nice to have your blessing, but if you feel you cannot give it, then we must go ahead with our plans, regardless of your feelings."

"In that case," said Daisy, looking at Kitty, "I must talk to you. In private." She spat out the last two words and they were accompanied by a baleful look in Faith's direction. It was as if she blamed her for the whole thing, just as she had done when she heard of George's death.

Kitty glanced at her son, and he nodded. Let them sort it out between them, he thought. He had great faith in his mother's powers of persuasion. He went to hold the door for the two women. Then he and Faith sat on the sofa, very close, still holding hands.

"I don't understand," said Faith. "What can she be saying to her?"

"I suppose she is trying to convince my mother that she, Daisy, is right and we are all wrong. It won't work, though. Kitty is simply delighted about us, nothing will change that. It is just unfortunate that for some reason Daisy has adopted this attitude. Let's hope my mother does the persuading."

"She is so sweet," said Faith. "I love her. She has not said a word against us."

"That is because she loves you," said Rex. He was irritated at this unexpected turn of events, but he was not particularly worried. He thought his mother would deal with the situation very well. Although he would not have said so much to Faith, he considered Daisy had a very narrow view on life and her opinion was not of paramount importance.

They did not speak after that, and the time went slowly. There was a carriage clock on the mantelpiece, which chimed the hours and the quarters. Twice the silence was broken by the tinkling silvery sound.

Rex said, "This is absurd." He got up and went to the door which he opened a fraction. "Mother?" he called.

They heard her faltering steps and the sound of her stick on the wooden floor of the hall outside. When she pushed open the door, closely followed by Daisy, they were astounded by her appearance. In the time she had been away from them, she had changed completely, aged. She looked like an old woman who has received a great shock.

"She is very upset," said Daisy reprovingly.

Rex and Faith helped Kitty to her chair. All the colour had drained from her face, and she leaned her head against a cushion and closed her eyes, as if she was about to faint.

"What is the matter, darling?" asked Rex, deeply concerned.

"Give her a drink," ordered Daisy. "Whisky and water is what she likes." She made no effort to get it herself.

Faith ran out of the room, across the panelled hall and into the dining-room. She found a bottle of whisky in the cupboard of the serving table and, with a trembling hand, poured the drink into a glass. She was very frightened. Was Kitty in the throes of a heart attack or a stroke because of the news they had given her that day?

When she re-entered the room, her mother tried to take the glass away from her, but Faith brushed her aside and, kneeling on the carpet beside the old lady's chair, she held the glass to her lips. Kitty drank a little, opened her eyes wide and stared long and hard into the girl's face.

"Oh, my darling," she said.

Rex and Faith were aware that Daisy was leaving the room. She went very quietly, closing the door gently behind her.

While they watched anxiously, Kitty seemed to pull herself together. "My darlings," she said, "please listen carefully to what I have to say."

"We are listening, Mother," said Rex.

"Daisy has been telling me such a remarkable story," she said. "I don't know whether to believe it or not. She says that her husband, George, who was an ARP warden during the war, went into the bombed house in Addison Road and found two bodies in a cupboard under the stairs, my daughter Mary and Donald Beeching. They were both dead and their bodies were shielding a very young baby. George knew there was nothing to be done for the poor young people and he left them there to be discovered later by the man in the fire service who wrote to us. The baby was alive, though, and George took it home and he and Daisy, who were desperate to have a child, pretended it was theirs." Her voice broke, and she took another sip of the whisky. She went on. "They moved to the country so that no one would suspect, and wrote to Daisy's family in Devon saying that she had given birth to a daughter. According to your mother, Faith, you were that child."

The significance of those last words did not dawn on Rex at once. He looked at Faith and saw her stricken expression. At that moment he felt only for her. As Kitty had said, it was hard to believe, and he wondered if Daisy was losing her mind. He had never thought of her as an imaginative person, and he did not think her capable of inventing such a story.

"If it is true that Mary and Donald had a child, and Daisy and her husband successfully abducted her," he said, "why did we, as a family, come into the picture at all?"

"Because Daisy felt guilty about it," explained his mother. "She found out that I needed a housekeeper and applied for the job." She looked at Faith. "I am grateful to her for that."

"It's nonsense," said Rex irritably. "How could she possibly find out that you needed a housekeeper?" He tried to remember the circumstances, eight, nine years ago? There was some muddle about the advertisement, which appeared in *The Lady*, but he could not recall the details.

"I don't know how she found out," said Kitty. She

was looking at Faith, and remembering the first time she saw her. She always thought it was a happy chance that she resembled Mary. Surely Rex could see it too?

"What about a birth certificate?" he was asking. "Have you got a birth certificate, Faith?"

"Yes," she said eagerly, "I have seen it."

He left her with his mother, and he marched into the kitchen where he found Daisy sitting at the table. He had to admit she looked utterly desolate.

His voice was kindly when he said, "I would like to see Faith's birth certificate if that is possible, please."

"Of course." She got to her feet and went upstairs. He could hear her opening and shutting drawers. She appeared with an old-fashioned tin cash-box in her hand. "I put all these things together when we moved," she explained. She produced a little key and unlocked the box. "You look at what's in there," she said.

He went through the contents carefully. He felt it was an intrusion of privacy, but the circumstances were so unusual he considered he had the right. He withdrew the items, one by one, and put them on the side. There was a faded cutting from a society magazine, showing his mother, Chloe and himself at the first night of *The Captive Audience*. Then he opened the report of the bombing of 1 Addison Road in the local paper. Scraps of paper revealed a note of the address in Harrogate, and scribbled notes about his father and himself. The next thing he picked out was a studio photograph of himself, torn from a theatre programme; it looked as if it had been crumpled up, and then smoothed out. He found photographs of Faith with her father, and one of the little house where they lived in Annesley. Touchingly, there was a pair of tiny shoes, Faith's first shoes, and down at the bottom of the box, folded neatly, the birth certificate.

The first thing that sprang to his notice was the name Beeching. Daisy Mary Beeching. "Was that your maiden name?" he asked, knowing with a cold feeling around his heart, that this could not possibly be the case.

"No," she replied, "my name was Daisy Flower before I married. George told me that the name Beeching was the only discrepancy. Discrepancy, that was the word he used."

Rex sat down heavily in the chair opposite Daisy. The birth certificate convinced him of the truth of the story. Somehow, that name Beeching had to appear on the birth certificate. The name of the child's father, and probably the name Mary used when she went into the hospital to have her baby.

Rex wondered how George had managed to carry out this amazing deception. He thought, he must have had a friend in the register office, someone who was willing to help him in exchange for a sum of money. It was wartime, and that made it easier to get away with something as outlandishly wicked as this.

It was as if Daisy knew what he was thinking, for she

said defiantly, "My George never did a dishonest thing in his life."

He may have been a fundamentally honest man, thought Rex, but the temptation to provide his wife with a much-wanted baby had proved too hard for him to resist.

He buried his head in his hands. The enormity of the situation hit him. It altered everything, and since coming to his mother's house, the world had become extraordinarily bleak. He looked up and stared at the silent Daisy, thinking about the first time he saw Faith – the tall awkward schoolgirl. He must have known then, but he had not been able to make sense of his feelings. He had loved Faith from the beginning because she looked like someone he had loved very much. He recalled his mother's expression when she first set eyes on her; she had felt the same way, that chance had made this child look like the daughter she had lost. Of course, it happens all the time, people look like other people. They had just put it down to a happy coincidence.

He put the papers back into the box. "I'll keep these for the time being, if you don't mind," he said. Daisy nodded.

Then he returned to the drawing-room to face the two people who mattered to him most, to tell them the truth, show them the evidence. In his distress he was almost brusque. In case Faith had not taken in the full implication, he spelled it out to her. "We can never marry and, as for having children, that is out of the question."

"We can live together," she said.

"No."

Kitty put her arm around the girl who had started to weep. "Is there nothing to be done?" she said, and then, realising there was no hope anywhere, "Are you sure, quite sure?"

"Quite sure," said Rex. "All Faith and I can do is to try and forget we ever met and wanted to be together." He was aware that he sounded brutal, but it was his last gift to her before he disappeared from her life. She had made no secret of the fact that she longed for children. She was his niece, there was no getting away from that, and the revelation made that an impossibility. Suddenly, the age gap resumed its importance in his mind. He could not subject her to a life with an old man and no family, and a terrible secret that prevented them from marrying. It was a secret that must poison their lives together.

He told himself that, without him, she would, in time, forget him and find happiness with someone else.

He said, "No one else must ever know about this."

Chapter Twenty-Seven

Faith wept and cajoled, but Rex was adamant, nothing would change his mind. Late in the afternoon he strode out of the house and drove back to London, alone. The two women and the distraught girl were left on their own, bewildered and hardly able to face up to what had happened. Then Daisy pulled herself together and started to prepare a meal. She had always insisted on eating in the kitchen, and she set two places there, one for herself and one for Faith. Kitty would get her meal on a tray in the other room.

"No, Daisy," said Kitty firmly. "We all eat together, and let's have no nonsense, please."

Faith finished the run of the play, but Rex did not come near the theatre. There was speculation about his absence, but no one suspected Faith of being the reason. As is always the case with stage people, the cast gossiped amongst themselves and unfounded rumours floated about – that he had become an alcoholic, that he was in the midst of a torrid love affair.

Faith found herself an agent, and on the strength of that one favourable revue she soon managed to get a major role in a play. She threw herself into the part, and she was a success. Her name began to be known.

It was a long time before she returned to Harrogate. She decided to go when she got a letter from Kitty imploring her to come.

'You must forgive Daisy, my dear,' Kitty wrote. *'It was kindly meant. She wanted me to know I have a beautiful granddaughter, and I cannot help but feel grateful to her for that. I have been reading about you and I am so proud. I miss you so much, and all Daisy's sacrifices will be wasted if we never see each other. You can be assured Rex will not be here when you come. My love to you, Kitty.'*

When Faith arrived the two women greeted her very differently. Daisy had never been demonstrative with her, and now she stood quietly to one side while Kitty embraced her. Faith turned to Daisy and hugged her, "It's lovely to see you, Mum," she said, purposely reverting to her childhood name for her.

The three of them sat down to supper in the dining-room. Kitty and Daisy always ate together now. Kitty had become even lamer, and Daisy who was younger than her employer, looked older than her years and had become a little deaf. Faith, looking at them, felt the sadness of old age creeping up on them both.

When she and Kitty were alone, she summoned up the courage to mention Rex. Even saying his name produced a throbbing in her ears. Kitty told her that he was in America. "He has been there six months, and he is doing something quite new, writing the lyrics for a musical. After . . . well, you know, after it happened, he wrote nothing for months and months. I began to think he would never write anything again. Then he was asked to do this, and it was a new departure for him. Perhaps he thought doing something completely different would be a good thing. Anyway, he accepted the offer, and he is living in New York. It's hard to imagine, Rex in New York!"

All Faith could think of was Rex's hard face when he told her they must part for ever. She tried to put it out of her mind, to remember the happy parts of their relationship, but it remained. Seeing Kitty again helped. It made her realise that here was someone who understood, and to whom she could speak openly about Rex.

"Of course it means," said Kitty sadly, "that I have not seen him for months and months. I can't tell you how much I miss him, so I hope you will come instead, my darling, whenever you can manage it."

The musical opened in New York to a rapturous audience, and then came to London. Tony Agnew telephoned Faith and asked her to go and see it with him.

"No, thank you," she said.

"I thought you'd be interested. Didn't you know Rex Patterson at one time?"

"My mother is his mother's housekeeper," she said. "That is the only connection. I'm sorry, Tony, but I'm not interested in musicals. I have no desire to see it."

"Well, could I tempt you to dinner one evening?"

"I'd like that very much."

She liked Tony, and she felt she knew him very well. She was comfortable with him. After all, he had been the first man to express love for her. She remembered with affection how, after they had slept together, he had asked her to marry him. At the time she had thought it a rather endearing emotional response, and she had not taken him very seriously. But he had continued to propose, at intervals, and it had become a sort of joke between them. He had learnt to expect a refusal. Now, she thought she could not spend the rest of her life warding off the advances of men; people were beginning to think there was something odd about her. She thought that sleeping with Tony again would not be an unpleasant experience.

Faith found it easier to have a man by her side. Soon it was an understood thing that they were always together. It was better than accepting invitations, which she regretted later. Tony was handsome and considerate. He had not set the world on fire with his acting, but he had persevered, tackling minor roles with enthusiasm, certain that he would achieve fame in the future.

He took her home to meet his family. She remembered seeing his father at the end of term play at the

Victoria Academy of Dramatic Art.

"That was quite something," said Robert Agnew.

"I cringe when I think of it," said Faith.

She wondered whether he would remember meeting Rex Patterson on that evening but, if he did, he did not mention it. She liked his wife, Jean, a respectable county lady, keen on horses and village fêtes, and he was a bluff agreeable man who had never got used to his only son becoming an actor. They lived in a beautiful house in Malvern, and there seemed no shortage of money. They would help Tony out if he became stumped for cash, like so many of his fellow thespians. The stability of his background provided a sense of security, which was an unusual feature for a career on the stage.

Then one day she read in the newspaper that Rex Patterson was getting married. She carried the newspaper to her bed, and lay between the sheets, sobbing. She thought there was no reason to live, but being an optimistic person by nature, she knew that she had to carry on. She wept alone, with no one to comfort her.

The telephone rang and it was Tony. "What's wrong? You sound strange."

"It's nothing," she said. "I think I may be getting a cold."

"Will it cheer you up if I come and see you?"

"I think so," she said, "and it's months since you asked me to marry you. Have you gone off me?"

There was a silence at the other end of the line.

At last Tony said, "Not at all, but I thought you weren't keen on the idea."

"It's growing on me," she said, "so you might try again."

She went into the kitchen and threw the newspaper into the rubbish bin. Then curiosity got the better of her and she removed it, and straightened it on the kitchen table.

'Rex Patterson,' she read, *'is marrying Elspeth Codlington, only daughter of Lord and Lady Codlington who live in Buckley Hall in Norfolk. Rex Patterson, as everyone knows, is the famous playwright and director. His new play* Summer Storm *is due to appear on the London stage in one month's time. Lord Codlington's claim to fame is Codlington Yellow, a fishing fly which he invented two years ago.'*

Next time Faith went to Harrogate she heard from Kitty that Elspeth had been brought home for inspection.

"Tell me about her," said Faith. "Is she pretty?"

"She is nice-looking," Kitty admitted, "not young, in her thirties I'd say. I am surprised she has not married before – no career to worry about and all that money. Not that it will matter to Rex," she added hastily.

There was a silence while Kitty thought, with reservations, about her future daughter-in-law and Faith decided, nice-looking or not, she hated her anyway.

Then she told Kitty that she was getting married herself, and Kitty was suitably happy for her. Both of them were aware of the spuriousness of their sentiments.

* * *

Rex had met Elspeth at a dinner party, and it was apparent from the beginning of their relationship that she adored him, not because of his fame but because of himself, and this endeared her to him. She was remarkably disinterested in anything to do with the stage, and he found this refreshing. Like his mother, he wondered why she had not married, and she told him that she had been engaged, but it was broken off. She did not offer a reason for this.

She took him home and proudly introduced him to her parents. He was fascinated by the eccentricity of this aristocratic family. If he had not decided to marry Elspeth he would have written a play about them. The bumbling old lord and his vague meandering wife were marvellous material for a writer. They had both seen the musical and loved it. He learned later that it was the only form of theatrical entertainment they enjoyed.

Afterwards, he thought he had been in the right mood to meet and marry someone like Elspeth. He had not liked New York, and the writing of lyrics for a musical had given him no satisfaction. Rex, that most English of Englishmen, was not at home in the States, although the Americans, American women in particular, thought a great deal of him. He had stayed in opulent hotels, and everything seemed on a grand scale; it was a relief to get back to his tiny house in London.

"Are you sure, darling?" said his mother irritatingly, when he told her of his forthcoming marriage. He visited the house in Harrogate less and less frequently; he loved Kitty dearly, but the presence of Daisy irked him. He remembered Faith shouting at her, "Why did you tell us?" He tried so hard to put these things out of his mind, it was essential for him to do so, but Daisy was a constant reminder.

"Don't you like Elspeth?" he asked pettishly, and Kitty replied calmly that she liked her very much.

The preparations for what seemed to be a big wedding were put in motion. Fortunately, Rex had little to do with it and, anyway, his mind was on his new play, which was about to be performed. He knew it was the best he had ever written. The sides of the London buses were emblazoned with the words *Summer Storm* and he felt the old excitement welling up in him. A romantic might have suggested that it was the memory of Faith which inspired this marvellous play but, in fact, he had put all his energies into writing it in an effort to forget her.

He invited his future in-laws to the first night as well as his future wife, his mother and, of course, Daisy. To his surprise Elspeth did not attend. The preparations for the wedding had so exhausted her she had retired to bed. "I'm so sorry, darling," she said, "but I don't think you will miss me. It's really not my scene."

Lord and Lady Codlington were staying at the Berkeley Hotel. After the performance Lady Codlington went upstairs to her room, and the old man stayed downstairs and he and Rex had a drink together in the lounge. Rex was a bit anxious about the time, as he knew he was expected at the usual first-night party.

"M'daughter is not here for a reason, " said Lord Codlington. "She wanted to leave the way clear for me to tell you something."

Oh, God, thought Rex, not another family secret about to be revealed . . .

"She can't have children. She had an infection when she was young, and everything had to be removed. There is no chance of her having a family. She was engaged before, as she may have told you, and the fellow broke it off when she told him. She's scared stiff you will do the same." The old man looked at Rex rather pathetically.

Rex found himself saying, "It makes no difference. Tell her it makes no difference."

He decided he could not face the party. He still owned the mews house, although it was about to be sold, and he let himself in with his key, and poured himself a large whisky. He made a resolution to get drunk. Only when he was drunk did he allow himself the luxury of thinking about Faith. In his sober moments he felt only bitterness about what had happened. When he was drunk he thought of her sweetness and how much he missed her.

The following day he telephoned the estate agency, and said that he had changed his mind; he was keeping the house in Peacock Mews.

Faith and Tony had a quiet registry office wedding, attended only by two members of the cast of the play they were both appearing in together. The fact that their time was occupied with the theatre was their excuse for not having their families at the ceremony. When the play closed they went to Ireland for a short honeymoon, paid for by the Agnews in lieu of a wedding present.

In contrast, Rex's wedding was a sumptuous affair. Billows of white flowed towards him as he waited in the church for his bride. He likened it to the musical, which was still playing to huge audiences all over the world. The Codlingtons had informed him that it was their intention to move to a small house on the estate, leaving Buckley Hall for him and Elspeth to occupy. Everything was to be left as it was, the priceless antique furniture, the valuable collection of porcelain and the paintings of hideous ancestors adorning the walls. Elspeth was overjoyed at the generosity of her parents; Rex kept silent. He did not really care. Accompanying his future wife on a tour of the vast place he reflected that it was like one of his stage sets, very impressive but not the sort of place where real people lived. Also, it was a very long way from London, a fact that Elspeth had ignored or did not find important. He was glad that he had decided to keep his house in Peacock Mews.

At the top table, the father of the bride made a speech. "We know little of the theatre in our family," he said, "and I only hope that my son..." All eyes turned to the son and heir, a chinless useless individual in Rex's view, lolling in the seat next to his mother. "... will not be influenced by my son-in-law, and want to become an actor!" There was laughter around the room.

Rex, sitting in the midst of all the flummery, suddenly realised what he had done. Desperately, his turned to Kitty, sitting on his right side. Their eyes met, and he knew by her anguished expression that she, at least, understood what he was feeling.

CHAPTER TWENTY-EIGHT

The Agnews were generous and purchased a house in London for Tony and Faith. Robert Agnew did not believe in newly-weds being encumbered with a mortgage so the house would belong to them. During the first few months of their marriage the couple were mostly on tour together, living in digs; then Faith became pregnant, and it was important for them to find somewhere more permanent for them to live. Tony talked to his father and asked him for a loan, which it was tacitly agreed between them would never be repaid.

Faith had nothing to do with the choice of house where they were going to live. Tony and his parents decided on 13 Cypriot Terrace, a very ugly little house halfway down a long unattractive street in an unfashionable part of London. They chose it because the Agnews were not prepared to put up any more cash, the house was in bad decorative repair and therefore cheap. They thought that Tony ought to be able to provide for his wife and future family, without having to come to them for any more assistance. Faith was dismayed when she saw the house, but she decided optimistically that it was a beginning, and they would move to something better when they could afford it. She had no way of knowing that it was to be her home for the next thirty-five years.

Tony was on tour when they moved in, and immediately Faith, with her rapidly increasing stomach, set about painting it from top to bottom. She would have liked to make other changes in the bathroom and kitchen – everything was very outdated – but that was impossible. Tony's cheque arrived each week, a proportion of his meagre salary, and she had to manage on that. There was a little untidy garden at the back of the house, and when her back ached so much she could not do any more painting, she went and sat on a deckchair under an apple-tree. It was quite pleasant, hovering between wakefulness and sleep, experiencing the reassuring little plops of the child within her. When the painting was completed, she turned her mind to furnishing the place. She went to Harrogate because she intended to ask Kitty if she could have the contents of her old bedroom.

Kitty was overjoyed to see her, and very excited about the prospect of a baby in the family. Even Daisy was enthusiastic; she had always been most interested in babies. She had softened over the years, and Faith found her easier to get on with than before. Perhaps a great weight had been lifted from her mind, and she felt free to be happy once more. She was very busy knitting garments for her grandchild. Perversely, she regarded this child as her direct descendent, the much-loved grandchild of herself and George. Fortunately, the two ladies were quite happy to share the honour.

Faith stayed there for three days and at the end of the time felt amazingly relaxed. She was not allowed to do anything, and Kitty fretted about her. Did she eat enough? Was Tony going to be with her during the birth? Curiously, she never asked the question that Faith would have found hard to answer. Did she have enough money?

Kitty had always had money, and found it difficult to imagine life without that comfortable bolster. Because it had always been there she never thought about it. Her husband, John, had looked after her finances, and now Rex was in charge of them. It simply did not occur to her that Faith might be hard up. It occurred to the more practical Daisy, and she gave Faith two hundred pounds out of her savings.

The old house was crammed with furniture, and Kitty hobbled around with Faith, pointing with her stick at the pieces she could have. Beds that were never slept in could be easily spared, and bundles of linen and towels were removed from the airing cupboard. "I don't need that any more," said Kitty, pointing at a cupboard, "and you can have the Welsh dresser, darling, no one else wants it."

"Practically all we have is a bed!" Faith told her. "I can't tell you how grateful I am."

Kitty even instructed Daisy to take pictures from the walls, leaving dark patches of wallpaper where they had once hung.

"Won't Rex mind you giving me these things?" asked Faith anxiously.

"Of course not," Kitty assured her. "He's surrounded by rubbish in that big house of his." She arranged for a carter to take everything to Cypriot Terrace. When the van arrived a few days after Faith's return, she wondered if he would expect payment. It was a relief when he said that he had been instructed to send the bill to Mrs Patterson.

She used the money Daisy had given her to buy things for the baby. She chose material for the curtains in the nursery, and posted it to Daisy to make up for her.

Tony did appear, at the last minute, for the birth of his child. When he held Ben in his arms, he wept. Faith, looking at this small entity, felt a surge of pure happiness. Things had not gone well for her, but she and Tony had managed to create this miracle. At that moment she loved her husband and her new little son with all her being.

There followed a time of great contentment for the little family. Tony had finished his tour, but he had been asked to take part in an advertisement for television, and this proved to be more lucrative than any of his stage roles. They bought themselves a little car, and made several journeys to see his parents and Kitty and Daisy. At both homes their visits were greeted with delight. Little Ben was an enchanting child, and the Agnews, Robert and Jean, genuinely loved their daughter-in-law. Kitty found Tony very attractive; he put himself out to be charming with her, and Tony could be very charming if he set his mind to it. It was hard to tell what Daisy thought of him. She was a person who had never been swayed by obvious charm; after all, she had recognised George's worth very quickly. She wondered what he would have thought of this personable young man, very full of himself and anxious to impress.

Tony had an agent who promised he would find him more advertising jobs, but these were not forthcoming. The situation became rather tense at 13 Cypriot Terrace, particularly as Faith was expecting their second child. Money was a constant topic of conversation for them; with one child to clothe and feed and another on the way the lack of funds could not be ignored.

At last Tony got a small part in a touring company from the North of England. This meant that he was a long way from home, and Faith saw even less of him.

Two weeks before the birth of Giles, Faith received a telephone call.

"Are you the wife of Tony Agnew?" said a woman's voice she did not recognise.

"Yes." She felt a moment of fear. Had something happened to Tony? "What is it?"

"I just wonder why you make his life such a misery," said the voice on the other end of the line. It spoke in a harsh resentful tone, and Faith did not know how to respond.

"I don't know what you mean," she whispered.

"Oh, don't pretend you don't know what is happening," said the woman. "You can't make him happy, and I can. Why don't you give him a chance?"

"Are you telling me that you are having an affair with my husband?" demanded Faith, finding strength at last. "Is that what you are saying?"

There was a little silence, and then the receiver was put down.

Giles was born one evening when his father was actually on the stage. Tony received the news of the baby's arrival soon after the curtain came down. He had to wait until the weekend before seeing his younger son, and by this time Faith and the baby were back home. Of course Daisy could not leave Kitty, but kind Jean Agnew came for a few days to help out.

When Tony arrived he was greeted with utter confusion. Giles was not the easy baby his brother had been, and cried solidly, without stopping, for hours at a time. Ben was a very active toddler, and extremely resentful of the new arrival, which did not help matters. A harassed Jean tried to keep some sort of order, but it was difficult. The poky little house was untidy, toys and clothes scattered everywhere, nappies hanging to dry on a clothes-horse in front of the old-fashioned gas fire. Tony stepped through the mess and turned on the television, a luxury that he had purchased at the same time as the car when his prospects seemed good. His mother turned if off, telling him that it would disturb the baby, hard to understand when the baby appeared to be permanently disturbed.

There was no sleep, no proper meals, no conversation, and it was Tony's idea of hell.

It had been a difficult birth, and his wife had not yet recovered from it. She lay on the sofa, looking distressed and palely uninteresting.

Sometime during that short visit she mentioned the telephone call.

"Who was that woman?" she asked.

Tony knew that denials would get him nowhere. "There was something between us," he admitted, "a member of the cast, you know the sort of thing. We see so much of each other during a tour. It meant nothing, and I'm sorry if you are upset."

"I can't understand why she telephoned me," said Faith.

"Oh, women!" said Tony, exasperated. "They behave so strangely at times. You don't know what to expect of them." He looked at her earnestly. "You can't tell me you have been faithful to me all through our marriage."

She was able to reply truthfully, "When have I had

the time to be unfaithful?"

Her sad defeated expression got on his nerves.

He felt a great surge of relief when Sunday evening came and he had to leave to catch his train to the north.

He kissed his wife, and thanked his mother for coming to their rescue. Then he embraced his elder son, and stroked the baby's cheek with his finger.

More than twelve years were to pass before Faith saw him again. Perhaps being catapulted into fatherhood, twice over, was too much for him. Whether he made the decision to leave them while he was staying in the house, she would never know. His farewell had been affectionate enough, so perhaps the idea came to him on the train journey.

It was a long time before she realised he was not returning. Once she was feeling better she pulled herself together and set about looking after her two little boys. Jean had to return to her husband, but Faith had always been good at making friends. She was the sort of person who chatted with people on buses. Her neighbours liked her and were supportive. When the weeks went by and no money was put into the account, she appealed to the single mother who lived next door, who worked at the DHSS. No money had been put into the account, but no money had been withdrawn either – at least Tony showed that much decency. The overdraft of nearly one thousand pounds, and rising rapidly, was Faith's main concern; she lay awake at night thinking about that overdraft. At that stage she did not think that Tony had gone for good. She thought he would suddenly arrive, possibly when the tour was finished.

Muriel, her neighbour, advised her to sell the car, which she did. Faith was all for getting rid of the overdraft with the money, but Muriel said that was not a good idea. Keep the money for emergencies was her sound advice. Put it into a building society.

Faith telephoned the repertory company and asked for Tony. She was told that although the play was still being shown, he was no longer in it.

"Why?" she asked. The voice at the other end told her to try and get in touch with the producer; he would explain what had happened.

"I'll never get hold of him," said Faith reasonably. "Please won't you help me? I'm Tony's wife, and it's important I know what is going on. You see, I have not heard from him for weeks."

So it was that she learned from a complete stranger that Tony had dried up in the middle of a performance, forgotten his lines. He had to go, of course, and his dismissal resulted in him having a nervous breakdown. He had ended up in some sort of hospital.

"Hospital?"

"Well, you know, the sort of hospital people go to when they have a mental breakdown. Poor old Tony, he was in a bad way. We all visited him from time to time, to try and cheer him up. Then one day he was gone. He checked out of the hospital, and no one has seen or heard from him since."

"Thank you for telling me," said Faith.

Muriel came over that evening, her arms full of clothes, which her boy, Sean, had outgrown. Garments for Ben, garments for the little one.

"You are so amazingly kind," said Faith, "I can't thank you enough." While they talked, she sorted out the clothes, putting them in piles.

"Of course you will be able to get supplementary benefit," said Muriel, "but first you must get in touch with Tony's parents. Surely, they must be wondering why they have not heard from him?"

"Not necessarily," said Faith. "He has never been good at keeping in touch with them." She looked fondly at her two boys, Ben asleep on the sofa, suddenly worn out by frenetic activity and, Giles, thankfully sleeping quietly in his carrycot. "I hope they will always be concerned about their mother."

She thought of Rex, and his warm love for Kitty. Rex, who was a constant presence, somewhere in her thoughts.

"Hi!" said Muriel, "Come back to the real world, will you?" She handed Faith a twenty-pound note. "That's for the journey. A loan. Pay me back when you can."

The train journey to Malvern was not a pleasant experience. They had to change at Reading, which meant heaving the carrycot through the door, at the same time keeping a tight grip on Ben's small hand.

Then they waited, a forlorn little group, on a cold draughty station, for the train to Malvern.

It was at that stage the journey took on a nightmarish quality. Giles became suddenly aware of the strangeness of his surroundings and he started to give voice. The carriage was full of well-meaning kindly people who offered advice, and then expressed concern. "Is he always like this? Are you worried?"

"It's colic," said Faith desperately, "he will grow out of it."

"Yes," said a woman sitting in the corner, "I remember my boy had colic, and then they said it was something called projectile vomiting. He used to hold his breath, like your baby. He ended up in hospital, he did."

At last, they tumbled out of the train, into the arms of Jean and Robert; both of them had come to meet them. Ben was fastened into his car seat, and the carrycot was stowed on the back seat. The movement of the car sent Giles to sleep. Both boys were sleeping when they carried them into the house.

"I have something to tell you," said Faith, without preamble.

"No," said Robert, "we know. We have had a letter from Tony."

Tony had written to his father telling him that he had withdrawn from the joint account he held with his wife and he had arranged for the house to be put into Faith's name. It was all he could do for his family. He regretted that he was unable to pay off the overdraft. He loved Faith and the boys, but he could not cope with the responsibility. He did not give an address, but his intentions were quite clear.

Robert covered Faith's hand with his own. "You have been worried, my dear," he said, "but Jean and I are your family, and we will see that you and your precious children are all right. I have already arranged to pay off the overdraft, and for a sum of money to be paid into your new account every month. The house is yours, and you have no worries about finding the money for a mortgage. I think you will be able to manage, and if you have any worries, Jean and I are here to help you."

What could she say? Such generosity went beyond the usual expressions of gratitude. She had not meant to weep. Up to this moment she had managed to keep tears at bay. Now she found them gushing out of her eyes, and she buried her face in her father-in-law's shoulder to hide them.

He patted her shoulder. "I am ashamed of my son," he said, "bitterly ashamed."

"He is not well." She offered this excuse to palliate the grief of Tony's saddened parents. She knew it was not enough, and she hoped that her two sons would make up for their loss.

Chapter Twenty-Nine

Kitty worried about Rex. When he came to see her, not so frequently these days, she felt he had changed and she could not reach him. Since that desperate look he had given her on the occasion of his wedding, he had not spoken of his marriage. When he did mention Elspeth it was with a sort of fierce loyalty, as if challenging his mother not to express adverse views about his wife. Of course, she had no intention of doing so, although she admitted to herself that she disliked her. She thought he must know that.

Elspeth had a special way with Kitty, displaying animation and interest in what had become a very sedentary life for the elderly lady. It was the sort of 'What have we been up to today?' approach which Kitty found patronising. Elspeth's smile irritated her too; a wide toothy smile, which Kitty decided was completely false.

She told Faith, who came as often as she could, that she thought Rex had become stolidly complacent.

"Neither particularly happy nor unhappy," she said. Faith was always eager to listen when she talked about her son.

To Rex she said, "You have put on weight."

He, who had always looked so spare and young, was beginning to look middle-aged and almost portly.

He did not reply, and she went on to ask, "Have you completely given up writing?"

"I do not think I can improve on *Summer Storm*," was his explanation.

The play was a classic and would never be forgotten. And his wife did not attend the first night, Kitty thought resentfully.

She decided she would not shorten his visit by reproaches. Time with him was too precious to spoil with controversial comments.

He was standing with his back to her, looking out of the window on to the stretch of lawn at the rear of the house.

"What's that?" he said suddenly.

"What?" She started to get out of her chair, a difficult manoeuvre these days, to join him and see what had caught his attention. She clung to the chair, and edged her way to his side. He made no move to help her, and for that she was grateful. However, she was glad to clutch his arm as they stood together.

"That," he said. "It looks like a ball."

"That's what it is," she told him, "a football."

"Why is it there?" he wanted to know.

"It's Ben's," she said, "Faith's elder boy. He was playing with it when they came over last week. When they left they forgot to take it with them."

She thought she felt a convulsive movement in the arm she was holding, almost like a shudder.

"You see a lot of them?" he asked.

"Not as much as I would like, but it's a long journey for them. I like to see Ben and Giles as often as I can."

"You have never mentioned it," he said.

"Well, I wasn't sure how you would react. I do my best to be tactful, you know, darling, but at the same time I am anxious not to lose touch with Faith and the children. It's hard for her being on her own, now that Tony has gone."

He had been told about Tony, and he was deeply sorry.

"You must remember," his mother was saying, "those two little boys are my great-grandchildren."

"I had not forgotten," he said.

Suddenly, she felt enormous pity for him. What sort of life did he have, she wondered, stuck in that enormous house, crammed with Codlington treasures, and only that silly woman for company? When she had met Lord Codlington at the wedding she had thought him a very stupid man, and the feckless son was even sillier than the father. They were not Rex's sort of people.

She pressed the arm she was holding. "I know it's hard," she said.

She knew at once that she should not have uttered those words. She sensed his withdrawal, and gently she was helped back into her chair.

"I must be off, Mother," he said.

She found herself pleading, "Please, do not leave it so long . . ."

"I won't," he promised.

As it happened, he returned within a few weeks. Daisy had become ill and needed care. She had cancer and would not live long. Rex arranged for two nurses to live in the house, one to look after his mother and the other to tend to Daisy. They were two young New Zealand girls, both healthy strapping young women and, in no time, the best of friends. They were so cheerful, so overflowing with life and vigour, he felt their laughter and jokes alleviated the sadness such a situation must engender.

Faith visited her mother as much as she could. One of the nurses was always happy to entertain the boys.

"Is Gran going to die?" asked Ben, and Faith, always truthful with her sons, said, "Yes, she is going to die, but we have to be brave about it. Everyone dies sooner or later."

She sat by her mother's bedside, and held the wasted hand. There had been a time when Daisy would have rejected such intimacy, but those days had gone, and Daisy and Faith were very close now.

"Where are Ben and Giles?" Daisy was fretful.

"They are with the girls. They will be with you very

soon." The boys came and stood by the bed, side by side, lost for words. They were terrified by the presence of death. Faith wanted to protect them, but there was no way; they had to face up to the reality. It was a hard lesson for them to learn. They had faced up to the absence of a father with equanimity, despite all Faith's fears. This was different: someone they had known all their life was about to leave them.

One day Daisy indicated to Faith that she wished her to lean forward so that she could hear what she was saying. Her voice had become very weak. "Rex thinks your father was a bad man. He wasn't. He did it all for me."

"I know," said Faith. "I loved Dad, remember?"

"Rex says . . . " The voice trailed off.

"It doesn't matter what Rex says," said Faith. "He is out of our lives now."

"And a good thing too," said Daisy, showing the last vestige of spirit she had in her.

She died soon afterwards, and arrangements had to be made for Kitty. The two nurses left, their duties fulfilled. Rex took over, put the house on the market, and organised his mother's move to a retirement home. She was given a spacious room looking over a beautifully manicured garden. She was allowed to furnish it with her own favourite pieces. "I won't last long here," she said gloomily. It had been a wrench leaving her old home, the home she had shared with John for so many years.

"Nonsense," said Rex, trying to hide the anguish he was feeling, "you will probably outlive me."

"Please God I won't do that," she said.

Elspeth came to see her. "Isn't this absolutely great?" she said. She was doing her best, but unfortunately the poor woman could not get it right.

"It will have to do," said Kitty, hating her.

* * *

During the years when she was bringing up her sons on her own Faith was contented. The allowance from Robert Agnew was credited to her account every month; she could rely on it and she was grateful. False pride could not enter into such a situation; she had two children to feed and clothe and that was her priority.

The little house in Cypriot Terrace was a haven of love. "I love you, Mum," called out Giles before he left for school. "Goodnight, I love you," they shouted to each other from their respective bedrooms before they went to sleep.

Faith worried about their lack of a father figure. Robert Agnew took them to Wimbledon once a year, but that was about all he could manage from a distance. Faith kept a photograph of Tony in the sitting-room, so that his image would be fixed in their minds. It was a theatrical study, and very flattering. Faith looked at it and tried to reconcile it with her last memory of him, a puzzled young man trying to deal with a houseful of women and wailing infants.

It was Ben who suggested the photograph should go.

"What is the point of it, Mum?" he asked. "Me and Giles can't remember him at all."

She felt it was a terrible deprivation. "Surely you must miss not having a father?"

Ben was eminently practical. "You can't miss something you have never known."

Faith removed the photograph and put it in the loft with all the other discarded family items; it joined the broken cricket bats, too memorable to throw away, and the car seats and baby bath which Faith was keeping for her grandchildren.

Despite the lack of a father the boys made remarkable progress. They did well at primary school, they smoked one cigarette each and then quit, they were not interested in drugs, and they felt responsible for their mother.

Ben moved to the comprehensive school, and then Faith's worries began. It was a vast concrete building in a very rough area. For an eleven-year-old, brought up in a gentle environment where no voices were raised, no blows were struck in violence, it was a cruel enlightenment.

Faith knew that he was unhappy. He did not burden her with his problems, but she knew of their existence. Giles would follow his brother in a year's time. He did not possess the stoical character of Ben; he was much more sensitive, vulnerable. His mother wondered how he would fare at that school.

For most of her life, she thought, she had depended

on charity from other people. First it was Rex paying for her time at drama school, then Robert Agnew taking on the burden of keeping the family afloat. She knew that if she mentioned it to Kitty she would agree at once to pay for the boys' private education. She would do anything for Ben and Giles. But Faith did not want to ask her; she decided she would find the money herself. She had trained to be an actress, and she would return to the stage. She did not like the idea of being parted from her sons for any length of time – after all, they were the pivots of her existence – but she thought it would not harm Ben and Giles to go to boarding-school when they were thirteen. Perhaps that would not work either, but it was a chance she would have to take. Seeing her elder child's increasingly worried expression made her even more determined to do something about it.

Muriel was sympathetic; her Sean had gone to that school and she did not like the way it had changed him. Sean was causing his mother a great deal of worry. "If I had the money I'd take him away tomorrow," she said. "You go ahead and do what you can, and good luck to you I say."

Faith had the drive, but the good luck was missing. She got in touch with the person who had once acted as her agent, and she was welcomed back by him with the exaggerated delight adopted by many stage people. Finding her a part? No problem. He remembered how good she was in the last role she played.

The trouble was that other people had forgotten, and it was a long time ago. She waited, day after day, for a telephone call that never came. She thought of her first job, which Rex had given her, and how thrilled she had been. Charity again! There was no one to turn to now, and her agent's voice betrayed signs of exasperation when she telephoned, over and over again, to see if he had found anything suitable for her. In the meantime, time was running out: Giles would be starting his new school in a few months' time.

One morning when she was tidying Ben's bedroom, picking up discarded clothes and dirty socks from the floor, pulling up the duvet on the bed, and thinking, as usual, that she had brought them up badly because, left to their own devices, they would live happily in the midst of a squalid muddle, her thoughts were interrupted by the sound of the front door bell. It made a melodic little noise, which she had always meant to change but had never got round to doing.

She ran downstairs and opened the door.

A man stood on the step, holding in each hand a bottle of milk.

"I'm your new milkman," he said.

It was Tony.

Faith was so taken aback by the sight of him that she could not utter a word.

"May I come in?" he asked.

She nodded, and he followed her into the house. She managed to take the bottles of milk away from him and stowed them in the fridge. She indicated for him to sit down, and they sat at the kitchen table, opposite each other.

At last she found her voice. "This is such a surprise. How are you?"

"I'm good," he said, and, it was true, he looked good. Not aged at all, and as handsome as ever. She felt he could not possibly think the same about her: no make-up, tousled hair and the old clothes she wore for doing the housework. Then she reminded herself that this was the man who had left his wife and children – it did not matter what she looked like.

"Would you like something?" she asked politely. "Coffee?"

"No, thank you."

"What are you doing now?" She felt she had to keep the conversation going somehow. "Not delivering milk, I take it?"

He laughed. "No, I still get the odd small parts. I'm fairly busy and, in between, I work at Harrods. They'll always take me back in the mens' clothing department. I'm very good at persuading Japanese gentlemen to buy outrageously expensive suits."

"I never go to Harrods," she said. "It's too expensive for me." Then she regretted the words, for they sounded as if she was pleading poverty, trying to make him feel guilty.

"How are the boys?" he asked. "I'd love to see some photos."

She got up and went into the little dining-room where one wall was covered with shelves for books. This was the room where the boys did their prep in the evening. She reached up and took down the latest photograph album. There were albums dating back to their infancy, childhood memories of birthday parties and special occasions. Surely he would not want to see these as well? She settled for the latest, and carried it in the kitchen. He pored over it, making exclamations from time to time.

"Ben looks exactly like you!"

"Yes," she said generously, "but Giles is like you."

"I hope he is a better person than me." She thought how easy it was for him to make that sort of remark. She was not convinced of its sincerity. It was inevitable that he should say, 'How I would love to see them!'

"That's up to them, isn't it?" she said. "I don't know how they would feel about it. Of course, I suppose you have every right to see them, they are your children after all."

"I would never demand that right," he said. "As you say, it's up to them. I realise they probably think I'm a bastard, and I could not blame them for thinking that."

"They don't know you," said Faith, "so how could they form an opinion about your character?"

"It sounds as if you have not painted too black a picture of me," said Tony, "and that is because you are such a nice person."

A nice person, thought Faith bitterly. At the end of

the day that is what I am, a nice person.

"Why did you leave?" she asked. "Had you fallen in love with someone else?"

"Yes," he said awkwardly, "that is just what happened."

She wondered if it was the woman who had telephoned her just before the birth of Giles.

"Are you still with this person?" she asked.

"No, I'm not. I've moved on to someone else."

"Do you want a divorce?" asked Faith. "Is that the reason you have come today?"

He looked at her sharply. "Do you?" he asked, parrying her question with another.

"No."

"Well, I don't either. I suggest we leave things as they are."

He left then, giving her a card with the address and telephone number of his club in London. "You can always write to me there, or leave a message," he said.

* * *

That evening, she told Ben and Giles about their father's visit. They looked at each other, saying nothing. She guessed that when they were alone together they would discuss it at length.

She said cautiously, "He wants to see you both. How do you feel about that?"

Giles spoke first. "I don't want to see him," he said.

"Ben?"

Ben thought for a moment. "We're all right as we are,

always have been. Why change things now?" Usually such a carefree child, he looked as if he was on the verge of breaking down. "I don't need this," he said angrily. "I have enough on my plate without this."

Faith felt overwhelmingly sorry for him, and sorry for herself because there seemed no way she could help him.

She wrote to Tony at his club. *'I'm sorry Ben and Giles are not keen to meet you at the present time. When they get older they will probably change their minds.'*

She hoped fervently that Tony would not press the matter, and she was relieved when she did not hear from him.

CHAPTER THIRTY

Rex and Elspeth were sitting in the sun on the terrace. Elspeth was half asleep, lying on a long wicker chair. Rex was hidden behind a newspaper. Before them stretched the garden, tended by two gardeners and immaculate. Somewhere to the right of them was a swimming-pool, discreetly hidden by a high hedge. The swimming-pool was built at Elspeth's instructions for her husband's benefit. She thought it was not in keeping with the rest of the property, but it was an indulgence she had allowed because she knew that Rex liked to swim every day during the summer months.

A man appeared, a servant.

"What is it, Fletcher?" asked Elspeth dreamily.

"A young woman to see Mr Patterson, Madam. Mrs Agnew."

There was an imperceptible movement of the newspaper.

Elspeth sat up. "Why, that must be the daughter of your mother's housekeeper. The one who aspired to be an actress? What can she be doing here, Rex?"

"I have no idea."

"Where have you put her, Fletcher?"

"In the drawing-room, Madam."

"Oh, heavens," cried Elspeth. She turned to her husband who had lowered his newspaper. "Is that safe? Perhaps she will take something."

It was at that precise moment that Rex Patterson joined his mother in disliking his wife. Or perhaps it was the moment he came to his senses, emerged from the torpor that had afflicted him for years. For the first time in over a decade he experienced a heightened emotion, and it was fury.

"I'll deal with her," said Elspeth.

"No, she has come to see me," he said, trying to keep his voice steady.

"Oh, darling, it is such a bore for you . . ."

But he was already treading his way along the creaky wooden floorboards to the drawing-room, down a long corridor and across a vast hall. He hurried his steps because he thought his wife might be following him. What was he going to say to Faith when he saw her again after all these years? The conventional words of greeting were on his lips, "What a surprise! What brings you here?"

She had been waiting for a while, and had filled in the time examining the objects in the room. There were some beautiful things to look at, and the pictures on the walls were interesting too. The room was very perfect, and unlived-in. No children to play havoc with its perfection, she thought. She turned round when she heard Rex enter the room.

He looked at her closely. Of course, as he had expected, she was older. There were fine lines around her eyes that had not been there before. But she had kept her lithe figure, and the blue eyes and the thin black eyebrows were what he remembered most about her, because they reminded him of his sister, Mary.

He found he could not utter the words he had planned.

Her voice betrayed her nervousness when she said, "I expect you will think it is an awful cheek coming like this, but I am thinking of returning to the stage. So far, I have not had any success, and I wondered if you had any ideas."

She thought the words sounded very trite and she regretted the 'awful cheek' bit as soon as she said it. It sounded so ridiculously outdated and even her schoolboy sons would not use such an expression.

"I have nothing to do with the theatre any more," he said stiffly, and then, more gently, "I'm sorry."

She stood in the middle of the elegant room, looking alone and vulnerable.

"I should not have come," she said, sounding utterly dejected.

He stepped towards her, and his arms encircled her. He gave a great sigh. "I made a mistake," he said brokenly. "We should not have separated in that cruel way. It was my fault, I see that now. We should have been more gentle with each other."

"Rex," she said, "your wife? She may come in at any moment?"

"Yes," he said, "I think, knowing her, she will not leave me for very long. We have to think carefully what to do." He stepped away from her, as if he could think more clearly when she was not too close to him. "Will you come to the house in Peacock Mews?"

"You still have that little house?" she said wonderingly.

"I did not have the heart to get rid of it." He urged, "Tomorrow?"

"So soon?"

"It is not soon enough."

"I'll come," she said.

"I'll be there all day waiting for you."

At that moment Elspeth entered. She bestowed her glittering smile on Faith. "What a surprise! What brings you here?"

"I am thinking of going on the stage again," said Faith, "and I wondered if Rex could give me some advice."

Elspeth looked at her husband. "He's rather lost touch with the theatre, haven't you, darling?"

"That's exactly what I told her," said Rex.

* * *

Faith told Rex about Tony's visit. "I could not have been more astonished," she said. "After all these years he turns up on the doorstep. First him, and then you, reappearing in my life. It is as if the past is coming back to me, full circle."

"What did he want?"

"I think he wanted to see the boys, but they are adamant that they don't want to see him. I thought he left me because domesticity and fatherhood became too much for him, but from what he told me it seems as if he had fallen in love with someone else."

"Did you suspect at the time?"

She told him about the telephone call she had received shortly before the birth of Giles. "I asked him about it, and he admitted at once that he had been having an affair with one of the cast. He maintained it meant nothing. I remember he said that he could not believe I had not been unfaithful some time during our marriage. I replied, truthfully, that I had not but, when I thought about it later, I decided I had lied. On every day of our marriage I had thought of someone else, and that is like being unfaithful, isn't it?"

"Oh, my darling," said Rex. He buried his face in her soft neck. They were at the little house in Peacock Mews, which had become their home. Rex found a pretext for coming to London whenever he could, as he had done that momentous day when Faith came to see him. They were completely happy and their love for each other had not been altered by the years spent apart.

Rex might have found himself in a very difficult

position as he was incapable of sharing his love between two women. He was fortunate in that Elspeth had not been concerned about sex for some time now and it was at her suggestion, a few months previously, that they had moved into separate bedrooms. They got on well, there was no animosity between them and they were genuinely fond of each other, but they led separate lives. She hunted during the winter and was busy all day long. He hardly ever saw her. When they met up for dinner in the evening, he listened politely while she told him of all the projects in which she was involved. The present one was a protest about building a housing estate on the outskirts of the village.

"Jack Hatherway is up in arms about it," she said. "The houses will adjoin his land."

"All five hundred acres?" said Rex dryly. "Surely, it will not affect him greatly?"

"He thinks it will," she replied with dignity. "We have lengthy discussions on the subject."

He could imagine that. Sir John Hatherway was the most long-winded old bore he had ever met. "I don't envy you," he said.

To Faith he commented, "Neither of us has made a successful marriage."

She replied, "And we are both entirely to blame. The people we chose hadn't a chance in hell of real happiness."

It was a sobering thought and Rex, the eternal worrier, was anxious about the outcome of their being together again. He was convinced someone would find out and turn nasty. In his view, the only good thing that had resulted from their separation was the fact that Faith had two sons. He had done the right thing in that respect. She could never have any more children. After Giles was born she had decided she did not want to risk having another child with Tony. He was too unpredictable and money was short. She had made sure it would not happen. She could not have foretold that he would leave her; she had anticipated them stumbling along together for the rest of their lives.

Rex and Faith went to see Kitty, and she was overjoyed to see them together. She was now in a wheelchair and resigned to the fact that she would never walk again. The carers in the home were fond of her, and treated her with great kindness. "I am getting so old," she said, "it's ridiculous." But her brain was as sharp as ever, and Rex was glad in more ways than one. He imagined a less acute old lady might have regaled one of the nurses with a very strange story.

He liked Faith's boys. Mary's grandsons. It was hard to believe except that Ben looked so like her. Rex could see a likeness to his sister in Faith, but his memory of Mary was of a sixteen-year-old girl, and Faith was a mature woman. This boy, on the other hand, was uncanny proof of the relationship. His brother, Giles, was slight like his father, as Rex remembered Tony, the only time he had seen him, on the stage for the final production at the Victoria Academy of Dramatic Art.

Faith had shelved her idea of going back on the stage to try and make money for their education. Rex would not hear of it.

He told his mother that it was his intention to send both boys to his old school, Gills. Kitty persuaded Faith that it was a right and proper thing for him to do. "If not for your sake, for Mary's sake," she said tactfully.

Rex wanted to make other changes in Faith's life. He did not like the idea of her receiving an allowance from Robert Agnew. He recognised that it had been necessary, but now he wished for it to stop. "You belong to me now, " he said. "I will look after you."

"Supposing Elspeth found out?" said Faith practically. "She would not be pleased, and no one could blame her."

"Elspeth has no idea what I do with my money and she is not interested. Because it has never been a problem for either of us, we never discuss finances. She need never know that I pay for the boys' education, and I hope she will never find out that you and I are together again. I did not think I would ever be party to such a deception, but I am far too happy to change it."

Faith knew that the Agnews would be relieved to be freed of the burden of the monthly payments. He was retired, and had lost a great deal of money invested in Lloyds. They had sold their lovely house in Malvern and moved into a flat, and it was there that Faith went to see them.

They greeted her with real love and affection, two loyal people who had stood by her and her children during many years. They had never let her down. They knew that someone was paying for the boys' education, but tactfully they did not ask questions. They guessed it must be Kitty Patterson.

When they were alone, Faith took Robert's hand in her own. "There is no need for you to pay me any more money," she said. "I have met someone who cares for me."

"I am so glad," said the old man. "You deserve some happiness, my dear. I hope Tony is not standing in your way of getting married."

"Not at all," she said. "That is out of the question."

Later, when Jean had joined them again, she asked them if they ever heard from Tony. She had never mentioned his visit to her.

"No," said Robert, his mouth a thin straight line, "and I think it's better that way."

Faith looked at Jean, and wondered if she felt the same as her husband. As a mother, she thought it must be very hard to lose touch with a much-loved son. When she left them, she embraced them both and thanked them, once again, for all they had done for her over the years.

"You and the boys will still come and see us?" said Jean anxiously.

"Of course."

"And will you be living in the same house, in

Cypriot Terrace?"

"I'm afraid so," said Faith, laughing. "I think I'll be living there for the rest of my life."

Ben went to Gills, and a year later his brother, Giles, joined him there. Contrary to Faith's fear they both did well there, and were happy. They were grateful to Rex for making it happen.

'Dear Rex,' wrote Ben.

'I was so pleased to see you at the match. I wish we could have made it worth your while by having a win, but perhaps next time. Mother always insists she enjoys watching cricket, but I don't think she understands it completely. It was nice having someone like you there who appreciates the finer points of the game. Looking forward to seeing you both soon.

With love, Ben.

During the summer holidays they went abroad with their mother. Rex would never accompany them. He thought travelling with Faith and her two sons would be fodder for the gossip columns, and also he did not know how his wife would react. There was an understanding between them; they gave each other space, but Rex was suspicious. He felt that her family watched every move he made, and any false step would put him in the wrong with them. He reflected that they ought to be grateful to him because when Elspeth's brother had been convicted for drug offences Rex had helped out the pathetic fellow. His father-in-law had never thanked him for his part in the wretched business. On the contrary he sensed he resented him for it.

Rex was given a knighthood for his services to the theatre. Ordinarily, he would have been pleased to receive such an honour, but it brought with it a public awareness and that alarmed him. His name and a photograph appeared in a newspaper, something that caused displeasure to a man who was obsessed with the press, always believing they were in the wings ready to pounce. He hoped that Elspeth would get satisfaction from going to the Palace with him, but she seemed strangely unimpressed. Secretly, he shared her lacklustre attitude to the whole event, which meant nothing to him if he could not share it with Faith.

Faith was lovingly tolerant, but she thought Rex worried too much. Over and over again he asked her if she had told anyone about her relationship with the Patterson family.

"No, darling, not a soul."

"Not even Tony, when you were first married to him?"

"No, not even Tony. He was the last person I would have told."

One day she told him that she wished she could tell the boys. "I think I owe it to them to tell them about their roots."

Rex was horrified. "Please, please," he implored her, "do not tell them. They will marry and tell their wives." Sometimes he despaired that the secret would be kept. He could not understand Faith's complacency about something he considered to be a shadow on their contentment.

"Don't you ever feel guilty about what we are doing?" he asked her. "Every time we make love we commit an offence."

"I love you too much to worry about that," she replied, "and no, I do not feel guilty. Our love is so sure and strong I can't conceive of there being anything immoral about it. Put all those thoughts away from you, Rex darling, and be as happy as I am."

He assured her of his happiness; every moment he shared with her was a joy to him. He decided she was right and resolved to try and forget his fears.

* * *

They were in the habit of taking Ben and Giles out to an eating-place near the school. All the parents and their sons congregated there.

Ben told them, "I am studying a play for English Literature."

"Not *Summer Storm*, I trust?" said Rex.

"No, *Juno and the Paycock* by Sean O'Casey."

"A wonderful play," said Rex. "I remember so well the first time I saw it. I was mesmerised. Beautiful language and drama fused together in a magical way. The man was a genius."

"Rather spoilt for students who have to remember an explanation for every word he wrote," said Ben.

"I agree," said Rex. "In *Summer Storm* I had someone

say, 'I felt so elated it was like soaring into a blue sky'. The note at the back of the students' copy said, 'RP is referring to his time in the RAF.' Absolute nonsense! I just wrote the words, and hoped they would get by. I had no thought of my time in the RAF when I was too scared to feel elated."

Faith looked at him, and saw that he was relaxed and happy. If only he could be like that all the time. She felt a tremendous feeling of well-being and pride for her two wonderful sons and the man she loved. She was blessed, and she could not imagine anything would spoil her contentment.

"Do you think you will write another play?" Giles asked Rex.

"I don't think so."

"Why don't you write your memoirs?" This was Ben speaking.

"God forbid," said Rex, looking at their mother. "It's the last thing I want to do."

CHAPTER THIRTY-ONE

'Dear Rex,' wrote Ben during his last year at medical school, *'there is something I would like to talk to you about. Is there any chance of our meeting in London? I will be there on Wednesday and can meet you any place you suggest and at any time.*

With love, Ben.'

Rex replied at once saying that he would be delighted to take him out to lunch at a restaurant they had often been to before. Of course Rex arrived first and sat at the table he had booked in advance, wondering why he had been summoned. He had not mentioned to Faith that Ben had asked to see him. In his usual way, he thought the worst. The boy had got some girl pregnant and did not know what to do, or he had got himself hopelessly in debt.

When he spied him coming through the swing doors of the restaurant Rex felt guilty for having had such thoughts. Ben had such an open cheerful countenance, and was so absurdly like his mother, both in character and looks, it was impossible to think anything bad of him.

It was obvious that the menu was more important to him than the news he had to impart, and Rex waited patiently while he chose. Ben was enjoying himself; he knew that the cost of the meal would not worry Rex, so he could have what he wanted.

"Well?" said Rex at last, after the order had been given to the waiter, and they both had a pint of beer in front of them.

"You know Mother writes to Tony from time to time giving him news of us."

"No, I did not know that," said Rex, noting that Ben did not refer to Tony Agnew as 'Dad', and reflecting that it was sad that he never had. "It is a kind thing for her to do, and exactly like her."

"She writes to him care of his club, and someone there sends the letters on to him. He never replies. She does not write often, only to report momentous events in our lives, leaving school, Giles getting into university, that sort of thing.

"Last week I was walking along a street in London I did not know, when I looked up and found myself staring at the name of Tony's club. It was written over the front door. I know that most of the members are in the theatrical profession. I do not know whether it was impulse or curiosity that made me decide to walk in, but that's what I did. The big hall was dark and gloomy, and there seemed no one about except two chaps behind the desk. I asked the older of the two if he had seen Tony Agnew, and he told me that he did not think Tony had been in the club for about two years. He called out to his colleague, 'Have you seen Mr Agnew lately?' and the man replied, 'Not for ages.'

You know how frustrating it is when you are prevented from doing something, even if it something you were not particularly keen on doing in the first place? That's how I felt." He paused while the waiter put a plateful of food in front of him. "My God! Lovely. Look at that."

"Don't let it stop you from telling your story," said Rex. He was interested.

"I asked the man if he had Tony's address, and he looked into a book and said, 'Yes, I do have an address for him.'

" 'Please will you give it to me?' I said.

"Then he told me that he was very sorry but it was the club's policy not to give out addresses, so I had to accept that and leave."

A pause for eating ensued. "This is *so* delicious."

After a few moments Ben took up the story again. "I decided to go to the theatre where I knew there was a play showing in which I thought Tony had a small part. I asked the man at the stage door if he was there, and he said, 'He's not in the play any more, son. Someone else has his part.'

" 'Do you happen to know his address?' I asked.

" 'No, I don't,' he said. It looked as though I would

have to forget the whole thing. It was early evening and the cast were arriving for the last performance. 'Here's someone who will be able to help you,' said the man suddenly, and he stopped a girl who was about to enter the theatre.

" 'Who wants to know?' she asked.

"I explained I was his son.

" 'Really?' she said. 'You don't look like him. I can give you his address.'

"I fished a piece of paper and a pen from my pocket, and she put the paper against the wall and wrote on it. 'There you are, darling,' she said, handing it to me. 'Give him my love when you see him. Sandra is the name. He'll know who it is.'

" 'I will,' I said. 'Thank you very much.'

"I took a bus to the address which was in a terribly rundown part of London. It was a flat in one of those high-rise buildings. The walls were covered in graffiti, and I walked along a covered way looking at the numbers, until I found the right one. Some people were standing in their doorways watching me closely as I went past. I had been for an interview that afternoon and I was wearing a suit and a tie. I wished I had been dressed more casually – I felt I stuck out like a sore thumb. It was all so eerie; I began to wonder if I was safe. Someone could have sprung out at me, and I would not have had a chance."

"And we would not have known where you were," said Rex. "Stop talking now. And eat up." He sat and watched Ben tucking in, and thought how different he was to his brother. Giles would have left that situation as soon as it showed signs of becoming difficult.

"It was a great relief, I can tell you, when I found the right number on the door. I rang the bell, and a young man opened the door. He had one of those joke aprons around his waist – you know, the one with a naked girl and big boobs, and he was carrying a saucepan in his hand.

" 'My name is Ben Agnew,' I said. 'Is my father here?'

" 'Of course,' he said, 'he'll be thrilled to see you.'

"I followed him into a dingy sitting-room, and there was Tony lying on a sofa. I recognised him at once from the photograph Mum had before we told her to get rid of it.

" 'Ben,' he said, jumping to his feet. 'I can't believe it is really you.' He seemed genuinely pleased to see me. Cans of beer were opened and I was invited to stay and have supper with them.

" 'There's plenty to eat, isn't there, Boris?' he asked. He did introduce me, but I can't remember the full name, only Boris.

" 'Yes, plenty,' said Boris.

" 'We must kill the fatted calf for the prodigal son,' said Tony. I wanted to remind him that it was he who had been prodigal for so many years, but the atmosphere was so friendly I did not want to spoil it. Besides, you know how awful I am about food - I can never resist a free meal."

Rex was amused to see that he looked embarrassed when he said that, and a blush came to his cheek. So like his mother, it did Rex good to be in his company.

"Boris disappeared into the kitchen to cook the meal. 'He's a marvellous cook,' said Tony.

"Up to that moment I thought they were two actors sharing a flat, all they could afford, then, something in Tony's voice when he said he was a marvellous cook, a sort possessive pride, made me wonder about their relationship.

"I thought I should come right out with my thoughts. 'Is it what I think it is?' I asked.

" 'Yes,' said Tony, 'we have been together for years. We met on tour. I suppose I should have told you. I'm sorry.'

" 'Does my mother know?'

" 'No, I have not told her. I thought she would not understand. For the same reason I have not told my parents either.'

"So, that was that," said Ben. "It's a funny feeling discovering your father is gay. I stayed long enough to eat the meal Boris had prepared, and I must say it was delicious. The flat was filthy though. Even I noticed it, and you know I'm not fussy. I decided I did not want to make another visit. The conversation flowed quite easily, mostly about the theatre and their reminiscences. They were like an old married couple. It was weird. I left early. I wasn't keen on making my exit from that block of flats, especially at night, but Boris accompanied me to the street outside. 'It's not safe in this building because the lighting is so poor,' he said. 'We are always complaining about it.'"

"Boris," said Rex thoughtfully, "it is such a masculine name."

"Tony looked fairly macho," said Ben, "but old Boris was your archetypal stage fairy. It would not surprise me to learn he had once been in the chorus."

"So, you are wondering whether you should keep this information to yourself, or tell your mother and Giles. Is that what is bothering you?"

"A bit," replied Ben. "You see, I don't think Mother will mind too much. She'll be astonished because we have always regarded Tony as a womaniser. But Giles, that is another matter, I think he'll be really upset about it."

"He must be told," said Rex firmly, "or he will find out some other way." He was always so certain it was impossible to keep a secret forever. "I'll tell your mother, and you tell Giles. How does that sound to you?"

Ben dug his fork into a mound of toffee pudding. "I suppose you would not tell them both? I have an awful lot on at the moment. I'd be so grateful . . ."

* * *

As Ben had said she would be, Faith was astonished. "I never thought of such a thing," she said, "but, of course, it explains so much. He's right about the Agnews – Robert would be heartbroken if he knew."

"Surely they are heartbroken already, never hearing from him?"

"Jean is, I know, and I'm sure she would welcome him back, but Robert would never tolerate it. I've heard him air his views on homosexuals – he'd rather his son was a serial killer than that."

She agreed with Ben that Giles would be upset. "He must be told though," she said. "My poor darling, the things you have to do for my family."

So Rex wrote to Giles and suggested they meet for lunch at the same restaurant. The two brothers had one thing in common, a big appetite. When the slight handsome Giles had finished a gargantuan first course, Rex gently broke the news about his father. As his brother had predicted he was devastated, and Rex wondered if he was going to break down in tears.

"It's disgusting," said Giles.

"It's very common in the theatre," said Rex. "People these days usually have a sympathetic view of it."

"Not if it happens to be your own father involved," said Giles bitterly.

"Ben did not seem too worried," said Rex kindly. "He had supper with them both, and accepted the situation. Do you think it would help if you went to see them?"

"It would make me sick. I have never seen Tony, and I never want to see him. He is a complete waste of time. I know he is my father, and I have to accept that unpalatable truth."

"I'm sorry you are unhappy," said Rex. He could not bear to see one of Faith's boys, his boys, so distressed.

"The only thing that would make me happy at the moment," said Giles, "is if you told me we are both adopted. I suppose that is not the case?"

"No," said Rex.

"You have been so good to us. And Mum, I wondered . . ."

"No," said Rex sadly.

CHAPTER THIRTY-TWO

One morning after he had breakfasted on coffee, toast and marmalade, Rex was neatly opening his post with a silver paperknife when he glanced up and saw that his wife, sitting opposite him, was in tears.

Alarmed, he said, "What is the matter?" He wondered what could possibly have made Elspeth weep. A very unusual occurrence. A mortal illness, the death of her brother, profligate but beloved or, more likely, the death of her father, now very old and no longer just stupid but senile with it, all these possibilities went through his mind as he stared at her, the paperknife in his hand.

"You must tell me what is wrong," he said gently.

"It is so dreadful, I don't know how to say it," she said.

"Please try."

"I want a divorce."

Later, much later, when he was telling Faith about the incident, he said, "She was distraught about what would happen, how I would manage without her."

Although both of them could see there was a humorous side to the situation, neither of them felt inclined to laugh about it.

"She wants to marry Jack Hatherway. They have been trying to quash a plan to build houses near his estate. He is a widower with an estate as big as hers, and lonely, I suppose, as no doubt she was. They have been in each other's company constantly during the last few months, but I thought it was just deciding the latest offensive against the planners. I had not the slightest inkling what was going on between them."

"What will happen about the house?"

"God knows, but it is not my responsibility. I live in it, but it is all Elspeth's. Two vast houses and all that acreage, how she and Jack will cope with such encumbrances I do not know, but it is their worry, not mine. I have no regrets about the house. I can see that it's very magnificent, but I have never liked it. The only thing that I shall miss is the swimming-pool."

He looked around at the miniscule accommodation in his house in Peacock Mews. "I much prefer this," he said.

He gave her a wry smile. "I wish Elspeth all the happiness in the world. I think, darling, that this is going to be one of those rare events that crop up from time to time, an amicable divorce. Neither of us has a grudge to bear, and we are both well-off enough not to have to squabble about money."

Faith was silent, thinking about what had happened. She had always known that Rex would never leave Elspeth. He felt guilty about marrying her when he had not been totally committed to her happiness. He was prepared to exist in a meaningless marriage rather than behave dishonourably towards her. Now, Elspeth had taken on that part, and he was free.

"People will feel sorry for you," said Faith.

"I know," he replied, "and please don't think I feel good about it."

He went to see his mother to tell her that he and Elspeth were parting. Kitty was now ninety years old. He found her, as he knew he would, sitting in her chair by the window, looking out on to the garden. Faith had given her a wooden bird table, which the odd-job man at the home had placed so that she could see it from the vantage of her chair. It was an inspired gift because Kitty got endless pleasure watching the birds, and one of her kind carers replenished the table every day with scraps of bread and bacon rinds, and kept the little plastic sacks full of grain for the tits. One day a small dog wandered into the garden and that was an exciting diversion, and something to talk about when she was trundled into the dining-room to share lunch with the other residents. She did not complain. She noticed that the people who were always grumbling did not get such good attention. It paid to be nice, and she found it easy.

When she saw Rex she held up her veined old hand

and he took it in his own. He told her that he and Elspeth were getting a divorce because of her wish to marry Sir John Hatherway.

Kitty became quite animated. "I can't say I'm sorry," she told him. "She was not the right person for you. Not from the beginning. Now, dear Rex, you and Faith . . . "

"Mother," he sounded a warning note. "You know that's impossible."

She replied in a quiet voice. "Of course I know. It is just that I am getting old and sometimes I forget."

"You have not told anyone . . . ?"

"No," she replied impatiently. "I may be an old woman, but I still have my wits about me, thank God. Really, Rex, you worry too much."

Mostly Rex and Faith visited her on separate days. They agreed to do this because it spread out the visits. Sometimes the boys went to see her, and that delighted her. She still thought of them as boys, although they were young men now and Giles, the younger, told her that he was going to get married.

"Morag," he said. "Her parents live in Edinburgh."

"Are you having a big wedding?" asked Kitty.

He flushed. "No," he said, "I'm afraid I put my foot down. We are just getting married, and that's it." It was so like him to come to that decision, thought Kitty; he was shy and sensitive. She thought he was far too young to get married, and Faith and Rex were inclined to agree with her. Rex could not help wondering if Giles was making a statement to himself and to his father.

They were married quietly in Edinburgh, not even the parents were present. Perhaps it was not what the bride had dreamed of for her wedding day, but she accepted it because she loved Giles and it was what he wanted. He had made sure that there was no possibility of Tony having to be invited.

It was a different matter when Ben married. By this time a doctor, he married a doctor and they wanted to invite everyone they knew to share their big day. An invitation was sent to Tony and Boris, but there was no response.

"You are coming," said Rex to his mother. The card stood in pride of place on her mantelpiece.

"Oh, do you think I can manage it?" she said. "In this wretched wheelchair won't I be an awful nuisance?"

"No, you will not," said Rex decidedly, "you cannot think of disappointing Ben and Caroline. Don't worry, everything will be arranged. You don't have to worry about a thing."

"I'll ask Faith to get me something to wear, and perhaps a new hat." She was very excited.

After the wedding Faith said, "Well, that's that. No more children to look after. They are on their own from now on."

Rex said, "I did not see the mother of the bride shed one tear. Is that customary?"

"I might have wept if I did not like the person he is marrying," replied Faith, "but Caroline is everything I desire in a daughter-in-law." She added hurriedly, "And the same applies to Morag. I am a very lucky woman. How could I shed a tear on such a happy day?"

Kitty thought it a happy day as well. She sat in her wheelchair and many people gathered around to talk to her. Faith had chosen a blue dress for her, the same colour as her eyes, and she looked beautiful. And Rex had devised something to make the day special for her. He had nudged the elderly Harris out of his retirement, and it was he who collected Kitty from the home, and delivered her back there after the reception was over. Two old people, whose day was made perfect by their reunion, Kitty sat in front with Harris, the wheelchair stowed in the boot. They chatted happily throughout the journey back about the old days, the Air Vice-Marshall (God bless him) and the years living in the house in Harrogate. They even touched upon Mary, but Harris was tactful here, just saying what a wonderful girl she had been. It would have been easy for Kitty, after so much champagne and conviviality, to tell her old friend what had happened. She did not, because he was a servant and because it would be a betrayal of Rex. She and Harris clasped hands and she returned to her room at the home. She had enjoyed every minute of her day, and could turn her thoughts to it whenever she pleased. It was good to have something to think about in the days ahead.

* * *

Faith received a letter, written in an unformed childish hand. It said:

'Dear Mrs Agnew,

Tony, your husband, is ill. Please will you come and see him.'

It was signed Boris Jenkins. A strange mixture of names, Faith thought; they did not seem to go together. On the top of the letter was an address.

She decided not to tell Rex for the time being. She never kept anything from him, but she thought he would dissuade her from going. She took her car and, surprisingly, had no difficulty in finding a space to park it outside the high-rise building. Like Ben, she walked along the covered way, peering at the numbers on the doors.

The young man who answered the bell was tall and fair, and very thin.

"Mrs Agnew?" he said. "Tony will be pleased to see you."

He led the way to the little sitting-room. "I'll leave you two together," he said.

Tony was lying on a sofa. The floor was covered with newspapers, dirty coffee cups and even a plate with dried-up food on it. He did not get up, but said, "I'm sorry about the mess. I didn't know you were coming."

"Boris wrote to me to tell me you are ill," she said. He was wearing a woollen cap on his head, so she surmised he must have lost his hair. That could only mean one thing in her judgement: he had cancer. She was shocked by his appearance. She found it hard to believe that anyone could change so much. The old debonair Tony had completely disappeared; he was painfully thin, and she could see the points of his knees underneath his trousers. His skin was flaky as if he had been sunburnt and was peeling, but his complexion was sallow and there was an unsightly lesion on the side of his face.

"You must be very run-down," she said.

"Yes," he answered, "run-down in every department of my body."

Staring at the sore on his cheek, something stirred in her memory, the remembrance of an article she had read or a film she had seen. "You have AIDS," she said. It was a statement, not a question.

"I'm afraid you're right," he said.

"Excuse me," she got to her feet and ran into the little hall. There was a door opposite, which she rightly guessed was a bathroom, and she went in and locked the door. She wanted to be sick but, strangely, the unclean state of the lavatory deterred her from this basic function. She turned away and held on to the side of a washbasin and retched. Then she wiped her streaming eyes, and splashed cold water on her face.

She found Boris in the kitchen.

"Are you all right?" he asked anxiously. All the rooms in the flat were so small and adjoining each other, he must have heard her, and anyway could see from her face, drained of colour, that she was not well.

"I'd like a glass of water," she said.

He held a glass under the cold-water tap, and then handed it to her.

"Thank you very much."

After she had drunk some of the water she began to feel better, and she said, "Have you been tested, Boris?"

"It's nice of you to think of me, Mrs Agnew. Yes, I have, and I'm glad to say it was negative."

She handed the glass back to him. "Please call me Faith," she said.

"Will you stay for a while?" he asked. "Have a cup of tea, or something?"

"No, I won't stay. I'll just pop in and say good-bye to Tony."

Tony was apologetic. "I'm afraid I have upset you. You are not alone in having feelings of repugnance. Most people do."

"It is not that," said Faith. "It was a shock, that's all. I'm very sorry this has happened to you."

"I'm very lucky to have Boris to look after me. He is not easily repulsed."

Faith said, "He tells me he is not infected. Please keep it that way."

Tony looked at her sharply. "I am not a complete monster, you know. I care deeply for Boris, and I am just so sorry that I was as unfaithful to him as I was to you."

"I'd like to go now," said Faith.

"Thank you for coming," said Tony casually. "Boris insisted on writing to you. I didn't think it was a good idea."

"I am very grateful to him."

"He will take you out of the building," said Tony.

"There's no need . . . "

"Oh, yes, we always escort our guests to the road. There are a lot of very strange people living in this block. It's safer with two people than with one, especially if that one happens to be female."

When Faith and Boris reached her car she found that a back window had been smashed and the radio removed.

"I should have warned you not to come in a car," he said.

The broken glass was collected in the well at the back of the car. She got into the driving seat. "It's perfectly all right for me to drive home," she said. She couldn't wait to get away from the place. "I'll telephone the police when I get back."

Boris was about to say that this was a waste of time, but he refrained. He lifted his hand in a gesture of farewell. In her mirror she could see his forlorn figure standing on the pavement, watching her drive away.

Chapter Thirty-Three

When Faith reached 13 Cypriot Terrace she ran into the house, and started running a bath. The house was too old-fashioned to have a shower, and she had never bothered to have one installed. There was something very comforting about a hot bath, and she washed her hair and scrubbed her nails in a frantic effort to get all the grimy unpleasantness of the afternoon rinsed away. Then she changed into clean clothes, right down to her underwear.

She decided she would go and see Rex and tell him what had happened, but before that she telephoned the police and gave them all the details, registration number and where the car was parked. Then she telephoned the garage and arranged to take the car the following day to be repaired and have a new radio fitted.

She let herself into the little house in Peacock Mews; she had her own key. The first thing that struck her anew was how clean and tidy it was, a complete contrast to the house she had left a few hours earlier.

Rex employed a woman who cleaned for him twice a week and, as the place was so small, she was able to keep it immaculate. He was a kind and considerate employer, and his cleaning lady thought the world of him. The pieces of furniture he treasured were polished until they gleamed. The silver always shone.

Rex got up from the desk where he was sitting, and embraced her. He was always touchingly pleased to see her. She pressed her face against his chest and took a great gulp of him, he smelled so clean. She remembered going to his house, Elspeth's house, after an absence of so many years, and how he had taken her in his arms. She had smelled then the fresh clean smell of him, and it was like coming home.

As she had expected he was horrified by what she had to tell him. The idea of the filthy house was an anathema to him. Also, as she had expected, he was compassionate about Tony.

"What can we do to help?"

"I have decided," she told him, "I'm going to go back."

"My God, no!"

"I can help, Rex." She had a picture in her mind of the lonely figure of Boris standing on the pavement watching her departing car. "When Boris wrote to me it was a *cri de coeur.* He was appealing for my help. How can he manage on his own?"

"Darling," said Rex patiently, "there are people who deal with a situation like this. You do not owe anything to this man. You are not a nurse, how can you help?"

"For a start I can clean the place," said Faith. "I think if I do that, I will feel better about it."

"It's in a terrible district – it is not safe for you. Look what happened to your car, on the one visit you made there."

"In future I shall go on the bus," she said. She tried to explain to him how she felt. "I was horrified when I realised what was wrong with him, but I know it is wrong to feel that way. I am beginning to see very plainly how wrong it is. It is Tony who has landed himself in this tragic predicament and I can't just abandon him."

"He abandoned you," said Rex dryly.

"I promise," she said, "that when things get too difficult I will hand everything over to people who know how to deal with such cases. In the meantime, though, I think I can be of help."

He offered to take her there in his car and pick her up when she was ready to come home.

"No, darling," she said, laughing, "that is such a bad idea! If they stole a radio out of my little runabout what would they do to your beautiful car?"

* * *

Boris looked astonished to see her when he opened the door, particularly astonished because she was holding a plastic bucket and mop which she had purchased at an ironmonger's shop near the building.

"What are you doing here?" demanded Tony from the sofa.

"I think Boris needs help looking after you," said Faith, "so I am offering my services. You are in charge of the cooking, Boris, and I will see that the place is kept clean. Is that a deal?"

"We can manage," said Tony.

"It's a deal," said Boris. He went on to tell her that two policemen had called that morning. "They operate in pairs in this area. They came about your car."

"What did they say?"

"The usual," said Boris. "They will never catch the thieves who stole your radio. Contact your insurance was their advice."

During the next few days Faith cleaned the flat from top to bottom. She scrubbed the floor, shampooed the dingy carpets and poured buckets of disinfectant down the lavatory. She carried loads of dirty sheets, curtains and covers to the launderette down the road; the flat did not have a washing machine. Boris accompanied her on all these journeys; he would not allow her to go anywhere alone. She was glad to be able to reassure Rex of this fact. They got into a routine; she arrived in the early afternoon and stayed until about six o'clock. As it was winter it was dark at that time, and Boris walked with her to the bus stop. He had a job, stacking shelves in a supermarket during the night; he went there at nine in the evening, returning at six in the morning. Tony was in bed, and usually asleep, by the time he left the flat.

Faith did the shopping on the way and Boris gave her the money for it out of his wages. Laboriously, he wrote out a shopping list for her to use on the following day. He was very anxious that Tony should have a healthy diet.

Tony spent most of his day lying on the sofa watching television. He did not read, as he said his eyesight had deteriorated; whether this was anything to do with his illness she did not know. A doctor called to see him quite frequently, and a district nurse twice a week. One day Faith followed the doctor out into the covered way, where they could not be heard. He indicated that he was not prepared to discuss his patient with a strange woman.

"I am his wife," said Faith.

The man looked embarrassed, and she could guess what he was going to say next. "We have been separated for nearly thirty years," she said, "and I have not slept with him since that time." What a relief it was to be able to say that. Supposing Tony had not left them when he did? What sort of existence would they have had then? Perhaps he had done the one decent thing in his life when he decided to desert his family.

The doctor told her that Tony's prognosis was very poor. In his view he did not have long to live. Faith decided she would not tell Boris what the doctor had said. It was true that Tony seemed to be declining rapidly. She and Boris decided they would hire a wheelchair, and they were able to take him for short walks. Mostly he sat with his chin on his chest, not looking at anything around him. He seemed to have lost interest, to have given up on life. Faith noticed an emptiness in his eyes which had not been there before. He did not grumble any more about her presence in the flat; he seemed to take it for granted that she would be there every day. He ate tiny portions of the food Boris cooked for him, and he swallowed his pills when they gave them to him.

Faith had been going to the flat most days for about two months when Tony developed pneumonia. She arrived one afternoon to find an ambulance parked outside the block of flats. People were standing about, curious to know what was going on. Tony was carried out on a stretcher, a red blanket covering his poor emaciated body.

Someone from one of the adjoining flats said to Faith, "Poor lad. He's in a bad way."

She was amazed by the kindness of the neighbours; they were always enquiring about him, sometimes even leaving titbits for him to eat. "I know he lost his appetite, but he might like this..." They knew what was wrong with him, but they were not shocked, just sympathetic. "Poor bugger," Faith heard a man say, "he's copped it this time."

Faith thought, and perhaps Boris did too, that Tony would not return from the hospital. She prayed that he would not return, that the nightmare would be over.

Miraculously, he made some sort of recovery, and he was brought back. He was accompanied by an oxygen cylinder, which followed him from the bedroom to his seat on the sofa, and attached to it was a mask which he put over his nose and mouth to enable him to breathe more easily. The idea was that he should put on the mask when he was in distress, and take it off for talking and eating, but it was hard to separate Tony from the mask: it was his lifeline. Because of the bulky oxygen cylinder, and his dependence on it, there were no more walks.

To try and inject some life in him Faith and Boris organised a party. She bought a big bunch of flowers and she arranged them in a vase she found in a cupboard. Boris made cheese straws and concocted tasty morsels on squares of toast. "You are a marvel," said Faith admiringly. "You should be in the catering business." He glowed with pleasure at such praise.

The party was a good idea, as Tony seemed to summon up a reserve of energy which enabled him to enjoy it. Boris had made a list of people to invite and this included old friends from the stage as well as loyal neighbours. The little room was crowded with chattering people, mingling well together. Faith heard Boris explaining, "Faith came and tidied us up. I was never any good at the housework. She's been like a mum to me." It was the biggest accolade he could give her. All were distressed, but all had the ability to hide their real feelings. It was a good send-off for Tony.

There came an evening when Faith and Boris detected a change. He had not eaten anything all day, just taking sips of water. He was now permanently in his bed, his place on the sofa abandoned. It seemed as if he had slipped into a comatose state.

"Don't leave me," said Boris pleadingly.

"I won't," said Faith.

"I think I'll ring the supermarket and say I'm not coming in tonight," he suggested.

"Yes, you do that," said Faith, "and ring the doctor at the same time."

They sat at either side of his bed, each of them holding a skeletal hand. At one point Faith tried to remove the mask from his face, but he showed his agitation by waving his hands, so she put it back again. When she did that he gave a great sigh of contentment. They noticed a change in his breathing, a slight rattle in his throat, then silence. Faith had always been suspicious about claims in the death columns about dying peacefully. Now she knew they were probably true – Tony had died peacefully. Despite a traumatic illness he had slipped quietly away with no signs of distress.

"I think he's gone," she said. She removed the mask, and this time there were no protestations.

Boris sobbed convulsively. Faith held him close and tried to comfort him. The doctor arrived and confirmed that Tony was dead.

"So that's that," said Faith to Rex. "Now we have to face the funeral."

The funeral at Golders Green was attended by a handful of people, mostly in the acting profession. If they had not been to the party they would not have known about Tony's illness and they would not have been there. Ben came with his mother and Boris and, surprisingly, Giles who had travelled down from Scotland to attend.

Faith had telephoned the Agnews the night their son died. She had asked Tony to let her get in touch with his parents, but he would not allow it. She hoped they would understand she had to respect his wishes. She looked across the room and saw them sitting together, not speaking, mouths pursed. She felt unspeakably sorry for them, especially Jean, looking so much older.

Faith wondered whether Boris would break down during the service which was short and impersonal. He did not; perhaps his former stage life made him appreciate the theatricality of the whole event. He watched, fascinated, as the coffin glided away through the velvet curtains.

They emerged into the spring sunshine. There was a knot of people waiting to take their place. Tony's friends stood about chatting and squinting in the glaring light or wandering between the avenues of flowers. They looked at the cards, but very few were for Tony. Lovely flowers, thought Faith, wilting and dying of thirst in the sunlight. Why should they die as well? She vowed she would never send flowers to a funeral.

She and the boys walked over to talk to the Agnews.

"Hello, Grandma, hello, Granddad," chorused Ben and Giles dutifully, kissing their cheeks. An awkward desultory conversation ensued, and to break it up Faith said, "Have you met Boris?"

He was standing alone, a few feet away from them.

Robert Agnew's mouth set in a hard line. "No, we have not," he said.

Faith looked at him. "Have compassion," she said.

He ignored the plea, but his wife seemed to think for a moment, and then said, "I'll have a quick word."

Faith watched her make her way to Boris's side, introducing herself as Tony's mother. When it was time to leave she noticed that Jean and Boris were still in animated conversation. What could they be talking about? She hovered around them to say good-bye. Boris smiled at her, "Mrs Agnew has been telling me about Tony when he was a little boy. Magic."

In the car park Ben got into the driving seat of his mother's car, and his brother sat in the back. Faith slipped in beside Ben. Eyes blinded by tears, she struggled with the seatbelt.

"Mother . . ." said Ben, concerned.

His sympathy was too much for her to bear, and she sobbed uncontrollably. Giles leaned forward and put his hand on her shoulder.

At last she was able to speak. "It was just so sad," she said, "that funny funeral. All those stage people talking about Tony. One woman told me she couldn't understand how we had not known about him years ago. Apparently it was common knowledge in the theatre world. And the Agnews turning up, just to look down their noses it seemed, although dear Jean changed her tune in the end. One can't help feeling sorry for Robert; people like him don't begin to understand Boris and the like."

"I feel ashamed," said Giles, "because I have been as bad as Granddad. I have behaved very insensitively. After all, I was Tony's son."

"Oh, no, darling," said Faith, "your behaviour was very understandable. It was Tony who was to blame for everything, not keeping in touch, not bothering about his children. Just because he is dead we can't forgive him that easily."

She blew her nose and recovered her composure. Ben started the car. "Where do you want to go," he asked her, "Cypriot Terrace or Peacock Mews?" Giles was staying overnight with him and Caroline before returning to Scotland on the following day.

"I think I'll go to Peacock Mews," she said. As she had expected, Rex was not there, and she remembered that he had gone to get his hair cut. She noticed there was a message on the answerphone and she pressed play. 'Sir Rex, will you ring the Home as soon as possible, please?' said a disembodied voice.

Faith wondered what it could mean; they never rang. Kitty had a telephone in her room, so she could telephone them if she needed anything or just wanted to have a chat. She debated whether to ring the number, but then decided against it. She sat in a chair and stared at the inanimate machine until she heard Rex's key in the lock of the front door.

She told him about the message at once. He did not bother to remove his overcoat but dialled the number straight away. He looked worried. He stood, listening to the voice at the other end, and then he put out his hand for Faith to take it in hers. He put down the receiver. "Died in her sleep," he said quietly, "early this afternoon."

Chapter Thirty-Four

They said all the usual things to each other, a wonderful way to go, an old lady who had a long life (she was ninety-two), she would have wanted it that way, but words were no comfort when it came to real grief. Rex, Faith, Ben and Giles clung to each other in their disbelief and feelings of loss. It was unrealistic , but they had begun to think she would be there for ever, sitting in her chair by the window, her head rising sharply when she saw them, her dear face crinkling into a smile of love and welcome. It was hard to take that she had been taken away from them.

Giles did not return to Edinburgh. He stayed in London for another funeral, and his wife travelled from Scotland to be with him. Caroline and Morag were sorry as well, they had grown to love Kitty, and Caroline was pregnant with her first great-great-grand-child whom she would now never see.

Rex received a telephone call from the family solicitor. "I know this is a bad time, but can you come and see me in my office?"

He knew it would be concerning his mother's will. He did not know the contents; Kitty had never discussed them with him.

"I suppose I shall have to go," he said to Faith.

The old man had the will on the desk in front of him when Rex was ushered into his office.

"Your mother left several bequests," he said, "to Ruby Banks, to Albert Harris and to three of the carers at the retirement home where she spent the last years of her life.

"She left sums of money to various charities; I need not mention them all. Then she left the sum of one hundred thousand pounds to Ben Agnew and a further one hundred thousand pounds to Giles Agnew. She writes *'I leave to my son, Rex Patterson, whom I love more than anyone in the world, the contents of my room.'* Presumably this means the contents of her room at the retirement home."

"Yes," said Rex, "when she moved there she was allowed to take with her favourite pieces of furniture. A chair, a desk, that sort of thing."

The solicitor continued. "The rest of her estate, and it is a considerable amount of money, goes to Faith Agnew. Her jewellery to be divided between Faith Agnew, Caroline Agnew and Morag Agnew." He looked over his half-moon spectacles at Rex, and said, "Are you happy about this?"

"If you are inferring that my mother was not in

sound mind when she made that will, you could not be more wrong," said Rex. "She knew exactly what she was doing."

"I had to ask the question, that is all. Sometimes old people do not realise how well off they are. Your mother inherited from her parents, her husband inherited from his; there is a considerable amount of money involved here, even after death duties are paid."

Rex knew exactly what was going through the man's mind: all this is to go to the daughter of a housekeeper. It did not make sense.

He took a deep breath. "My mother did not leave me money because she knew that I have enough for my needs. More than enough. As far as I am concerned, I am perfectly happy with her decision. One of the things she has left me is a Sheraton rosewood writing table, an object of considerable beauty I have always admired. It was in constant use, and I can visualise her sitting at it. It is all I ever wanted."

"There is nothing more to be said, then. You have answered my question."

Rex said, "Is there some way we can keep the will private? I would not like the press to make something of it."

"I'm afraid not. If they are interested they can easily find out. Wills are in the public domain and there is no secret attached to them. Let us hope they will not be interested, although with your name it is always a danger."

"The name does not mean as much as it used to," said Rex shortly.

"I would not say that. Hasn't one of your plays been recently revived in London? I heard it was a great success. My son and his wife went to see it, and they raved about it. No, I do not think the name of Rex Patterson has been forgotten at all."

When Faith was told about her legacy she was flabbergasted. It was the last thing she had expected. Her sons were ecstatic. Both of them could think of ways the sum of one hundred thousand pounds could alter their lives.

"It will make all the difference," said Ben, an underpaid junior registrar, about to become a father. "Good old Kitty."

Sadly, so many of Kitty's friends had died before her. Rex, on impulse, wrote to the Beechings. He found their address, but had no idea whether they were still alive. He found out that they were, but only just; a letter from a daughter informed him that her parents were both beyond taking in the news of Kitty's death. Thank God my mother never became like that, he thought. The people in the church attending her funeral were mostly of the next generation and the generation after that. Harris was there in his best suit. Several members of the staff at the retirement home were present. Faith thought it must be part of their job, attending the funerals of their patients. Many of Rex's theatrical friends came out of respect for him. Ben and Giles read the lessons, and Faith felt a surge of pride when they spoke so loudly and clearly, never faltering. She had been blessed with the most wonderful sons.

She knew that Rex felt it deeply, and she longed to protect him from grief. That was impossible, but when Ben came across a paragraph in one of the more popular newspapers he was normally unlikely to read, she hoped she would protect him from that intrusion into their privacy. The item was written by a group of journalists who wrote under the name of 'Spider'. It was a predatory menacing name, and many reputations had been destroyed in their web. It was gossip, but of the most scurrilous nature. Rex would have heard of Spider, but would never lower himself to read the column.

'An old lady called Mrs Kathleen Patterson died a few weeks ago at the age of ninety-two. She was the mother of Sir Rex Patterson the playwright. She was possessed of a considerable fortune and she left the bulk of it to Faith Agnew, the daughter of Daisy Foster who was employed as housekeeper to Mrs Patterson for many years. Faith Agnew's two sons came in for their share as well: they were left one hundred thousand pounds apiece. Sir Rex inherited a few bits of furniture from his mother. One could be forgiven for feeling puzzled about an old lady's last wishes, and for hearing, perhaps, the faint rattle of a skeleton in the Patterson family cupboard.'

"What does it mean?" said Ben, bewildered.

"They are suspicious because I have been left so much money," said his mother.

"She left it to you because she loved you," said Ben. "Surely, it is as simple as that."

"Not quite, darling, there is another reason as well."

"What reason?"

So she told him. Sitting opposite him at the kitchen table at 13 Cypriot Terrace, she told him the whole story, every detail, about the air raid and her father going into the bombed house in Addison Road and finding a baby, shielded from certain death by the bodies of its parents. She told him, as Daisy had told her, making out that George was more of a saint than a sinner. She could not explain how he had managed to get her a birth certificate; that must remain a mystery forever. Rex had always maintained that he bribed someone in the registrar's office, but Faith could not believe that of her father. She told her son that Daisy had felt an overpowering sense of guilt; she thought the child's grandmother should be given the chance of seeing her, getting to know her. Daisy achieved her dearest wish by moving to the house in Harrogate, to be near Kitty.

"Rex and I were going to be married," she told Ben, "but of course that was impossible when we found out the truth. I wanted to live with him, but he would not hear of it. You know how obstinate he can be. He walked out of my life. I married Tony and, years later, when Tony was no longer around, I turned to Rex once more. He has always lived in terror of the press getting the story. It would be meat and drink to them, there is no doubt about that. I think it has become an obsession with him. At the beginning he was more concerned with himself and his reputation as a well-known figure in the public eye, now he thinks only of me and you two boys, how it would affect us if it became known."

"That's unlikely, isn't it?" commented Ben. "Something that happened all those years ago – nothing could ever be proved." He paused. "Why didn't you tell us, Mother? Surely, we had a right to know."

"Of course, darling, you had every right," replied Faith, "but Rex did not want me to tell you. He thought you would tell your wives, and somehow the secret would be out." She added hastily, "I want you to tell Caroline, and Morag must know as well. There must be no secrets from wives."

"And Giles, Giles does not know anything of this. Who is to tell him?"

"Would you do that, Ben darling?"

"Yes, I will." He wondered what his brother's reaction would be. He was unpredictable. Ben did not want his mother to be more upset than she already was.

"In a way I can understand how Rex feels," he said thoughtfully, "and it explains something that has always puzzled me: why you two don't live together."

"I hoped after his divorce from Elspeth came through, that we would, " said Faith sadly, "but soon I realised that nothing was further from his mind. The fear never goes away, and that is why it is so important that he does not see this newspaper cutting. It would destroy him. Fortunately it is not a paper he ever reads."

But when she went to Peacock Mews she found that Rex had already seen the paragraph relating to Kitty's will. "It was sent to me by my solicitor," he said. "He knew I would be interested."

"It's speculation," said Faith. "They know nothing."

"It's the thin edge of the wedge," he said. "They are scavengers, these people, they search for meat among old bones. How did they get their information? Daisy's name for example – nothing is beyond them when they are on a trail."

His air of deep gloom made her task even harder, but she knew there was no escape.

She took a deep breath. "I have something to tell you," she said.

"Oh, dear, when I hear those words I fear the worst."

"I'm afraid you may think this the worst," she said. "It is that I have told Ben everything about us. I have told him the whole story, from the moment my father stepped into the house in Addison Road."

There was a little silence, and he looked at her with a sorrowful expression. "What made you do that, after so many years?"

"I was sitting in church at Kitty's funeral, thinking about it. I felt it right that the boys should know she was a blood relation of theirs. I think she wanted it too. By leaving all her money in our direction she was ensuring that they would have to know the truth. Of course they will understand the importance of keeping such a thing to themselves. In my view, it is a justifiable risk."

"Don't you think you could have spoken to me, before you spoke to Ben?"

"I knew what your answer would be. You would say that they will tell their wives, and their wives will tell their friends, and so on."

"And you don't think that is likely?" asked Rex. "Especially after that newspaper reference to a skeleton in the cupboard."

Faith was on the defensive. "The newspaper item made me even more determined they should know. We must face up to this thing as a family."

There was an edge to his voice when he said, "I'm afraid you have not the least idea what it would be like if the truth were known. I have lain awake at night thinking of the questions that would be asked, the innuendos made about our relationship. A relationship that would be frowned upon in every aspect of society." He gave a little shudder. "It would be intolerable. Our lives would not be worth living."

"It has worried you so much that your life has been affected by it already," she said, "and it has been the same with me. Sometimes I can understand how criminals who get away with a crime go the police, years later, and confess to it. A secret is a terrible burden."

"It is better to have the burden of secrecy than to have your private life laid bare in the national press."

She sensed that he was trying hard to keep his temper. He had never spoken harshly to her in all the years they had known each other, and she felt cold with fear. Her action had made him like this.

He went on speaking in a voice that was strange to her. "We have committed no crime, my dear. The crime was committed years ago – we just have to pay for it."

"Don't compare my father to a common criminal!" she shouted. "I loved him!" She started putting her arms into the sleeves of her jacket.

"Where are you going?" he asked.

"I am going to my home in Cypriot Terrace. And, by the way, that is something else I have to tell you. I intend to sell it. It is a soulless house, and I never liked it."

"Isn't that rather a rash decision?" he asked. "What are you going to do? Buy another house?"

She was already at the door, ready to leave. "Well, I can't come and live here," she said. "That *would* give you cause for anxiety."

He did not move from his chair, and she let herself out by the front door. When she reached home she was weeping once again. She thought that during the last few weeks she had cried more than during her whole life. She wept for her father whose integrity was being questioned, she wept for Kitty whom she had loved and she wept for Tony whom she had not loved, enough. She wept out of loneliness and despair. She looked at her tear-stained face in the mirror, and thought, perhaps I am having a breakdown. She hoped that Rex would telephone her, but he did not.

He did not telephone her the next day either, and by that time she was feeling frightened and a little defiant. She went to see Ben.

"I'm being a nuisance," she said. "Mothers-in-law should keep their distance."

"Not this mother-in-law," said Caroline. "We love to see you." She made an excuse to leave mother and son together.

First of all, Ben told her that he had spoken to Giles and told him everything.

"How did he take it?"

"He was surprised, of course, but grateful to you for deciding to tell us. He said he was sorry there was no time to see you before he and Morag went back to Scotland. He told me to tell you he loves you very much."

Faith felt the tears starting to flood her eyes.

"Mother!"

"I have wept a river," she said. "I can't stop. I don't know what to do about it."

"There must be a reason."

"The main reason is Rex," she said. She told him of

their conversation the previous evening. "He was so angry with me, Ben. I have never seen him like that before, and it shocked me. What future have we together? Living in separate establishments, always looking over our shoulders? I love him so much; I have loved him since I first saw him when I was a little girl. I know I will never love another man. If only we could just be happy together, free of all these complications."

There was a danger that she might start crying again, and Ben noticed at once. "I'm just going to go and get you a drink. I think you need one, and I will join you."

"What about Caroline?"

"She'll come in later."

He came back with the drinks. He sat down opposite her. "If I were your doctor, I'd say you need a holiday. You have been through a lot lately: Tony's illness, Kitty dying and now this. How long is it since you went away?"

"Rex…" she began.

"No, not with Rex. On your own, and with a project in mind to make it interesting." He took her hand. "Listen carefully, Mother, for I have a plan."

Chapter Thirty-Five

Ben Agnew and his wife, Caroline, were in the kitchen of their little house in Shepherd's Bush. They had bought the house when they got married with the help of Caroline's parents and Rex. Ben was cooking pasta bake which was what he did best, and Caroline was sitting at the wooden table sipping an apple juice. From time to time, Ben was slurping red wine from a glass standing on the surface near the stove. He was harassed; cooking had that effect on him. He was using a lot of saucepans and kitchen utensils, and his wife knew that it would be her task to clear up after him.

Caroline was in a state of blissful discomfort. The hand that did not hold the apple juice rested on top of her enormous stomach. The rest of her, slim as ever, had learned to cope with the additional burden, although the strain caused the backache that had been troubling her during these last few days of waiting. Hence her husband's offer to cook the evening meal. They were both in a state of high excitement about the imminent arrival of their first child. George Patterson

Agnew lay curled up in his warm spot, ready to emerge into a complex world. They were both sure it would be a boy; a girl would be equally welcome, but a surprise. George had been chosen as a first name because, by a happy chance, George was the name of Caroline's father.

There was the strident noise of the front door bell.

"Damn!" said Ben.

"I'll go," volunteered his wife, already heaving herself into an upright position.

"No, no," he said, "you stay where you are." He was determined to be considerate, helpful.

He opened the door, and there stood Rex. Rex, urbane and elegant as ever. Ben, dressed in old jeans and a moth-eaten jersey, felt at a loss. It was so out of character for Rex to arrive unexpectedly and, if they had known he was coming, he and Caroline would have made preparations for the visit. He was that sort of man.

"Rex!" he cried, hoping to sound welcoming. "Come in!"

Rex followed him into the sitting-room which was a shambles. Ben made inadequate efforts to tidy it, straightening the cushions and removing the newspapers strewn on the chairs. It was the weekend and they had not expected a visitor, least of all Rex. Ben noticed two dirty coffee cups on the floor, and he hastily removed them and put them on top of a book-case.

"Please sit down, " he said, indicating a chair which had nothing on it.

But Rex remained standing in order to say what he had come to say. "Has your mother left me?"

Ben was startled. "What a question, Rex. Of course she has not left you."

Rex sank into a chair, and it struck Ben, for the first time in his life, that he was quite an old man. Despite the immaculate suit and the handmade shoes there was a despondent almost down-at-heel look about him. His shoulders drooped, and the hand resting on the arm of the chair was frail.

Ben flew to the kitchen. "It's Rex," he whispered, "and he's in a bad way. Have we any whisky left?"

Caroline might have shrugged her shoulders and murmured, "Your family!" but, being Caroline, she did not, and instead rooted around in one of the kitchen cupboards until she found a bottle of supermarket whisky.

"I'll stay here," she said conspiratorially.

"Do you mind?" He was pouring whisky into the glasses, adding a dash of water, as he knew Rex liked it. "Just put that in the oven, will you?" He pointed to the uncooked pasta bake.

Back in the small sitting-room with Rex, sitting opposite each other with glasses in their hands, Ben could not help remembering he had done the same with his mother a few weeks earlier. It was then that they hatched their plan.

"Have your heard from Mother?" he asked.

"Not a word."

"We got a postcard." He leapt to his feet, and started looking for it on the mantelpiece which was as cluttered as the rest of the room. Behind scraps of paper, envelopes and another dirty coffee cup he found it at last.

He handed it over to Rex, who read, *'I am in Valencia, surely the most beautiful place in Spain. Today I am going on a boat trip. I hope Caroline is well. My love to you both, M.'* Rex handed the postcard back. "It doesn't say very much," he said.

"But it sounds as if she's happy," Ben insisted. "She wrote to you before she left?"

That had been part of the plan, that she would write to Rex and tell him she was going away. She had wanted to confront him with the plan, but Ben had dissuaded her. He said it was time she showed a bit of initiative for a change.

Rex brought out the letter. Ben was touched to see that it was crumpled as if it had been read many times over. The old man carried it around in his pocket, like a love letter, a talisman. He took his spectacles from his breast pocket and put them on the end of his nose. He read the letter aloud. " *'My darling, I am going away for a while. All that has happened lately has upset me, and my doctor son thinks I need a change of scene. I am sure he is right. I shall miss you terribly, but it will give us both a chance to decide what is best for our future.'* "

Ben had taken no part in the writing of the letter. "It doesn't seem like a letter from someone who is intending to walk out of your life," he said.

"What sort of life do we have together for her to walk away from?" He sounded bitter. "I have no right to want her to stay. And yet I do, I am completely miserable without her." He folded up the letter and returned it to his pocket.

"I have to confess I did urge my mother to go away," Ben told him. "She was very stressed, which I think you will agree is not like her."

"She could have suggested my going with her."

Ben reminded him gently, "You have never wanted to accompany us on holidays. You had your reasons, I understand now, but why should Mother, on her own, think you feel any differently?"

"No reason. That is what I mean. It is a very unsatisfactory arrangement."

"There is another decision Mother has taken, perhaps without your knowledge. She has put the house in Cypriot Terrace up for sale. I am in charge of that while she is away, and already there has been an offer."

"But why do that?" asked Rex querulously. "What will she do when it is sold? Buy another house?"

Ben began to feel exasperated with him. Was he completely blind? "That is her affair. You must admit it is not a house with much going for it, although it was adequate for us when we were children." He nearly added that now his mother had the money to do as she liked, but he could not believe that Rex had forgotten about the inheritance.

As if reading his thoughts, Rex said, "My mother saw to it that Faith could make changes if she wanted to. I fear that these changes may not involve me."

"I don't think you need feel so depressive about it," said Ben briskly.

"It is just that when we parted . . . " Rex began. He finished lamely, "It was all my fault."

"Rex," said Ben, "lighten up, for God's sake."

He could not believe he was uttering these words to the famous playwright. He was relieved to see that Rex did not seem at all put out by them. Rather, the words seem to pull him together. His face actually broke into a smile, and Rex's smile reflected the innate charm of the man.

"Thank you, Ben," he said. "I'm glad I came. You have done me a lot of good."

"And now I hope you will stay for supper. I have cooked the meal this evening in deference to my wife's increasing discomfort. I always cook for an army; I don't seem capable of catering for just Caroline and me. There is always masses of food left over."

"I don't think . . ." said Rex.

"Please help me out." He went to the door, opened it and called for Caroline. She had been sitting patiently at the table, sipping her apple juice and reading a paperback. She sat in the most comfortable position possible, legs splayed, the bump almost level with the tabletop. She got up heavily, and walked into the sitting-room. Rex rose to his feet.

"You look wonderful," he said. It was an involuntary remark and said with great sincerity. He felt tears prick his eyes. He always felt sentimental about a heavily pregnant woman. "Sit down, my dear," he said.

She lowered herself into a chair. "You are such a special person, Rex. Please stay."

He could not resist such an offer.

"Did you drive here?" asked Ben, throwing cutlery and tablemats on to the table in a haphazard manner.

"No, I came in a taxi."

"Then you can go home in a taxi," said Ben decidedly. "Which means that we can drink lots of wine, except for poor Caroline, of course."

"I think I'll have a glass of red wine," she said dreamily. "At this stage, George Patterson Agnew is ready for a party."

They explained about George Patterson Agnew, and Rex could not believe that his name had been included in the family thing. For the second time that evening his eyes filled with tears, a phenomenon not unnoticed by the future parents. He was thinking that it just proved how right Faith had been to tell her sons the truth, and how wrong he had been to doubt her wisdom. It was a perfect evening, only marred by her absence. When feeling distinctly mellow, he was pushed into a taxi, he had already resolved it was time he made changes too.

Ben felt he should accompany him back to Peacock Mews, but he did not want to leave Caroline alone.

"Don't you worry, son," said the cabby with a wink, "I'll see your dad gets home safely."

During the following days Rex looked carefully at his little mews house. It contained all his precious possessions. The comfortable leather chair he always sat in during the evening, paintings on the wall which had at some time appealed to him, and which he had purchased for large sums of money. His little study, the room where he had written most of his plays, adorned with pencil sketches which he had collected over the years. A study of a girl's head by Augustus John, a sad pencil sketch of Marie Antoinette on her way to the guillotine, worth almost the whole amount of one of his productions. There was no theatre memorabilia to be seen, no framed posters advertising his successes, no programmes, no autographed photographs of famous people in the acting profession. Hidden somewhere was the prestigious award he had received for his contribution to the theatre. The knighthood granted to him a year later had not affected his life in the slightest. He supposed Elspeth had been pleased, but she had readily abandoned it for a more permanent and less merited title, a baronetcy.

Now, he thought, he had to decide what to do with the furniture left to him by his mother. The superintendent of the home had kindly stored it in a shed until he was able to collect it. Kitty must have known he had no room for anything more. It was as if she too was sending him a message: it was time for a move. He thought of Kitty's desk, which had been in the family for as long as he could remember. He did not want to part with that.

Ben telephoned. They had been right; it was George Patterson Agnew after all. Everything had gone well. Rex felt a surge of pride at the thought of this much-wanted child. Surely Faith would return now?

He sat one evening watching a programme on the television. It was so trivial he wished he had the energy to turn it off. He felt indescribably lonely. That morning in the mirror in his bathroom he had seen an old man looking back at him. During his marriage with Elspeth he had put on weight (wryly, he remembered Kitty commenting on it) and then when he was reunited with Faith he had taken more exercise, led a happy fulfilled life, and consequently shed pounds. Now, since her absence, he seemed to have shrunk. The old objection, long since discarded, came back to disquiet him. He was too old for her. What right had he to hope that she still loved him?

He heard a little noise in the hall, the unmistakable noise of a key being turned in the lock. He knew there was only one person, besides himself, who had a key to the house. His hand reached for the remote control and he turned the sound down. He felt his heart begin to hammer in his chest.

She entered the room, looking tanned and healthy

and, he noticed with a pang, youthful.

He managed to say, "I thought you had gone for good."

She put her arms around him. "No chance of that," she said. And then, "I have something to tell you."

He sounded amused. "And what might that be?"

"It's not bad," she said. "In fact, it's very good. I have spent some of the money your mother left me, and I have bought a house. A house on a Spanish island, and I can't wait to show it to you."

PART THREE

Chapter Thirty-Six

"Why did you tell me this?" asked Christabel. "What made you, after years of secrecy, decide to tell me the whole story? You have only just met me, and yet you chose me to share this wonderful story, which belongs to you and Rex."

"Rex is gone," said Faith. "It is no longer important who knows it. Although, of course, I prefer it remains a secret, and I know that you will not shout it to the world. When you came to dine with us that evening, the night before Rex . . ." she paused as if the words were hard for her to say, "the night before Rex died, I thought you had a very sad expression. You looked defeated, as if you had resigned yourself to something inevitable. Bell had already told me the reason for it. I had no intention, then, of telling you about Rex and me, but I felt there was a similarity between the decision you have to make and the decision I made nine years ago."

"I'm afraid the decision is no longer up to me," said

Christabel sadly. "I forfeited the right to decide when I came here."

"Perhaps you are right," said Faith thoughtfully, "and I hope your Ambrose Silveridge has the nous to seek you out and take you home, but I would not count on it. Sometimes I think that men are slow to face reality. It needs a woman to give them a nudge. That old Lady Silveridge will not live forever, and then what will have been lost? You can't allow that to happen because of her silly out-dated attitude. Rex and I came near to losing each other, and my comfort now is that some strange twist of fate brought us together again. But I am talking theatrical nonsense when I say that. It was not chance that we found each other again. I went to see him that day, at Elspeth's house, with the pretext that I wanted his advice about getting back on the stage. The truth was I could not bear to face a whole life without seeing him again. I did not want to part him from Elspeth; I was not that bad. I just wanted to be with him again, even if it was for a few minutes. Which is what I am trying to say to you: happiness is worth fighting for."

"I understand," said Christabel.

"We had nine years here," said Faith. "Nine years! That is a big chunk of a life to be happy, and I am so grateful for those years."

"I did not realise that you had been here for that length of time," said Christabel.

"We came here in 1998, the year that Kitty died. Rex

had no reason to stay in England, but I did – I had my sons and, at that time one grandchild. Later there were more grandchildren, and I travelled to England twice a year to see them all. Rex had his little mews house, which he kept, and I stayed there while I was in London. I shall go there now until I decide what I am going to do next. I used to try and persuade him to come with me, but he would not hear of it. He preferred to stay here, anxiously awaiting my return. In the summer Ben and Giles and their wives and children came to stay here – it is the perfect place for a holiday when the children are small."

"Will you mind leaving this place?" Christabel asked.

"Of course, and I shall miss this tree most of all. It was the first thing Rex saw when I brought him here all those years ago. His mother had one in her garden in Harrogate, not as big or old as this one, of course. He liked sitting under it, for longer periods as he grew older. It was the best decision I ever made, buying this house. Rex fell in love with it as soon as he set eyes on it. The lovely garden you see around us now, he made it. It was his pride and joy. For years he had led a stultified existence, only made real by the presence of my sons and me. Suddenly, there was this beautiful garden to do with as he liked, and here there was peace of mind. The English newspapers are not bothered with people who live on the Isla de la Fuga. The inhabitants of the island accepted us, and did not ask questions. It is an inborn characteristic of theirs not to probe into other people's business. Remember the soldiers of Napoleon who escaped from Cabrera to come here? They knew what they were doing. The handful of their compatriots who managed to get back to France found a hostile welcome waiting for them. They had not been forgiven for being defeated by the Spaniards. The men who came to this island found contentment. They married and had children and became respected."

"Did Rex write anything while he was here?" Christabel asked.

"He wrote short stories and poetry. He refused to do anything about them; he said the world had had enough of Rex Patterson. But I managed to persuade him to agree to letting me give them to a publisher, should I outlive him. It is one of the things I shall do when I return to England."

"I hope I see you again," said Christabel, "but I have been thinking lately that I should go home. And you have convinced me it is the right thing to do. I have so enjoyed staying with dear Bell. Now I can visualise her in this beautiful place. You may be sure I will come again to the Isla de la Fuga."

"Sadly, I don't think I will," said Faith. "This lovely old house will belong to complete strangers, and I don't think I could bear that."

The big leaves of the Catalpa tree were darkening over their heads. The light was fading over the island. Although it was getting late it was still warm. In

England at that time of day, even in summer, the air would have become a little chilly; cardigans would be put on over flimsy clothes. Here, the balmy air enveloped them like a soft warm blanket. When they were not speaking, it was quiet, except for the sound of the little waves falling on that small stretch of silver sand.

"I suppose," said Christabel reluctantly, "I must return to Bell's house. She may wonder why I am so long."

"I know," said Faith. "Thank you for listening so patiently. It is amazing how much better I feel having told you, a sort of catharsis. I need not tell you that Bell knows nothing of what I have said to you tonight."

"And she will not hear it from me," said Christabel. She rose and Faith rose as well.

"Are you going into the house?"

"No, I am going to sit under this old tree for a while. I have a lot to think about, not all sad thoughts I assure you."

Christabel took her hand. "Thank you," she said fervently.

She walked slowly. It was so still. The air was filled with small sounds, rustlings and the scrunching of leaves beneath her feet; the island enveloped her with its warmth and tenderness. She felt as though she belonged there. Darkness was beginning to fall, but it was not a menacing darkness. Her feet trod confidently on the path leading to Bell's chalet.

"You were not worried, I hope?" she asked her.

"No, I knew you were with Faith, and I was just glad she had your company. I have put a glass of *jerez* and some olives on the terrace for you. I have already moved on to the red wine."

When Faith walked out on to the terrace she saw that there was a letter propped up against her sherry glass. "It arrived this afternoon," said Bell hopefully. "Francisco and Fernando have been here."

Christabel saw at once that handwriting on the envelope was that of her brother. "It's from Andrew," she said.

"Oh, that's lovely," said Bell, plainly disappointed. "I'll leave you to read it on your own." She went slowly into the house to prepare their supper.

Dear Chrissie,

I thought I should write and tell you what has been happening here. Yesterday Ambrose Silveridge arrived, quite unexpectedly. Of course this put Mother into a flutter. He had come for one reason only, to ask for your address. Father got on his high horse and said he would not give it to him. He said that you had not given him permission to do so, which sounded pretty high-handed to me. Then Brose said that you are engaged to be married to him and therefore he had a right to know. Father replied that he had not been told that the engagement was still on, therefore he had assumed it was off.

Mother offered him coffee (it was mid-morning), but he

refused. Then I chipped in and asked him if he would like to come to the nets for a few balls, and he accepted. We walked to the pavilion saying nothing. I could not think of anything to say to him, and he seemed depressed. I must say, he was pretty good, he bowled some good balls, and got me out, twice. He seemed a bit puffed, so we had a rest and sat on the bench outside the pavilion. Then I gave him your address. He was very grateful and wrote it down on the back of an envelope in his pocket. I like him, I think he is a good chap, and I hope all goes well from now on. Don't take any notice of Father, his ideas are from the Dark Ages.

With love,

Andrew.

PS It would not surprise me if he arrives before this does.

Christabel held the letter in her hand, and read one passage over and over again. *'Brose said you are engaged to be married to him, and therefore he had a right to know…'* The implication of those words filled her heart with hope and joy.

Bell returned with plates of food. "Well?"

Christabel said, "When is the next boat due from the mainland?"

"The day after tomorrow."

It seemed an eternity.

* * *

She stood on the jetty for half an hour before she saw the speck on the horizon which was Francisco's boat.

Her eyes ached from staring at the shimmering sea. Around her were excited people talking at the tops of their voices. The owner of the shop waiting for provisions, a local bride expecting the material for her wedding dress, many island inhabitants waiting for mail.

The boat came nearer. She could make out that someone was standing beside Francisco, a passenger. Near and nearer came the boat and taller and taller appeared the passenger. He dwarfed the other occupants of the boat. She felt as if her heart would burst.

When he jumped ashore she could not utter a word. He looked tired, dishevelled and she guessed at his frustration at having to wait at Colonia de Sant Jordi. She put her arms around him and laid her face against his chest. The top of her head reached to a spot below his chin.

He took her hand, and the ring sparkled in the bright sunlight. "We are still going to get married? Everything is the same as it was before?"

"Yes," she said.

"Thank God." He sounded tired but so relieved, as if a great burden had been taken from his mind. She felt like bursting into tears, not tears of grief, but of happiness. At that moment she made up her mind: she would make certain that neither of them would go through an ordeal like that again. She regretted with all her heart that she had put him in an impossible position. How could he be anything but loyal to his mother? In future she would have more understanding and she would do her utmost to protect him from further contention.

"Nothing must come between us," she assured him. "Your mother and I will just have to get used to each other, that's all."

He nodded. "Don't worry," he said, a positive note in his voice. "It will be all right. She will learn to love you, as I do. It is just a question of time."

PART FOUR

CHAPTER THIRTY-SEVEN

It was the usual Friday night gathering, but with a difference, the difference being that it was a celebration, the celebration in the year two thousand and thirty-five of her one-hundredth birthday.

It surprised her to think how much had happened during her lifetime, a life that had spanned two centuries, witnessed one major war and some minor ones, and seen many changes. She had been married to a great man, a financier and a philanthropist, now dead for nearly fifty years. How long she had lived after him! And she had never wanted it that way. She had survived a dangerous illness, which she had thought, at the time, would reunite her with him.

Looking around the crowded room, there were many more people than usual because of the occasion, she could not help thinking of the absent faces. She had outlived most of her contemporaries. Eager young men had replaced the old rabbis, and she did not know any of them. There was not a beard to be seen. They were brought to her side to be introduced, but she could not summon up the energy to be interested in them. She had once thought Rabbi Daniel Wiseman a man of the times, a free spirit, and therefore a suitable person to instruct her future daughter-in-law, but he had long departed this life, and she still grieved for him.

All her guests were seated at the long table in the dining-room. Presently Ambrose would tell them that his mother tired easily and must leave them. He would say that this was not an indication for them to leave, the party was not over and he hoped they would remain in their seats. It would be a short speech and the only one he would make. It was tacitly agreed between them that he would not get to his feet and speak eloquently about the virtues of his mother. She had forfeited that pleasure when she distanced herself from his wife. Even the occasion of her hundredth birthday would not make him untrue to himself, but he managed to remain loyal to both of them and nothing would alter that. Sometimes she felt she had put an awful strain on him that he did not deserve.

She put out her hand, and he grasped it. He was her precious son, and he stood by her wheelchair, a solid dependable figure, towering over everyone else in the room. He had broadened with age, but he had never grown fat. No doubt his wife had seen to that. Someone, a woman, had once said to her, "How could you, a frail little person like you, have produced such a son?" and she had replied modestly, "He was a big baby." Later, she had remembered that she had not actually given birth to Ambrose, another woman was responsible for that, and it was a fact she found difficult to believe now that she was getting older. His strong warm hand in hers was a comfort. He understood what an effort it was, trying to remember names and be polite to everyone.

He had come to see her every Friday, year after year, mingling with the guests and then staying for a quiet supper with his mother and, on occasions, his sister. He had never missed a visit, except when they were holidaying in Spain or it coincided with the birth of one of his many children or the indisposition of his wife. Whether she wanted to hear or not he had recounted the details of his life, the arrival of a new baby and, lately, proudly he had told her of their first grandchild, a boy. The years had passed so quickly she could not remember when it was they purchased the house on the island near Mallorca. Perhaps it was before they were married. She had been invited to stay with them there – in those days she could have managed it – but she had refused. At first they went there twice a year – the house was big and could accommodate all the children – now the visits became longer and longer. Ambrose had retired; leaving his two sons to run the business. There was nothing keeping him in England, except herself. She reflected bitterly that when she was gone they would probably go there for most of the year. He spoke glowingly about the house, the strip of sand that belonged to them, the giant Catalpa tree in the garden. She had been to such places when she was married to Marcus; now she was bound in the trammels of old age, the wheelchair held her captive.

Suddenly she was aware of a child standing near her chair. He sidled closer and closer, until he was so near that she could have put out her hand and touched him. She did not do that because she knew that it would frighten him. He fixed her with a blue gaze and she noticed his hair, the colour of corn. Ambrose called out to him, but he was gone, running on his short stout legs to someone sitting at the other end of the table, probably his mother. Of course, she realised, this must be the grandchild, no longer a baby, and the passage of time had eluded her as usual. The hair should have told her who it was. Marcus had been so proud of their sturdy blond boy.

She thought, as she thought so often, that Marcus would have dealt with the situation differently. He possessed a tolerance, which she did not have. She always hoped that Ambrose would accompany her to the evening service at the synagogue; she had tried to persuade him over the years, but he would never agree to go. They had remained two stubborn people locked together. She knew that he loved her: that was her only consolation.

She saw the woman, his wife, sitting several places away down the table. So she had deigned to come to the birthday party then. Ambrose, who had been responsible for the seating arrangements, had seen to it that she was not too near. He was fiercely protective of his wife and very proud of her. Unlike Ingrid, who had become fat with age, she looked slim and elegant. That fact could not be denied. There was a faint smile on her face when she caught her looking in her direction. Self-satisfaction or a genuine desire to be friendly? She could not tell, and she was too weary to care. She longed for the moment when her two carers would arrive to take her home. They would help her into her coat and then into the waiting car, and the ordeal would be over.

If she had not felt so tired she would have told Ambrose she wished to greet his wife. She knew he would never ask this favour of her; he had given up doing that years before. Old age had fined down some of the bitter feelings of the past. And death, she thought, death would eliminate them altogether, and they would disappear like thistledown in the wind, having served no purpose in the mystical workings of the Torah.

She was wheeled out of the room, and a great cheer marked her exit. The guests raised their glasses to a game old girl and the memory of her husband, with his flamboyant red bow tie, looking down at them, epitomising all that was good and real in the world.

Acknowledgements

La Isla de la Fuga is a fictitious island, but Cabrera is real and I was fortunate in finding a book, *Mallorca and Ibiza, Menorca and Formentera,* one of a series called *Inside Guides* where the plight of the Napoleonic soldiers is very well described. Published by APA Publications, it is edited by Andrew Eames and the Editorial Director is Brian Bell.

Poem: 'Life I know not what thou art . . .'
by Anna Laetitia Barbauld (1742-1825)
in *The Golden Treasury.*

Judaism - A Very Short Introduction
by Norman Solomon.